CROWN OF BONES

"I saw Sabnock," Nick said. His gaze went inward. "The guy is tall. Seven or eight feet. Dark. At first, I thought he had the head of a lion, but I was seeing him from the side, and he's got this piece of armor, this shoulder thing poking up high, that's shaped like a head of the lion."

"A pauldron," Johnny suggested.

"Yeah. Only like it's above his shoulder." Nick held the palm of his hand six inches or so off of his own shoulder. "It's golden, and from the side it looks like a mask, almost.

"He was directing some of the trucks. Or telling people where to take what. It was close to the stadium there. There's a lot of construction. He was standing on a corner and there was this shadow next to him..." Nick's voice became thoughtful. A little quiet. Sarah's hands reached around and held him. "I almost took a shot."

CROWN OF BONES

A Grimm Story

CHRIS J CRANFORD

Forged Iron Press

BOOKS BY CHRIS J. CRANFORD

First Paperback Edition Dec 2024

Cover Design by J Caleb Design

Published by Forged Iron Press
www.forgedironpress.com

www.chrisjcranford.com

Acknowledgements

2023 was a rough year for me. I hurt a nerve in my back, the pain grew until I kind of lost the ability to move my arm… and everything seemed to get worse from there.

Most of my stories—the ones I really enjoy writing—have the hero overcoming the darkest of evils. Breaking through the hardest of walls. After my injury I wondered if I really could write again. Not just because I couldn't physically move my arm, but because if I couldn't beat this on my own, then how could I write the kinds of stories where someone else could?

I want to live in a world where my stories mean something. Where at readers can escape to them, and at best they offer a little hope. Life is hard for all of us, we all fight *something*, and we should all hold onto the hope that we can beat whatever it is that holds us down.

It took some good people to remind me that as much as Grimm wants to battle evil on his own, he has friends he counts on. I'm laughing as I type this, remembering Bronwyn saying those exact words.

A big light came on. Family were there. Friends were too. And of course I overcame all of it, with a lot of hard Grimm-like work.

And since then I've tried to reach out a bit more. For the most part. I mean, there is a bit of Grimm in me.

So thanks again Bronwyn, and Frank. Thanks for picking me up a bit at the Big Bad Breakfast, hope you and your families are well. And thanks to a few other cool people up in Cool Springs who checked on me, Rourke and Brian.

This is not the book I thought I'd thank you all in, that one still needs to be written, but this one might be the more important one for me, for now.

CHAPTER ONE

I t was hot in Mexico.

It shouldn't be, not this time of year. Not in the middle of December. Not with Mexico City being a mile above sea level. It should be cool, mildly warm at the worst, a nice seventy degrees, with a breeze blowing inland from the water carrying a hint of salt. It should be a place people walked around in chinos and white, blousy shirts, drinking and celebrating and looking in stores for the occasional thing that caught your eye.

After all, Christmas was around the corner.

That was before the change though. Before the Dead Zones appeared. Before large cities became empty corpses, bastions of the dead, where creatures rose up from hell and found themselves a new place to live. Before the demons, one demon in particular, hatched a plan to create his own real estate company. If heaven and hell existed, and Earth was the in between, then Azazel had become a middle-king of a new middle-Earth.

So, the Dead Zones. Azazel had brought some friends with him, freed them from Solomon's Key, and given each a place to rule.

Cities to bring their own particular flavor of undead. Their own rules and laws. Monstrous armies with which to protect each demon, nestled in their citadel.

And, sadly, humans willing to work with them.

There was a flutter in the air, a stirring that might once have been a breeze, before it had traveled the long distance over a barren land, before the breeze died, before it had become the gasp of something cool from an ocean too far away from here to matter. I looked up at the cloudless pale blue sky, so pale it was almost gray, so empty and alone the sun looked ten times its normal size. It hung overhead, swollen, tinged a little red, angry and beating down on all of us underneath. Maybe screaming, *how could you let this happen?*

It was fair to blame me. But it wasn't for a lack of me trying. And I was here now. Here anyway, with my friends. Still at the plate and swinging the bat, though we were down in the count. Standing on a hill, as high as we could find, and looking at the first of the Dead Zones we were going to try to tackle. The first of Azazel's friends we were going to kill.

Mexico City.

Sabnock.

The builder. The architect. The demon of sickness and disease.

Seemed as good a place to start as any.

I returned my eyes to the set of binoculars, the glasses heavy in my hands. The metal casing was hot under the sun, but I brought them up and gazed across the city spreading out below me. Where I looked was too far away for the binoculars alone, even high-powered, but I had found using the glasses with a little bit of ethereal energy, power I took from a ghost, I could focus my gaze much further.

Miles upon miles upon miles further.

So I could see far into Mexico City from outside the Dead Zone, even forty miles away, even if we were far northeast of the city's center. The elevation helped, and my focused ethereal gaze took in the sprawl of buildings that had homed millions of humans.

No longer.

The first thing I caught was all the high-rises. Tall structures in the center of the city, dark towers stretching high into the air, scraping the sky. New buildings, built by modern man, covered in glass on every side, the glass shiny under the sun. One wide building might have been the World Trade Center of Mexico, back when Mexico City had trade to speak of.

All the metal fingers pointed high into the sky, as high as man had built them, but now there was something at the top of them, something too far even for my ethereal gaze, some smudge of grimy green darkness climbing even higher. A bulbous growth, like the towers were sick. And spreading their disease.

I lowered the glasses, letting my eyes pick out some of the older buildings. Shorter things built of rock and stone. By old man, long ago. These shapes were smudges in the distance, dark blocky smudges of gray, blurred smudged columns of white, old buildings of granite and basalt. Palaces, old temples, cathedrals.

The cathedrals were smudgier now. Darker. As if some sticky substance covered them, had been thrown or spattered on the walls. The columns too, were stained, one in particular, a tall white column in the center of a square, topped with what might have once been a golden figure with wings. An angel, once, but no longer. It was something stained and dark and broken, smudged, though the figure was too small and too far to really tell.

None of the older buildings climbed toward the sky. None of them had that finger-climbing blackness at their top. Those were just for the high-rises. The older buildings sat there below, well under the pale blue sky, old bones of times long past.

All around these monuments were smaller buildings. There were the high-rises, towering into the sky. Then the monuments below them. And then, even smaller, blocks of older apartments and homes and business complexes.

Wild color schemes colored the homes in some places and held a faded and reserved palette in others. Mixed among the homes were gas stations and markets and cafes and restaurants. Scattered buildings of aluminum roofs and metal sides, of plaster and wood, buildings where people had once lived. Graffiti here and there, splattered on walls and bridges, though I couldn't make out any words. It was just the color and the shapes.

Everything was blurred with the distance. Diminished by the high-rises. And everywhere high the tarrish, greenish substance lay. It stuck here and there, swelling at the top of the buildings, bulbous. It grew like algae or bacteria. Something dark, maybe crimson, maybe green, maybe brown. Something that spoke of rot and decay. Something that spread over the surface of glass and stone and steel alike, a slow crawl of a mindless monster that ate and consumed and never, ever gave back.

And more besides. We had watched trucks headed in over the past week. Big eighteen-wheelers for the most part, some earth movers, dump trucks. Among all that rot and decay, something was being built. Even now, I watched one pick its way south through the city, rumbling along a street that had been cleared of all other vehicles.

That was Sabnock. Builder. Raiser of armies. Builder of weapons. Demon of Rot and Decay. And Number One right now on my list of demons to kill.

Boy, I sure can pick them.

"You figure it out yet?" a voice asked from behind me.

Nick. Hanging out with me again for the seventh day this week. Quiet for the most part while I studied the city, and he was easy enough to hear in the day. It was at night where Nick was danger-

CROWN OF BONES • 5

ous, a shadow walker, a person who could move from shadow to shadow in the blink of an eye, kill, and move on.

As Johnny had once said, a dark fucker.

But also the best of friends.

I spat to the side. Nothing really came out. It was that warm and dry. Lowered my glasses. Even as hot and barren as it was, the elevation reminded me of another time, another place, where I was dressed in ranger gear and with another team. Where this fight with Azazel had really begun.

A team long gone now. More than a team, a group of people that had depended on one another. If not friends, then brothers and sisters in arms. People who had once had my back.

All dead.

"Nah," I said. "I keep telling you guys, I'm not good at the planning thing."

I never had been. In the Rangers, I had been a good scout. An elite scout. An elite killer, even. Though I wasn't a killer like Nick, who was surgical in his precision. I was more of a taking a beating and keep on ticking kind of killer.

Back then, I had never been in charge of a team, though. Of leading anyone. Of walking through the various scenarios and plotting a course. Of making sure everyone made it home alive.

I was just a guy who took an order and winged it from there.

Winged it. Hah. Perhaps a little inside humor. Though it was hard to tell what I was laughing at, because it was hard to tell what I believed and didn't believe. I found the whole situation a little too out there to really take in.

Some folks thought I was an angel.

I was maybe coming around on that idea.

But if I was an angel, then that meant other things might exist. Things larger in scope and meaning. Things high above and below.

Which I refused to think of now, I wanted to believe all of that was beyond me. For now.

"I'm not talking about that," Nick said.

Oh. Nick meant the other thing. Which he had mentioned once or twenty times in the past week. I probably needed the reminder. I mean, if I was bad at planning…

I shook my head. The other thing was something I was putting off. Which, honestly, was like me. But I had good reasons. It wasn't like there was an easy place to shop. Not like I could waltz through the Dead Zone, through the dying city, with all its empty stores, and pick something out. Even if all the monsters of hell living there, even if all the minor demons and undead and Sabnock would let me.

Even if Christmas was right around the corner.

CHAPTER TWO

I kept staring at the Dead Zone. At the city and the hidden pentagram underneath it. If a person pulled up Google Maps and looked at the satellite view, they would have seen the city, sprawled across the map, all its blocks and streets and buildings and monuments haphazardly built. They wouldn't see it, but underneath the satellite view of the city would be thick red lines, running criss-cross over each other, forming a star-shape pentagram the size of Texas over Mexico.

A pentagram built of silver cable and powered by the desecration Azazel had engineered in New Orleans, a literal hell on Earth. Like all the zones, the undead had risen, old ghosts and demons and anything evil that had found its way below. Even monsters, monsters existing so long ago that they may have been forgotten, had found their place to the new digs. Real estate for evil had become really, really cheap, and creatures were still moving in.

Sabnock's kingdom was big, larger by far than the Dead Zone in Louisiana, big enough to capture all of Mexico City and miles beyond. The tinge of red in the air, the red only I could see in my ethereal vision, stretched from where Nick and I stood, south past the Pyramid of the Sun, past Mexico City, and further south to all the old places, all the old temples and forgotten cities, over where Aztecs and Mayans had once lived, where tens or hundreds of thousands or even millions of sacrifices had been made.

That was a lot of Evil. Evil, with the capital E. Of dark people and dark times, waiting to rise up and live again. Tortured souls and the torturers. I saw them all through the binoculars, coming out mostly at night. I saw the humans too, the humans that had remained in the zone, who wanted to work with the demons, who saw a chance to get to a higher rung on a different ladder. Corrupt politicians, cartels, gangs, the modern-day Jeffrey Dahmers and Ted Bundys of the world. I saw them all, tiny figures in the distance, sometimes shooting guns, sometimes throwing bottles of fire through a broken building's windows. I saw and watched. I kept seeing and watching, until night fell, waiting for a plan to come to me.

It should have been easy. After all, the city had a center. And the pentagram enclosing Mexico City, the symbol dug in the ground, built by Azazel across thousands of miles, it had a center too. And that center—the center of the pentagram, if we could locate it, that would be where we had a chance of powering the Dead Zone down. Nullifying it.

So we watched and looked. Tried to find the center, following the traffic in. Searching for something that should have been easy to find, but wasn't. Not just the center, but a real plan to get there, to neutralize the Dead Zone and kill Sabnock.

It was all I could do. Each day for the past week. Not having a great military mind. Not having a real experience to relate to in order to tackle a war like this. It wasn't like there was a *Banish Dead Zones for Dummies* book I could pick up at the local bookstore.

Jason Bradley could have done it. Could have planned it all. My master sergeant, back in the army. He would have had me and Lilly walking perimeters, marking possible entries. He would have had Suzy and Patty Ice up on a rooftop somewhere, or a hill, on overwatch. He would have had Joe, and the two of them would have come up with something from all the information they gathered, and it all would have worked.

Except that they were all dead now. Dead because of me. Well, not me, but Azazel. But they had run up against something that no one could have planned for, because no one had ever planned for something supernatural. And it had killed them all. And it had left just me. Just me, then. But not only me, now. Now I had my own team, my friends, the group of us that were going to take on Azazel and his demons on their own turf.

If I could come up with a real plan, that was.

Nick usually came with me, mostly quiet. Throwing the occasional stone. Sometimes disappearing, practicing his shadow walking from the shadow of an old boulder or a cactus. Never complaining. Just trusting I would come up with something.

And I was coming up empty. Not for lack of trying. I felt like my brain was working on overdrive, but maybe I wasn't seeing things right. It happens. Sometimes we all get so focused on a goal that we start missing things on the outside. Sometimes we need to shift our perspectives.

And I was having trouble with that. With shifting perspectives. I had been the run away guy. Then I had been the guy shouldering too much of the load. Lately I had been the take-things-on guy. But with the hundreds of millions of undead below, with all the various monsters that kept popping out, with the cartels ruling parts of Mexico City during the day, there wasn't a viewpoint I could find that would suddenly make any plan seem viable. Especially with Sabnock likely waiting for me to try.

And of course, on top of all that, Christmas was coming.

So I answered like I always did. "Man, there's not any shops around to even shop in."

"It's Christmas, dude."

"I know it's Christmas." I know I sounded frustrated. I couldn't help but feel responsible for everything that had happened. For the Dead Zones and the demons, for the millions of people dead when the zones had first appeared, the restricted flight zones, for all the broken shipping lanes and all the interstate jams, the abandoned cars, the closed stores. It was hard to come up with a gift with all that on my shoulders. Shopping just reminded me, when I saw another broken-glass storefront, that I could have stopped it all, if I had just been smarter than Azazel.

But I hadn't been. Azazel had beaten me. But I was back at the plate, here in Mexico. A Mexico City strangely empty of people, but not empty of monsters. "It's Christmas, yeah, but we're in Mexico," I said. "With monsters all around us, and a demon to kill, remember?"

"I remember," Nick said, like he had every time before. Patiently enough. "Just saying."

And he was. He was a good friend. And he was probably getting feedback from Sarah, Jen's sister, and letting me know that while Jen had told me not to get anything, that, just like everyone in every relationship in the history of the world told their loved one not to get them anything, Nick was telling me that Jen was looking forward to something special.

From me.

I snorted. You would think saving a person from death would be gift enough.

Then I shook my head. That thought wasn't fair. That thought came from the old Grimm, the old guy who had been on the run too long. A guy who had thought more about himself than others. Who ran when he should have fought. Who hadn't forgotten, or perhaps never really understood, what friendship really meant.

This Grimm was different. He had learned from his friends. From Danny, who had sacrificed himself twice for me. From Jen, who had given her life once as well. And from all my friends, Nick and Johnny and Sarah. From my parents, who had given their lives as well.

I was keeping that tally. As my mother had told me, I was becoming something more. So were my friends. *We* were all becoming something more. I thought even Gabrielle. There was a group of us, a committed group, picking up people here and there so that we could rise to this challenge.

What that final becoming would be, though? I had no idea.

The stone on my chest tingled, briefly. A cool, electric buzzing that emitted a scent of honeysuckle. Letting me know Jen was thinking about me.

The stone had been part of Solomon's Key once. Now it was a broken half of an amulet. Broken after I had somehow put Jen into it, and held her there, alive, until I could find a way to bring her back. After the final battle in Denver, where I had been finally freed from the geas my people were under.

My people. I know. I still can't quite say the other word.

Now each half of the Key was teardrop-shaped, and held a blue shimmering that was almost ethereal in the right light, or tiny streaks of blue lightning in another. Jen and I both wore a half, and through a process I didn't quite understand, something residual from when she was in the Key, the stones let us communicate, to be together, even over distance. To share feelings and thoughts.

I broke away from my thoughts. I found myself standing a little straighter, and I couldn't help the slight grin that broke across my face.

Jen did that to me.

Everyone should have a Jen in their lives.

One thing I knew now, I was no longer a runner. I was a guy who would take a stand. I was a guy that would make evil pay. I would protect my friends, let them protect me, and together we would all stand against the demons. We would threaten Azazel himself. The mastermind demon behind the Dead Zones. A demon that had caused more pain and death over the past few thousand years than the Black Plague. He probably had created the plague.

He was the head of the group of demons on Earth. He had helped cause the Fall, so long ago, of those angels that had been in heaven. He had started the war and the disappearance of the rest of the angels.

And he was the demon who had killed Jen.

He would also be the demon I killed last. After I took everything from him. After I broke every plan of Azazel, brought him to ruin, surrounded New Orleans and then marched in to finish what Azazel had started.

But first, Sabnock. The guy with a large army and a city that seemed like a thousand miles of humans by day and monsters by night. Massive in their count, bloodthirsty at the best of times, and probably on alert for someone with my description. All standing between me and the demon ruling Mexico City.

It wasn't like I could plan an assassination, either. My powers didn't work inside the Dead Zone. Like everything else, I was learning what I could do, why I could do it, on the fly. I thought the reason I couldn't make my sword appear in the Dead Zone was because it was an "off-limit" zone.

Maybe an angel's powers couldn't work in hell. Maybe a demon's powers couldn't work in heaven. Maybe both places were an "Olly Olly Oxen Free" kind of zone, where if a person from the other side visited, they had to do so with the understanding that there would be no harm. Maybe that was how heaven and hell had been originally set up, to keep the sides fair.

Of course, those were things I wasn't trying to think about. Because if there was a heaven and hell, if there was a demon named Belial, who I had met and was close to another demon named Lucifer, if those demons existed, then there had to be another guy.

That guy hadn't really been helping me or my friends lately.

I sighed. And pushed those thoughts away. For the millionth time.

None of that mattered now. All that mattered was finding a way to get into Mexico City somehow, get Sabnock's citadel in the middle of his Dead Zone, and slay a demon. And here was as good as anywhere. We had to start with one, because there were more Dead Zones out there. More demons to kill.

And maybe, if we could find it, maybe even revert the Dead Zone itself. Evict the monsters and the undead, kill off the cartels, and restore each zone back to humanity.

A tall task.

And, as Nick kept reminding me, I also had to find a Christmas gift. For Jen, who had told me not to worry about it. So I hadn't, and then I found myself still putting it off, for—as I've been explaining—some very good reasons.

Or so I thought.

I had no idea why it was so difficult to figure out a gift for Jen. Maybe because I had never really gotten her one before. Sure, there had been the occasional bunch of flowers I had gathered as a teenager. And the birthday gifts we all gave each other as kids.

But I had left not long after we had become something deeper. I had run away from Grafton, right at that young time in our lives, where dating a girl in school became something much, much more. Where just seeing them took your breath away. Where every thought you had was of each other.

So, a gift. At a time where I had no idea what to give someone who made you feel taller every time they smiled at you. It felt like flowers weren't enough, that earrings or a pretty necklace weren't the right fit for where Jen and I were in our relationship.

We had passed that point in our lives. We were in a different realm. It was hard to tell which thing was going to bite me in the ass worse. Figuring out how to kill Sabnock and rid the world of a Dead Zone, or finding this special gift Jen was telling me I didn't need to get her.

But I knew what I was betting on.

CHAPTER THREE

Night was going to fall soon. I could see the purple of it in the thin line of darkness swelling along the horizon to the east. Soon, that darkness would cover the towers to the west, the towers with the bulbous rot on the top of them. It would hide the construction in the middle of the city and conceal the trucks moving in from the north.

There was nothing here I hadn't seen all week. I put the glasses down.

"Strike eight?" Nick asked, grinning.

Eight, nine, twenty-six? Four hundred and thirty-two? I had lost count.

We both got into an old truck, a beat-up Ford F150, something that was a mishmash of colors, but mostly tan, with balding tires and a passenger window that wouldn't roll up. It smelled musty and a little like burned motor oil inside, and I was glad the window on my side was stuck down and not up. The truck was at least two decades old, the hinges of the doors squealed as they opened and shut, the truck always rocked a bit when our weight was added to it. The seats so old we sunk into them.

I missed the Camaro, but that was stuck back in the states. Hidden in a storage unit as we all fled the United States. Which was another story in itself.

The short part of it? Well, there was a warrant for our arrests from a cop in Grafton, a cop who was actually a demon, one of Azazel's finest performances. That had led to another warrant from a town in Tennessee, where we had found a group of witches to help Sarah. A little misunderstanding with the local police there.

Then there was video of us from a rest-stop in Alabama, the devastation there after we had fought off Kimaris's first attack. A second video of me in an airport in Denver, in the middle of a fight with my father. That one had been taken by the SRF, some kind of new supernatural federal agency. Who now declared me a "person of interest."

And to top it all off, there was a recent deal between Azazel and the President of the United States. The one where the United States would help find us, my group of "fugitives," and turn us over to the demon. In exchange, the demon promised no aggression from his little territory around New Orleans.

I mean, demons never lie, right?

Right.

Neither did politicians.

Yeah... I know. I know.

We had to ditch the Camaro somewhere in Texas. Then we fled across the border, where the Dead Zone in Mexico City happened to be waiting. And since I had just bragged to Azazel that I was going to shut him down, kill all his friends, tear apart all his plans, well, Mexico City seemed like the place where we were going to start.

If I was being honest, I wasn't sure what their plans really were. Or if the demons had plans. Azazel had been trying so long to free his friends, build these Dead Zones, these places between heaven and hell on Earth, that I wasn't sure he really had a plan after that.

I'd be lying if I said I wasn't worried about that part. Azazel had plans for his plans. Plans for after a plan failed, plans for if they worked. Schemes and designs and backup plans for anything and everything that could or might happen. It didn't feel right to me that the demon would have these Dead Zones as his endgame. But I also wasn't sure where he would take things from here.

Part of that was not knowing what had happened in the beginning. What had caused the Fall, what had started the war between the angels and the demons. It might have been what I thought it had been, that Azazel was just that kind of asshole, but I worried it could be more. That the demon wanted more.

Nick fired up the F150. It chugged a bit before rumbling, like all eight-cylinder Fords do. A throaty, off-beat chugging that had me missing the Camaro more. He took off, the cab vibrated with the motor's lopping beat, and I put my arm on the dashboard and braced myself as we rode down the dirt road.

The seatbelts were missing. One had been cut. The other torn and shredded. Some of the stains in the seats were dark. I didn't want to wonder about the *why* of either. I just settled myself for having a vehicle that blended in.

"You know," Nick said, "we're going to have to do something."

I sighed. "I know."

"Why not send me in?" he asked. He had asked it before. Many times. "Let me go in at night. I'll find him and kill him, and then we're done."

He wasn't wrong. His powers worked in the Dead Zone. It was me that was more vulnerable, anything remotely angelic in nature straight out didn't function once it crossed over the thin red line surrounding Mexico City.

So Nick's plan was solid. Or, at least it was a plan. Perhaps a good plan. But even Nick, as dangerous a fucker that walked the Earth, would have trouble killing a major demon on his own.

I might have been the only person around who had done that in the past few thousand years. As far as being able to kill a demon.

And I had actually killed two.

But the sword I could call, the sword that was the symbol of who I was, what I stood for, the sword that was powered with everything I believed of myself, that sword couldn't be called inside the Dead Zone.

And of course, Sabnock wouldn't come out of it. Which was the problem. I wasn't sure we could lure him out, and we just didn't have the force to go in. And by force, I was including the low number of people on our side, but I also meant… me.

"I wish it was that easy," I said.

Nick looked over. The truck bounced up and down on the hard dirt road, and we both bounced with it. "You're still having trouble."

I knew what he meant. Not trouble with my powers, or trouble with putting myself in danger. I had a problem with letting my friends take a bullet for me. I mean, Jen had done that literally. It was a feeling I didn't want to have again, not for Jen, not for any of my friends, but I understood that I had to.

I understood some of us would die.

The odds weren't in our favor.

But there was something between letting someone take a bullet for you and acceptable risk. I just couldn't find it. And I couldn't just let Nick go on a plan that had—at best—a very slight chance of success. I couldn't.

My friends were dealing with that too. That part of me. They wanted to take the same risks I did, but I could heal myself. I could tap into ghosts and live, as long as a spirit was around, and as long as I was alive and conscious. My friends, as powerful as they might be, as *becoming* as they were, couldn't do that.

So yeah, it was complicated.

"Maybe," I said. Then looked at him, my tone a little different. More serious. "Maybe."

Nick got it. I was finally coming around on sending him in. There was no way I could see to get to Sabnock myself. Or to get the demon to come out of the Dead Zone, where he was safe.

His eyes widened. I had surprised him. "Really?"

I did something that was a combination of nodding and shaking my head. "I don't know. But I can't see any other way. So we should at least talk about it."

I wasn't fully committed to Nick's idea. Not yet. If we were going to do it, we would do it my way. Fully armed to the teeth. We would get a beachhead somewhere in the zone. We would have a way out, for all of us.

I would have to start with that. We all would have to. And we all would understand, if Nick failed, one of us would have to rescue him. Or take our own strike for Sabnock, if Nick were dead.

Like I said, I wasn't fully committed yet. I was still trying to find another way.

That way just wasn't revealing itself fast enough. The Dead Zones weren't going away. More and more evil found its way to each every day. I could almost see them swell with it. The sheer size of the task was daunting.

And, of course, it didn't help that all of that was clouding my vision. Stopping me from starting the task. Stopping me from seeing this task through, or seeing any other way to accomplish it.

Though I would see it through. Or die in the attempt.

Nick seemed to grow larger next to me, just for a brief moment. Like he had taken a deep breath and was holding it in. Like he was steeling himself for what was coming. His hands tightened on the wheel. His voice even, pitched a little higher, for all he tried to keep his tone casual. "Just let me know."

I would. And I wouldn't like it, when I did. If I did.

The truck bounced down the road. Nick and I bounced in the seats with it. Evening was coming, purple on the horizon, swelling toward us. Dirt and dust flew behind us, various shapes of cacti stood out, casting dark shadows on the dark desert among clumped gatherings of agave. Montezuma pine trees mixed with cypresses as we wound down the hill. Off to the northeast stood a large Ahue-huete, a monster of a cypress, its thick trunk jutting into the sky until it split into shorter trunks, dozens of thick arms bowed underneath the darkening night. I imagined the leaves shivered under the dying breaths of breeze from the east.

The radio in the truck didn't work. Neither of us spoke. There wasn't much to say, really. We would go, or we wouldn't. I would send Nick, or I wouldn't. My friends would let me make the call, and they trusted me to make the best one.

A burden I found it hard to live with. No matter what I had said in the past. No matter what I wanted to accept. I was made one way, to put it all on myself, and anything else for me was a struggle.

Long ago–at least a few months–Nick had punched me. Called me a traitor. Blamed me for everything that had gone wrong in Grafton. For Danny and Sarah, Raphael.

Since then, he had been a real friend. A true friend. He had stood with me and Jen in New Orleans against three major demons, he had tried to pull me out of my despair after Azazel had shot Jen, and he had even followed me into Colorado. Trying to save me.

Nick had had my back. Many times. Maybe it was time I had his.

That was going to be a tough pill for me to swallow. There was always a wide gulf for me between the *knowing* and the *under-*

standing of a thing. Chasms I had a hard time crossing. I knew, I *knew,* no matter what I did, people I loved were going to get hurt.

I just didn't want it to be now. I didn't want it to be Nick. I didn't want it to be any of my friends. I wanted it to be me, facing every demon, because I was the guy who could. I was the guy who not only could kill them, but who was also the hardest to kill.

I just couldn't see another way at Sabnock.

So, that was how we made our way back to our hidey-hole. On the edge of trying *something*, but not knowing what that would be. Or when.

Sometimes, that's the way things are meant to happen. Some people called it letting things come to them. Some people attributed it to a hidden plan, one governing our lives, driving our fates.

I wanted to call it bullshit.

CHAPTER FOUR

Like all large cities, super-cities, megacities, whatever they were called, Mexico City sprawled from a densely populated center to suburban outskirts, from suburban outskirts to smaller town-like areas, from smaller town-like areas to the surrounding county. The city was like a hub, a dense concentration of buildings and population, and the spokes of that hub met other little cities that surrounded it.

These little mini cities attached to Mexico City through thick threads of crowded streets, these streets wound out and became roads, passing trailer parks and smaller towns until most of them started to pass sparsely populated fields and farms. These farms thinned out as well, into desert-like areas, with large stretches of tan dirty, dusty, large ahuehuetes in the fields, those tall cypress trees mixed with cacti and agave plants, the plants thick in places, thin in others.

Then the process reversed. The desert-like fields to farms, to trailer parks, to towns. Smaller towns, way outside of the megalopolis that was the center of Mexico. We had found one of those to stay in, a smaller town a far distance from Mexico City. Larger than Grafton, but tiny compared to the population centers inside each of the Dead Zones.

This town was mostly empty and abandoned, like most of the places we'd found in Mexico, though a few people remained here and there. In this town a bar remained open, a neon light flickering above its front, naming the place El Muerde Amargo. There was also a small market, open mostly twenty-four seven. A gas station. All connected to Mexico City by a road leading southwest, with empty apartments and businesses on either side fading into the distance until the road hit the Dead Zone.

I didn't like staying here. I had argued for something more remote. Something like a farmhouse, all on its own. Out in the country. A place we could bunker in, if we had to, and fight it out.

Again, if we had to.

Jen had just looked at me then. For a long time, one eyebrow slightly arched.

"What?" I had asked.

"If something comes for us," she had explained. "Does it really matter where we're at?"

Did it? If something came for us, chances were that something was nasty. And if not nasty, then they were coming by the thousands. Or the hundreds of thousands.

She saw me see where she was going. She let me get it, then continued, with a small smile that said I would get it too. One day. "Gus, people are going to die. This is a war. But we can't stay remote. We can't just hide. We've got to find friends. We've got to get more help."

The smile had grown a little larger, a little more devilish. "Or... were you still thinking of doing all this on your own?"

I took a breath and blew it out with that accompanying exasperated sound people make when they are called on something. I had been thinking that, and of course, Jen had known exactly what I was thinking. She would have known it even without our connection through the Key.

So here we were. In a place where a few people still lived. Maybe not the best of people, but certainly not the worst. People who couldn't afford to leave, the old and the young, all poor.

Not the best place to gather an army. But definitely a place we could build a base, if that's what we were doing. An abandoned fort we all could huddle and stand together against Sabnock and Azazel and whatever demon or evil, whatever monsters had surfaced out of hell, whatever twisted spirit, hungry vampire, or just generally bad person stood in our way.

Yeah, I know.

I was thinking it too.

Maybe a hundred people left living here, people too old to care, too old to move, or to flee. Just them, basically bystanders, and just us, our little group, against the millions and millions of monsters and demons in Sabnock's army.

And that was just what was happening here in Mexico City. Not the rest of the world. Not the other Dead Zones.

It seemed wildly disproportionate, the scales seemed inhumanly unbalanced, but as I had recently learned, these things started small.

We entered the town, Nick driving us down the street, the blacktop lit by an occasional working streetlight and colored store-front signs. There was the smell of spicy chiles frying in the air, heat on heat, mixed with cinnamon, all of those scents blowing through the open windows of the truck.

Even with nightfall coming, and even in this dead town, there were some signs of life. The first thing we passed was the store, the open storefront facing the street, the few people inside looking back out at us. Picking up a few pieces of fruit or vegetables or meat before going home for the evening. The shop could have been a grocery store, but felt more like a farmer's market.

Then a few older buildings passed by, made of an old clay, none of them reaching more than four stories in the air. Nick waved to someone coming out of the bar, the bartender, and the man waved back. He was an older Mexican with black hair, cut short, and a short-sleeved flowered shirt, just the bottom two buttons buttoned. The man smiled a gap-tooth grin, Nick gave a last little two-fingered wave back, and the whole interaction surprised me, because I hadn't known him to be that outgoing.

Nick kept the pressure on the gas pedal light, the truck rumbling its way along before he turned into an alley that led to our hideout. A three-story building with faded yellow walls, blocked, old in the way that buildings can be, with open stone arched windows on the bottom level and newer, flat glass windows ringing the top. Floor-to-ceiling ones that someone had put in for some reason.

We had found the place empty, abandoned, and moved in. Whoever had lived there before was either dead or gone. It was three levels, the top one being some kind of condo, opened up in a way that spoke of the prior tenants really buying into the open-house concept, with even the bedroom walls having been taken down.

All of us had a place on the second story, there were six empty apartments there, and each couple had taken one to sleep in. With the top being our command center, we had left the first floor open, blocking up the front door and leaving just the rear entryway for us to get in and out.

As soon as we pulled down the alley, both Nick and I saw another car there. In front of the rear door. An old silver sedan, gray. Dusty from travel, with American plates.

The two of us looked at each other. I didn't think we were expecting guests. Nick parked the truck behind the sedan and both of us got out, Nick checking his vest. Something he made months ago, and as tattered as it looked it still did the trick. It was black, thick, with all kinds of knives layered around it, blades lying on top of one another.

One of Nick's hands laid briefly on his Glock, holstered at his hip. Somewhat of a surprise for me, Nick carrying a gun. He was more of a knife guy. Which you could see from all the knives sheathed in his homemade assassin's vest.

Anyway, Nick waited, watching me over the roof of the truck. I wondered when I became the guy who made all the calls. It wasn't so long ago Nick had punched me in the face, called me a coward.

It seemed like years, but, like his vest, it had only been months ago that this all had started. The path from Grafton to New Orleans to Colorado to Mexico.

I nodded.

He slipped into a shadow and disappeared. To a normal person. it may have seemed like it happened in a blink of an eye. I knew from using my ethereal vision that his body kind of slid into the darkness. Flowed, all at once, too quickly to see.

I was already reaching through the Key to Jen, but Nick was back before I had finished. Just a few seconds, and he was opening up the rear door at the bottom of the complex, having unbarred it from the inside.

Locks were never a problem for Nick.

He was smiling. Which was a change, but Nick was changing. We all were changing, but maybe him the most. From a reserved, shy kid, to an angry young man, and now someone a little less nervous and a lot more confident in himself.

Maybe Sarah was the crux of his change. Like Jen was for me. Like I said, everyone should have a Jen in their life. It makes it worth living. Sarah was closer to him now, the closeness he had wanted with her since we were kids. Actually, she was closer to everyone now, after her time with Raphael. Especially Jen.

Speaking of her, or at least thinking of Jen, the Key buzzed a happy thought back at me. Something that felt like a smile, or a warm hug. So I knew they were okay, that the car wasn't trouble, but still asked Nick, "We good?"

"Yeah," Nick said. "Friends." And, before I could ask, he shook his head, a small smile on his face. Which for Nick was as big a grin as it got. "Jen wants it to be a surprise."

We headed up through the door, stopping to lock it and lay a few iron bars across the back of the door. The bars fit into slots of the metal frame around the door, and were hard to find in the dark of the hallway. Nick had taken the light bulbs out here, leaving him a little shadowed area he could always travel to, if needed.

Then the two of us went up the stairs to the second floor. They were covered in plaster. I was betting they were concrete underneath, walking on the steps always felt more like walking on a hard stucco than wood or steel. The second floor held a short hallway with three doors to either side, each of them a separate apartment, and then a second set of stairs on the far end of the hallway leading up to the top level, the open-air condo.

There was a door at the top of those stairs. Jen waited there, the door open, one hand on the knob. Her smile lit into me like a bullet. Piercingly hard and physically shocking each time I saw it. I don't know how people survive without that kind of love in their life. I don't know how I had. It was amazing that every time I saw her, I felt that same electricity. The same stomach-churning. The desire to be better, all of that and more...

Taller.

Stronger.

Lucky.

I smiled back, one of my goofy grins. Jen slid into my arms and kissed me quickly on the lips. Her body was warm against mine, and I caught her scent, honeysuckle, something only Jenn smelled like, that sweet honey of the flower mixed with the scent of a cool rain.

She was tall for a girl, almost as tall as me, built with strong shoulders and graceful curves, some combination of rugged athlete and runway model. Blonde hair framed her face, long, and although her skin had darkened under the Mexican sun, her hair had stayed the same golden-yellow it had always been. Maybe a touch lighter, more corn-silk than yellow blonde. It was a good look for her, but then, all her looks were good.

Her blue eyes locked onto mine, twin irises of the bluest Caribbean water, translucent, deep, with a shimmering of something at their bottoms. She winked at me, a quick wink between us.

"Figure it out?"

The same thing Nick had asked me. I groaned. Jen knew Nick would have to do this, but she let me try my way. She wasn't rubbing that knowledge in; this was more her way of letting the idea wear me down. A gentle reminder that all of this wasn't all on me. Her version of an ocean surf quietly washing against the rocks of the shore, slowly wearing the stone away.

"No," I said, then admitted aloud. "We're probably going with Nick."

She nodded, as if that was the decision she had expected me to come to, given enough time. Nick patted my shoulder and slid between us and the door, looking back only when I had mentioned his name, nodding as if me saying it all it had to be.

He was ready to go in and die in a half-ass plan, just because I had said it. He believed in our cause. But more, he believed in me.

Just like the rest of my friends.

Just like Jen.

It was a lot of weight. A huge burden. I took a deep breath, let it out in little shuddering steps, feeling my chest push up briefly against Jen's, feeling the warmth between us, how her body fit against mine, the press of her breasts against me, her hip, the feeling that neither of us would be separate from another again.

Like I hoped for my friends. That none of us would be separate from each other again. That somehow we would succeed at this herculean task, succeed with no casualties, and good would finally triumph over evil.

Evil was rarely that easy.

The pendulum would swing both ways. It was a fact of life. Good overcame evil, evil overcame good, that merry-go-round seemed like it would just keep circling. First there was the garden. Then the serpent. Noah. Sodom and Gomorrah. Azazel, then Solomon and his creation of his Key, the same Key that Jen and I wore around our necks. All of these events in history, all swings of the pendulum, the back and forth, leading to the *now* of this day.

To here. Mexico City. To Azazel and his demon cabal. To Sabnock. To me and my friends. To our growing powers, to our becoming more, all the while knowing as we became more, the force opposing us would also grow in return. Knowing that the stronger that evil grew, the more powerful we would have to become to defeat it.

I felt like in the end the winner would likely be whoever was the most stubborn. The hardest head. Which fit in my wheelhouse, and gave me some hope.

Jen pulled a little back from me, taking her scent with her, her comforting warmth. She had a little smile on her face, maybe sad, maybe regretful. She understood what I was feeling. About the weight I pushed myself to carry, about keeping my friends safe. And if not safe, at least alive. As easy as she wanted to make that decision for me, she always let me work through it on my own.

Instead, Jen grabbed my hand and tugged me through the open door. "Come," she said. "I've got a surprise."

CHAPTER FIVE

I should have realized who the surprise was, given the gray sedan beside our apartment building. After all, I had once borrowed the car. And had not liked the driving of it. Probably the reason the sedan hadn't registered.

Tabitha was on the large burgundy couch in the center of the open-concept condo that was on the third floor. Next to her was her daughter, Zoe. The couch itself, a dark red leather, circled the center of the floor in a big U-shape, the open end facing the floor-to-ceiling windows. A big coffee table sat in the middle of the U, so big it made it hard to navigate around the couch. Every time I tried, my shins cracked the table's edge.

Tabitha looked older. Much older than she had appeared back in Lewisville. More like when I had first found her in Grafton. A little hunched and more worn, her salt-and-pepper hair tied back in a tight bun, much like a librarian might. She had the thin, stern face for it, and even wore the glasses, round ovals perched on black frames.

Her daughter seemed more energetic, her hands moving in her

lap, her leg bouncing up and down. Huddled next to her mother, but also sitting straighter. Zoe was a spirit witch, one of those people that would charge for seances and palm-reading. Other than her energy, she was a replica of her mother, the same thin, stern face, lips a severe slash. The same style of hair tied in a bun, though Zoe's hair was all black, with no hint of gray.

Zoe held her talisman in one hand, an opaque globe the size of a billiard ball. Something that one might use to communicate with spirits. It looked like a smaller version of the crystal ball that sat on a gypsy's table. Smaller than those large globes, but somehow it also felt more focused. The way Zoe held it, the ball seemed to have a certain weight, as if the globe contained something greater hidden inside the swirling opaqueness of its surface.

At one of the ends of the couch stood the witch I called—in my mind—the Valkyrie. The tall blonde stood by windows and stared outward through the large panes of glass into the deepening purples of the evening. Maybe wondering why she was here, or maybe, like myself, wondering what the future held.

Gertrude had been much thinner back in Grafton, starved from her time as a prisoner in one of the cages in the factory there. She had filled out her muscle again, and looked more imposing than I would have believed, dressed for battle just like the legend of the Norse. Leather vambraces, armor, leggings, all were tied tight around her form. The hilt of an axe poked over her shoulder, the double-crescent blade low on her back. The metal of the axe was intrinsically carved, tiny runes I could see, but not make out, or understand.

Witch stuff.

I thought.

Maybe Norse stuff.

Maybe both.

Tabitha smiled tiredly at me. Jen patted me on a shoulder and walked over to the kitchen, digging into the fridge. I nodded back at the witch and her daughter, tried a smile. Then tried to put more energy into it. "We meet again."

Tabitha's smile turned real for a moment. Then wistful. "Jen called us. Said you might need a hand."

I looked over at Jen, who was pulling out a few beers from the fridge. She winked at me. She knew what I was thinking, and not just because of the bond. She would always know.

More people to lose.

More people to worry about.

And maybe, just maybe, the survivors would become something more.

What few were left.

I glanced back at Tabitha. "It's going to be dangerous."

The old witch's eyes flicked over to her daughter. Briefly. Then back to me. "We know."

So Jen had given them the real deal. The breakdown of what we were trying. And they had come anyway. Likely because I had saved them from the factory in Grafton, at a time when I was just trying to rescue Jen. They had happened to be there, and I had unlocked their cages, but I had never felt comfortable with Tabitha's gratefulness for the act.

I was there for Jen. They had been just a lucky happenstance. I had saved them because I was there, and truth be told at the time, if more policemen had been coming, or vampires, or demons, I would have left all the witches, taken Jen, and run.

"You don't owe us anything, you know."

Tabitha's smile was real, this time, even if her eyes still were worried. "I know you think so."

Jen walked over, her hips shifting ever so slightly in the way some women have. She held two bottles of beer in one hand, their bottlenecks crossed in her fingers. I tugged one from her hand. The bottle was wet on the outside, a cool frostiness that left a wet chill in my palm.

The beers were Medallas. Pale lagers. I took a sip, then another. They had a light and crisp taste; the beer was cold and left a little hoppy aftertaste on my tongue. Refreshing after the day out in the sun, and I breathed out a little relaxed sigh.

Jen bumped my hip with hers. Looked at our new guests. "Worried?"

She knew I was. "How are you not?"

Jen shrugged, a little elegant motion of one shoulder that tightened her shirt around her breasts. She took a sip of her own, her throat working delicately with the motion of her swallow. "I guess it comes down to belief."

"Yeah?" Belief was a tricky word.

"Yeah."

I remembered the first person who had really brought belief up to me. The process of it, at least. Father Benjamin, back in Grafton. He had spent years walking around the town during the day, tracing symbols against doors and windows, leaving little golden trails against the glass that only I could see, all through the power of belief.

He believed those symbols would keep demons and vampires out. And they had.

They just hadn't kept him alive.

He had talked about the Miracle on Ice. How a young group of kids from the United States had beaten the overwhelmingly talented Russian team. They had scrapped harder, fought longer, and had fit together in a way that a team should fit. Where the sum of the parts together was greater than the count of their individual skills.

Because they had believed.

Jen watched me. It was as if she could feel everything I thought through the keydrop binding us. What had once been Solomon's

Key. The prison for the demons before they had been released. And then Jen's prison, after her death. Or near-death.

Our eyes connected. There was a physical sensation to it, like a punch to my gut, and I was the first to look away.

Her voice was soft. "Gus..."

I wasn't going to say it. I wasn't going to ask her what she believed. About her belief. In whatever power in the word, in me.

I had failed her once; in all honesty I had failed her a number of times. All of my friends, when I had left Grafton. I've made up for it since, at least some of it, but I also felt like I had a long way to go.

I knew who Jen believed in.

And *god,* I wanted to be that person.

But I knew I was a long way away. I was the guy who looked at Father Benjamin and his belief, who had seen the ghost of the dead priest kneeling in the parking lot of the King's Lodge, and wondered why he thought he could have stood up to Azazel.

I was the man who had seen a Templar die, who had been eaten by wights, for no other reason than he was trying to help me. Another man who had believed in a greater good. A greater purpose.

I had watched another priest, the archbishop in New Orleans, fail him. He had believed in his purpose so hard he had ignored the signs around him. And that mistake had gotten him killed.

Belief seemed to be a double-edged sword. Neither side was safe to be near. And standing in the middle only got you cut faster.

I didn't want to fail Jen's. Not ever. I didn't want to be the one that my friends believed in, and have that belief cost them their lives.

Jen's hip bumped mine. It felt like an age had passed, and her look was knowing. "Haven't we already talked about this, Gus?"

She meant back on our trip to New Orleans. When we were

hiding in a garage. About things like belief and sacrifice and being together. About letting others take the bullet for you.

Literally.

I did not like that talk.

I did not like what happened in New Orleans.

I didn't like the vision of a ghostly Jen floating forever above me, mute, sad, and possibly climbing the steep stairs over the horizon.

But all I could do was roll my eyes. Try to find a way to deal with it. Because this was us. We were together. And we all wanted to beat the demons at their own game.

Maybe you're wondering why I still wrestle with this. After all, I had seen what doubt could cost me. And hell, I was an angel. Or part angel. Or something.

I can only say that I didn't know I wouldn't always wrestle with it. It being the concept of worthiness and belief. Maybe we all should wrestle with the idea more. What life should mean. What our lives should mean. And if someone believes in you that much, how we can find a way to be worthy of what they believe of us.

I think we all know about those people who are so self-absorbed they already believed they were worthy of everything life gave them. History is littered with the lessons those people left for us. Those same lessons weren't something I wanted to make the mistake of doing. Or being. I was comfortable being on the other side, taking little steps to feeling worthy of what my friends believed of me.

Hell, I'd settle for just finding a way to keep them all alive.

CHAPTER SIX

The evening outside had become a deep purplish black, a darkening miasma hiding all sorts of intentions in cloudy, black depths. The pressure across the horizon swelled with the night, the plate-glass windows a thin barrier between those of us inside and the thickening darkness outside. The blackness pressed down, pushing the sun below the horizon, and if I placed my fingertips on the cold glass I thought I would feel it bowing inward, straining under the evil out there, hidden in the murky, angry night.

The moment froze in time. No one else moved. For some reason the floor-to-ceiling windows faced south-west, toward Mexico City, and while a few stars pinpricked the night sky, what dominated the western horizon was the blackness, pushing down on a thin arc of a brilliant red glow. Like the sun had been murdered by the night, leaving a puddled sunset of blood, a dark sliver of crimson that drained from the end of the Earth.

Something only I thought I could see in my ethereal vision.

Something I kept from others. None of them would like the negativity of my thoughts, the dark train my mind rode, the dark passage of what my life had been and what I believed it would always end up being.

Gertrude turned from the window.

"I like none of this," the witch said. Her voice deep, deep for a woman, deep even for a man.

"None of what?" Jen asked.

The Valkyrie waved her hand, the motion encompassing the group, flowing over the window, over the horizon, and ending so that her arm lay southwest. "This. All of this. Us. This city. Sabnock. The army of demons between us and the demon. None of it."

I couldn't help but feel a burst of happiness at the Valkyrie. Finally, I had someone on my side. Someone who saw the task for what it was. If not suicidal, at the very least impossible. I caught Gertrude's eye and gave a slight nod before looking over at Jen, a small smile developing on my face.

That smile froze when I caught Jen's expression.

Jen was upset. Not so Gertrude could tell, but in a way I could. Definitely something I sensed along our bond along the keydrop, but also something I could sense from the stiffness in her expression. Something friends could tell about other friends, a controlled exasperation, or an anger, something that brought a low rumbling echo along the windows, a soft warning of thunder from a cloudless, dark night.

"Gertrude," Jen said. Her voice cool. "If you feel like this is something you can't do, or won't do, then you are free to go."

The tall witch froze, cocking her head. Mistaking the moment. Her tone curious. "That's not what I said."

Jen's voice remained cool. She looked at the witch, but her words were for Tabitha and Zoe as well. Maybe even me, with the keydrop radiating the same chill against my chest. "Nevertheless, I want to be clear. If you feel like the task is impossible, or if you aren't up for it, then…" She motioned the neck of her beer toward the door, leaving the sentence unfinished, but likely understood.

Gertrude scoffed. Perhaps the worst thing she could have done in the moment. "You think I'm afraid?"

"Fear has nothing to do with it," Jen answered.

I spoke up when I shouldn't have. "Jen, she's just saying the same thing I've been saying. There's no easy way to do this." I lowered my voice, leaning in a bit. "There may be no way to do this."

And Jen knew what I meant there. I didn't mean killing Sabnock was impossible. I didn't even mean reverting the Dead Zone, turning the land back to Mexico City pre-undead was impossible. But doing it without anyone dying, well that was the task we all spoke of.

"Gus," Jen said, her reply quiet. Just between us. "Was I speaking to you?"

I pulled my head back. Surprised.

This was a different Jen to me. I didn't know why she was angry. Why she had immediately jumped onto Gertrude. For a moment I wondered if there was some jealous feeling involved, some dislike because I had been happy that Gertrude was saying the very thing I had been saying.

But that didn't seem like Jen to me. Jen wasn't petty. Or jealous. She had no need to be. Jen was, well, Jen was Jen. Jen was enough. Jen was more than enough.

And right now she was looking past me. Still dialed in to Gertrude. "I appreciate you coming out. You and Tabitha and Zoe. None of you had to."

Zoe went to speak up, but Tabitha reached out and grabbed her daughter's arm, and the young witch remained silent. Gertrude the same, quiet, standing silent, the haft of the Valkyrie's axe and hilt of her sword poking out at angles from either shoulder, a darkened metal cross outlined against darkened glass windows, a thin transparent film holding back the darkness of the night.

Finally, Gertrude spoke. "There is no fear here. None in me. I have done things like this before. Battles. Wars." The witch paused. "Maybe you haven't."

"Whether I have or haven't," Jen said, "is not the point here either."

Gertrude waited.

I waited. I could feel the tension along Jen's bond with me, though I couldn't identify the cause. I could only remain still, afraid that any motion of mine would tip Jen over into some darker place.

"There's going to be a cost here," Jen said. "A cost here, just like there was a cost in New Orleans, in Lewisville, even back in Grafton. There's going to be a cost here just like there's going to be a cost in Paris, in Italy. That cost is going to grow. It's going to be dear. And every time we do this, every time we go up against these demons, each time we stop we're going to have to pay that cost. From here on out, we're not getting anything free."

Jen's hand motioned the bottle to the door again. "So I don't want anyone here not ready to pay it. We don't need that here. We need people committed to that cost. I can understand you not liking it, but if you're not ready to pay it, if you don't think this is something that can be done, or if you're not sure you're the person to help do it, then go."

She tilted her beer to her lips and took a small sip. Let out a sigh that wasn't a *this tastes good* kind of sigh. "No hard feelings."

I felt for Jen then. I thought she was trying to protect me. Because she knew that if someone died, I would blame myself. Just like I had blamed myself for Jen back in New Orleans. I reached out a hand to Jen, to lay it on her shoulder and tell her I understood.

Jen leaned back from my hand so that it fell away. Her gaze was still locked on the Valkyrie. My hand fell through empty air, my outstretched fingers barely brushing the cotton of her shirt.

The Valkyrie nodded, once. As if formalizing a bargain between her and Jen. "Death holds no great mystery for me."

Jen nodded in return. Took another sip of her beer. Then turned to look at me, her expression tight and controlled and still exasperated or angry or *something*.

At the same time, Nick came in from one of the side rooms of the condo. Rooms that used to be bedrooms, and still kind of were, I mean, they did still have beds in them. We just didn't use them to sleep in. For us they were private areas, for private conversations. An occasional nap during late-night planning sessions. Or—if we needed to—a quiet place to call someone.

Sarah was with Nick. Her faced worried, one hand on the back of his shoulders, the other hand fingering the little amulet she had on a chain around her neck. Something she fingered more and more lately. Her eyes found Jen's, and I could see the worry in them.

Nick held a cell phone just a bit from his ear. A tiny sound trilled from the phone's small speaker. He looked at me, his gaze unreadable behind the reflection of his glasses.

"They're not answering," he said.

CHAPTER SEVEN

The small speaker kept up its shrill tone in that on-and-off rhythm all calls had, *rinnnggg, rinnnggg, rinnnggg*. The entire condo filled with the sound, the trilling, then the quiet, then the trilling. The tiny sound faded around us, into the thick carpet of the condo, fading before touching the dark windows, fading before hitting the pressured glass.

The only other sound was the clunking of the icemaker in the fridge as ice tumbled out into the tray. A loud sound that made us all glance into the kitchen. Still, no one spoke, or drank, or did anything until the last ring of the call finished and Johnny's voice came on. Tiny in the room. "You've reached Johnny. Speak up, drink up, or hang up."

Then the beep for voice mail.

"Man, get back to us," Nick said. Then ended the call.

Maybe it shouldn't have been a surprise that Johnny didn't answer. That we couldn't reach him. After all, the networks were spotty at best now. The Dead Zones had been quite the service interruption. Phones, power, supply trains, all lines we had depended on, relied on, all lines that had been broken or overloaded with the appearance of the Zones.

What goods that could be made or farmed were still hauled by truckers, but the routes had funneled in, and the roads were swamped. The homes with power were lucky they lived in a different grid than Louisiana or Alabama or some of Texas. Cable television was just for the major cities now, most people had gone back to having rabbit ears on their tv sets. At least, the televisions that could actually hook up to a set of rabbit ears.

The phone calls people could make, they had to push past millions of other calls, people trying to connect to their loved ones. Every network, every grid, every road was slammed, and what worked for the most part was barely functional. Companies scrambled for fixes. Everyone had a plan.

The power companies were cutting parts of the grid off and trying to consolidate. There were emergency rules in place for travel, especially on the interstates, allowing eighteen-wheelers the right of way to try to get goods to places faster. Hell, even the President was in on a quick fix, trying to work out a treaty with Azazel for supply routes—both land and sea—to pass through New Orleans.

All of that took time. And the phone companies might have had the worst of it. After all, the roads and power lines hadn't been used to make the Dead Zones.

Cell phones didn't work in the Dead Zone, and for the most part anywhere around it. Signals couldn't penetrate the barrier erected around them, and any lines passing through the zones were basically cut off.

Building a new infrastructure to go around those zones would take years. Maybe decades. Putting more satellites in space would take even longer. Building the satellites was only the first step.

Finding a launch window, planning trajectories, coverage, all of that would take more time than people could wait.

And while there was urgency, there was no real plan of action. A lot of words though. By now you've seen different senators and governors talking about what they were doing, but an election was coming up, and those words were basically just words. I mean, the companies were still trying to build out a top-of-the-line internet network that the United States government had promised to build voters back in the nineteen eighties.

Taxes well spent.

So phone calls were spotty. Email even was chancy, with sendings and replies falling into the great spam folder of the overworked internet. Texting worked better, short bursts of characters from one screen to the next.

With that knowledge, reaching Johnny and Gabrielle shouldn't have made them worry so.

Except for they all knew where the two had gone.

And they all knew what was at risk.

So even if it was just a network overload, the fact that Johnny hadn't answered or texted worried us all. Because it was more of a matter of *couldn't*, than *hadn't*, with our friends.

I waved at Nick. "Go."

Nick nodded, stepping back into the side room. Sarah backing in with him. A moment later the door shut, there was a click of a light switch, after which the door reopened. Sarah stepped back into the room, alone.

"Don't worry," I told her. "I'll be right behind him."

I headed towards the front door. Jen made a motion as if to stop me, or say something, and I paused. She swallowed, her throat seemed to catch on something, and whatever she wanted to say didn't come out.

Which was weird, because Jen knew exactly what to say. Every time. All the time.

"Later," I said. Trying to convey everything was okay with us. Whatever she was angry about, or working through, I would be there. Just like she always had been for me.

Later, she echoed back along the bond. And tried to smile.

I got it then. I thought. Jen didn't want anyone here that might die that wasn't ready for it. Because it was bad enough that I was worried about protecting my friends. I thought she felt like having others along, people who didn't want to be here, if those people died, she thought I might feel even worse about their deaths. Worse, because they hadn't even wanted to be here.

It would definitely spread me out. Would thin out the area I had to cover. The people I had to protect. Like Johnny and Gabrielle.

I rushed out of the apartment and ran down to the far end of the hallway, opposite the stairs I had come up. A door there led to a ladder, that ladder led to the rooftop. One of the things we had liked about this building was the roof access.

I quickly climbed up the rungs, slid the bar on the steel door to the side and swung it open. I pushed too hard, the door was heavy enough, and it landed on the stone of the rooftop with a hollow granite-like tolling sound.

Then I hopped up. Quickly swung the door shut, knowing Jen would be locking it behind me. I ignored the rest of the roof. The people before had left a nice setup here, a worn tiki-like bar top with a tent-like top covering it. Some beach chairs, and other lounge chairs laid flat, a place for people to lay out, and a few side tables. The beach chairs were those yellow-ribbed ones, with the plastic bands that stretched when you sat in them, and folded all the way out so people could lay on them.

I took a few steps past all of that and reached for some ghost.

There was no lack of spirits here. Not in this town, not closer to

Mexico City, not anywhere in Mexico at all. Not just because of the large concentration of the population, in combination with tens of thousands of years of people living in the general area, all the way back to the Aztecs and the Mayans and the Nahua. People had been dying here for century upon century, for longer than the Egyptians were building pyramids.

There were ghosts here in waves, the area was flooded with them after the Dead Zone erupted. So many people had died. So many more had been killed. It was as easy for me to find a ghost as it was to find a ripe apple walking through an apple orchard.

So I found one.

Then I braced myself. Nick was already way ahead of me, and who knows what Johnny and Gabrielle were in the middle of. I would have to travel fast and likely far.

And, finally, I pulled.

CHAPTER EIGHT

I could see all the spirits around me. They appeared like little blue dots on a radar screen in my ethereal sight. Some of these dots were bright, stronger ghosts that had a larger connection to the ethereal plane. Some spirits were dim, weak, barely hanging on to the tap connecting them from this world to the next.

Some seemed to have a fiery redness center to them, a deep flickering of hate or anger. Those spirits I had learned to avoid, carrying a darkness I didn't want to experience, though they weren't always obvious at first glance. Sometimes the evil was buried too deep in the spirit for me to see it. Sometimes these angry spirits were the only ones around I could use. And sometimes I had no choice, I could either tap into the dark spirit and use it, experience those memories, or I could pass onto the afterlife from whatever life-threatening injury I was suffering for.

So I had used those angry spirits from time to time. I had lived their lives. Experienced their memories. Each of those times I... I can't really describe the evil. I can't describe how my whole body wanted to reject what I had lived through. I could only say, well...

let's just say the memories of those experiences stuck with me. Hell, I still couldn't eat gingersnaps, after that old lady in Lewiston.

And I was in a hurry. It was one of those times where beggars couldn't be choosers. The first bright ghost, the first strong one that appeared on my ethereal radar, that was the one I immediately went to tap. It might have flickered a little red, but still I leaned that way, ethereally, stretching my senses towards that bright blue dot. I needed that deep well of energy. I was likely going to have to travel far and wanted to top off my tanks right from the start.

So—as prepared as I could be, and with the tiniest of winces—I tapped into that spirit and pulled...

The warrior stood, panting. Breathing heavily. Him. Me. I. The two of us became one, inhaling a deep musky scent in the air, something primal, with an underlying odor of feces... all of which was somehow threaded with the coppery smell of blood. Altogether, the smell of it almost choked me as I inhaled, and still the warrior panted in hard, expelling breaths. His chest rhythmically pulsing with the effort.

There was a stone axe in his hand——my hand——the wooden shaft polished from years of use, the flintlike-edge of dark rock dripping dark, red fluid. Something pink and globule-like hung onto the bottom of the blade, finally dropping to the ground with a plopping thud. My other hand held a head, a head without a body, sweaty strands of thick black hair tightly wound in my fist.

The head leaked, the blood trickling onto the ground, sounding a little like someone pissing on sand. The stream slowed, then stopped, until there were just the tiny dripping drops of blood smacking into the thick puddle below. The warrior loved the sound—I loved the sound—and we both stood there in reflection until the screams of a woman lying a few feet away disturbed the dark tap-tap-tapping of the drips.

Still, that sound made him grin. Made me *grin...*

I tore myself out of the memory, away from the ethereal power, choking on the bile rising in my throat. I found myself on one knee, my chest swelling with a deep breath of the warm air around me, the air that was too warm for Mexico, but still much cleaner, much cooler than the wet hotness of fetid death I had been breathing as that ghost.

All the spirits in the area, and I find some kind of ancient Aztec warrior.

Great.

This spirit, like some of the other darker ones, now *wanted* the fight. Wanted me to try to take him on, to tap the ethereal plane through his memories and burn through the ghost with as much energy as I could pull. Even now I could feel the ghost's eyes on me, feel the warrior trying to reach towards me, and though I knew he could never really reach *me*, I also didn't want him standing around for the next person to touch. To live.

A person like Zoe. Witches, or fortune-tellers, or anyone else that could touch the afterlife. Other people who might be able to communicate—in some way—with ghosts. So even though there were a thousand other dots around me, some as bright, some less so, I readied myself to tap the warrior's ghost, even as the warrior was reaching back to me.

Some concern radiated along the keydrop from Jen. *Gus?*

I tried to push a feeling of okayness through it. However that feeling was supposed to feel. A thumbs-up kind of thing, maybe, through the Key. I got the idea she wasn't buying it, as well as feeling the worry about Johnny and Nick out there, and the slight wondering of whether or not to tell me to hurry behind all of those thoughts.

Funny, what our bond allowed us to feel from each other. More than words, more than tone, something deeper bound us. And while

I would never hide anything from Jen, I also didn't want her to worry more about me than she needed to.

I could take it.

I could take anything. I would take anything.

For her. For my friends.

So while I wanted to find someone else, some other spirit, I knew that wasn't what I was going to do. I was going to burn through him and send him on to the next plane, wherever that was for him. Whatever ghostly hell he would end up in.

It was part of who I was, after all. Vengeance. Judgement. And while I could question someone's choice to make me the final arbiter of someone else's fate, I would also make sure I made that judgement based on who I was, what I felt was right, and wrong.

I set my jaw. Reached back to the warrior. Felt the ethereal energy flow through the spirit's tap and burn through my body, a cool heat that rose goosebumps along my flesh. I felt the ghost laugh, the warrior flex, and I pulled more, feeling energy push through my body, fill it, fire along my nerves, pulse along my veins.

The warrior laughed harder. *His/my grip tighter on the smooth handle of the axe, growing erect by the screams of the woman, our chest going in and out, our breath almost panting with excitement, the warrior throwing our head back and letting out a scream…*

I gritted my teeth and screamed from the rooftop, feeling the energy fill me, feeling the warrior's memory slam into me at the same time…

The woman before us screamed. Her legs spread apart as she scrambled back along the sand, her feet kicking up little tufts of white spray. My grin grew larger, I grew hard at the same time, and I tossed the head aside. Wiping the man's blood—her mate, weak man that he had been—off my chest. Feeling my nipples tingle as my wet thumb brushed over it. Feeling myself almost come just at that.

The woman's scream died out, choked off, and she stared up at me in fear. Fear I had seen before, fear from a hundred other spirits just like this one. She stared up, her mouth open partly, her hands, her chin, even her eyes shaking ever so slightly.

It just got us harder.

Her back was against a thick stone, a square black basalt thing. Almost like an altar. Her feet dug in the ground like she could keep backing through it, little baby-like motions with no real strength behind them.

Weak, the man protecting her. Weak, the woman. All was prey, for him. For us. We stopped, standing in front of her, hard as the altar behind the woman, letting the axe plop to the ground. He grabbed her foot, tugging her leg to the side, breathing deep with the thoughts of what he was about to do, his other hand holding himself, massaging himself, even as he stepped inside her other leg and pulled her close to him, dragging her back along the sand, feeling her other leg strike his, weakly…

So weak, this woman. Her mate. So weak, all of them.

All were prey for him. He could take anything he wanted. And he would.

He would.

He grew harder and fell on top of the woman. Feeling her scream, her teeth bite into his shoulder, tearing his flesh, and he did come then, but he would take her still, he would take her and her mate and everyone—

He would take them all…

I came back screaming. The scream ended in a gasp of air. The warrior's ghost ended in the same moment. I could feel its realization and rage along with the sudden bubble-bursting sensation of the spirit… disappearing, wherever those things went.

Good riddance, bitch. Hopefully hell was real, and hopefully the people there knew how to handle ghosts like the Aztec. Like Jo in the past. Like so many others...

Energy coursed through me. Energy I had pulled from the ethereal plane, through the tap of the ghost, energy that had surged through the spirit along with thousands of other memories the warrior had held, all released when his spirit had disappeared, memories that slammed into me one after another, each a ninety-mile-an-hour fastball to the chest.

The memories of the Aztec's life, believe it or not, grew worse, and worse, and still worse until all I could see and feel and smell was death. Murders and rapes, of the living and the dead, were just the beginning for the warrior. He had lived quite the life, and as always, I wondered why he had remained. If hell was a real place, the warrior certainly deserved to have gone straight there. Without passing go. Without collecting two hundred dollars.

Through those quick moments, the sliver of time I had lived the spirit's life, the spirit became me in some way. Even as I was living his life, he was living mine, there was some interchange there where I could feel the ghost mock me. Where I could see the spirit looking at who I was, what I had done in my life, what I was trying to do, and then laughing at all of it. As if my efforts were futile. As if *I* was futile.

It was those brief moments I worried. Did doing what I do leave me with some darker stain on my soul, some dark blot that would not rub off, or wash out? Could I live something like that, these memories, and *not* be affected in some way? Could the stain be permanent? And not just permanent, but growing with each use of power? Each tap into the plane? If I peered too long into the memories of these ghosts, if my need or desire or *want* for the power I could access through them grew too great, would I then become them?

And not just them, but the collection of all of them? Some dark jigsaw puzzle of evil lives, of a million spirits, all pieced together into… something?

Maybe that's why they laughed each time I lived them. Why they were eager to fight me. Why they were eager to share who they were. Because they knew, over time, the sea always washes away the shore.

Still, Johnny and Gabrielle were in trouble. Nick was on his way to help, with no idea of what was going on. It could have been a blown tire in a bad coverage area, or Sabnock could have attacked the pair with an army of demons. There was no way to tell, but it was likely my friends needed me.

And needs must.

So I pushed confidence through the keydrop, feeling Jen's concern. And I roared defiance at the spirit, at its evil, its spreading darkness, at the murder and rapes and vileness, I screamed at it all and leapt into the air…

…feeling ethereal wings expand behind me, flapping like a feather-light cloak, the wings catching invisible currents of air and shooting me like an arrow southeast.

CHAPTER NINE

I had flown like this before, once I figured out who I was. What I was. What, I guess, I am.

There was still video of me at the time, speeding through the night in Colorado, like an F-14 Tomcat soaring over the Earth. Pulling energy from spirits as I passed, powering my flight. Maybe I looked more like a comet, because those videos, and the few pictures, showed a furious blue-white ball of lightning searing through the air, the overflow of ethereal energy I was pulling streaming a shower of white sparks behind me.

So while I was looking to get to my friends quickly, I also didn't want to announce to the world where I was headed. Where I had left from. Because I was sure demons were watching. I needed to fly, but fly a bit more stealth-bomberish, not all F-14 Tomcat.

So I flew closer to the ground. I tried not to pull so much ethereal energy that I would erupt in that blue-white ball of lightning. I went as fast as I dared, only occasionally letting out a shower of sparks when I pushed the pedal a little too much to the metal.

I was still learning, after all.

Still, my wings were out. Translucent wings, outlined in shimmering blue-white, so thin I could see through them. Bright enough that if someone were looking at me as I passed, they might have thought me a UFO. Because I wasn't shaped like a plane.

The countryside slid by underneath me, a dark ocean of darkness, flowing quickly. Occasionally populated by the occasional flutter of lights and lamps. The quick flash of headlights on a road. Sometimes illuminated blocks of a town rolled underneath me, windows lit up against the night like a leviathan surfacing from the deep.

I avoided the towns I could. Flew quietly and less... brightly where I couldn't. And tried to follow, the best I could, the route I knew Johnny and Gabrielle were traveling.

They had been circling around Mexico City. Heading to a town called Cuernavaca. Gabrielle's family had a base there, where the Antonados had ruled over most of the United States. South America was much older, vampires had come over with De Soto, and so a lot of Mexico and Brazil had ties to Gabrielle's family in Europe.

Gabrielle had thought she could find us a small army. Not a real army, but more of a guerilla force. Vampire SWAT teams, like she had brought to Grafton. And whether it was ten soldiers or a hundred, we needed them.

Of course, that was all dependent on whether her father was looking for her. Or hadn't—at the very least—kicked her out of the family after what had happened back in Denver, at Red Rock. No one had seen him in the aftermath, and who knew what could have happened to him after the geas had been broken between he and I.

So, Johnny and Gabrielle had taken a chance. A big enough chance, but one with a lot of help if they had made it there and back.

True night had fallen, the deep purple—so purple it was black—of midnight. The land rolled underneath me, dark swells of hills, deep stretches of sandy earth. I followed the road I knew they were heading back from Cuernavaca, a big looping route wide of Mexico City and the Dead Zone there, a route taking them close to the Gulf of Mexico and north along the shore.

There was a part where the Dead Zone almost reached the Gulf, and that was the dangerous part of the route. A narrow strip of land between the zone and the beach, with just one road paralleling the shore, winding north-northeast.

I flew and pulled ghosts as I passed overhead, and searched.

In the distance, sparks appeared. The horizon, southeast of me. Not sparks, but flashes. Quick repetitive pops of light that grew brighter as I neared.

Gunfire.

I closed in. The flashes were accompanied by the thumping sound of automatic weapons. Assault rifles. Fired in coordinated patterns.

I reached ahead for ghosts, seeing plenty on the radar. Vampires were undead, so none of the spirits there were from the fight, but also, as far as I could tell, none were Johnny's. Thralls, after all, were human.

The route had passed through a small beach town. I could barely make out the small homes and houses that littered the shore, tiny shops and restaurants, brightly colored tarps hanging here and there. Everything was muted, hidden in shadow.

Everything but the fight.

Cars littered the street, passing between the homes and shops. Old beat-up trucks covered in rust. A few sedans, colored much the same, mixed with a few newer, sleeker cars. And up front, first in line, a Cadillac Escalade, black, windows busted out, flipped upside down, the front grill and engine looking crumpled, as if it had struck something at full speed and the vehicle had flipped over.

Johnny and Gabrielle's truck.

People were huddled around the Escalade. Some moved among the older, rusted cars. All of that I could see, outlined in the flashing strobe-like pattern of gunfire, so that everything almost looked like one of those stop-motion animated films.

The pops and thumps became pops and thumps and whizzes through the air. *Pings* as bullets struck metal. *Thwacks* when they took a chunk out of rocks. Someone sat by the corner of a fender, holding an assault rifle close to their body. The next flash of light they were firing that rifle over the hood. The next flash of light, they were bent back, huddled by the tire well of the car.

Other shapes ran through the street. People running, firing guns. And larger shapes, much larger, the size of the cars they moved between.

And then a dark shadow flew among the rusted vehicles. A shadow that appeared and disappeared in the night. A shadow that, when it appeared, fired a few shots, or let a knife fly out of his hand.

Nick.

Wherever the man went, the other figures fell to the ground. In many cases I saw a ghost appear. In some I did not, and in those cases Nick would bend down and do something more with his knife. Something that left that figure headless.

Nick stayed away from the larger shapes. Now that I was almost overhead I could see them. Red, thick-shelled figures with long arms stretching out to either side. And legs, many legs, along both sides of the creatures.

I shook my head. Closed my eyes. Opened them again.

Saw the same thing.

So I fell to the earth. Landing behind the Escalade. Where Johnny and Gabrielle sat, one behind the crumpled engine block, one at the rear. Johnny held an assault rifle, an M-16 he had picked up back in Colorado that he liked. Gabrielle had an Uzi in either hand.

Both the Uzi's and the muzzle of the rifle swung my way, until the two recognized me.

"About time brother," Johnny said, with his trademark flash of a smile, a big pearly white grin. Blood trickled down from his forehead, running along his dark skin.

I took a peek again over the truck. "Nice driving."

"Yeah," Johnny laughed. "They forgot to use the crosswalk."

"Who?"

Johnny nodded behind me.

I looked back, saw the huddled mass of shattered red shells there. Broken in long cracks, revealing a whitish interior, the white of fishy flesh, with a yellow-white liquid trickling out of the breaks. The long arms were there too, ending in huge pincer-like claws. And the legs, the many legs, to either side. Some of them twitching, and even one of the claws still working open and close, open and close...

It was surreal. That thing was just as large as the Escalade. I turned back to the truck, taking a peek over it. The other car-like shapes were there, scuttling from side to side, never running right at the people shooting at them, but more of coming at them from the sides, as if the shapes were circling around to the shooters. "Are those...?"

I couldn't say it. It didn't seem possible. I mean, I had faced wights and vampires, other forms of the undead. Demons. The mob of rakshasa over in the Hindu Kush.

There were hints of things like this, though. Ever since the Dead Zones rose, they had not brought just the denizens of hell, but other creatures too. Creatures since the beginning of time. The media was all over a dragon in Paris, making its nest in the Eiffel Tower, and then I had seen something deep under Lake Pontchartrain, a blue-white glimmer of life hiding in the depths of the water, something so large I couldn't begin to fathom what it was.

Still, to see something like this, in person. To be here now, fighting them... it made me wonder where they had come from. Were they some kind of evolutionary branch that had died out? Would dinosaurs come tromping down the beach next? What other creature could surface out of the ocean?

"Yep," Johnny laughed, seeing my face. Knowing what I was thinking, where my mind had gone. And, being Johnny, cracked a joke, "We've got a bad case of crabs."

Gabrielle just snorted.

It was a bad joke. Johnny knew it. I knew it. Hell, even Gabrielle knew it. She rolled her eyes and made a nodding motion to Johnny, signaling something like *hey, keep shooting*.

Johnny winked at me, then turned back around the front crumpled fender of the Escalade. Took a few shots, then looked back.

I was still standing there.

"You helping?" Johnny said, taking a blind shot or two down the street. The best I could tell, the bullets thwacked the shells of the crabs, sometimes penetrating, sometimes not, not killing them, and most of the time just angering them. "You know, do some kind of angel thing?"

"Right."

I shook myself out of my thoughts. That was why I was here, after all. I could wonder about the whole thing later. It was time to get to slicing and dicing.

I pulled at a ghost, someone nearby. One of the men that had come in the rusted cars. I was relieved and also a little ashamed to live a memory of a man who only liked punching his wife instead of something like the Aztec warrior. Or some kind of baby-killing grandma who baked a hell of a cookie.

I'd wonder about the creatures later. The crabs, the dragon, the leviathan in the lake. It was all bad, and each of those things would have its moment with me.

For now, though, it was crabbin' time.

Yeah, that was a bad joke, too.

After all, Johnny didn't have a monopoly on them.

CHAPTER TEN

I lived the ghost, briefly. The spirit was weak, thin, the dot barely blue on my radar, and popped as quickly as I pulled.

Bitch you listen when I tell you…

I hate saying this, but "if I had a nickel." I couldn't begin to count the amount of wife beaters I had sent to whatever after-after-life they went to. There seemed like millions, and I was happy to send them all, and this one too.

Speaking of—the spirit popped, taking its ugly memories with it; I took the energy it gave me and willed the sword into existence.

It felt like a sword, a flat blade, edged on both sides, all the way to a long, sharp tip. It even looked like a sword, though the metal was more translucent than any kind of steel, shimmering a bit with a blue-white energy, the edges of the blade colored a more intense blue, like a sharp streak of lightning splitting the night.

It weighed nothing, though it balanced in my hand. I tried not to think about that, because it threw me off, like swinging a bat that was lighter than air. In my mind I made it feel like a sword, so that my hand gripped a hard, heavy hilt, and I fixed that thought there.

I leapt over the Escalade. Landed in front of a scuttling giant crab. Ducked its backhand swing of a claw. Swung my sword in return and almost fell when it hit the shell of the creature and rebounded.

Can't picture it? Grab one of those wiffle bats. The ones with the plastic balls. Then swing it as hard as you can at a tree. Put all your force into it like you're going to chop the tree in half. Put all your weight into it, so that as you step into the swing you're leaning forward, putting everything you have into the motion.

See what happens.

I didn't fall, but I did stumble a bit. Towards the crab. Which, in the pinching way all crabs have, came back with its other claw and snapped me up.

Those claws hurt. Jagged rock-like pincers cut into me before I could harden my skin with ethereal energy, although I snapped up another ghost and did just that, pouring ethereal energy into my muscles, my bones, my skin, hardening everything. Making myself a tough nut for this crab to crack.

That was a sentence I never thought I'd think.

The claws had me good. Both arms were trapped inside it. I couldn't push the claw open, and though I still held my sword I couldn't swing it much.

A large part of me worried about that. About the sword, and why it didn't just slice the crab open like it had sliced open vampires and demons and other dead and half-dead things. But that worry could be later. Right now I wanted to focus, it was hard to breathe, the claw kept up its crushing, cracking motion, and it was everything I could do to keep myself in one piece.

I was in trouble.

The keydrop flared a bit with worry. It was all I could feel, this far away from Jen. The bond only communicated so far. And, of course, not wanting to worry her, I tried to radiate a *fine*-ness I didn't quite feel back to her.

Men, right?

The claw crunched in further. The serrated tip pinching into my chest. I stopped breathing, my chest was too compressed, too tight around my lungs. I pulled from another ghost, and another, trying to counter the force crushing me. Hardening skin and bone. But it was a losing battle.

I was *really* in trouble.

So the keydrop really worried.

No babe, I'm fine, I'm fine... I thought, and even though I was having a hard time breathing, I laughed, maybe a bit delirious with lack of oxygen, thinking this is where it might end. Not death by Azazel's hand, but cut in two by a crustacean.

The shadows in front of me swirled, like I was about to pass out.

But the swirling shadows weren't me going down for the count.

It was Nick, stepping out of the darkness he was a master of, face and vest covered in spattered blood and a yellowish-white liquid, his glasses missing. He still held a gun in one hand, a thick Bowie knife in the other. A real knife, not translucent like my sword. A knife he plunged right behind the hinge of the claw cracking me, into the joint, where the shell was thin and weak.

The creature screamed, a horrible gurgling sound. The claw split wide open, letting me fall to the ground. The bottom hinge of the claw hanging in the air above me.

"Thanks," I said, looking up. Trying to take a deep breath.

Nick was already gone.

That man was all business when it came to killing.

Speaking of—I rolled to the side, feeling more than seeing the crab behind me swoop in with its other claw. The good one. The shell cracked into the pavement and rattled behind me as I rolled up against one of the older, rusty cars.

And I thought, this will do, in a pinch.

Get it?

Yeah, we can't all be Johnny.

I scrabbled to the back of the car, pulling at another ghost as I did. The crab came up beside me, raised up on its rear legs, both arms in the air, one claw hanging from the end of its arm. Screaming its gurgling cry.

I picked up the car and slammed it down on the giant crab.

Twice.

Three times, for good measure.

I went through the rest of the fight that way. Picking up the older cars and trucks and slamming them into the giant crabs along the way. One after the next. Until, like some collective brain flipped a switch, the remaining grabs scuttled east. Past the houses there, into the darkness of the beach, disappearing into the waves.

Weird.

I stood there, chest heaving a bit, hands on my knees. Covered in the crab-gore that had spurted out each time I had slammed a car down on top of the creatures. Looking around, seeing a bunch of dead men and women wearing jeans and T-shirts, some with bandanas, most not.

A number of vampires too. Most of those better dressed, in dark tactical gear, albeit headless. The few undead that weren't missing their heads, Gabrielle was trying to help up. I guess what was left of our help.

Nick materialized next to me, right out of the dark, standing and looking east as if he had always been doing exactly that. "Weird, right?"

I knew he meant the crabs. I was wondering the same thing. I couldn't see the swells of the ocean that had swallowed the creatures, and if those waves hid more, we could be in trouble.

Still, we were okay now. With the crabs on the run. "Yeah."

"What happened to your sword?"

"Didn't work." It had bounced off that crab like it was concrete. "At least, not against those things."

We both were silent for a bit. Contemplating that. For me the sword had become, well, not a talisman, but the reason I could do what I was doing. I had discovered the rules to summon it, rules I lived by now. To be someone who lived by their promises, who kept their word, to protect those I should be protecting.

And so, it had become my symbol of vengeance. It had killed Kimaris. It had killed Buné. It had killed vampires by the score at Red Rock.

It was belief for me. Belief we could kill Sabnock. Belief we could kill the rest of the demons and get rid of the Dead Zones.

Ultimately, it was the reason Azazel was worried about me. For him, I was a symbol of something he had beaten thousands of years ago. Angels.

Though I wasn't really an angel myself. I didn't quite believe in that. I was part angel, the way some people were part Cherokee or part German. Some of the same blood flowed through me, and that linked me to them, but I wasn't a banner-carrying trumpet-blaring guardian of the heavens.

Still, the sword had been a symbol of sorts for me. Like I said, not quite a talisman, but an idea. After a decade of running from Azazel, I had something that could fight back. Something he was scared of.

And now, it didn't quite work the way I believed it should.

It worried me. Maybe Nick was worried too. It was quiet enough I could hear the groans of those still alive behind us as they picked themselves off of the road. It was quiet enough I could hear the checking of cartridges. It was quiet enough to hear the breeze, kicking up from the Gulf, bringing the taste of salt and something... *tangy*, in the air.

The taste twisted my mouth, and I spit out saliva. Some of the crab's fluid too. And even a bit of shell.

Nick looked over at me. "You know, there's a dragon in Paris."

I knew. The thought had recently occurred to me. "I know."

Another groan. Another click of a cartridge being loaded into a rifle. Another puff of a tangy, salty breeze.

Nick faced west again. "Just saying, you can't hit everything with a car."

He had been there in the parking garage back in Denver. I looked over at Nick. The corner of his lip might have twitched. What passed for humor in my friend, and dammit if it wasn't funny.

I grinned too. There were no rules to this game. We would get stronger, and so would the demons. We would keep fighting, and so would Azazel.

In the end, the winner might just be who can hit the other person with the largest car. I didn't know. All I could say is I planned to be the person taking that swing. "Who says?"

Nick's lip twitched again. He glanced over his shoulder, towards Mexico City. "Think it's something they did? Or something they might know?"

I shrugged, pulling myself up. A few feet away lay a head, staring at us. The eyes angry, the mouth sneering, sharp canines exposed.

I summoned my sword, punching the tip through the skull. Watched the eyes roll up, the mouth drift open, as the vampire gave up its ghost.

Well, not literally. Just figuratively.

I let out a slight breath I hadn't realized I was holding. The sword still worked. At least on undead. And demons. Just not on weird ass Dungeons-and-Dragons-like creatures.

Nick grunted. Looked at me with a slight shrug, glancing up with his eyes as if saying, *what did he know?*

He disappeared again into the shadows. Reappearing back down the road, next to a few buildings that looked like boarded-up shops. He took a peek into one and disappeared again.

I smiled to myself. Nick liked to do a little shopping sometimes, especially in stores that were, let's say, permanently relocating. Sometimes bringing Sarah back something.

I would too, if I could do what he did. I should at least take a peek. Christmas was coming around, and Nick kept dropping those hints that I knew he was getting from Sarah…

Speaking of, I put a hand on the keydrop. It seemed to help some over long distances. Feeling it. I gave an all-good over the bond and waited until I felt something back from Jen. A sense of relief, and a tinge of something else, something I couldn't identify but worried me. Exasperation? Frustration? Anger?

It was none of those, and a little of them all. So hard to tell, this far away. And so unlike Jen, I wondered if it was something I had done. Was it jealousy, that I sided with Gertrude? Was it her being angry at someone adding to what I had to be worried about?

Later… I had said.

Later… she had returned.

But later what, Jen?

Hell, I didn't know. All I could tell, it was making this Christmas gift more and more important by the day. Which was a kind of pressure that made me squirm a bit, made me shy away. Because I really had no idea what to get Jen.

I headed back to the Escalade. Johnny was leaning against the folded-up bumper, the stock of his assault rifle on the ground, one knee holding it against the truck. Looking past me and down the road.

"Hell of a thing, right?"

"Glad you guys are good." I looked at the truck, I could flip it back over again, but it wouldn't do any good. It wasn't going anywhere.

"Me too," he laughed, it was the kind of forced laugh that came when all your adrenaline was gone, and you felt lucky to get out of whatever you had been in. "The first one," he nodded to the one I had seen first, that he had hit with the Escalade, "it came out of nowhere. And I was already driving a bit fast anywhere, trying to get away from those guys."

He meant the older sedans and trucks. The dead thralls and vampires in them. "Never thought something like that would happen. Being attacked by crabs. Glad you guys got here."

I slapped his shoulder. "Wolverines, right?"

Johnny's laugh became a snort, but his smile was real. "Wolverines."

"How'd it happen?"

He explained it, briefly. They were heading back from Cuernavaca. Gabrielle had contacted a few groups that were actually happy to hear from Victor Dumont's daughter. Paris had been where the Dumonts had their headquarters, and when the Dead Zone had showed up, well... the clan's infrastructure was shattered. A lot of the family missing or presumed dead. And then there was Red Rock, where a lot of the higher-up Dumonts and Antonados had been straight out killed, and where Victor had disappeared. So the clan down here, they had been on their own.

It had been a large clan, but the vampire families down here were broken up much like the cartels. And, just like cartels, they looked for any weakness in each other, and if the weakness was found, they pounced. After the past few weeks, the main cartel—the one serving the Dumonts—realized they had a weakness. They had no support from Paris. No support from the Dumonts. From their head, Victor Dumont.

The other cartels had pounced.

They had sensed weakness and had gone on the attack, carving out pieces of the Dumont territory for themselves. Well, the pieces left after Mexico City became what it is now. The fighting had been all over the south of Mexico, working its way up to Cuernavaca. Between the Dead Zone and the rest of the vampire clans, the family here had been whittled down.

They had still been doing okay until one of the other clans had formed a pact with Sabnock. Had switched allegiance to the demon. Johnny didn't know the details, the clan didn't know the details, but apparently Sabnock held a human cattle-farm inside the city, something he let the vampires feast on. The demon also had fortified the border between Mexico City and Cuernavaca, giving his new allies —La Familia Diablo—a protected home base. And, finally, the Jalisco's started getting, well, b*ackup* out of the Dead Zone.

Like the crabs.

"So Gabrielle contacted the clan here, and those that were left joined up with us." Johnny looked over the remains of the nice sedans, the vampires in tactical gear. "Such as it was."

I followed his gaze to those huddled around Gabrielle. Thirteen men and women kitted up. And now being patched up.

"This is it?"

Johnny gave his trademark shrug. One shoulder. "There's more, but it's tied up protecting what they have left. They've been in a hell of a war."

Well, that made both of us.

What I wouldn't give for more. For an army. Hell, while I was wishing, an army of Templars. But those that were left were in Italy. Lost, or dead, inside the zone surrounding the Vatican. The Templars had gone in to see if anything was left, after the Dead Zone had swallowed Rome whole.

Like the zone here had swallowed Mexico City. The city sat northwest of us, encased in a glow of red, a bloody bubble hovering over the horizon, tinted crimson in my sight, even against the black of night. All the stars in the sky behind the bubble were tinted red by the zone, and they pulsed and twinkled in an ominous bloody pattern, like the beat of a thousand hearts.

This is what we had. A baker's dozen of vampires from a vampire cartel. Three witches. Johnny and Gabrielle. Nick and Sarah. Jen and me.

Against all that. Against not only that but things like dragons. And giant crabs. And whatever the fuck else might exist in this new world of hell on Earth. Whatever else Sabnock might have waiting.

If we were going to grow stronger together, if we were going to be *more*, then I felt like we needed to do it in a hurry. Because the other side sure didn't seem to be slowing down.

CHAPTER ELEVEN

The breeze kicked up, whipping across us, across the road, heading west. The few lights in the town that remained lit threw shadowed globes of light here and there, tiny spots of illumination against the black night. The few storefronts remained black, where the windows weren't already boarded. This town was a ghost town, not figuratively, but literally, blue dots spreading out across my ethereal radar.

If anyone still remained in the town, anyone alive, they hadn't, and likely wouldn't, come out. Not now. And likely not until well after daylight.

One of the doors swung out though, from one of the storefronts. Johnny and I looked over, watching Nick come out, twirling something around his index finger. He couldn't keep the twirl going, whatever it was didn't quite have that balance to it, and as he neared I saw it was one of those clips people used to clamp on their guitar necks. The ones that changed the length of all the strings, so the guitarist could raise the pitch of their guitar.

This clamp was pink, with little butterflies scattered across it.

All in the act of flight, with black-trimmed wings, inset with dark orange and white wedges.

I was staring. Nick had paused his twirl. "What?"

Back in Grafton I had gone through the Cooper's house, looking for Jen. I had checked every room and remembered Sarah's. There had been a distinct goth feel to it, all vampires and black leather. Posters of heavy metal bands.

"Gift for Sarah?" Johnny asked.

Nick looked at the pink clamp with the butterflies. "I think she'll like it." He caught Johnny and me exchanging looks, and he shrugged. "I like it."

This from the guy who walked shadows. A *dark fucker*, as Johnny once had called him. And probably as deadly a man as I had met. Hell, a minute ago he had saved my life, stepping out of the darkness, stabbing the claw of a giant crab, only to disappear to another kill. All with a face of focused intensity.

A great friend, sure, but not a guy—I would've bet—that would have freely admitted *liking* butterflies in the past.

I guess we all have to have a little sunshine, to balance the night.

"They got this thing here, in Mexico," Nick said. "A flock of butterflies, like a migration. I think millions of them, maybe billions. Monarch butterflies."

He caught our looks, tried to explain. "It's happening now. They're all over the place."

"I—" I said, and stopped. Nick was standing there, covered in crab and vampire gore, torn-up vest smeared with it. He had wiped his face, but his glasses were still a little smudged. The only thing clean on him were the handles of his knives.

And here he was, twirling a clamp and talking about butterflies.

"I don't know what to say," I finally said.

Johnny grinned, did his eyebrow thing, adding, "You be you, bro."

Nick snorted. Saw where we were going. Pocketed the clamp. "Go fuck yourselves."

There was the old Nick, and I grinned at it.

"You should go in there," he told me, nodding back to the store. "Find a little something for Jen."

"I know," I said, almost routinely. I purposefully didn't look at the store. I turned to the east. It was hours to sunrise, but after the flight here, using my powers here to fight off the crabs, I had something more to do. "I'm thinking on it."

Johnny and Nick exchanged glasses. They knew I was putting off the gift. But what do you get someone who means everything to you? What can possibly show that kind of connection? Anything I thought of didn't seem like enough. Or right.

And I felt like it had to be right. In other worlds it was the thought that counted, but in this one, *mine*, the only thing that mattered was that it would show Jen what she was for me. Who she was, to me.

Both of them were grinning now, watching my face. I knew what I was thinking, they knew what I was thinking, and I knew they were laughing at it all inside.

So I stole Nick's line.

"Go fuck yourselves."

And hell, we all laughed. And it felt good to laugh. It felt good to be among friends.

Gabrielle wandered over, bringing one of the vampires with us. She looked at Nick's gift, and a little smile curved over her Italian features. One of her eyebrows, elegant and thin, arched slightly up in a good approximation of Johnny doing the same expression, as she looked over at him.

His smile got a little smaller.

Turnabout was always good play.

Gabrielle introduced the vampire, Alejandro. He was shorter than the rest of us, though more compact, and had the well-tanned skin of a Mexican. His face was pocked, a small, black mustache trimmed nicely, and a tiny soul patch below his upper lip. His hair was shaved tight on the sides, leaving thick straight hair pointing up on the top, like a porcupine.

A vampire followed him as well. A smaller woman with thick black hair tied back in a bun. Compact but built, with glossy black eyes and a white scar running down the side of her face, down from her temple, along her cheek, and down her neck. Most vampires could heal those types of wounds. She must have gotten that before she turned.

Alexandro performed a motion that was almost a bow. "Many thanks for the rescue," he spat to the side. "Those creatures, they lay in wait."

"We lost ten," Gabrielle said.

"Half of my team." Alejandro's jaw flexed. "My apologies, señor."

The woman vampire looked angry. Alexandro was looking at me, as if for forgiveness. Or direction. I still had to get used to that look, the one where people waited for you to make a decision, to lead, but his look seemed more... intense than others. "No apologies needed," I said. "Just appreciate the help. Wish we could've gotten here sooner."

"You strike at Sabnock?" The vampire asked. His accent, if not thickly Mexican, still present.

I nodded.

"Then we are with you," he said, spitting again. Waving to the dead vampires, the ones in T-shirts and headbands. "The La Familia Diablo, they side with the demon. He gives them places to hide in the Dead Zone. People to feed."

His jaw remained tight, as if he clenched it. "What they do is wrong."

It felt weird to me some, that I was looking to vampires as allies. Not only because of all the stories, the movies, Dracula, etc... but also because they fed on humans. That seemed unnatural to me, as much as I wanted to get past it.

And they not only fed on them but made them thralls. Turned them, in some cases. I only had to look at the Dominic Antonados and the Victor Dumonts of the world to see how that kind of power corrupts.

But power was everywhere. I was learning that some vampires, if not the shining example of goodness, also weren't evil. Gabrielle. And now Johnny. A thrall for a while, and now a vampire. At least, one in waiting.

He still hadn't taken blood, and that had led to some... difficulties with Gabrielle. Where she wondered if what she was, wasn't good enough for him to be as well. And if that was the case, if the thought of drinking someone's blood made Johnny sick to his stomach, well, what did that really say about how Johnny felt about who Gabrielle was?

He looked thinner. Johnny. He was eating real food, but it wasn't really giving him nourishment anymore. He was just forcing food down. And when he wasn't doing that, it was drinking.

Lately it seemed like a lot more drinking, than forcing any food down.

Johnny had told me he had the thirst back in Colorado, after Red Rock, and he had said it in a way that I could tell he was worried about it. At the time he had also told me that he could see ghosts, more and more as his thirst grew. Almost hear what the spirits were thinking. I could see him seeing the ghosts around us now, right after the fight, and yet trying *not* to see them.

And other than that, it wasn't something he discussed with

anyone. The thirst, the hunger. He fought a silent war, and if any of us mentioned it, he ducked his head at the table and kept forcing food down. Drank another beer. As if doubling-down on how he felt.

It wasn't like Gabrielle chose to be a vampire. She was born into the family. Raised to be someone who continued the line, someone who would have kids who carried the Dumont name, their DNA. And then turned into a vampire when her older brothers were killed.

It wasn't an easy thing, not for Johnny, not for Gabrielle.

It wasn't something I could do either. Be a vampire.

The raised eyebrow of Gabrielle, even if she was trying to join the fun, hid real pain. I felt for both of them. He had been happy to be her thrall, happy to provide her blood. I guessed there was some kind of thrill in that, being there for her, maybe it was even love… and that led him to not be able to drink someone else's blood for himself.

It was sad. I wasn't sure where it was headed. Gabrielle hadn't wanted to be a vampire, but had accepted it, and she had found someone she loved who may not be able to do the same.

Alejandro broke up my thought. "Señor, a question?"

He didn't need to ask permission. "Ask away."

"Are you really the angel?" he asked. "The one they showed above Colorado?" His accent made the word Colorado sound different, even exotic. In a way, more tropical. He strung the syllables together quickly, barely pausing at the hard consonants, the letter C, the D.

Funny, I guessed none of us were comfortable with who we were. Who we might be. I shook my head. "I'm no angel."

Alejandro looked confused, glancing at Gabrielle, who gave a roll of her eyes. "He is."

The man looked back at me.

"It's me on the video," I admitted. "I'm just not an angel."

I wondered which one he'd seen. The shot of me blazing across the sky, or the one where I had descended into Red Rock. That one was a little clearer, having been taken by one of the video cameras on a stand there. Apparently the vampire families recorded Conclave meetings, and someone had found the video and released part of it. The camera had been damaged, a lot of the fight was missing and the audio was gone, but there was a good ten-second clip of me landing in the middle of Red Rock, blazing white sword in hand, wings shimmering in an outline of ethereal blue-white energy.

You couldn't see my face in the shot. The light was too bright. It washed everything out. But you could see the form. And hell, I was there, so I knew it was me.

And sure I had wings. And a sword.

Being an angel was a part of me, but I wasn't sure I was all of it. Like I said, having a Cherokee as my great-great-great grandfather didn't make me a Native American. It was just something in the mix.

I pushed the thought away. Like always. I remembered my mom, sitting in a cell in Grafton, scratching out pictures of a trumpet, of wings, in the concrete floor with the tip of her sword. I remembered her scars, scars that should have healed, scars left from fights scattered throughout her long life. I remembered her sacrifice, her and my father's, back at Red Rock.

That was still too raw. Whatever she thought I was, whoever she thought I was, that was something I couldn't handle. Just another life taken, a life of someone I had barely known, and maybe a life I wish I had known as a real mother and son.

"It's me," I said again. A little more roughly.

Alejandro nodded. For some reason accepting it the second time. His eyes, though, still glittered in their intensity. "Until the extermination of our enemies, then." He paused, wanting to add something, but looking at my face, he settled for, "There are more of us. Just a few protecting our home. But we're here to serve."

If he had said something like *my lord*, or angel, or father, or something like that, I wouldn't handle any of those words well. I already didn't like the word serve. It wasn't me.

But, speaking of all of this, there was an angel thing I needed to do. I had done this three times already, each time something had happened down here in Mexico. Each time I had to use my powers, in a way that Sabnock might be able to tell where we were at. A principle I had learned from my Ranger team lead, Jason Bradley.

Always distract, he had said once. Our team sitting above the edge of a city, lying flat on our stomachs, staring down at the old stone buildings, the chickens in the yards, the reddish-brown dust fluttering along in the slight wind. *If you think you're going to be seen, distract. Ping the enemy. Hit him constantly from various directions. Circle back to the same place occasionally. Until they are sure that's where you are at. Where you're coming in. Knock on that door, knock on that door, knock on that door, and then take the window.*

I remembered that lesson. Well, didn't remember, but the memory had surfaced, and I used it. Every other night, I would circle around another part of Mexico City and ping them. I'd knock on the door there, kill some of the undead around the Dead Zone, make a show of it. Always in a different location, sometimes circling back to the same place, but always, always away from where we were hiding.

That way, Sabnock couldn't be sure of where we were. Short of sending out an entire army, which granted, he probably had, and having that army march outward in all directions of the compass, search every town, scope every farmstead, he had to wait until we came in.

Or I made a mistake.

I put my hand on Alejandro's shoulder. "I'll help out your family, however I can."

It wasn't quite a promise, but they were words out of my mouth, and as I had learned, the words were the deed. Sometimes the words fueled the deed. Cuernavaca would be a good place to ping Sabnock today. Going there would kill two birds.

The vampire worried, his gaze past me, his eyes even more intense. As if there was an internal fight inside the man, or some force, wanting to break out. It made me... uneasy. Not because I felt as if the man was good or evil, but because it was unknown.

I radiated the signal to Jen. This far, it was something we had worked out between the two of us, since we could only feel thoughts and emotions and not really hear each other. It wasn't a true message, it was more like morse code, just three quick beeps of thought along the keydrop—*doing the thing, doing the thing, doing the thing*.

And back, from Jen—*understood, understood, understood*.

I didn't know that was the actual word she used, but I could feel the rhythm of her thoughts, the three syllables repeated in the same pattern. So didn't know it, but I *felt* what she was saying. Like a song you know the sound of, that someone is humming next to you. You know the chords, the melody, but the lyrics are hiding in your hindbrain, refusing to come out.

This song was a bit frustrated. A little concern, the kind of feeling of a mother wanting to bundle her kid up in a nice heavy coat before sending them out into the snow. And some other emotion, the one I couldn't quite put a name to but was worried about. All of that, underlined by acceptance.

Barely.

All of this was more unknown for me. More uneasiness. More

things to juggle when walking the tightrope was tough enough. Sometimes, I was glad to look for a fight.

"You doing the thing?" Nick said. Knowing the routine.

I nodded. "You guys got it from here?"

Johnny looked over at some of the older cars. Some of the nicer sedans, the Cadillacs with the blacked-out windows, sitting amongst the older rusted-out trucks and cars. The few cars left I hadn't used to crack open a crab. Seeing which ones they could take. "We'll be traveling in a little less style."

"You can get there, though, right?" I looked east. It would still be half a dozen hours before sunrise. I thought the vampires would be safe enough. While the sun itself didn't kill most vampires, sunrise itself was deadly. That moment of transition, from night to day, had a power to it.

"The way he drives?" Gabrielle said, moving her hand back and forth. "Maybe."

It was a joke, said in Gabrielle's dry way, almost like an elegant statement of fact. Her eyes sparkled a bit, her thin lips curved a little at the corners.

Nick snorted. I grinned a little, and Johnny smiled at her, a real Johnny smile, as she leaned into him a bit. He pulled her a little closer.

It made me feel better about them. And hopeful. About everything.

CHAPTER TWELVE

Cuernavaca had once been called the city of eternal spring.
It was far from that now.

Once a city for tourists, retirees, and people of means and wealth, it had fallen on hard times lately. Cartels battled over the city, leaving a tally of dead that grew by the day. And that was before the Dead Zone had appeared.

Still, the enchantment remained. I could see it, feel it, even in the late hours of the night, the mid-morning hours when the sun was beginning to appear over the horizon. There were the sandstone walls, tall walls built of brick, the beautiful, red-painted buildings poking out from broken-down frames of homes and stores and historical structures abandoned long ago. There was a beauty of a place that had existed for longer than humans could remember, with all the little pieces of time hidden here and there around the city.

There was the Palace of Cortés, a tall square fort-like palace, arches built into the stone entry way, with crenellations running the top. It had started as a seat of authority hundreds of years ago, became a factory, then abandoned, turned into a jail, then became a place of government, and finally abandoned again. There were the stair-stepped pyramids of gray stone, built for purposes not quite understood today.

There was the Cathedral of the Ascension, a red brick building topped with a crimson dome, sitting on a tower of white. There were hidden Aztec collection centers, where tributes had been brought a thousand years ago or more, these places long buried now under the ground, but leaving bluish-red dots across the landscape in such masses that I shuddered, thinking of the warrior earlier that night. There was the lush vegetation that gave the city its name, a dark green in the night, clumps of trees and bushes and vines that crawled over the city as if Mother Nature was staking its claim on land originally hers.

There were the gunshot streets, upon which sat a mishmash of expensive Lamborghinis, Humvees, Jeeps and trucks and broken-down sedans, windows broken out. There were bikes all over the place, not motorcycles but ten-speed bikes, the kind you pedal, maybe used for messenger-services. Most of Cuernavaca was empty, though parts of it held humans, and an even smaller part hid vampires.

It was those I was looking for. Alejandro had given me a little background. Where his clan was, the few that were left, and where the La Familia Diablo clan had its headquarters. Not surprisingly, in a part of Cuernavaca that was run down. Where a lot of the gunshot streets were. Where not only people seemed to be scarce, but a place even the vegetation pulled back from, as if even nature didn't want to reclaim what lived in that block.

I hovered above it all. Looking down and surveying, ethereal wings spread out wide against the night. Not just finding and locating spirits to tap, but trying to pick out the less psychotic, the less murdery ones. Trying to plan ahead so that I didn't accidentally stumble and grab something like the ghosts back in Lewiston.

Just the run of the mill bad spirits, please.

I also watched and looked to see who was there. There was a mass of ghosts under a large brick building. Dots gathered in such a way it seemed to me to signal a place where the vampires of the cartel fed, or killed, or both. The seemed to be people on watch, some of them having the dark purple glimmer that said *vampire* in my ethereal sight. And, from what I could tell, nothing screaming *it's a trap*. No large glimmers of life-sparks. No reddish-tinged sparks of demons. Nothing that said I would get down there and find a bunch of crabs waiting for me.

To the east a faint light appeared, the precursor of dawn, still hours away. The time where most vampires came back home. The time where they would be getting ready for their slumber, waiting for the next night to come around, sharing blood of a person or two, laughing in the quiet of the morn, satiated and ready for rest.

It was time.

I summoned my sword, the blazing ethereal blue light brighter for the darkness I hovered in. I pulled more and more ethereal energy from the spirits below until streamers of blue-white motes swirled up through the sky and into me. I pulled until I became as bright as a comet, a bright pulsing blue-white star in the dark of the night…

Then I plunged.

The wind whipped around me. It buffeted my face. I pulled energy and hardened my skin. Hardened my bones. Strengthened every muscle, every tendon, every ligament.

And I crashed through the ceiling of the building with all the dots. Pulled from ghosts as I crashed through each floor. Stones and bricks and wooden two-by-fours exploded around me, clouds of dust burst upward over the building like a mushroom cloud until I landed through the bottom floor, taking the landing on the hard bottom of the building with a flex of my knees.

I looked around, using my ethereal sight. Coughing hard into my hand, trying to breathe as shallowly as possible. Sometimes I don't quite think these things through.

Flickering purple glows lay around me in spots, fuzzy in the thick cloud of dust, as vampires tried to pull themselves out of the debris. A few blue-white glows, too, some of them tinged red, thralls. Some of them moving, others not.

Broken stone and wood landed around me, smacking into some of the vampires, knocking out some of the thralls, hitting the bottom floor with deep thuds and thwacks, followed by the tricking tick-and-tacks of smaller pebbles and rock. There was so much dust that the only thing I could really see was the sparks in my ethereal sight, the sparks and the reflection of my sword in the swirling motes, blazing bright.

I started killing. The sword—thankfully—worked as it always did. Slicing vampire and thrall alike, cutting them in half in various places, taking off limbs and heads and powering through midsections. It wasn't a glorious battle, most of who I fought were still trying to gather themselves, but I wasn't a glorious battle kind of guy. I was more into winning.

And not dying.

So I carved my way through the building. I didn't meet a lot of resistance. In fact, I didn't meet any. At first I killed by the score, then by the dozen, until in the end I was hunting down sputtering purple life-sparks trying to hide from me. Hide in terror. Hide in the unknowing of what death was coming to them.

I got a little queasy. I wasn't a murderer, after all. Or at least, I didn't think of myself as one. I was someone who protected his friends. I was someone who took vengeance seriously. I was someone who didn't let others fuck with those he wanted to protect. Like his friends, the Wolverines. Like Gabrielle, who I had met and liked because of Johnny, and who now fought our fight with us, and

—because of Johnny, and through Johnny, Gabrielle—now Alexandro.

I pushed the queasiness down. Sabnock was building a vampire army, and I was going to whittle that down some here. Vampires or thralls.

So they all died. As many of the La Familia Diablo as I could find. I was going to wipe them out and let the rest of them hide inside the Dead Zone. But they were going to know Cuernavaca was a deathly place for them.

It wasn't a long battle. But it was a long hunt. A lot of thralls, those who could, fled. A lot of vampires hid, at the end. It was messy work, and a small part of me didn't like it, but the larger part of me, the one that did what needed to be done, pushed through.

I finished around sunrise.

Left anyone I had missed—any vampire—to that moment.

Any thralls that were left, I let them run. Someone should carry a message back.

Ugly stuff. And not clean. But the necessary work usually is.

I took a moment and leaned against the wall. Watching the sun come up. Feeling the first warm rays hit my skin. Wiping my face and feeling all the dust and rock and blood and goop on it. Trying to wipe it off with a dirty curtain I pulled from the rubble, and smearing my face more than cleaning it. Then I walked away. A little north, along the street, passing bikes tossed aside in the street, a car flipped over, the ground rippled up like a wave of stone had flowed outward from where I had landed in the building. The street broke up here and there, like crests of concrete, and I navigated those with slowly moving feet.

I was tired. All-nighters did that to you. I could pull as much ethereal energy as I wanted, but all of that energy in all the world couldn't replace a good night's sleep.

Trust me, I had tried.

Somewhere I found a bottle of water. Poured it over my face. Tapped my keystone and let Jen know I was okay. Another rhythmic pulsing of feeling to her, hoping that the distance wasn't too far that she could get it, so she wouldn't worry.

I thought I felt something in return, but we were far enough apart that it was hard to tell. I wanted to believe it, though, so I did. Allowing a sense of relief and *I miss you* to wander back down the key.

It took a bit, but I came up to the edge of the Dead Zone. It sat in the distance, glimmering crimson in the early morning light, a wall of bloody air separating the northern part of Cuernavaca from the southern part. I walked until I got on the very edge of it. Until I stood right before it. I stuck my head in, briefly, feeling the change in the air inside the zone. The dry heat. The soul-sucking feel of hot coals burning deep beneath the earth. And somehow, for some reason, the smell of gingersnaps.

Odd.

I pulled back, looked around.

The street was wide where it met the edge of the city. Like it had once been a major life-carrying vessel between Cuernavaca and Mexico City. In the distance, deeper into the zone, cars piled up on either side of the road, building a tiny wall of destroyed vehicles, cockeyed across the road. The wall of vehicles was three or four cars high and broken in the center where an eighteen-wheeler sat cockeyed. The cab of the truck faced Cuernavaca, the back end jackknifed and twisted, as if someone had been driving it out of the Dead Zone. Through the wall of vehicles.

It reminded me of the trucks up north. The long train of eighteen-wheelers mixed with construction rigs, dump trucks, backhoes and earth movers. Had it started here? I looked at the truck. The writing on the side was in Spanish, there was nothing I could read, no symbol telling me it was carrying vegetables, fish, or all the tools needed to build a modern-day demon palace.

So I stood there, at the edge. For a while. Where the wall of cars was. One of the cars there, a sleek white sedan sitting by the wall, sat facing me, its hazards blinking. On and off. On and off. Like a buoy, indicating the deep currents in the channel. Or a lighthouse, warning those that approached of sharp rocks ahead.

On a whim I pulled out my sword. Poked it, tip first, through the red wall. Watched the tip of the sword disappear, then inch-by-inch the rest of the blade, as I pushed it further in.

I pulled it out. Watched the blade reappear. All the way back to the tip.

Then I repeated the process.

I couldn't feel anything when the blade disappeared. Perhaps a slight sense of loss. A coolness in my hand. A slight twinge of uneasiness, as a person might get walking down a dark, lonely alley. But all of that could have been my imagination, each of the feelings were that slight.

I knew I could pull ethereal energy, fill my body with it, and walk into the Dead Zone. But once inside, I couldn't pull any more. I would have what energy I came in with, for as long as that lasted. I remembered the last bits of it in my fight with Azazel back in New Orleans, bleeding out of me, punch by punch.

Whatever the sword was, it couldn't exist in the Dead Zone. None of my powers would work there. Whatever the Dead Zone was, it was close enough to hell that anything angelic in nature had no power there.

And that was what I needed. The sword, to kill Sabnock. As far as I knew, it was the only way to kill a demon. It was the only way *I* had killed them. Anything else, silver, blessed bullets, all of that seemed to just injure them. Sometimes enough, like when I had shot Azazel, to get them to leave.

But he had always come back. And Sabnock would as well. The Dead Zone would make it easier. I assumed that however Azazel had regenerated, after me shooting him, that process would work just as fine in Mexico City in the center of the zone as it had in hell.

Something about the fight with the crabs stuck with me. My sword. Nick's knife. One worked where the other didn't. I had to figure this out. After all, I was on the clock. Six hundred and sixty-six days since I said I would kill Azazel. Since I had signed that contract.

This wasn't just about taking everything from Azazel before I did that. Making him pay for everything he had done. It was also about figuring out how to kill a demon in the center of their place of power. Because—at the end of this, when it was me and Azazel, I knew where he would flee to. Where he would hide.

So I stood there for a bit, a bit foggy-brained, trying to think of something, test-plunging the sword into the zone and out again. Thinking of the vampires and the thralls and how easy it was to kill them. Thinking of the crabs and how impossible it had been to use the sword on them. Thinking of the zone and wondering why I couldn't use the sword there. Looking north, at the center of where Mexico City would be, and Sabnock, and getting the feeling that something there was staring back at me.

A little lost in all that. A little puzzled. Reaching out and trying to see if what I was feeling was real or if it was something imagined.

I almost jumped out of my skin when someone coughed. When a little *kuff-kuff* kind of sound, as if someone was covering their mouth with their hand, came from behind me.

CHAPTER THIRTEEN

I spun, quickly. Sword out.

I had walked far enough north to be at the edge of Cuernavaca. A nicer part of town. Some people there, waking up and getting around. Though—for the most part—not here. Not at the edge of the Dead Zone. Everyone knew enough to get away from that.

So nice buildings lay around me. Some vines and bushes and other vegetation, green for late in the fall, hung down sand-colored walls. Some of them still blooming, which they shouldn't be this time of year, dark red poinsettias and pink-and-yellow dahlias. Yellow Mexican poppies. Just around where I was standing, though, as if I was in a manicured garden, something outside normal seasons and time. Something I had not noticed, walking north as I had.

The garden circled a small little patio. The patio held small circular tables built of wood with tiny folding chairs of the same. The tables all had holes in their centers, holes for umbrella poles, and there was an umbrella in the center table, a big pale blue umbrella, open and shading the person sitting there.

He was a tall man. Or at least I got that feeling. Long legs, laying out to the side, crossed at the ankles. His clothes were so clean and… bright, so bright in the sun that I couldn't help but feel how dirty I was, covered in crab muck and vampire gore and dust and debris from the building's collapse.

He wore a nice pair of tan linen pants, a thin gold belt around his waist, and a blousy white cotton shirt that couldn't hide a large pair of shoulders. His shirt was buttoned halfway, letting a tanned chest show. His face was lined, weathered, with pale blue eyes and short-cut brown hair, shorter on the sides than the top.

His smile, when he gave it, pearly white.

He held a wide-rimmed cup in his hand. White. A faint whiff of expresso and milk came from it, brought along the same breeze that carried the scents of poppies and poinsettias and dahlias. Watching me over the mug, he took a small sip and then motioned to the chair across from him with one large hand.

Naturally, being me, I didn't take it. I did take a few steps onto the patio, holding my sword off to the side. The man remained seated, watching me as I looked around, wondering how I had missed this when I had initially walked by. It seemed, well, out of place.

The patio was encircled by a low-running white wall. Stone or alabaster. The encircled area held a smattering of tables and chairs. Some green brush dotted the whiteness, here and there along the wall, and there was a flourish of poinsettias that Mexico was known for. A dogwood lay off to the side, flowering white blossoms overhead, a few petals floating down from above.

Behind the man, the low-running patio wall ran into the corner of a building. Two taller walls, also white, meeting at a wide angle. The left wall had a colored window, something someone might put up to let the sunlight scatter pretty colors inside. The right side held a large flat window right next to a door.

Through the flat window I saw a counter holding an expresso machine. A coffee shop. A small mom-and-pop place, with a man and a woman inside working a large machine. An old couple with gray hair, the man with a large salt-and-pepper mustache that drooped to either side of his lips. The woman thin, her hair tied up behind a thick red and yellow bandana. She waved at me through the glass of the shop and smiled.

I wondered how I had missed them. Had the store just opened while I had been standing a little bit north, testing the zone? Were they some kind of coffee stop-shop for people heading in and out of Mexico City?

It didn't make sense. Not the lady's cheerful wave. Or the man in the chair in front of me. Coffee shops seemed to be where things became more complicated for me. At least, lately. I didn't like how they marked things in my life, because I did like a nice cup of coffee. So my voice was rougher than I intended. "What do you want?"

"Just to talk," the man said. His voice was rich and carried a timbre that could easily be heard on this patio, or in a ten-thousand-person theater.

I hadn't had much luck with just talking with people, either. Especially ones that could be demons. Especially in a coffee shop, where the demon could be Azazel.

"Then you won't mind?" I asked, moving my sword up, holding it so the blade was parallel to the ground, but putting the tip of the blade between us.

The man raised his eyebrows, then gave a little shrug. A little smile. Set his cup down, the china cup tinking against the little white saucer. Held out his arm, the one closest to me, forearm facing up.

I placed the flat of the blade on his arm.

The man remained. Didn't turn into a demon. Or another demon. Or anything else.

It was the test I had. Don't knock it. Azazel had a million angles, a million ways to hide what he had coming, and that was the one demon I really *knew*.

I rotated my sword ninety degrees and pulled it back with a quick flick. Slicing his skin a bare hair on the edge of the blade.

The man, again, didn't disappear or moan at the cut. So far the demons I had stabbed with the sword had all, well, died. But those blows had all been killing blows. I didn't know what I expected with a tiny cut like I had just done, but I figured a demon would respond in kind.

This man didn't move at the cut. Didn't shout at the quick move. Just kept his eyebrows raised as we both watched the tiny cut on the skin. Watched until a drop of blood beaded up.

"Good enough?" the man asked.

I let the sword disappear and took the chair opposite him.

There was a huge cotton napkin tucked beside the saucer holding the man's coffee cup, the man pulled it out, flapped it open with a quick flourish, and pressed it to his forearm. His smile remained, kind of tilted to one side of his face, a knowing smile, as if everything that happened was what he expected.

I looked past him, back into the coffee shop. It had been a long night, and I was tired. It would be a lot longer day, with me driving back to our hideout. A cup of espresso would be nice. The old woman caught my eye, I waved and mimicked a coffee cup drinking motion, and she nodded.

I turned back to the man. He still lay back in his chair, the one arm lying in his lap, the white napkin covering it. A small red dot or two blemishing the napkin. His other hand held his cup of espresso, and as I watched, the man took a tiny sip. His eyes closed for a moment as he savored the taste, and then opened, refocusing on me.

"So," I said. "You wanted to talk?"

"That, and to meet you."

"Meet me?"

"That is how people meet today, correct?" he asked. "By talking?"

He sounded like he was partly-asking, and partly—well, it wasn't a sarcastic type of tone. But something along those lines. As if the man was used to a different kind of reception.

"Well," I said. "You know me, then?"

"By reputation."

Something in his voice caught me, and it was then that I noticed his sword. Leaning against the back of the chair next to him. A tall silver blade in a leather scabbard, the cross of the hilt poking well over the top of the chair. It looked like something else rested on the ground between the back of the chair and the sword, something like a heater shield, tall, flat along the top, both sides curving down to a point at the bottom.

Another thing I had missed, walking in. "Then maybe you'd share yours?"

"Of course," he said. "I was named Michael."

That gave me an odd feeling. Something fluttered at the edge of my brain, some thought I couldn't catch right then. One of those things you know after it hits you slam in the face, but right now, the understanding eluded me.

The lady brought the coffee out. Actually, a latte. Closer up she was older than I had guessed, her face dark with a healthy tan, wrinkled from years under the sun. Her irises a dark black, but her teeth in a bright smile.

I took the cup, a wide china cup like Michael had. It was heavy with espresso and cream and foamed high to the rim, with a little pattern decorating the froth. What looked like a poinsettia, with a black outline of espresso sinking into the cream.

Nice.

I took a sip, and the sweet warm cream blended with the bitter coffee just right. It was both bitter and sweet on my tongue, dark and hot in my belly, the caffeine racing outward from my stomach and pulsing along my nerves like a shot of adrenaline.

It was delicious. Almost heavenly. And well-needed after last night.

I took another sip and savored it. The lady set the saucer next to me, the tiny plate to hold the cup, and tucked a thick white cotton napkin next to it. I placed the coffee on the plate and reached for my wallet.

"Let me get it," Michael said, waving the lady away, the lady nodding a few quick times.

I paused mid-motion and then shrugged. Went back to the latte and drank. Some mornings a well-made coffee could make a world of difference.

"So we've met," I said. "Or talked, or whatever. Want to tell me why?"

"Can't you guess?" His eyes were blue. Pale blue. And they twinkled a bit. "After all, a lot of people have been wanting to meet you lately. You've been causing quite a stir."

I looked at the sword again.

The hilt, in particular. The cross of the hilt held a smaller, golden cross inlaid in its center. A hint of fiery red in the metal.

I leaned a little to the side of my chair, catching the curve of the shield. The shield was white, a brilliant white, and gold inlaid around its edge. At this angle, I saw the beginning of a thick golden line curving horizontally across the shield. I knew, without knowing how, that there would be a matching golden line crossing that one vertically. A golden cross on a white shield, a shield of heralds, and a tall sword with a matching golden cross.

Then the missing thing hit me.

That elusive understanding circling around my brain.

Jen and me, standing in a church in Lewiston. Trying to get help from the priest there. Her and I waiting, me standing there looking at a stained-glass window with an angel in it. An angel with a blazing yellow cross on a shield, a blazing glow around a silver sword, and a tall angel there, leading the fight.

I think that's Saint Michael, I had said to Jen then, *The Archangel.*

The lead soldier against Lucifer, Jen had said.

I smiled now at the memory. Because of what I had said next. *Yep, if you believe in that kind of stuff...*

So much had happened since that moment. I had learned, but not enough. I had grown, but not nearly enough. And I even believed, but maybe not nearly enough.

"I see you understand," Michael said.

I understood. I saw the man, the *supposed* archangel, in front of me. With his sword and shield and delicious lattes. The white patio, the white napkin, even the colored-glass window that sat right behind him from where I was sitting.

All that was missing was the glow.

I leaned forward, flicked his napkin off of his arm.

The cut, slight as it had been, was gone.

I leaned back. I wasn't sure how I felt. Here was someone who could have been helping a long time ago. Before the Dead Zones. Before Azazel had killed Jen. Before my parents had given their lives to end the curse.

The next sip of latte seemed more bitter than sweet. "A little late to the party, aren't you?"

Late was an understatement. Here I was, fighting a demon and a war started millennia ago. Michael was the chief of the angels, it was he who had helped cast Lucifer out, it was he who led that battle between Lucifer and Belial and Azazel and the soldiers of heaven.

I still remember my mother healing me back in Grafton. Sitting next to me. I remembered the thick white line around her neck and all the other tiny scars in her skin, barely visible, marks of wounds that had been inflicted on her so many times that she couldn't heal herself completely.

This guy could have helped her. Long before all this had gone down. Long before Azazel created the Dead Zones. Perhaps before the demon had even hatched his plan.

The slight crook of his lips told me he understood. That this was something he heard plenty. So his eyes remained steady. His words like iron. "My—*party*, as you call it—started thousands of years ago. Maybe it is you who is late to it."

Well, turnabout was fair play. It also could be a son of a bitch.

His stare never wavered.

I didn't like it.

I sipped my latte. It remained bitter. The cream seemed to have lost its battle in the cup.

The patio was quiet around us. Nothing went on around us. There was a breeze, it stirred just enough of the dogwood that the tree shivered, and a few white petals took the opportunity to drift to the ground.

Michael remained just as quiet. Though he seemed to be enjoying his coffee more.

This guy had been around when Azazel had created the geas. He had been around, he had been the person to cast Lucifer out of heaven. So he had a lot of power. Power he hadn't used when he could have.

Maybe enough to break the geas.

Maybe that thought showed on my face.

"I tried," he said. And left it at that.

He could have. I had tried myself. I thought I could do it with my ethereal blade. I had sliced through the tendril of the curse, and for a moment thought I had done it. Thought I had freed my father.

But the curse had grown. Multiplied, like the mythical seven-headed hydra. I had cut it, and the tendrils had both split and grown larger. Had thickened until they had reconnected. And then had taken it out on my dad.

So maybe he had done the same at some point. Maybe he tried to break the curse and watched it grow stronger. Maybe—even if he was the strongest of the angels—he feared being trapped in the same way as the others.

I worked through all of that. Michael watched me. It wasn't but a month ago that my parents had killed themselves, in the same moment, at the same time, and by doing so allowed the geas to eat itself up. Well, eat itself up, inside me, the geas from the Dumonts and the geas from the Antonados each killing the other.

While my parents lay dead in front of me.

Michael spoke, his words still like iron, but also softer. "I knew them, you know."

"My parents?"

He shook his head. "Not them. Not personally. But who they were. Who they came from. Seven of our strongest. I knew each of them, each of those Azazel trapped.

"Seven friends." Michael set his cup down, the cup making the slightest tink against the saucer. "Then each of their descendants. Their lineage, all the way down to you."

"So, what?" I asked. "You've just watched from afar the past few thousand years? Doing nothing?"

He sat up a little. He was tall and bent forward to be a little closer. His words still as hard as iron. "I've watched you, poking here and there. I know what happened back at Red Rock. I know—" He tapped his chest. "—who you communicate with, and why. I know your struggle. The burden of protecting your friends.

"Imagine having to do that for a whole world." His eyes narrowed. "How many places can *you* be? How many people can *you* protect?"

I shifted in my seat, uncomfortable. That fell in line with the kind of thinking I had been doing on my own. I didn't need it reflected back at me. Almost thrown in my face. I didn't like hearing it aloud. My jaw set. Or I set it.

He had been there, he said. He had watched me at Red Rock. Probably New Orleans. Even watched me as far as back as when I had first found the Key, back in the Hindu Kush. More importantly, he had seen me come after Jen. In that white clouded land, and those stairs that led forever upwards.

It made me wonder.

It wasn't fair, blaming Michael for the geas. For my parents. But I wanted it to be fair. I wanted to have someone else to blame. Someone that could have been there. Who could have maybe stopped everything, before that everything came to rest on my shoulders.

Turnabout really *was* a son of a bitch.

I set my coffee down as well. The cup rang a little harder on the saucer than when Michael had done it. The tink cut through the silence on the patio. "Fair enough."

Michael smiled then. A smile, not a grin. "Fair enough."

We could have sat there for an hour. Or a few minutes. The silence wasn't oppressive, but it was thick. Here I was, talking to an angel. An archangel. Perhaps even *the* archangel. Someone who had been there when all this had started. Someone who had opposed Lucifer and Belial and Azazel.

And now he had picked this time to meet. After the past year, this particular moment. And he hadn't come to us up north, me and Jen and Nick and Sarah and Johnny. He had come to me, alone, here in Cuernavaca.

"So, we've met," I said. "And talked. Is that it?"

His eyebrow twitched, just once. His lips pursed as if he was forming a word that came from an as-yet fully realized thought. Then he blew out a breath, long and slow.

"Maybe," he said. "Maybe."

I grinned, but it wasn't a happy grin. It was an *I-should've-known* grin. One side, this one, seemed happy to tell everyone there was a heaven and that people could get there, and then step away to see where all the chips fell. They had no problem not showing up if they were needed, and—like Michael had just explained—couldn't help *everyone* anyway.

The other side, if Belial could be believed, didn't want anyone to know anything. Didn't want people to know if there was a heaven or a hell. Wanted people to act how they were going to act, and then settle the score after they passed from the Earth. And while Belial's side didn't want anyone to know about heaven or hell, they had no problems being around all the time, throughout human history, to tempt people in their particular direction.

That was the top layer of that particular cake. There were many more layers there, I was sure. But that was the most obvious, to me.

And if Michael wasn't going to help, if he wasn't here to offer his sword in my battle against demons, then sitting here on the patio wasn't doing anything but wasting driving time. I had a home of sorts to get to, and Jen waiting.

I nodded to the Dead Zone. The invisible line between Mexico City and Cuernavaca. "So you're going to let us go in there all on our own?"

The angel looked past me. I wondered if he saw what I saw, the tinge of red, the bubble over Mexico City, stretching far to the east, far to the west, far to the north. Perhaps as large as Texas.

"You've been in there," he said, finally. "What *can* be done?" His face twisted, very unangel-like. "I can bring no army into Hell. There, my powers have no sway."

We were back to the beginning then. Me and my sword, the thing I needed to kill Sabnock. The thing that I couldn't bring with me into the Dead Zone. I understood his frustration—even fear— but I couldn't understand the giving up.

And then it clicked. I think it was the fear that clued me in. If Michael really felt responsible for the world, and if he was one of the few angels left after thousands of years maybe he was questioning every step he made. Those thoughts would slow down anything the angel wanted to do, especially if he lived with the fear of a single misstep being his last.

Not just his last, but also the last for those who believed in him.

A corner of my mouth turned up slightly at the recognition. I may have been looking in the mirror. At what I might have been, had I not had friends. Had I not had Jen.

Funny, the things that helped us fear, could also make us brave.

"Well, can't say I'm not disappointed. Here I am, fighting your fight, after all. The end of the line of all your friends, going in to kill Sabnock and right some wrongs," I said. And leaned forward a bit, to underscore my next point. "Seems wrong, somehow. Seems like I'm cleaning up your mess. Because Azazel was your problem long before he was mine."

If you had told me I was going to start the day insulting an angel, I'd have laid long odds against. I'd have thought it more likely I'd have fought giant crabs. So these past twelve hours or so were more out of the norm than usual.

Michael's eyebrows thundered down. His eyes flashed. He moved to speak, shifting a bit in *his* seat. His eyes flickered back and forth, over my shoulder to the Dead Zone, then to me. Then seemed to hold his tongue. "Fair enough," he repeated. Softly, this time. As more to himself.

That was that, then. "Fair enough."

I had a long drive, so I finished the latte, downing what was left in a quick gulp, the coffee neither bitter nor sweet, the last of the foam almost tasteless, tepid in the way foam gets when it's been left in the cup too long.

Then I got up. "I'd say it was nice to meet you…"

Michael nodded from his chair. "Understood. Perhaps next time."

Perhaps next time, what?

Hell, next time maybe he offers some help. It was the least he could do. He was the supposed commander of the heavenly armies. The angel paratroopers looked to for help. He was the guy who commanded the other angels, and he was the guy who shepherded all the souls to heaven after their death.

I could use some of that.

"Appreciate the coffee," I said, and waved to the old people in the shop. I wasn't sure if they were real people or some other form of spirit summoned by Michael, but either way, the latte had been delicious.

I walked off the patio, back into the world of Dead Zones and vampire gangs and thralls and half-empty cities. Of dying vegetation, brown brush, and withered trees. Of bikes and cars parked in the street, empty, sometimes even in the street, as if people had got up and left with their car running.

It was going to be a long enough drive now as it was. I tapped my chest, the keydrop there, and tried to radiate the feeling of me coming back. Then I found one of those empty cars, one with a full tank and a set of keys, and I headed north.

CHAPTER FOURTEEN

I t was a long ride home.

Well, home such as it was. The hideout. Where we had begun our planning for Sabnock and trying to figure out how to get into the Dead Zone in Mexico City. In a small town whose name I didn't know, a place that would likely fade from existence in the coming years, if not months. If not weeks.

I wasn't going shorter.

The road was worn with use, and I followed it east until it circled around north, following the coast. The sunlight was bright on the windshield, definitely bright for a morning after the night I had just had, and absolutely too bright for a short visor that couldn't quite hide the sun behind it. I dug around in the glove box, found some sunglasses, a pair of Maui Jims, oval lenses a bit wider than tall, and put them on.

Then I drove. The car had a half tank of gas, plenty to get some miles on. I left the windows down and took off, hanging my hand out and feeling the morning dew on the wind. Feeling the tires roll along the road, the rubbery bite of them as the Camaro dug into a steep turn, feeling the smooth acceleration of the modern car, the push of force, pushing me back into the seat as I accelerated out.

It was nice. Relaxing, to a degree. The open road, with very few vehicles on it. There had been a white truck I passed earlier, an old man behind the wheel. A few other cars all headed the opposite direction. The blue sky, the bright yellow sun, the roaring sound of the wind whipping through the car, bringing the smell of fresh country air and occasionally, the tiniest whiff of salt.

In my search that morning for a car, I had ended up stumbling on a newer Camaro. One of the body styles that was a more modern representation of the older version of the muscle car. Painted gunmetal gray. The door had been unlocked, the keys on the seat, window down. As if whoever had been in the car had just left.

So I had thanked whoever it was and taken the Camaro. Fired it up, with the more modern purring rumble that eight-cylinder cars had. Not the rumbling roar of my Camaro, safe in its storage unit, but something in this newer car that seemed more bark than bite. As if its sound had been engineered in the lab, and wasn't the result of me goosing the gas pedal, wasn't the result of almost four hundred horsepower powering the pistons, but some trick of a pre-programmed engine and manufactured exhaust.

It was nice. Relaxing. But I still missed my car. My Camaro. The older, beat-up version of this one. Funny how you learn to count on some things, even material things. Objects, not alive, become a kind of emotional crutch. Something that made you feel better just by driving it, or wearing it. A lucky coin, a favorite shirt, an older car. These things become a part of you before you know it, and when they are gone, it's like a piece of you has been torn away with it. Something you couldn't believe you'd miss, or something you'd believed made you better. Luckier. Faster. More confident.

Belief.

It kind of came back to that.

And seeing—for me—meant believing.

Still, I wasn't sure what to think of Michael. Of the whole angel thing. I wanted to put what I thought about the archangel in the same place I thought about myself. But I couldn't because, well, he was really an angel. Born an angel. Or created.

Unlike me, who had descended from angels, who just had some of the same genetic pieces, Michael was the real deal. One-hundred percent Grade A top-shelf angelic.

I wondered if he saw spirits like me. If he used them, tapped ghosts for ethereal energy, like I did. If that was how angels got their power. After all, he was supposed to be the guy who brought spirits to heaven at the hour of their death.

I guess I should have asked him more questions. I should have thought more about why Michael had showed, then and there. But that whole thing was still hard for me to think about. I believed I was part angel, but that was where I left it. I didn't want to bring deeper thoughts into it. About me, and angels. Especially after the moment with Jen. In the ghost-dream. The water tower high up among all the white clouds. Her and I talking, before I jumped off in an attempt to take her place.

As I've said before, it's easy to put off that kind of thinking. Especially when I was fighting demons. It was easier to look at what was right in front of me, and not wonder about where Jen might have gone, had I let her go. What the water tower in the clouds had represented, or whether or not that whole thing had been real. It was easier to focus on Azazel, and Sabnock, and my deal with Belial.

Those were Demons that I had seen. Demons I had fought, or fought with.

Easier to fight them than wonder if—because I was fighting with those demons—if what they represented was real. Things like a real hell. Things like a real prince of hell. Things like Lucifer.

Because if Lucifer was real, then the opposite was likely to be real too.

And I had just met that guy's chief enforcer.

My mind skittered around the realization. I focused more on the road. The sinking of the Camaro in the curve, the acceleration out. The smooth pull of the car down the road. The mesh of the tires on the asphalt.

Deep breaths of fresh air.

Open hand surfing currents of the wind.

Foot angled across the gas pedal.

Beams of sunlight breaking through the windshield.

The good side seemed to be happy to just exist. They weren't showing up, leading the charge. At least for the past three thousand years, more or less.

While the other side had taken their fight to Earth. Always there, always tempting. There's a reason people say things like the road to hell starts with good intentions. Demons like Belial, like Azazel. They were happy to offer a carrot, just a little bit down the way. And when you took that carrot, they offered another. All the way until you were too far down that road to see a way back.

I was on that road, in a way. With a firm destination in place. I had a few years left, but I had signed a contract, after a carrot had been offered. Six hundred and sixty-six days from that one, I had to have killed Azazel.

I wasn't too worried. Not yet, not about the contract and fulfilling my side. I had six hundred and thirty-some days left. I had plenty of time to do what I needed to do.

But the carrot had been taken. I had taken that first step. And part of me wondered, when I got to the end, if I'd be able to find my way back.

I think a part of me wanted Michael to be that, for me. The way back. A real archangel with all the powers thereof. A beacon to light my way back, in case things got too dark.

But that didn't seem to be the case. He had just wanted to meet. Michael might have had a reason for not being around. He could have been just as scared of being entrapped by the geas as his friends, though his sword and shield seemed to say different.

Why wouldn't he help? Why wouldn't he come out and offer that, at least? That was the thought that bothered me. Contract or not, Belial had been more help to me, hell Raphael had been more help to me than Michael's side. And that didn't *feel* right. Not to me. And that was the worry. That was my concern. That I had taken a carrot, had gotten the help I needed, had gotten to Red Rock and my mother, had even survived it, with my friends, with some assistance from Belial. I had taken that first step down that road paved with good intentions.

And my mother had died. Had sacrificed herself, her and my father, for a chance for me to live. Free. And for some reason, the image of my mother wouldn't leave me. Not the one, at the end, with her falling away from me. With my father falling away. Both of them dying, and by dying, freeing me from the geas.

Not that image, but the memory of her at my bedside, back when I had first met her, in Grafton. She had been nervous, meeting me for the first time. Her hand slightly trembling as she waited for me to wake, after she had healed me, after Dominic had almost killed me.

That was the image of her that stuck with me. The trembling hand. The thick scar around her neck, white with age, and all the other tiny pale scars crisscrossing her skin, scars from so many wounds that even with my mother's healing ability, the scar remained.

Much like the one over my heart from Dominic's stab.

That image I couldn't get rid of, and it made me sad. Angry. Sad again, then furious. The missed time. The hopefulness of the rescue. And then, the pain of loss.

I had once asked her how she had made it. Being a servant of evil. And she had replied that you find some part of yourself that you just won't compromise, you won't let go, and you hold onto it. For as long as it takes.

I wondered about the kind of love a mother had for her child, that she could weather those kinds of wounds and hurts. And put in motion a plan to free her child from the geas that had trapped her. And—ultimately—sacrificing her life, my father's life, for me.

I pushed the Camaro faster. My thoughts, now dark, stayed that way. I wasn't happy with Michael. We needed help, and here he was, the leader of all of Heaven's armies, and he had just wanted to meet. To talk. While I was here on Earth, cleaning up his mess.

Michael had lost his fight with Azazel.

His friends had been the ones captured back then, the angels put under the geas.

And he had walked away.

I could assign the mess to him. I could blame some part of him for my parents' death, while he remained away. It was the lives of my friends on the line now. It was my life. And a solid chance at eternity in hell.

He had waited three thousand years, and shown up now.

Just to meet me. Just to talk.

So yeah, my thoughts got dark.

About halfway through the trip, I stopped to fill up. There were still stations in service, even with not as many people on the road, and there I picked up a few candy bars. A couple of energy drinks. At least, I thought they were energy drinks. They were shaped the same, tall, brightly colored cans, the words were just all Spanish and I couldn't read them.

The first one, an orange can, was more grapefruity than orange.

But it was cold and carbonated, and I swallowed it down quick after I hit the road again. After a moment I looked at the empty, then crumbled the can and tossed it in the back of the new Camaro, in an homage to the older days. Back when I had used cars as a means to stay ahead of Azazel, as a place to sleep, really as a way just to stay alive another day.

The air got a little rank as I neared the crab ambush place, and I rolled up the windows and made sure the recirc was on. The smell got worse, like a skunk's scent seemed to, as I slowed down to navigate between bullet-riddled sedans and decomposing mountains of shell and meat, of crab and thrall and whatever was left of the dead vampires after sunrise. I felt things pop under the tires, hopefully pieces of crab and not pieces of human.

No people around still. Even though I thought there were a few alive in that town. It was weird, for as many people as Mexico had, as large of a population, to see so few. It seemed those that remained had either fled or gone inside the zone, leaving only ghost towns encircling Mexico City.

I accelerated out of that town quickly. I had been holding my breath and couldn't wait to roll down the windows and get fresh air whipping through the car again. The sun was directly above. It wouldn't be but a few more hours until I got back to the hideout.

Soon I got in range of the key, to where Jen and I could talk along the connection, to send more than general feelings. She was up, having not slept the night either, and she let me know that everyone got back okay. Laughing a bit at the butterfly guitar clamp Nick had given Sarah, and I laughed too, although Jen mentioning it made me wonder if there was another reason behind it.

She still felt like Jen. Like my rock. But there was something in the background, something troubling her, and I wanted to ask, but I also wanted to be there when I did, so I put the thought away and talked about my night. I started out with the ghost. The ancient

Aztec warrior, and how it made me feel, subsuming him. How I was worried about how those ghosts fought me, how they seemed to hide behind what appeared to be more placid spirits on my ethereal radar, and I wondered aloud what those ghosts were trying to do.

I moved on to the crab fight. My worry about the sword and how it had no effect on the creatures. How that mistake had almost cost me, and how no matter how much ethereal energy I pulled, the crab seemed to be almost a match for that raw power, how I could not harden myself enough.

Armor had popped out of my skin, once. Back in Grafton, in the factory where I had rescued Jen. The... material, for lack of a better word, had slid out of my skin. I had watched it, encircling my arms like gauntlets — *vambraces*, that was the word I had thought back then.

The vambraces had felt like a hard leather, actually harder than leather, and smooth like metal. It had been like titanium, bullets flattening as they struck it, but the armor had been flexible, too. It had moved when I moved.

That had been back in Grafton, and the crab's pinching claw had brought that back. I hadn't thought about the armor sense. The sword had been enough. And I wondered why the thought occurred to me now.

Jen let me keep talking along the key. Just let me let it all out. That fight, and the next. The vampire nest in Cuernavaca, the brief fight there, taking out the base of the La Familia Diablo. All the thralls and the vampires I had killed there.

Then I talked about the patio. About meeting Michael, and what he had wanted. I talked about Red Rock, and wondered what all that meant, the two of us in that water tower in the ... dream, limbo of clouds, whatever that place was. And though I started there, I wandered far off that course. I talked about what I thought that meant, how angry it had made me, that he had been there and done nothing these past few years. These past few centuries. These past few thousands of years.

I talked about my mom, about waking up to see her on my bed. The trembling hand. The nervousness. The deep scar that would never go away, the tiny pale scars that couldn't quite be healed.

I know my voice got hard again talking about it. I know I was full of anger, and that I was having trouble letting it go. I know she got it, and knew that I felt almost betrayed that Michael hadn't been there to help, and that I would have to keep carrying the burden I had been carrying. The burden of saving the world, of rescuing it from Azazel and his demon friends. From Belial and her machinations. And Raphael, too.

And Jen just listened. Without telling me what to do, just listened and was there, which maybe was what I needed most. I could feel her across the key, just like I had known as a kid, back in Grafton, staring up at the night sky, seeing the stars, that Jen was doing the same where she was at.

Some of the dark thoughts left me.

But not all.

I got more and more tired. It had been a long night. A long day before that. And a long day today. Physically and emotionally. But I finally got home. When I did Jen was waiting, in our apartment. The windows blacked out, hiding us from the afternoon sun. She welcomed me with open arms and held me, silent, just enfolding me in her arms and pulling me close so that I could feel the beat of her heart in her chest, so she could feel the beat of my heart in mine.

We stood there that way for a long time. Some of my breaths were deep. Some shuddered a bit, coming out. One of my hands was clenched, and I worked it open, taking my palm and sliding it across Jen's back, feeling the warmth of her body through the thin cotton T-shirt.

She pulled me to the bedroom. Pulled me down onto the soft

mattress. Took my shirt off, then hers, and pulled the cool sheets around us.

Then it was her breathing. Heavy. And mine. Her warmth, against me, and mine. Nothing was between us but warm, smooth skin. Warm, wet skin. Panting breaths.

The key resonated between us, the connection between us vibrating with an awareness of the other. Little warm wet kisses became tingling aches in each other. I could feel her, feel her over me, feel her feeling me, me in her, and I felt her awareness of that, of *us*, and for some time there was just that awareness and the feeling and the breathing, the feeling and the panting, the long motions between us becoming quick, frantic strokes. The heavy, deep, pulsing inhales becoming quick, shuddering breaths.

Our connection shuddered too. The feelings of each other too intense for the key to hold it all, and at the final, trembling point, everything spilled over. Nothing but that moment existed, it all overwhelmed us, it was everything we could do to hold each other, tight, feeling each other shake. I felt Jen bite my shoulder, hard, and I felt her awareness of me as I felt it, and I pulled her tighter to me, the two of us trembling and feeling each other tremble and feeling each other be aware of each other in a new, different way.

And then quiet.

Our breathing slowed, from the frantic pants into something longer, slower. Jen's body curled into me, her chest lying across mine, her forehead tucked into the nape of my neck, so that I could feel her breath across my chest, warm, stirring the hair there.

The tip of her finger traced something on my belly. I watched it, and watched her, until she looked up and our eyes met. Like every time, I could feel that connection. Something more than the key. Something more than her and I. There was an us there, when we gazed into each other, an awareness of something more we became, together. Something *meant*.

"Hey," she said. Her voice a near-whisper, yet the word something I could feel her speak, feel through our bodies, feel through the key, a deep resonation.

I turned a little and snuck a kiss to her temple, my hand cupping the back of her head, her hair thick against my palm. My voice much like hers, a whisper, but the word also something that resonated between us. "Hey."

Like I've said many times, she made me stand taller. Smile wider. Want to be more than who I was.

I had no idea what life would be like if I had never met Jen. I suspect I would have gone along, missing something, knowing I lacked a part of myself, never knowing what that part would be, or how complete I would feel with it. I would walk around, knowing that I wasn't who I was supposed to be, but not knowing how to get to be that person. Where to begin. Where to head. I would have been lost, unknowingly so, in a sea of life that stretched forever, empty.

Everyone should have a Jen.

I had almost lost mine.

Never again.

CHAPTER FIFTEEN

I woke up the next morning smelling bacon. The bedroom door was partly open, and the sizzling of fat on a pan drifted into the room, along with the softer smell of pancakes, the sweet smell of butter and batter frying in a pan. More sounds came in: the tinking of silverware, the rubbery slap of a spatula here and there, the hollow thunk of a big spoon dropping into the bowl, the occasional rushing of water in the sink, and Jen's voice, talking to someone softly.

It surprised me she was out of bed first. She was the late sleeper between the two of us. It told me how drained I had been from the past two days.

I took advantage and slowly worked myself out of the bed. The mattress was a little too soft for me, the thing seemed to suck me in, and I was still a little sore from the night before. No matter how much energy I pulled, how many times I healed myself, there still seemed to be a piper to pay the next morning. Still aches and pains, sore muscles, crackling bones falling back into place.

So getting up was a little work. Some groans here and there as I pulled myself up. A sharp gasp as my lower back tweaked, a brief shout from the muscles there warning me to go slow. Careful.

A lot of times I would make sure to heal myself after a fight. I hadn't, after Cuernavaca. I had forgotten, after checking out the Dead Zone. After my talk with Michael. Likely I had forgotten on purpose. The ghosts out there felt more like landmines, and despite how I saw them on the radar, I never really knew what I was stepping into until I tapped into one.

I should just stretch more, instead. Take up yoga. Do some Tai Chi each morning, greet the sun standing on one leg like a crane.

I snorted.

Or not.

It was groaning and tweaking for me. I did the first and watched the other, pulling myself off the mattress and standing. I put on my jeans and stretched, tall, raising my arms high in the air and feeling my back muscles resist the motion, then, after a moment, letting go in relief. I did it a few times, and felt a little bruise by my collarbone, looked at the mirror on the dresser and saw Jen's bite mark there.

T-shirt too, I guessed. I pulled one out, something gray with a band name on the front, with a few triangles and the words Dark Side of the Moon. Then I wandered through the open door into the living room slash kitchen area of the apartment.

Jen was there behind the kitchen counter, standing before the stove, flipping pancakes on a griddle. Using a fork to flip bacon in a cast-iron pan. There was a plate of bacon next to her, the meat dark in places, some of the bacon a bit chewy, with crunchy bits on the ends.

She winked at me and smiled. There was another pan next to the bacon, holding the pancakes, and she grabbed a spatula to flip a golden brown over in the pan. Waiting a moment for it to brown, then placing it on a plate, the first of a stack there. The pancake was a nice golden brown from the center outward, leaving just a bit of the edge here and there a little blackened.

The pancakes were cooked like the bacon. Golden brown in the center, but dark around the edges, crusty bits of batter around the edge. Just the way I liked them. A little bitter with the sweet.

Sarah was in the kitchen, sitting at a stool by the breakfast counter. Both elbows on the counter and hands wrapped around a large mug of coffee. It had been her and Jen speaking that I had heard. Sarah looked a little worried, and a little sweet, reminding me of how I had felt like she had been a younger sister back in Grafton. She was like Jen, just thinner, more fragile. Her hair was a little disheveled and tied back behind her back, wisps of it floating out, her brow creased with a few lines, though she smiled and waved a few fingers from her mug at me as I walked out, she still frowned occasionally at the bacon.

Sarah was a vegetarian. The world takes all kinds. Something that had happened after I left. She had a plate in front of her with a half-eaten pancake on it, two largish bites out of one side, the pancake smeared with melted butter and grape jelly.

The kitchen was small, almost like a galley. The sink and counter on one side, with Sarah sitting on the opposite side of the counter, and then the stove opposite the sink on the other, right next to the fridge and a coffee maker.

Jen bumped hips with me, smiling a little smile, and handed me a cup of coffee, already made. Something with cream and sugar and a sprinkle of cinnamon on top. It was delicious. And felt good. Warmed me, inside. Nothing felt more right than a delicious cup of coffee after a good night's sleep.

I had slept the whole night. As well as the afternoon before. Slept like the dead, apparently. I looked at the window, seeing the blue sky of midday, with the yellow sun well above the horizon.

"Nick and Johnny went last night." Jen had noticed my glance, knowing that I would have wanted to go out last night. Back to the edge of the zone to look for a way in. To make sure nothing was coming out. To watch activity and try to make some kind of plan.

"Good," I said. And meant it some, even though I wished I hadn't slept as long as I had. I took some more coffee in, letting the bitterness of the bean and the sweetness of the cream dance on my tongue before swallowing. Little sips of heaven.

Which had me thinking of Michael.

So I pushed that aside. Instead reached around Jen and snagged a piece of bacon, popping it into my mouth, at the same time chewing it and trying to make sure it didn't burn my mouth.

It was smoky and fatty and delicious.

Jen fought off me going for a second piece, then hip-checked me when I tried pulling a pancake off the plate, elbowing me aside with an "I'm making it, I'm making it," and laughing the whole time.

Sarah laughed with her, so I changed sides, stealing what was left of her pancake and stuffing it into my mouth. Her scream of *Hey* came seconds too late. I was chewing. Normally I was a maple syrup and butter guy, but the grape jelly and butter was delicious. It had me thinking of doing the same.

Sarah guarded what was left on her plate with her elbows. Jen did the same with the stack of pancakes and bacon.

"I've got to keep up my strength," I protested, after being fought off from the bacon again.

Sarah snorted, looked at Jen over the rim of her coffee cup. Her eyes twinkling. "So I've... heard."

I paused mid-swallow, feeling my cheeks get warm. Jen was holding back a laugh, smiling at me the whole time, not smiling but grinning, as if she had told Sarah everything. Which was something I hadn't thought of before.

My cheeks got even warmer. Hot. I was suddenly very glad I had put on the T-shirt.

"Look at that," Sarah said. "A man who blushes."

Jen did laugh then, waggling her eyebrows at me. "Cute, isn't it?"

For some reason, a feeling of youth came over me, a memory that wasn't a memory, more of a gathering of hundreds of memories into one image. Sarah and Jen and I at their breakfast table in Grafton. Mrs. Cooper cooking us all breakfast, pancakes or waffles or French toast, bacon and sausage or eggs. All of us laughing, being kids. Jen and I, even then, feeling that connection between us. Not knowing what the future held, and not caring, just being kids, being us.

I finished my swallow. Widened my eyes, feeling them twinkle, knowing there was a spark there, something mischievous. Jen paused a moment, holding the spatula, looking back at me. Sarah cocked her head, both of the girls still holding back chuckles.

A few minutes later we were all wrestling in the living room. I had a few pieces of bacon in my hand, and I was sitting on top of Sarah, having pulled her off her stool. We were wrestling around, I was pretending to make her eat the bacon, and she kept her lips pressed together tight, turning her head back and forth. Trying not to laugh and screaming through her pressed lips, *no no noooo—*

Jen grabbed me from behind. Trying to pull me off, but at the same time trying to tickle me. Her fingers dug into my ribs, into that spot between the ribs, and all of a sudden it was everything I could do to stay on top of Sarah.

Bacon was everywhere. One of my hands still held crumbles of a piece. I kept that hand near Sarah's lips. At the same time, I was trying not to scream myself. Jen was digging into my ribs with the fingers of one hand, the other arm around my chest, trying to pull me off of her sister.

A plate flipped over. A coffee mug hit the floor, and all of a sudden coffee and pancakes and bacon were everywhere. Somehow there was more food on me than Sarah, bacon bits smeared my cheeks, pancake fell out of my hair.

I was losing the fight but making every moment count. Wriggling to stay on top. My hands searching the floor for bacon. Sarah laughing and screaming, Jen's arms around my belly, tugging—

The door to our apartment slammed open.

We all stopped. Looked at the door. All breathing heavily, trying to catch our breaths. Me swallowing some smeared pancakes that had ended up half-in, half-out of my mouth.

Nick stood there. Looking half-asleep, but also looking fully alert. Like he was ready for battle, seconds after jumping out of bed. His face all Nick, composed, serious.

He cocked an eyebrow at us.

Then he grabbed a piece of bacon and joined the fight.

CHAPTER SIXTEEN

I took a shower after that. It was a new routine for me. Just a few months ago, I only took a shower when I had a safe, free moment. Which was rare, with Azazel hunting me. I never knew how much time I had, running from the demon, and even five minutes under some water could have proven fatal.

Like I said, showers were a rare thing. So when I had the time for one, I enjoyed it. Thoroughly. And I enjoyed the routine that came with it. Getting up and getting a cup of coffee, a hot shower. A moment or two with Jen. It was new and exciting and something I could see enjoying every day of my life.

The water was hot, and the pressure was high; the streams from the showerhead struck my skin. I felt like I needed the pressure. Somehow during the bacon wrestling I had gotten covered in grape jelly and maple syrup, and my T-shirt had come off like a large piece of Saran Wrap, sticking to my skin and peeling off in one big *schnicky* sound. The more water and soap the better.

I took some time, toweled off, scrubbing my chest and arms thoroughly. Put on some deodorant, something Jen got, some scent called Captain. It smelled too spicy for me. Almost like a pine scent.

Jen came in, smiling a little secret smile. Somehow she hadn't got any bacon or jelly or syrup on her. I wasn't sure how that could happen.

"You missed a spot." She took the towel from me and got some of my back and then the back of my arms. I guess I had missed spots. I hadn't been as thorough as I thought.

"I'm not sure about the deodorant," I told her. And at the time of saying it, thinking how domesticated that sounded. Here we were, getting ready to take on a demon deep in his stronghold, and I was having a discussion about scent.

"Why not?" she said, still smiling. Still toweling me with one hand, though I knew I was dry. Her other hand on the back of my shoulder, her palm soft and warm against my skin.

"It's too piney," I said. It came out a little whiny, but hell, I smelled like a Christmas tree. "I smell like one of those trees that you hang in your car."

"It's not pine," she said. "It's sandalwood."

Her eyes caught mine in the mirror. Her fingers slid over my shoulder, finding her bite mark from the night before, and lightly danced across it. "Some women find that sexy."

Well, who was I to complain to that?

I turned towards her; her lips found mine. She folded into me, and our bodies melted in that way a perfect couple does, hips fitting each other, bellies flush together, her arms snaking under mine. The kiss went on long, and when it finished, she tucked her head against my shoulder. Speaking of scent, I found hers, that smell of cool rain and honeysuckle that just always seemed a part of Jen.

"Want to talk about it?" I asked. Feeling what she was feeling through our bond. Feeling the mix of frustration and worry and the emotion underlying all of that, the emotion I couldn't quite identify.

"Maybe," she said, her breath warm over my arm. "I know we said later…"

She wasn't ready yet. I could understand that. It had taken me a long time to be ready to talk about some things, and when I had, those things had come with tears. With a racking emotion, with me crying into Jen's shoulder. Danny, leaving, fleeing Raphael. My time away, my time on the run. And the time back in the garage, when I had realized that my friends weren't going away, that they were with me, whatever the cost. Whoever the cost.

Those had been dangerous thoughts. Dark. That responsibility I wasn't ready for. Still wasn't ready for, honestly. A burden that only got heavier.

So whatever she was going through, she wasn't ready for that. Wasn't ready to unburden herself. As much as I wanted to know, as much as I wanted to be there for her like she had been for me, I knew that pressing now wouldn't help her.

Only time could do that.

So I wrapped my arms around her tighter, holding her close. "Okay."

That was all the two of us would ever need. Each other. Together. Forever.

After some time, she took a breath, let it out. It shuddered a bit. Her voice quiet. Reflective. "Most everyone else is upstairs."

The daily meeting. I'd say planning session, but it was more of a get-together-and-talk-things-out, than any kind of military operation. They were probably waiting on us.

Jen kind of hinted at it. "They think they saw something."

Nick. Or Nick and Johnny, with Gabrielle then. Watching the same thing I had been watching out above the city.

We moved into the bedroom. I got dressed. Again. Throwing on another pair of jeans and another T-shirt. Something white this time, and not from the dark side of the moon. Also not jelly-covered. Jen tossed me some socks, I slid them on with my shoes, and then the two of us were headed up to the third floor.

Jen paused there. One hand on the doorknob, the other on her chest. Over the key. The lights were dim, one of the bulbs above flickered a bit, throwing fluttering shadows behind her. She pulled the door shut, the latch making a light snicking sound that seemed to echo up and down the empty hallway.

Her eyes still looked worried. Not worried, but concerned. As if there was something going on she didn't understand. Something to do with the way she touched the key on her chest.

I wondered if that was what she was worried about. I didn't think so. Like me being an angel, our connection wasn't something I thought hard about, but for different reasons. I didn't want to know what it meant, being an angel. But I knew what Jen and I were together. It just was. It was us. We were something that was always meant to be, and there was no need for me to think about that.

Whatever was coming, we would face it. Whatever rose before us, we would defeat it. The two of us would always be greater together.

I grabbed her hand, threading my fingers through hers, her palm warm against mine.

Her other hand played with her key a bit before tucking it back into her shirt. She let out a breath and seemed to relax. And then came her smile.

I grew a little taller. Felt a little stronger. Smiled that smile that came naturally, the way that happens when you and the person you loved connected on that level no one else could.

Jen seemed taller as well. Stronger for sure. Firm, in my hands. And her smile, well it was the thing I wanted to see first when I woke up. See first whenever I saw her. And the last thing I saw before I closed my eyes at night.

A moment or two later we pulled apart, though still together. The two of us headed upstairs, Jen's hand in mind, our fingers tightly entwined, an unbreakable bond. Both of us nervous, with the shaky unknown of Sabnock and Mexico City before us, the vampire army he was building, the other humans inside, all the humans missing outside. The crabs and creatures rising from some unknown hell.

Nervous, but also ready. For whatever was next. At least as much as we could be.

After all, we had gotten this far.

CHAPTER SEVENTEEN

The upstairs room was full. Jen and I walked into the low murmuring noise a lot of people made when they were sitting around the room, speaking in pairs, low talking in various personal conversations. Nick and Johnny, standing to the side. Gabrielle and Gertrude by a wall, Gabrielle using the wall to hide from the sunlight in the windows. Alejandro in the doorway next to Gabrielle, a bottle of Modelo in his hand. Zoe and Tabitha on the couch, Tabitha getting up as we walked in.

There was a little music in the air, Sarah sat at one end of the big U-shaped couch, on the arm of the couch actually, legs crossed onto the sofa and her acoustic guitar in her lap. It was the one Nick had gotten her back in New Orleans. From a pawn shop up there. I smiled to see the pink butterfly clamp hanging off the neck of the guitar.

Sarah's eyes were closed, she was playing something soft, lightly strumming the chords and humming underneath the sound of the guitar. Her head weaved back and forth, just slightly, and I looked away to see Nick standing by Johnny, watching Sarah as well, with a tiny smile on his face.

Jen hip-bumped me, just slightly, and let go of my hand. She moved to the island in the kitchen, where some bagels and cream cheese sat, some chips, and a bowl of fruit. Small apples and ripe bananas. She grabbed a banana and a bagel, and Tabitha caught her there, bringing them into the conversation.

Zoe was on the couch. The side of the U across from Sarah. She motioned me over, patting the cushion next to her. For some reason I felt reluctant to walk over, but there was really no reason not to, so I maneuvered around the big coffee table in the middle of Couch U and sat, seeing that someone had laid out the huge map of Mexico City on the table. It was what we used for our planning sessions; I had drawn in a large red circle around the city, representing the edge of the Dead Zone. This zone was far larger than the one in Louisiana, stretching almost all the way down to Cuernavaca, west past Toluca, east almost to Puebla.

A tall empty glass held one corner of the map down, a plate with a piece of toast held down another. A matchbox car on a third, a tiny black Porsche 911. Some bottle caps were scattered across the map, representing where we had seen concentrations of vampires, humans, landmarks, or other items of interest. We used what we used.

"Hey," Zoe said. I was struck again by how like her mother she was. Hair tied behind her head, thick strands but also a little frizzy, so some hair escaped the bun. Glasses, just like the ones you see every librarian wear, perched on a pert nose. Closer, I noticed a scattering of freckles across her cheeks.

I nodded, looking back at Jen, who seemed to be trying to eat the bagel and at the same time answer whatever Tabitha was asking her. The bagel had a bite in it, but she was doing more talking than eating.

I looked back at Zoe. And wondered if this had been planned.

"Jen told me a bit about your ghost," Zoe said. "The warrior one that you took in, before you left."

It *had* been planned.

I let out a breath.

Zoe smiled.

"Yeah?" I said. Not quite sure what else to say.

"I think we should go out together sometime," she said. "And have you find one of these spirits. The really malignant ones. It might be while you're absorbing it, I can find out more about it. About why they are fighting you."

Jen had told Zoe more than I wanted her to. More than I wanted anyone to really know. While I was worried about it, worried about the spirits like the warrior, Jo, the grandma with the cookies, to me it was too small concern leading up to the fight with Sabnock. It was something I could put aside. Something I could deal with later.

Zoe seemed to understand. "It doesn't seem like that big a thing, right?"

It wasn't something I wanted to explain. "Whatever it is, it's something I can deal with. There is evil in this world, and then there is *evil*. We all know it. It's no surprise to see it in the ghosts. To have one or two fight me."

Fighting me was one thing, but living their memories was another. I left that part unsaid. There was a difference there, a difference between fighting evil and internalizing it, and while that part had me worried, again, it was something I felt like I could deal with later.

I smiled, inside. Not a smile really, more of a sarcastic grin. There was always something I could put off later.

"I understand," she said. Her voice was a lot like Sarah's. There was an ethereal, fragile quality to it. Like her voice might crack or break in any word. Though it never did. Odd as it was, it kept me focused on what she was saying. So her next words, I fully received. "I always think the worst of evils start out that way. Something small. Something that can be put aside till later. Something that festers and grows until it becomes so large that the dealing with it is no longer easy, but something that becomes a real fight. A fight of life or death."

Her words hit me. She saw it in my eyes. My smile this time was on the outside, a you-got-me kind of smile.

"So," she said. "Tonight?"

"You're very pushy," I said. "For someone so small."

She was small, and thin. The very image of a spinster, just in her twenties. Her eyebrows raised as she waited. A knowing kind of look in her eyes.

"I've got to go to the city tonight," I said. Like I did every night here. Like Nick and Johnny had done the night before. To figure out the plan.

"My understanding is that's been covered," she said. Her eyes going to the very people I was thinking about.

I had been right. This had been planned. But not just between Tabitha and Zoe. I looked back at Jen, who was suspiciously *not* looking at me, and still seeming to try to find a way to answer Tabitha and finish her bagel. Without cream cheese, but with the banana still in hand.

A lot of food there, for someone who had just eaten.

Dammit. "Fine."

Zoe smiled. Patted my knee. "Good."

"I've got something I want to do first," I said. I had a thought, with the connection that Jen and I had through the key. The bond there, of something that had used to be Solomon's Key, but now was something else. Something that held energy that bound Jen and I together.

"Nighttime is still far enough away," Zoe said. "We'll be here."

"Okay," I said, getting up. Pulling myself out of the soft couch. Feeling like I should be a little more... not grateful, but that I should say something to someone trying to help me. All I had was the one word. It might have come out a little gruff. "Thanks."

Zoe laughed. "We're not pulling your teeth tonight."

Maybe we weren't, but we weren't picking daises either. "I'll be here at sunset."

I walked over by Sarah, who watched me get up from the couch. She had a slight grin on her face, though her eyes had a little twinkle. She seemed sad; she always seemed that way lately. She was playing something different, her head still bobbing slightly to the music, her fingers plucking each string, slowly, to a familiar rhythm. In fact, the song struck a chord, a memory, a slower version of something I had heard a lot as a kid, each note drawn out in a melody, a jingle, the name bouncing around in the back of my head—

The Twelve Days of Christmas.

Nick must have told her about me and Jen and the Christmas thing. I knew it when Sarah winked at me, and her humming became a soft singing to the song, soft enough only I could hear the words in her ethereal voice... *Four calling birds*, *three French hens*, *two turtle doves*—

I found myself singing along, on the inside.

Dammit.

Sarah laughed and played on. The song became something else, something you might hear in a coffee house. I looked for Nick and found him making sure that he was *not* looking over at me. But he seemed to have a wide smile on his face, talking with Johnny.

Jen hadn't heard though. Hadn't seen, I didn't think. She was still at the island with Tabitha, and the two seemed to be in the middle of a good discussion.

I'd find something. I was sure of it. When the time was right.

I snuck around the corner of the couch, between Sarah and the window. The sun outside was high in the sky, the sky itself was blue, and there were fish scales of clouds patterned across the horizon, telling me a warm front was incoming—even though it was already too warm for the season—and that a storm was on its way. If not a storm, at least winds and some rain.

Tonight was going to be more fun than I thought.

Gertrude and Gabrielle stopped talking, both looking my way. Alejandro tilted his Modelo to me. His eyes thankful. Word must have gotten to him about Cuernavaca. I nodded a return.

Gabrielle looked tired. Still a little bruised. I guessed she hadn't drank much lately. Or at least not much from Johnny. Her eyes looked over my shoulder, and I knew she was looking at him before coming back to me.

"No problems getting back?"

She shook her head. "None. Though I didn't thank you for coming."

"No thanks needed," I said. "We're a team."

"Yes." Her words were pronounced elegantly, in the way Italians had. Carrying a different timbre. "I... believe I am still getting used to that."

I probably understood. She had been raised to breed more of her family before her brothers had been killed by Dominic Antonado in revenge for being ostracized to the United States from Europe. After that, she had a child, apparently at fifteen, and turned a few years later and raised to take over for her father.

A father she was now trying to kill.

And who was trying to kill her.

And I had been a loner a long time. On the run after Grafton. It had taken coming back, and Jen, and Nick and my friends, to show me this way. The working together way. Which I still had some trouble with.

"It takes getting used to," I said. "But you're a Wolverine now. So no thanks required. No apologies. Whatever we have to do, we do it together, right?"

Her eyes watered a little. Her voice lowered, even though Gertrude was close enough, the witch could surely hear. "Is being this Wolverine, is it permanent?" She looked over my shoulder again. "What if…?"

I knew she was worried. And it was something I couldn't pretend to understand. After all, vampires drank the blood of humans, even if they were "quote/unquote" good vampires. And Gabrielle had been raised to believe in that bond between human and vampire, and treasure it as part of her family.

A family that had been a lie. That had turned on her. A family that had been a mask for the geas and what it had done to my family.

Johnny was having a tough time with that part. He hadn't talked about it much, but I got the feeling he had liked being Gabrielle's human. Her thrall. I was sure there was something sexual in it, something about the taking of blood, and the feelings and excitement that came with it, that had attracted him at first. Something about being that, for her.

Something he couldn't do with someone else.

It was a tough nut to crack. And I couldn't do it for them. All I could do was be there.

"Once a Wolverine, always a Wolverine." Was all I could say. She nodded, blinked a few times. While she did, Alexandro finished his beer. Asked us if any of us wanted one.

Gabrielle looked back once more over my shoulder. "I could use a drink."

The two of them went to the kitchen. Grabbing a few beers from the fridge. Getting caught up in the Jen and Tabitha conversation on the island. Which left me and Gertrude.

"I am not a Wolverine," the witch said, in her deep voice. "So I may need to offer an apology."

"For what?" I glanced back at the kitchen. Catching Jen looking at me. I winked.

"For what I said before," Gertrude said. "About how tough this is going to be."

I snorted, looked at Gertrude. The Valkyrie was as tall as me, one of the few women that I could look straight in the eyes. I realized she was older than I thought, she looked as if she was in her forties, though witches could be older, and though she carried muscle she was also weathered. Weathered from fights, would be my guess.

She wore her armor but was missing her gear. The sword and axe not crossed over her shoulders. The scabbards that I had seen, with all the symbols painted over them.

"Every fight I go into is tough," I said. "Hell, not so long ago I ran from every one."

The Valkyrie smiled. "Not many people are smart enough to run when needed."

I felt Jen behind me. Felt her smile from back down in the hallway. "That's true," I said. "But sometimes running gets to be a habit, when standing up to things should be instead."

Gertrude nodded an acknowledgement. "It's a fine line, isn't it? The balance between running and the fight."

"It is. But I used to lean more towards running. All I'm trying to do now is lean more to the fight."

She laughed a bit. "A younger me would have liked you a lot."

"Well," I said. "The current you is enough. You're here. You're helping." I had come to my question. The thing that had been bothering me since the fight with the crabs. "Listen, you helped Sarah a lot, back in Lewiston."

Gertrude had been one of the first to see that the symbols, the tattoos on Sarah's back, had been built as a construct to hold the energy of a demon in her skin, to tie that energy to her vampiric control, so that as the energy built inside her, her blood would be more and more craveable, so that the vampires who had drunk her blood could control other vampires who had drunk the blood created in the factory.

Those tattoos had reminded me of Solomon's Key. Of the patterns there, when I had stared at it. Not just the patterns of the demons, but the overall pattern etched into the stone.

"That tattoo on Sarah's back," I said. "The one binding all the energy. Can you create something like that?"

"A tattoo?"

"Not a tattoo," I said, although I did file it away for later. "Maybe something like an etching. In stone or metal."

Her hand reached up and rubbed her chin and cheek in that thinking motion a fighter did before entering the ring. "Not that specific one. The one we found on Sarah, that one was evil. Not something we dabble in."

"Oh."

"But I could do something else," the Valkyrie said. "There's something called the Five-Fold Symbol."

"Nordic?"

"No. Celtic." She smiled, then shrugged. "There's some crossover in that part of the world. You take what works."

"I understand that."

"It's something I could etch onto metal," she said. "Something I could empower to hold energy, I believe. Are you talking about what you use? What do you call it, spirit energy?"

"Ethereal," I said. "Ethereal energy. I pull that from the spirits. Well, from where the ghosts are tapped into the ethereal plane."

"I wonder about that. This plane, it seems like it's a bridge between the worlds." Gertrude let out a small smile. "Like the Bifrost bridge."

Could it be? I wasn't going to tell someone what to believe or not. I was still getting used to the idea of the ethereal plane being there, about the spirits that I tapped there leaving and moving on to their next place. The worlds that awaited them, good or evil. Heaven or hell.

Maybe it was all related. But that part didn't matter so much to me. What mattered was if Gertrude could build me something like Solomon had built in his key.

"This Five-Fold Symbol," I said. "Let's do it."

"Now?"

"Some time today, if you could," I said. "The sooner the better."

One of her eyebrows arched.

"In what would you like me to inscribe it?"

"Got a knife you can spare me?"

She smiled. "I have many knives. But I prefer the sword."

"A knife is fine," I said. "If you think the Five-Fold Symbol can hold energy, inscribe it there for me. And then let me borrow it for a bit."

"I'm guessing you're going to borrow it for more than a bit."

I smiled. Wondering if she was giving up an heirloom. All her armor and sword and axe spoke of long use. Something handed down from her father or mother. We didn't have a lot of money, and I was sure that I didn't have anything Gertrude really wanted. "Wolverines?"

The witch snorted. "I have no need to be part of that. All I want is a promise."

I froze at the word. Gertrude saw me do it. After all, I had learned that the word was the deed. That a promise was more than just speaking it. Probably for everyone, but especially if you were someone like me.

"Does it have to be a promise?"

She nodded. "Your word."

A chilling feeling ran down my spine.

And Gertrude saw me almost physically step back. She shook her head. "I'm not asking for much, Grimm. I just want you to tell me, the moment you think we should run."

The Valkyrie paused. Looked back at Tabitha and Zoe. At Sarah and Jen. "That is all."

She felt responsible for them. For Zoe and Tabitha, maybe Sarah and Jen, maybe witches in general. I had never asked, because the Valkyrie was just one of a couple dozen witches I had freed. She had just been another witch when we had showed up later in Lewiston. I had assumed they all were from the area, but Gertrude had come from somewhere else. It could be she was part of a group that protected witches, those that didn't have the power to protect themselves.

It was something Jen would know. But for now, the promise. The second time I had given my word in one day. A commitment to Zoe. And now, my word to Gertrude. About running. Something I thought about enough already, with trying to figure out a safe way for us to attack the Dead Zone, to neutralize it, to kill Sabnock. Of course I'd want to run, if that was any kind of real option. And I told Gertrude that, in so many words.

The side of her mouth curled in a tiny smile. The grim smile of a warrior waiting to be overrun by an overwhelming force. "Not those moments. We all have those. I want your word on the real one. The moment where we need to commit and win or run and fight another day. That's the time I need to know. That moment."

I shook my head. Honestly, that could be anytime. I mean, we really didn't have a plan. Well, something had occurred to me, but that idea was in its infancy. Who knew what would be happening tomorrow? A few days from now? A week?

Would I be around Gertrude? Would I be close enough to tell her? She seemed the type to be in the middle of a fight, with the sword and the axe, and that's usually where I would be. That was all I could count on.

And I was overthinking it all. I could try. I would try. And that would have to be enough.

Still, I tried to put a condition on it. Some of the old me, hanging on. "If I can."

That was enough for her. "Your word?"

"You have it."

We shook. Her hand was strong and firm and callused. Her voice was just as firm, if not as callused. "Then you'll have your blade."

I held her hand a moment. Her words struck me. She meant them for the knives she was going to etch for me, but they applied to a different blade as well. My sword. My blade. The one that came because I did the things I said I would do.

I let go of her hand. Looked back over the room. Saw Nick standing there next to Johnny. Johnny, holding the neck of a bottle of beer with his fingers. Saw Jen breaking away from Tabitha and Alexandro and Gabrielle.

I wondered how many of the knives I could make. We certainly could use more if they worked. I turned back to Gertrude. "Maybe a couple of knives, if you can. Nick might have a spare."

"I'm sure I have enough," the Valkyrie said. And the way she said it, I found I was sure she had enough too.

So I let out a breath. Another promise given. And I was still standing. I was still leery after discovering how much my word really meant to me. Meant to what I could do. Meant to how strongly I could defend my friends and attack our enemies.

Jen came up, standing next to me. The palm of her hand rubbing up and down my back. She looked at Gertrude, and I got the feeling that while Zoe and Tabitha had been part of something planned this morning, the Valkyrie hadn't.

Jen's voice was Jen. Calm, relaxed, yet with a hidden timbre, a light rumble, more than a purring. Like a sound a puma or a lioness might make, if their young were threatened. That kind of rumble. Her hand paused, and her fingers dug just a tiny bit into the back of my shoulder. "Everything good?"

The Valkyrie seemed not to notice. Or at least pretended not to. "As good as can be."

I looked aside at Jen. Her gaze and Gertrude's were locked. Not in one of those right-before-a-fight kind of stares, but in something measuring.

I felt awkward standing there. "We're good. Gertrude's making me something."

Jen's eyebrows rose.

"It's good," I said. "It'll help."

Jen smiled then, as if it *was* good. She steered us back to the couch. I realized Sarah had stopped playing the guitar, and the room had gone mostly silent. Everyone was sitting in or around the U-shaped couch, looking back at us.

Planning time.

Mentally, I shook my head. It had been a long couple of days. And last night with Jen, and this morning, had kind of recovered me a bit. So it was kind of crazy that I already felt like I had been through a ringer today.

And the day was just starting.

CHAPTER EIGHTEEN

J en tugged me over to the couch. We snuggled into a corner, her leaning back against me. She had brought me a beer, and I held the cold Modelo in one hand, feeling the cold beer sweat against my palm. The lager was crisp, with not much of a bitter aftertaste, and it was growing on me.

Sarah still sat on the edge of the couch, to my left. Her guitar was put up, and Nick sat in front of her so that her legs were wrapped around his stomach, and she leaned a little against his back. Zoe remained where she had been, her mother next to her, and Gertrude standing behind them both. On the other end of the U was Johnny and Gabrielle, Johnny sitting closer to the window, Gabrielle wearing a large pair of movie-star sunglasses. His hand was in her lap, held tightly in both of hers, and though they sat close together, I saw how tired Johnny was. Wan. Too thin.

As if he had been thinking the same thing, he reached out to the table and grabbed some of the chips there. Eating them mechanically. His throat working them down after all the chewing. He finished the swallow with a sip of beer and a grimace.

He didn't see me watching him.

Alejandro seemed to not know where to sit and ended up back at the kitchen island, which sat behind the U of the couch. Facing the windows. He leaned back against the island, squinting. The female vampire had showed up, the shorter one with the scar down her face, wearing sunglasses that reminded me of the Terminator movie.

I had learned her name was Millie. She didn't say much, and looked unhappy when she did. But Nick had said she was good with a blade and a gun; he had seen her fight back against the crabs. The scar must have been something she earned. And she was alive after whatever had done that to her, so she was a fighter.

It wasn't like we could afford to turn down anyone, really.

Then it was the group. And though I was the man green-lighting all the decisions, I wasn't the type of guy who ran the sessions. That kind of structure and planning wasn't me.

Jen remained leaned back against me. Her back warm against my chest. There was a comfort there I would always notice and always enjoy, a kind of her-and-me existing in all places and all times. So when she spoke, I felt it. Her voice a mix of lilting contralto and a purr.

"Nick, catch us up."

Nick had his glasses on. The wireframes. A beer in his hand, though forgotten. He leaned forward, glancing at me. The lenses of his frames flared up as the sun caught it, a quick, bright flash of light, and then it was gone.

"So Johnny and I rolled out last night to take the watch," Nick said. By watch, he meant the thing I did when I went out there looking for a plan I could never find. "There was a lot of activity. And by activity, I mean trucks. More than usual."

"Yeah," Johnny added. "A long line of them, coming from the north. All eighteen-wheelers, running single file."

Nick kept looking at me. "For miles."

I frowned. None of us knew what that meant.

"We know Sabnock's a builder," Johnny said. He had done the research there. "An architect. And we know he's building something."

"We just don't know what," Nick said.

"But it seemed like last night was a big event," Johnny said.

They looked like they were trying to convince someone of something. I realized then that they were. They were trying to convince me of what they had done. That it had been the right thing to do.

"You went in."

"Yeah," Nick said, at the same time Johnny was saying, "No."

Nick glanced at Johnny. "Well, I went in."

And there it was. I could feel it. The moment that this mission wouldn't be something I would do. The real moment where I knew —I *knew*—Sabnock wouldn't be a demon I would kill. For better or worse, Nick was taking the lead here.

The feeling was much like riding a rollercoaster. One of those that went way up high, the cart clickety-clacking as it climbed, pushing you higher and higher until you crested the top and sat there, balanced for a brief moment on that edge, seeing the Earth far below you, all the tiny figures standing in the crowd, waiting and watching.

I could almost feel the wind at the top, the rocking of the cart, the slight tip of it over the precipice, and then I would be plummeting down, racing down the rails, the cart shuddering and rocking as if it might break loose at any moment.

I wanted to get out, I wanted to stop the cart from moving, but I knew I would have to ride this ride to its end. There was no stopping what would happen now. Nothing I could do except be there and help where I could. And hope I was enough.

Hope that Nick would be enough.

Hope that we all would be enough.

I wish I could have fought the fear inside me better. It swelled in waves, the fear I wouldn't be there if someone needed me. The fear that when the demon struck, I wouldn't be able to help. Just like what had happened back in New Orleans. My hands opened and closed. Once. Twice.

Jen noticed. Felt the fear from me, whether from a change in my breathing, or the key, the bond between us. She shifted, one of her hands going to my leg. Rubbing it softly.

I made sure my voice was even. Knowing Nick was someone I could count on. Wanting him to know that too. "What'd you find?"

He looked at me. His face serious. Composed. It was as manly a look as Nick had ever given. Not a glance full of testosterone or anger or rage. Just something that said he was ready. For whatever came next. He would handle it.

"I saw Sabnock," Nick said. His gaze went inward. "The guy is tall. Seven or eight feet. Dark. At first, I thought he had the head of a lion, but I was seeing him from the side, and he's got this piece of armor, this shoulder thing poking up high, that's shaped like a head of the lion."

"A pauldron," Johnny said.

"Yeah. Only like it's above his shoulder." Nick held the palm of his hand six inches or so off of his own shoulder. "It's golden, and from the side it looks like a mask, almost.

"He was directing some of the trucks. Or telling people where to take what. It was close to the stadium there. There's a lot of construction. He was standing on a corner and there was this shadow next to him…" Nick's voice became thoughtful. A little quiet. Sarah's hands reached around and held him. "I almost took a shot."

He shook his head. Glanced back over at me with a boyish

smile. Something I might have given to a teacher if I had been caught doing something I shouldn't. "But I waited. And watched."

I grinned back. I could feel what he was talking about, standing in the shadows, seeing the demon, pulling out a knife and wondering if he could end it all, right there. Right then.

"Anyway, I didn't," Nick said. "I watched them. They are building something there at the stadium. Or maybe adding to the stadium; it was hard to tell. There was a cover over the top, a frame-work of steel girders collapsed over it all, and more."

Johnny took it from there. "We know he's an architect. At least from the research. A builder. He's supposed to have built the Pande-monium in hell."

"Didn't he have other powers?" Zoe asked.

"Sickness and rot," Johnny said. "We've seen evidence of that on some of the skyscrapers."

"I saw it up close," Nick said. "The closer you get to the center of the city, the worse it is. Covers all the buildings at their tops. A dark greenish snot thing streaked in black. Hard too, not liquid."

"But is it disease? Gangrene?" I asked. Remembering us talking about Sabnock, back on a farm, a long time ago.

"Who knows?" Nick said. "Reminds me of *Aliens*. That part in the movie where the big egg things open up. That kind of snot."

That movie never brought a good feeling when it was mentioned. I had a friend in the Rangers who had liked it. She had wanted to shout the big *Game Over Man* scene during our last fire-fight. And had missed her moment.

Jen leaned closer. "You good?"

"Yeah," I said. "Was remembering something."

Something big and eggy and gangrenous. I didn't like the feel of it. I didn't think it was just a disease Sabnock brought with him. The buildings had a purpose. A reason to be covered with an eggy snot-like substance.

"We know he's building something. Or has built something," Johnny said.

"There's more," Nick said. "I know we've been wondering a bit where everyone is here. There should be millions of people here, hundreds of millions, and most of the towns are like this one. Just a few people here and there.

"Mexico City is the same. There are a lot of workers, but not a lot of people," Nick said. "So I looked around."

His voice had darkened some. Whatever he had found must have been bad. Alexandro had mentioned that the clan had made a deal with Sabnock, that the demon had granted the vampire clan asylum inside the Dead Zone, but that he had also gathered farms of humans together to feed them. Maybe to build his own vampire army.

But, I thought, surely not a hundred million people.

I looked at the map. "Was this Aztec Stadium?"

Nick responded with a thumbs-up.

He had gone far last night, traveling the shadows. Aztec Stadium was south of Mexico City. Closer to where I had been the day before, in Cuernavaca, than our safe house. I grabbed a bottlecap and marked the stadium, and noticed when I did how close to the center of the Dead Zone it lay.

"Do we know when they built it?"

Like he usually was, Johnny was the first to answer. Looking at his phone. "Sixty or so years ago. Nineteen-sixties."

He paused, his thumb sliding along the face of the phone.

"Renovated just a few years ago."

That cinched it for me. "That's the center," I said. That was where Azazel had broken ground with his pentagram. Where he had laid the cable underground and built the pentagram connecting Mexico to New Orleans. I would bet any amount of money that part of the upgrades had been upgrades to the cell service and wi-fi in the stadium.

We all knew the center of the symbol would be where it was powered. Jen had told me that, but it also made sense in another kind of way. A memory from childhood, silly enough. Drawing on a piece of paper in class. If you take a pentagram and connect all the points on the inside of it by drawing a line between those points, you'll end up with a star. That star is five points with another pentagram inside of it.

You can do it again, connect all the points of the new pentagram, and end up with another star. With another pentagram inside. And then do it again, an infinite amount of times, or at least until you end up with a pentagram so small you can't see the center anymore.

That was how the symbol worked. The pentagram. Its center would always be the place of the most power. The most concentrated part. So we figured that would be where we—if we could— would be able to destroy it. Release whatever powered the Dead Zone, and send that piece of hell back to… well, hell.

In a funny way, it's how symbols worked. They were built up of lines, walls, protecting the center. Or holding the power in the center from getting out. And even if those walls were unbreakable, if you could get to the center and unlock it, as we did with Sarah with exorcising the demon inside the tattoo on her back, you could void it out. Nullify it.

We had figured out the center was somewhere in the southern part of Mexico City but didn't exactly know where. It's a little hard to pinpoint something when the Dead Zone was a thousand miles wide. But, looking at the map, the stadium was it. At least, it was our best bet.

"So that's where we need to go," Nick said. "That's where we break the Dead Zone."

The center. Pentagrams inside of pentagrams. The place of power for the Dead Zone, smack dab in the middle of the Aztec Stadium. A coliseum, maybe even a monument, for the warriors of today, built to honor warriors of the past.

The ghost of the Aztec warrior flashed through my mind, the murder and the raping, the blood dripping from the head the warrior held in his hand. The pure glee, mixed with malice, and not quite hate, but a thirst. A thirst to do worse.

I shivered. I think I went pale a bit. I felt cold inside, just for a moment. Zoe watched me from across the table. Jen shifted and turned her head so that it ducked underneath my chin so that I could feel her breath there, warm, and I took comfort from it. Her arm reached around my back, gathering me in.

If we can. I didn't say the words. But I thought we all were thinking them.

The map was the center of all our attention, for a moment. The stadium was far from where we were now; it was southwest of us, towards the bottom of Mexico City. If Sabnock was building something there, if that was the real center, then we were on the long side of it, northeast of the city. It would be a long trek to breaking the Dead Zone and killing the demon in charge of protecting it.

Though I had an idea. And the stadium was close to Cuernavaca. I thought the idea worked even better if that's the spot we needed to hit.

The idea coalesced. Became a plan. A real plan. Something I could be a part of. Not this bystander on the side, not someone who was sending in Nick without any help or protection, but the avenging angel I was supposed to be.

I leaned forward. "What if we broke the Dead Zone first?"

Nick looked at me. I couldn't tell what he was thinking.

"What's the right word?" I asked.

"Void," Jen said, the word warm on my neck. "Nullify."

CROWN OF BONES • 145

"That," I said. "You think we can get in there and void the Dead Zone's power?"

"All of us?" Johnny asked.

"Hear me out," I said. What I was thinking made sense to me. "I've been shock-and-aweing from that side of the Dead Zone for a few weeks. What if we really attacked from that side?" I looked at Alexandro. "From Cuernavaca."

"We would be going through south Mexico City," the vampire said, his voice somber. "Through La Familia Diablo."

We would be, but I thought that would make the attack seem more serious. More real. It would be a natural escalation of what had been happening in Cuernavaca. "We would. Just a few of us, but we'll dress it up like it's more."

The room had fallen silent. Everyone seemed to be thinking. The whole group seemed to lean forward a bit, looking at the map.

Even Jen, who was frowning a bit. "Dress it up?"

"Yeah," I said, thinking of the wall of cars back in Cuernavaca, the eighteen-wheeler jackknifed across the road. I grabbed the toy car, the Porsche, and set it down at the bottom of the map. Facing north, along the road from Cuernavaca to Mexico City. "We'll get a convoy and Mad Max that motherfucker."

Nick was nodding. Jen still frowned, though she had let out a *humph* of realization. Johnny, too, gave a smile. He was the big movie buff.

But some of the group didn't get the reference. Gabrielle and Alexandro. Gertrude. The Valkyrie's head was cocked. "Mad Max?"

I looked for more toy cars and settled on a few beer bottle caps, lining them up behind the Porsche. "We'll build up a convoy. A lot of big trucks. Drive them straight through, like we're headed right for the stadium. Make Sabnock think we're attacking him in force."

That would be the plan. Make Sabnock have to retaliate. Have him think we were committing everything in an attack, and have him respond. Force a pitched battle, drawing the demon's attention to me.

I was good at that kind of thing.

"It would be a suicide mission," Gertrude said, looking directly at me. As if wanting me to already tell her what she wanted to hear.

I shook my head. I didn't have the whole plan, but I knew this part would work. I could figure out the details later. "All we have to do is make it seem like an army is attacking. Then hold his attention. If we time it right..."

Nick knew his part. "I'll be sneaking in the back."

I nodded. "And null out the Dead Zone."

"At which point Sabnock will be vulnerable."

I nodded again. Feeling more in control. I wasn't sending Nick in to face Sabnock alone. If he could break the center of the Dead Zone and annul it, well, then I could summon my sword. And with the Dead Zone gone, there would be no place for Sabnock to hide.

"I will go," Alexandro said. He tipped his beer to me. "We may not have many fighters, but I can find drivers. We will Mad Max this motherfucker."

The female vampire next to Alexandro glanced at him. Maybe it was the scar, but she didn't seem happy. There was a tug of his sleeve, and the two pulled back from the rest of us, deeper into the kitchen, conversing quietly.

The planning session devolved into more group talk. Like when I had walked in, but now people figuring out the next steps. Kind of a brainstorming session, where people broke off and talked about ideas, things they wanted to try, plans of attack.

Nick wanted to go back in tonight and grab pictures of the stadium, figure out a way to get in. Plan his route. Johnny was interested in the pictures to try to figure out what Sabnock was building. Alexandro wanted to get back to Cuernavaca, not only to check on his clan but to start building up the convoy. Tabitha thought she could do to some of the vehicles like she had with my Camaro, strengthen the metals so they could take a beating.

Sarah remained a little quiet. Staying behind Nick, being a part of his conversation with Johnny without saying anything. Glancing over at Jen, her eyes a little sad.

Gertrude left, letting me know with a nod of her head that she was going to inscribe the knives for me. Which was good. I planned on trying my thing with the knives later, and that meant taking Zoe with me. I would kill two birds with one stone.

Jen remained quiet a bit, leaning against me, still frowning, and I could sense her struggle along the bond as people talked. She knew I would be in Cuernavaca. Details to figure or not, the convoy would be the deadliest part of the plan. The part where the most people who could die, would.

It struck me then that it felt odd for her to worry about me. Usually, she was my rock. She believed in me more than I believed in myself. For her to worry was in part natural, but also in part not-so-Jen.

This wasn't the normal worry. This was something else. Something that tingled along my spine. A deeper tolling of unease stirred, then rippled inside me, like the waves rippling the surface of a pond after a large rock had plunged into its depths. Whatever had Jen off, it wasn't simply jealousy of Gertrude, or something I could explain simply. It was deeper.

It was only right for me to be with the convoy. Not just because I was me and because of what I could do, but because it was something I was good at. Picking a fight big enough that it couldn't be ignored. I would be the carrot to lure Sabnock from his hiding space. A chance to take me out, while I was powerless, inside the Dead Zone.

I could understand how Jen felt. It didn't take a rocket scientist to see why she didn't like it. But it wasn't long ago she believed I was capable of anything. That I could take care of everyone.

For years after I ran from Grafton, she had tracked me through the news and had never been worried. I had found clips of newspapers she had cut out from events across the world, places I had been. She had known where I would be, she had known I was fine, and she had known I would be there. I would come back when I was needed.

She had found me, and even had made that call. Trusting me. Counting on me.

What had changed?

What was she worried about?

I could feel her wrestling with it some, the bond between us thrumming a little with tension, until she forced her feelings back down. Down where whatever else she was dealing with lay. So when she finally looked at me, it was with a grudging kind of acceptance, leaving one eyebrow raised.

She had returned to mostly the Jen I knew.

"It'll be fine," I said. "All we have to do is make some noise, just hang on until Nick cuts the power."

I was surprised to find that I believed it. Not only believed it, but that I had a plan for that, too. That made two plans in the same day, for someone who wasn't really good at that kind of thing.

It seemed like I was on a roll.

CHAPTER NINETEEN

The evening seemed chillier. And it wasn't. The air was still hot, dry, the kind of heat that belonged more in a desert than a small town outside of Mexico City. The kind of heat that baked rather than blazed. Something that you were always aware of, where any shirt was too heavy, too thick, where even the lightest piece of cotton darkened quickly with sweat.

The promised storm from earlier hovered closer on the horizon. It seemed to hold all the coolness that a coming rain might hold. Maybe it was having trouble pushing onto the land, pushing into the dry heat surrounding us. Maybe the Dead Zone itself fought the natural course of weather, the demon-infested earth pitting itself against Mother Nature.

I shivered in a shirt that suddenly seemed too thin and too damp for the night. The air was thick with heat and nerves and the scent of Aztec marigolds, which shouldn't be blooming this time of year but were. Heads of them were everywhere, bobbing a little in the air, yellow and orange in the fading light. They had a spicy scent, yet still sweet and flowery, a smell I only had found in Mexico in all my travels.

I took another breath of them and looked up. The night looked back, dark, pinpricks of light scattered across its face from the earlier appearance of a few stars. I thought I could make out Ursa Major, a square block of stars with a tail leading from it, and I searched for Ursa Minor, which looked much the same, just lower on the northern horizon. The big and little bears, wandering across the sky. Waiting for the moon, low in the horizon, to follow.

"You ready?" Zoe asked. Patiently. For the third time.

The knives Gertrude had inscribed were in my hands. Knives might have been leaving them a little short. That thought had me grin. They were closer to short swords, long elegant pieces of metal, each piece as long as my forearm.

Both of the blades rested in leather sheaths. If I pulled the blades out, I would see the Five-Fold Symbol inscribed on their hilts. Five circles, all the same size. A center circle, with each of the other circles placed north, south, east and west around it, drawn so that the looping arcs of each intersected the center circle, creating what appeared to be a four-petal flower inside the center circle.

I thought it was a flower. When I had mentioned it to Gertrude, she had laughed. She had told me it could represent a lot of things, but that she had meant it to represent the four elements. The inner circle would be the one that bound the others, as ethereal energy.

Then she asked why I thought it was a flower, and was that something men normally thought of. Making fun of me, if not in a mean way.

In the moment, my grin had slowly turned upside down.

It did look like four petals though. The five circles together, bound together, did. So I was going to stick with the flower.

The breeze picked up briefly. A quick whisper of wind that

stirred the marigolds and chilled the sweaty parts of my shirt. I tried not to shiver, and failed.

I wasn't sure why all the marigolds were here. They were wild here in Mexico, but they almost looked planted, the bushes of them circling the small stone wall of the graveyard both Zoe and I stood in front of. A graveyard close to our safe house but outside of the city. A place with plenty of ghosts.

A place where I could tap into something evil, and where Zoe could see what it was that was happening. Thinking she might be able to help me.

The shiver wasn't just because of the wind.

I had grown to hate the evil ghosts. Hate how the ones like the warrior and Jo and the grandma made me feel. Hate living their pasts, their memories, what they had done. Hate feeling that part of them stayed with me after I banished the spirit, and that I had become tainted with the evils they had done.

But, I looked at the knives, needs must. It was the key that made me think of this. The key and the sword. Both made of my power, but also different.

When Jen had died, I had taken her in. I remembered it as holding on to her as long as I could. Pulling her closely to my chest, gathering her to me. Somehow in that moment, with whatever energy I had left, whatever spirit energy she had left as a ghost, I had put her spirit into Solomon's Key. A stone with symbols inscribed on it, symbols of power, symbols meant to bind powerful beings into the stone.

A stone that held Jen, and held ethereal energy, as well as a demon. As well as seven demons. A stone that lasted back through my trip to the Dead Zone in New Orleans, that had held Jen all the way to Denver, even though it had begun to crumble under the weight of that bond.

Which told me something of Jen's strength. My strength. The

power of us, together. The power we still had, in or bond between us. In the keydrops each of us wore.

Then there was my sword. Something I could summon. Something strong enough to kill a demon, something that would kill vampires by the hundreds, like up at Red Rock, but also something that would not appear inside the Dead Zone. A weapon that seemed to kill things supernatural in nature, but also a weapon that could not pierce the shells of the giant crabs. Even as Nick had punctured the claw of the crab with a quick stabbing motion of his knife, just regular steel.

So I was going to put them both together. The ethereal power of my sword, into the steel of a regular knife. Like Solomon's Key, I hoped the symbols Gertrude had inscribed, had empowered onto her blades, would hold ethereal energy and carry that energy into the Dead Zone.

If it did, then we would have weapons against Sabnock. Against all the demons. We would be able to take the fight into their homes.

I looked back. Zoe leaned against her mother's sedan, waiting patiently. I guess when you speak to spirits for a living, you learned a little of that. She held her little orb lightly in one hand, a smaller version of what you might see a gypsy use to tell your future. A glass ball, with a gray mist turning inside.

It was just the two of us. Nick and Johnny had gone back out to look at the Dead Zone, and Nick was going to try to get pictures of the constructions around Aztec Stadium if he could. Jen had wanted to come, but Sarah had come out as we were leaving, a little distraught. The sisters had talked, and Jen had given me a quick kiss and let me go. Telling me it was nothing, and also telling me to be careful. In her mom voice. Which had me smiling.

The two of them seemed much closer now, which I thought was good after what had happened in Grafton. For a long period of time, after I had left, they hadn't been.

So it was just Zoe and I.

And a lot of ghosts. Spirits were around during the day, the strong ones at least, although they were hard to find. At night was when they came out, dotted my ethereal radar much like the stars above pinpricked the night, and the stronger ones became... more powerful. As if the night fueled them.

I slid one of the short swords out of the sheath. Looked at the Five-Fold Symbol for like the hundredth time. Definitely a flower.

Slid the knife back.

Yeah, I was putting this off.

Spirits stood above some of the graves in front of me. Most of them, actually. Ghosts that were trapped between heaven and hell, bound to the earth by the ethereal plane, waiting for something that had never come.

Waiting for judgement, I had learned. For someone to come along and live their lives, live their memories, and make the call. To send them up or send them down.

So far, most of the ones I had lived, I had sent down. Or that's what I thought I had done, living them until they disappeared. There were ones like Jo that I had banished, that I had wanted to send somewhere, but I thought me living them had been enough to send most. I thought how I felt was the key. For most of the spirits, it had been revulsion, disgust, anger. Mixed with despair, despondency, a deep, loathing sadness.

Those feelings—to me—had pushed them on their way. Sent them down as I used up the energy that bound them to the plane. The revulsion was enough, I thought, as I banished them. Used up their tap, so that when they were released, they could go on down. Certainly, that's where I wanted them to go.

All of them but Danny.

He had felt different. I had felt different, living his life. I had felt much like I did around Jen. Taller. Stronger. More powerful. I thought those feelings were the key to where the spirits went. Most of us have that inner compass that tells us if something is good or bad, whether we listen to it or not.

There just weren't many Dannys left, though, in this world. In the spirit world. Most of them left; I guessed they had headed upstairs of their own free will.

It seemed like Danny had stuck around in Grafton, just for me. Waiting for the moment I would need him. Which spoke of a knowledge I wasn't sure he could have had.

And that was as far as I would think about that.

I slid the knife out. Checked the Five-Fold Symbol again.

"We can come back tomorrow," Zoe said.

I know she was saying it in a nice manner. As if she didn't want to rush me. But she was also letting me know that we would be back, that she was going to do this with me tonight, tomorrow night, or sometime next week. Next year. She was small, thin, and looked like a librarian. And had a librarian's mighty perseverance.

Dammit. I had given my word, after all.

Now was as good a time as any.

CHAPTER TWENTY

W e had come here because I had felt them. Felt the spirits, and the angry ones, gathered here. There were plenty of other ghosts, the easier ones, but my ethereal radar pinged two large blue dots, blue threaded with red, so red they pulsed.

This would be as good a test as any.

I walked into the graveyard. Which was as easy as stepping over the low stone wall. Graves lay scattered around me, large granite blocks here and there lying among smaller squares of lighter patches of darkness, barely visible against the black of the night.

I blinked on my ethereal vision, seeing them. Young and old. Men and women. Almost never a child, anywhere I had been. Usually, the spirits I saw were older, they had time to accumulate their own personal evils. The older they were, the worse they got. Though there were exceptions.

I wandered a path, heading to a particular pair of headstones. Tall granite blocks, relatively new. The first headstone had the name Maria Lupez on it, a short sentence in Spanish underneath it, and then the dates of her birth and death.1972-1992.

The second headstone was identical to the first. Same size, shape, and color. That was mostly all I could tell. Someone had shot up this one. It looked like hundreds of bullets had struck it, so that the stone looked pocked with disease. I brushed my hand over the cold stone as if that would clean up the surface, every divot in the rock an empty pit brushing under my palm.

I thought I could make out the word Hector, but wasn't sure.

I could see his spirit, though, lying in front of me, arms tight to his sides. His face a mask of rage and anger, so mottled his head looked like it might burst. Wounds on his face and hands, tiny open wounds, like stabs, or bites. He was young, too, maybe in his early twenties, though I guessed he had died around the same time as Maria.

His eyes connected with mine, and I felt the madness there in that spirit. Felt the anger, and the rage. And behind all of it, that recognition I had started to feel in these spirits. The knowledge of who I was, and what I was there to do.

And how they were going to stop me.

This was going to be fun.

"Is this it?" Zoe asked, standing off to the side.

I took a breath, let it out. "Yeah." I motioned to the grave. "This one here, he's going to be trouble."

"Good," Zoe said, her orb pulsing inside like a storm of clouds. "That's what we're here for."

"I don't know why I let you talk me into this."

"You don't?" Zoe smiled. "I suspect it was because you knew Jen wanted you to try it."

Well, a home run on the first swing. And she got right back up at bat.

"But you know, as well as I do, that evil is an insidious thing. It takes many forms. It's not just something that kills. There are the murderers, and the rapists, and the drug lords, and then there is the low-lying evil, the snake in the grass, the thing that watches you get worn down, that waits while evils stain your soul, darker with every passing moment, and strikes only when you are weakest."

Yep, she was knocking them out of the park. But like anyone suffering from anything, it wasn't something I wanted to face. It was the initial reaction as soon as anyone felt sick, or felt an unusual pain, like a sharp, hot stabbing in their stomach. They never wanted to go see the doctor. They wanted to see if the sickness would go away on its own. They would take antacids day and night, for years, until the cancer put them on their deathbed.

So I knew where Zoe was going. And, like having a doctor around, I was thankful to have friends that looked out for me. But liking it was another matter. "Can you see him?"

Zoe shook her head. "Not yet. Sometimes I can, during the seance. But not right now."

I didn't know if that was a good or bad thing.

I unsheathed a blade, held it in front of me, pointed at the ghost of Hector. The Five-Fold Symbol gathered a hint of light and reflected it, briefly. A sparkle of moonlight. Or even starlight. Maybe light from Ursa Major, wandering millions of light-years away.

I wanted to sheathe it again, but I stabbed the knife into the ground instead. Next to Hector. I saw his eyes flick over to it, and that made me nervous. Normally the ghosts I saw weren't so... *aware*. This one was, like Jo, like the warrior.

I repeated the process with the second blade. To the other side of Hector. The symbols on each hilt facing the spirit. I was going off feel, there was no rhyme or reason or ritual for this. I just wanted the knives close by so I could try to push as much energy as I could into them.

It was all about the energy. It was why I wanted the strongest spirit I could find. I wanted these knives bursting with power. And the most evil spirits seemed to have the largest taps, like they had burrowed themselves into the ethereal plane, as if they meant never to leave this Earth. That was why I was in the graveyard with Zoe, in front of this bullet-riddled grave.

I found some space between Hector and his headstone. He began to thrash, or wriggle, or beat, but his arms couldn't move. His legs flailed a bit, like someone sick, like his feet were tangled in a blanket and couldn't move freely. But that was it. I placed one hand on either knife and stared down into the eyes of madness.

Then looked away.

At Zoe.

"Ready?" I asked. Even though I was not.

She nodded. She looked calm, though her fingers seemed tight around her orb. Her knuckles white against the night. The orb, gray and misty and swirling.

I took the longest breath in the world. Let it out. Looked back down at Hector.

And began.

CHAPTER TWENTY-ONE

I was Hector. Hector was me. It was dark around us, the pitch blackness of absolute night. Like deep in a cave, or well. There was a dankness around us, the musty smell of old earth and older blood. There was a squealing, or squeaking, in the black. I felt a pinch of something on the back of my hand, and I tried to move, and that's when I felt the wrapping. My arms were bound to my side, bound tightly, just like my legs...

The spirit realized I was there. I laughed. Hector laughed. We laughed, madly. And wriggled, and then we both left wherever we were to wherever the spirit wanted me to go. A journey of our past. There was no transition, no fading to black, no drawing back of the curtain. One moment we were in the darkness, and the next we were in the sun.

I was young. Hector was young. We stood outside a run-down house. A bike lay on the lawn nearby, well, not a lawn, but patches of grass mixed with spots of brown dirt. We were holding some pesos. Down the street was a house we would run to, a trap house,

*a little-ramshackle thing that had all the drugs in the world in it.
People would come up, I would get their money and exchange it for
what they wanted.*

*But I wasn't focused on the man in front of me. The young man,
with the bandana around his head, who had pushed his pesos into
my hand. Who was pushing me for more than what he had given me
money for. Who would learn that if he pushed harder, I would stab
the motherfucker right here, right now, no matter that he was twice
my age and twice my weight.*

*My eyes were across the road, at the ramshackle houses there.
At a young girl there. Long black hair. Tiny. Small. The family had
moved in last week, a mother and father, brothers and sisters, and
she was in their front yard, always playing in the grass, looking at
me and waving occasionally, waving even as her mother pulled her
back inside. I felt something stir in my groin—*

And I almost threw up, back in my body. My hands on the hilts
of the knives. The hilts warm now to the touch. As if the memories
had burned through each blade.

Hector hadn't been eight years old, I didn't think. Not too early
to think of sex, but he wasn't thinking of sex, or a woman's body,
how it might feel to love someone. He was thinking of the power he
could exude over a tiny child, of someone smaller than him.
Someone he could take, something he could have, something he
could force whenever he wanted, because he was older and bigger.
Because she was younger, much younger, and smaller.

Sex. Murder. Drugs. So many times my trips with the ghosts
boiled down to these things. So many times, I had experienced the
same thing, in a slightly different form. It was like being stained
with a different color ink. The more I lived these things, the darker
and deeper the stain became.

I looked for Zoe. She seemed frozen in front of me. Her hand still on the orb. The orb's mist still swirling, though slowly. As if time was slowing down.

I didn't want to go back in.

But that choice wasn't something I could make. I had begun it, and I would have to finish it. Whether I wanted to or not.

Hector's arms broke free from his sides, and he pulled me back in.

Screaming.

Bodies lie around. Some moving. Some not. I walked around them, and I knew I was older now. In my teens. Hector's teens. My teens. Our teens... It all mixed together now.

The knife in my hand was hot with blood. I walked around, stabbing the living. Stabbing the dead. The family across the street. The mother and the father. Brothers and sisters. A couple of cousins. She had a large family. Some bodies moved. Some didn't. Some might have gotten away.

There was her brother, wriggling on the ground in front of me. Staring up, gurgling a no-no-nooo through a blood-filled throat. Spurts of the blood coughing out of his mouth.

I stabbed him again, and again, until he stopped moving, stopped coughing, and I laughed. Loud and hard.

It was dark outside, and I had left the lights off. Found my way to the room. Her room. She waited, tiny and small.

Her door was locked.

I laughed and beat on it. Heard her scream behind it. The tiny voice thrilled me. Excited me. I beat on the door harder and harder. Felt the door jamb give, just a little. Just like she would give in to me. I beat on the door and grabbed my groin and screamed, "little sheep, little sheep, let me in", over and over, like this was all a nursery tale and I was the big bad wolf.

The screams grew louder. Her voice cracked in the middle of one. I could hear her breathe. Feel her breathe. Taking a large breath in. And I couldn't wait any longer. The door broke open and she sat there, in the corner of her dark room. I could see and feel her in the night. Trembling. Eyes open. Blood ran down my arm, mine or her family's, I didn't care. It was warm. She would be warm. She would be mine...

I took a step in—

And I pulled away. Or tried to. Hector's memories were too strong, and I wrestled with them. Wrestled with the knives, trying to pull away, but my hands were stuck to the hilts. The Five-Fold Symbols were brilliant with ethereal energy, so bright they were hard to look at, and I felt that energy course through me from Hector, a stream of it. A river. A raging river pouring off the cliff of a mountain.

The other ghosts stood around us. Around Hector. Some angry, some sad. They had gathered from the graveyard, piled together into a crowd, almost as if they formed a pit. I pulled from them all, the ones that were closest, feeling their memories race through me and get taken away with Hector's. Some brief thoughts surfaced, stealing from a cash register, beating up a kid in an alley, kicking a dog, all of those were quick bubbles of thought that came and went as soon as I recognized them.

Hector thrashed underneath me. The ghosts stared at both of us. I pulled harder. More. From everything. Wanting the strength to beat Hector, to break the connection *he* had formed. The two of us struggled at the bottom of a pit of ghosts. I pulled more. Little ethereal streams from each of the spirits came together and joined the river of madness from Hector.

I could no longer see Zoe around me. No longer see her misty orb. Or the gravestones. It was just me and Hector and a bunch of nameless ghosts gathered around us. Pressing in, tighter and tighter. Keeping Hector there, locked in. Keeping me there. Keeping *us* there.

Hector reached for me, and I resisted. I pushed away from the ghost, but the knives held me in place. I screamed and pulled more from the spirits around me, my body burning with all the energy, but I wanted nothing more than to break away from Hector, from his memories, even as I felt him pull me back down into himself and I tried to pull away.

The ethereal energy blazed around us. Lit up the night. Lit up each and every ghost pressed around me. And deeper underneath them, deep below me I sensed something... more. Not singular, but many. Hundreds. Thousands. Millions. I didn't understand what or why, but I know something, many somethings, were there. Drifting around me, drifting underneath me, perhaps lost.

A train whistle blew. I could swear I heard it, ghostly, forlorn, a cry across the ethereal landscape from somewhere deep below us, echoing along the spirit world. The whistle went on and on, mournful in its call, breaking over the shades around me in the spirit world, seeming to give them strength. At least, the ghosts pushed harder against me, or fled further from that whistle, drowning me in a swamp of ethereal bodies. I screamed with the train's cry, screamed and pulled on the spirits, struggling up each of them, pulling like I was trying to claw up their ghostly forms, climb over their spirits, trying to find a spark of light. Hector held me though, the angry ghost pulled me back down, his mad laugh mixing with my scream, with the mournful cry of the train, and I wondered how I could hear all of that, hear Hector laugh, when the spirits had always been so silent around me...

I was in a chapel. Or a church. Some kind of small building with a tiny altar in the back, Christ on a Cross behind it. Holes in the sides of the building, bullet holes, letting in beams of sunlight that crisscrossed the air.

Wooden pews were to my left and right, littered with bodies. Bodies scattered across the aisle. I saw the knife in one of my hands, and a gun in the other. A little compact submachine gun, an Uzi. I laughed and raised it and fired it into the air until the magazine ran dry with a single click.

Dust scattered the air, little dark motes that the sunbeams caught as they drifted along. Bits of the roof fell around me, tiny splinters of wood, and I walked to the altar. Stepping on the wriggling bodies.

There was a man there. Bigger than me, but most men were. Size didn't matter to a gun. I didn't recognize him, but I wasn't sure I could since parts of his face were gone, his skull was half-empty, little pink wriggly things and white bone were all that remained.

Though she was there. Still tiny and small, even now, years later. She was lying on the ground. Moaning. Crying. Her eyes recognized me and glazed over in the look I recognized from back then. The place she went to, her hidden place while I did what I did to her.

She was dressed in white. She shouldn't have been. I snorted and cut down the side of her dress. I was too eager, and I might have gotten too deep, there was more resistance than there should have been, and I jerked the blade some. The knife came back out, the edge of it red, and the dark liquid stained parts of her dress crimson.

Well, I was eager. I smiled inside. Felt the thing that moved inside me, inside my groin. It had been so long. I pulled her dress aside. Her legs moved, weakly. Already given up.

I had told her she was mine. She had run. She should have known. I had told her she was mine and she should have known.

These people, the dead people, she had thought they would protect her, but she should have known.

There were moans and gurgles behind me, but no one moved. Some crying somewhere, weak, fading. A last sob from whoever was left, slowing drifting into death.

I smiled. Hector smiled. We smiled.

I pulled my pants down, eager. Always eager. Watching her eyes close.

She was always mine—

I clawed and clawed. Climbed and climbed. Tried to get away, but the spirits pressed tightly around me. Holding me down. Holding me down with *him*.

Energy, crisp and blue, surged around me. I was deep in a dark hole, spirits around me, and even though my stomach churned with bile I felt my groin go hard, and hated myself for it. For the burning desire in me, the fake desire, Hector's mad lust.

I struggled, but I felt as if I was weakening. As if I couldn't fight it any longer. Fight Hector. Fight the madness. The ghosts piled around me, piled so high I couldn't see above them, like I was deep in a hole of my own making.

A squeaking grew louder, like a dozen rusty hinges, quickly swinging back and forth. The smell of earth grew stronger. And the coppery scent of blood. And something else, something like the musky scent of semen.

The bile in my stomach roiled. My stomach protested, and I threw up. I had forgotten about the knives. I was trying to pull myself out of there, up the mountain of ghosts. Each ghost I touched disappeared under my hands and was swept away in a torrent of ethereal energy. The torrent swirled underneath me, and like a whirlpool in the ocean, spinning and spinning, it kept dragging me back to the bottom.

Each ghost I touched was a memory. Someone else in that church. Another family member screaming as a bullet blew through them. Someone in the house, Maria's house, when Hector had stabbed them. All angry. All wanting vengeance. The dead and the living.

I screamed and pulled and wondered where Zoe was. I wondered if she was just gone. If time had stopped and now I was living in Hector's world, if he had pulled me into his memories, and that's all I had left to live, where it was just him and me and all the spirits of all the dead he had killed.

My world no longer existed, and it was just him and me. Just him and me and his mad thirst for Maria. Just him and me, with him pounding Maria in her wedding dress, with him pumping until he collapsed on top of her, with him pumping until…

I was bound. Hector was bound. We were bound. My legs belted together, my arms tied tightly to my sides. My side hurt, and blood thickened the shirt there, like semen covered my pants.

People looked at us. Small. Dark. Tall. Old. A small group of people, few, but enough. Enough to have pulled me off of Maria. Enough to have beaten me down. Taken my knife and my gun. Enough to put me in a coffin nearby, something sturdy and thick, and dig a hole nearby.

They all spat on me. One at a time. I laughed and cursed them and told them she was mine. She would always be mine. That she was in a place that only I could find her, and I would always find her.

They kept spitting. Some signed the cross. And right before they closed the lid of the coffin, they tossed in the rats.

I screamed. Hector screamed. He kicked and screamed and tried to butt his head against the coffin. I kicked and screamed and tried to butt my head against the coffin. He split open the skin of his forehead. I split open the skin of my forehead. The rats bit him, they bit me, they skittered and made noises and nibbled everywhere it was wet, the creatures bit into my hands, my face, my groin.

Hector screamed with rage and anger.

I screamed with fear and despair—

"Stop," came a voice, like the tolling of a bell. Large, and so voluminous, the sound carried through the air, vibrating every molecule. I felt it on my skin, *my* skin, and I was me again. The me in between the knives, one hand on each, the Five-Fold Symbol glowing a bright blue-white, the keydrop glowing too, three points of brilliant light.

Hector froze. Looked at me. His eyes unfocused in his anger. His hands, looking for a way out of the coffin, one of them squeezed tight on a rat, had squeezed so tight the rat had popped in his fingers, blood all over the place, the rat still wriggling, and his thought, my thought, our thought was still on finding her. *I could feel him pull at me, feel the whirlpool, the ethereal quicksand, suck me down again.*

He would find her no matter what. I would find her, in this world or the next. We would find her, body and spirit, body or spirit, and keep doing it, doing it again, and again, and again—

"STOP." The tolling voice came again. More commanding this time. Voluminous in its power. The word echoed through Hector, through me, through the spirit world, and some of the spirits around me faded away, one by one, until only a few were left.

It was a commanding ring. The vibrations shook the world. Shook Hector and me apart. Vibrated along my skin, and the hairs on my arms lifted as if from a static charge. It broke everything apart, and as the ringing word slowly rang away, the world stopped.

I stopped.

And, for the love of everything, Hector finally stopped.

CHAPTER TWENTY-TWO

Zoe appeared. She didn't look like a librarian anymore. She was more ethereal in this place, in this time. Wispy, thin threads traced along her clothes, her skin, her face. The threads drifted away from her, up into the air. White streams, thin but also bright in the darkness.

They gathered greatest around her orb, the globe no longer gray, but a cloudy white. The whole world around me lightened, turned into a misty fog, like we were *inside* her orb. Which didn't make sense, because it was still in her hand. Swirling, faster and faster.

She walked, slowly, pausing to look at the ghosts remaining, the few left surrounding me. Victims all, of Hector. Talking to some, though I could not hear her words, nor the spirit's answers. The orb pulsing in her hand. The streams of white wisps gathering, brighter and brighter.

Some spirits disappeared. Some walked away. Zoe came closer, pausing, still, when a ghost caught her attention. Casting quick looks in my direction, sad looks, but glances that asked me to be patient.

Like I could do anything else.

I was back in the graveyard. Kneeling between the bullet-riddled headstone and Hector. Both of my hands remained on the hilts of both knives. The blades with blue-white energy like beacons, with all the energy I had pulled from Hector, from all the spirits around Hector, from everything I had pulled trying to get away from his madness. It wasn't just the knives glowing but also the keydrop. As if each of the three items resonated with the power I had called.

I seemed frozen. I couldn't move. Like time had really paused. For me. For everyone, for all the ghosts here. The ethereal energy I pulled from the spirits remained, trails in the air: the thick stream of it from Hector, the individual torrents of blue-white energy leading from all the surrounding spirits into me. The torrent divided itself, raced along my skin, along both of my arms and into the knives.

All the spirits were empty. Their taps gone. All of them, even Hector, were in their final moment on Earth.

Hector lay before me. He, too, seemed empty of energy. Moments from his own banishment. His madness, his rage, paused. His eyes looked past me, at Zoe, and she slowly knelt beside him. Her face looked sad, and sick, as if she had seen everything I had experienced.

She leaned her head forward. Whispered into Hector's ear. He shook his head over and over, and she whispered more urgently. The orb in her hand glowed a brilliant white glow, and that glow pulsed whiter and whiter, and she brought it closer and closer to the mad ghost.

He shook his head and finally screamed something into her ear. Right when she brought the orb into contact with his ghostly flesh. I could hear his words, this time, though what he said was quick and in Spanish. He screamed it over and over and laughed and looked at me with his crazy eyes, like he was promising me something.

Zoe brought the orb back. Looked at me. Her eyes worried. I still could not move. I could only sit there as Hector suddenly, violently bent forward. His ethereal form connecting with Zoe and knocking her back. She stumbled backwards, the orb flying out of her hand; the whole world around us violently shifted from white to black, black to white, like the strobing lights of a bad nightclub.

I tried to get up, tried to help, but remained a statue. Frozen in time, frozen in this weird spiritual freeze-frame world Zoe had built around us. She recovered quickly, scrambling to her knees and reaching back for her orb, screaming something at Hector.

There was a sound in the air, in the weird spirit world I found myself in. A faint screeching from far away. A screaming of a many-throated whistle. And underneath that, a many-footed rumbling, like a stampede. A staggered stumbling of millions threading their way through streets like a maze. It was all faint, the whistle, the rumbling, as if I heard it all, felt it all, from many miles away.

The train was back. The one I could only hear and never see. From far below.

I thought Hector heard it too. I thought he liked the sounds, the faint burning cry, the mad rumbling, as if a train of a thousand cars roared over some mountainous track. The lost stampede of spirits underneath us, as if fleeing the train. The spirit was laughing as he turned to face me. His eyes open and mad, but also gathering information. The Five-Fold blades, the knives and the ethereal energy, they pulled his gaze and his eyes widened, like a kid walking into a candy store. He stuck his hands into the river of ethereal energy around us, cupped them together as if going for a sip of water, and *pulled* some of the energy back.

Zoe was almost to her orb. Her fingers stretched for it. A ghostly wind whipped around us, stirring the wisps drifting from her, stirring the ghostly air but not touching me or Hector. The hellish many-throated whistling, the mad stampede, all of it faded far into the background in that moment.

Hector's hands met his lips. His eyes met mine.

The evil spirit drank.

As he did, his ghostly tap reconnected to the ethereal plane, boring, burning a new hole there.

Hector disappeared, laughing. Taking his tap with him. Gone.

I sat there, stunned.

Zoe had the orb in her hands. The wind whipped harder around me. The white wisps swirled around us all. She screamed something into the air. The orb grew brighter and brighter until the misty ghost world was blown away, until the night around us was blown away, until it was all whiteness and no dark.

Until it was just me on my knees, in the soft earth of the grave, in front of the bullet-riddled headstone, my hands on the knives, what was left of the ethereal energy blown around us in the ghostly storm.

Until it was just me on my knees, in front of the bullet-riddled headstone, hands on the knives. White wind with blue ethereal energy swirling around us.

Until it was just me on my knees, hands on the knives.

Wondering what Hector had done. What Zoe had done. What had happened.

White wind swirling around us.

Until it was just me on my knees.

In the darkness.

CHAPTER TWENTY-THREE

I was back in the real world. In the graveyard, in the dead of night.

A graveyard empty of spirits.

Kneeling on the earth. Hard earth, here. Hard and packed and baked from the morning sun. The two knives stabbed into the dirt, one to my left and one to my right, looking like knives. Like metal, the Five-Fold Symbol on their hilts glittered a bit, the metal of the symbol glistening as if catching some unknown inner light. I looked at the blades quickly using my ethereal sight and flicked that sight off quickly. The glow of energy in the symbols was too bright to stare at. Like staring at an ethereal sun.

My knees ached, and my hands lay in my lap. The front of my shirt was wet with everything I had thrown up. The taste of the bile remained in my mouth, thick and sour.

Still, I was alive.

I looked over. Zoe stood in the same place she had earlier, when I had begun tapping into Hector. Her hand on her orb, the orb quiet now though, the gray mist inside barely moving. She looked stunned, her eyes lost, her legs shook, and she weaved a little as if about to fall.

I groaned, getting up. All my muscles were knotted, as if I had been bound in place for years and not moments. It seemed like it took forever, but I made my way over to Zoe, steadying her with a hand.

Her eyes flickered to me. She blinked. Once, then twice. Took a breath. "Wow."

I nodded.

"That… has never happened before."

"Which part?" I asked. Some things had never happened before to me either.

"I would say…" She looked at her orb, looked at the ground where the spirit of Hector had lay. Looked around at the entire graveyard. "Most of it."

"Great." I laughed, and the laugh sounded too much like Hector's. I hadn't really been hoping for any kind of answer from this experiment, but it was something Jen had wanted me to try. And I was hoping something would come of it, for her.

All that had happened was that I had banished a spirit. A mad young man who had a thing for a smaller girl. Who had loved the power he had over her. And now that spirit had found a way to create his own ethereal tap, had re-bound himself to the ethereal plane, and now, as I searched my ethereal radar, was nowhere to be found.

That couldn't be good.

And that left me. More stained than ever. I had bathed in more evil and come away dirtier for it. Muddier. Not some white knight, not some avenging angel, but something darker, something with a broken lance and mismatched armor.

But, needs must.

I went back over to the blades. Pulled each out, wiping them on my pants. My palms tingled, holding them. I could feel the power in each. I blinked my ethereal vision on, and both of the blades glowed so brightly I could almost see nothing else. Just a brilliant blue-white glow, swirling, like a whirlpool centered over the symbols of the knives, swirling blue-white energy concentrated so much each knife appeared like an ethereal sun.

At least the mission was accomplished. I had made some weapons. Hopefully, weapons that could be carried into the Dead Zone. Hopefully, weapons that—if we couldn't null the Dead Zone—could kill Sabnock. They were a bastard mix of metal and ethereal, something from this world and the world of my powers, and they were the best I would have, I thought.

Though the keydrop felt stronger, too. It had absorbed some of the energy I had pulled this night. I touched it and felt Jen, crazy worried. I even thought I felt her, searching for a set of keys, getting ready to head towards me, though she had no idea where I really was.

I'm okay, I thought. *It's okay.*

I felt her pause. I could feel her hide something, an emotion, a fear. *You sure?*

The chuckle, my chuckle, went along the bond. Something a little bitter. *Sure enough.*

Gus… I could feel her self-recrimination, and that shocked me, because Jen never second-guessed herself. She was the rock.

So I tried again. Worked hard to make sure she could feel the *okayness* that I didn't really feel. *Really. I'm good. We're good.*

Her hand found some keys in a bowl in the planning room.

Jen. I thought. *We're coming back now.*

There was a long pause. A long breath. I could almost feel her chest expand with it. Her mind race with whatever she worried about.

Okay, she said. *Okay.*

And, *hurry back*.

The bond went quiet.

I sheathed both blades. The power seemed to dim in each as I did so, but maybe that was something only I could feel. I held both in one hand and turned to Zoe.

Who was still standing there.

"That was what you do?"

"Yeah," I admitted. "Most or better. Some are worse."

Her face twisted a bit. "Worse than that?"

"Yeah," I said. Thinking of Jo. He had been the worst for me. Although the grandma in Lewiston had been bad. She had murdered so many kids, so many children. But Jo had been the worst, because he had been the first to really come after me. To fight me. And when I had lived his memories, they had stuck with me more. Harder. Those memories were in my brain somewhere, and they would never let go.

We are what we do. If you worked in a factory twelve hours a day, there are things you become over time that you don't realize. Some of that might be cursing, you might pick it up, feel more natural about a cuss word here and there. Some of it might be stopping by a bar after work, picking up a few beers. Your sleep cycle gets messed up. You're drinking in the morning and night. Those beers become shots over the years. Your temper gets a little short, because night is day and day is night, and because Mandy needs braces, and that means overtime. And, as the bills pile up and the work becomes not enough, you might say things, drinking, you would never have else.

Or you might be a soldier. You deploy a lot, you're on the front lines. You've killed a number of people. Over the years, you've had a lot of friends die. Either way, death becomes natural to you. It might even, over time, become the answer to certain problems for you. Not because it is an answer, but because you've lived in a world for years, a world that says when peace cannot be held, violence is the answer.

Or you might be a teacher. In a small town. Over the years, kids might stop listening in class, and you fight it. You try honest discipline, honest grades. You might miss a raise or two, or get called to the principal's office because some of your kids are doing bad. But you can only do so much. Parents need to do *something too*, and as more and more of the grades drop, you realize that no kid being left behind means lowering the bar and teaching *less*. Over time, that stains you, and you might give less than you had ten years before. Or twenty.

It's not right or wrong. Not for any of us, not for a factory worker, a soldier, a teacher, or an angel of vengeance. It's just what happens. We all get stained by what we do. What we do becomes us, it's *who we become*. It's who we are. We all get worn down by the waves of our work. And, if we aren't careful, we'll get swallowed by them one day.

I couldn't help but feel like all that was left was my head, barely above the water. I was buried in the sand, up to my neck, and the waves crashed in, higher and higher, with each spirit I tapped.

But, needs must.

I gathered Zoe, and we went back to her mother's sedan. Tossed the knives into the backseat, in the little well behind the driver's seat. I drove us back. The car was like I remembered, weak to respond when I pushed down on the accelerator, the brakes spongy. It was such an odd car for a person to have, for Tabitha to have, when she had grown up with muscle cars.

Anyway, the road leading away from the graveyard was a small, hard-packed dirt road. Tiny rocks scattered across the ruts of older traffic, the deep swells in the road worn in by other cars and trucks, of others coming to visit this tiny graveyard over the years.

I hadn't noticed coming in, but a church sat off to the side. Well, off of the road. A tiny thing with a small chapel. Wooden and worn, and even this far away, I could see boards crossed over the windows, the front door. I imagined, if I got closer, I would see tiny holes punched in the walls and roof.

The car lurched. I fought the wheel. Pushed the accelerator to get the sedan out of a particularly deep hole. The engine whined.

Zoe sat there. Lurching left and right with the car. Lost in thought. In what had happened. I wanted to ask her what Hector had told her. What he had screamed in the end, but if she had seen or felt anything that I did, I also wanted to give her time to process it all. To work through it, and forget what you could of it. To get clean again.

It's what I needed too, after all.

Jen sat there on the couch in her apartment. The one she shared with Gus. The couch was small, a little hard, the pillows not sinking under her, but—unusual, for her—she didn't notice how uncomfortable she felt. Didn't notice the quiet in the room or how chilled she felt.

She was alone, for the moment.

Her gaze was caught on the windowpane. It faced east and north, and somewhere out there was Gus. About to enter the graveyard, with Zoe, with those knives. Jen could feel the fear and trepidation from him through the bond. She could feel him push that fear down and ready himself like he always did.

Her hands tightened on her thighs. Her fingers pulled at her jeans. She hated this. Hated it more than she could tell Gus, hated it enough to ask Zoe to help, to see why the spirits came after him so much. She thought it would help, and now, now she worried she had pushed it too far.

She worried a lot more, lately.

Coming back from being dead seemed to bring baggage back with it. Baggage she hadn't had before. Jen hid it the best she could. Not wanting to worry Gus. Not wanting to add to his fears. He already worried enough about all of them. Their group. But her …

He was scared now, scared in that graveyard. He didn't master the fear, he never did, like usual, he just readied himself for the fight. For whatever it might take, to try something that might help them defeat Sabnock.

Oh Gus…

It was the name she had always called him from the day they had met. Even when the other kids had called him Grimm. Grimm was a nickname, one everyone had used. Even Parker, when he wasn't calling Gus boy.

It was even the name he had given her, back when they had first met, as kids. Right after Jen had sat next to him in class.

She closed her eyes in the memory. The teacher, in the front of the room, had pulled the principal aside about something. Jen, as a little girl, had told the boy smiling might make his face look better. She had smiled as she said it, and the boy seemed frozen.

Then she had taken the seat next to him, Girl-Jen introducing herself. It had taken a moment for the boy to respond.

I'm Grimm, he had finally said. They were both eight years old, and even then, Jen saw why the name had caught. His face was serious, focused, to the point of where he appeared like his nickname. His smile barely cracked his façade.

That's your name? She had whispered back. Drawing out the last word.

He looked embarrassed. *It's Fergus. Everyone just calls me Grimm.*

Well not me, Jen had proclaimed, in the way kids do. *I'm calling you Fergus.*

The boy's eyes winced. *That's my trouble-name*, he said. *The name people use when I'm in trouble.*

How often does that happen? Girl-Jen had asked.

His eyes rolled. *More often than I'd like.*

Girl-Jen had laughed then. Loud enough that the teacher broke off her conversation, and both she and the principal looked at her. At them.

The teacher's voice carried a weary tone. *Fergus.*

The boy looked at his book with his too-serious face. Girl-Jen, under the teacher's gaze, found her book and opened it to a page. Any page. And looked at the book until they both felt the gaze turn away. The conversation between the teacher and the principal restarting.

See, came the boy's whisper.

Girl-Jen burst out in a laugh.

Which had the teacher yell at Fergus again.

Which had Girl-Jen laughing harder. Other kids turned to look at her, and she didn't care. Her mom had moved them here, Jen and her sister, away from Boston and the kids there. Her mother hadn't even spoken about it. One day they were in Boston. The next day they were packing a truck.

So she had needed a laugh. And a friend. The serious boy would do. And while the teacher was explaining to Fergus the proper way to behave in the classroom, while Girl-Jen tried to smother her laughs behind two hands pressed to her face, inside the girl Jen had promised to always call him Gus.

CHAPTER TWENTY-FOUR

A fair enough compromise, Jen had thought at the time. Girl-Jen had fallen in love with Gus in that moment. Maybe even that word, the whisper, the frustrated sound of a kid who knew he was going to get into trouble but had to have the last say: *See*.

Her life might have been much different, had she sat somewhere else that day, but she hadn't. She had been drawn to Gus, even as a kid. Drawn to the combination of childlike stubbornness on his outside with a hidden, just-for-her smile inside. And Jen wouldn't have wanted it any other way.

Now, though, she had fears. Now her eyes were open, and she saw things in a different light. Worried about things out of her control. Things she couldn't predict, and couldn't handle maybe if they happened.

The couch still held her. The pillows too soft, pulling her into the cushion, not letting her go. She felt the bond, worried about Gus. About what he put himself through, to help his friends. What he had put himself through to save her. What he worried about having to do again, if something happened to her, *again*.

Jen should have gone with him. But there was Sarah, and Sarah had wanted her, had *needed* her, so Jen had stayed. Something in Jen had needed her to stay, to be there for her sister, for her sister's worries. Something in Jen that hadn't been there before.

She had always been there for her sister. For her friends. But there was a need now. There was something in the back of her head telling her this day could be her last. That if she didn't help Sarah now, or Johnny, if she didn't settle things with Gertrude, or take care of whatever problem popped up, then she may not be around tomorrow to fix what needed fixing.

Jen had always been the person to take care of things. The mother of the group. But she hadn't had the *need* to, like now. Before, she had helped because she wanted to. Now she helped because she feared if she didn't, she might not be around later to do the thing she had put off.

It was frustrating.

And Jen didn't understand it. She knew she had died, and she knew—in her brain—that was the reason she had this new fear. Intellectually she understood it. But her heart didn't understand. Her heart drove the fear. And it bothered her, that Jen would let Gus go out to the graveyard without her, just so Jen could help her sister with her feelings and fears.

Gus, being Gus, had understood.

He was like that. Jen was like that. It was why they were a good pair. They both took on a lot, but how could she ask him to change, to lean on her, to lean on his friends, when she was having trouble walking that same path?

Being dead had changed more than how Jen felt about herself. It had changed more than this driving fear that she might die today and not be able to help her sister tomorrow. Or set Gertrude straight. Or be there, if Gus needed her.

None of the Wolverines talked about it, but she could see it sometimes in their gazes. See it in the way her friends hung around, when they should have left. Feel it, the uncertainty her friends had around her, the knowledge they might be next, and the questions of what might happen after that. See it, in her sister's eyes, if Jen turned Sarah away.

The group felt different too. They had seen Gus bring Jen back. Did they think he could do it for each of them? Was Nick not worried about going into the Dead Zone and facing Sabnock on his own because he thought Gus could bring Nick back if he failed? Did they all think death was no longer the final escape?

It was a lot to place on Gus. And, for his part, Gus left that question unanswered. Jen thought even he didn't know. Maybe what had happened, with the key, with Jen, with Gus there on the water tower on the end, maybe that was a one-time thing.

Those questions were always there, the fears of the group, hidden, unspoken, but there in the quiet moments. In the little glances. In the lay of her sister's hand on Jen's shoulder.

And always being there, it led Jen to her own questions. Personal ones. What might happen if her sister died? Or Nick? Would they come back? *Could* they?

The problem was, they would never know, until the next one of them died.

Jen's fear would always be in the forefront. It had her rushing around trying to fix problems before they became larger. Had her looking for problems in an otherwise normal day, like with Gertrude. Had her looking for problems before she might not be around to take care of them.

Her fear was driving her to some unknown destination. She didn't know how to fight it. To turn the car around. To head somewhere else. It was why Christmas had become a big thing for her. Why she had found the perfect gift for Gus. Something that would bring back the laughs and the hidden smile, the one just for her.

It was only Christmas. It was coming soon. And it was silly, this need of hers. But the idea had hit her. The gift had jumped into her mind, and in that moment, she knew she had found the perfect gift for Gus. And maybe even for Jen. Something Danny had gotten for him, for Christmas, long ago. Something Jen had helped Danny order, something that might bring a little pain, but also a lot of healing.

A football card, silly enough. But Danny had seen the player, some football lineman named Russ Grimm. A big man with dark hair, a little like Grimm. A man who stood in the center of the field and defended those around him. Danny had laughed and laughed, seeing the name on the television once. And he had told her about it, and they had ordered his rookie card.

They were just waiting for it to arrive when Danny had been killed. When Gus had run away. Jen had gotten the card and cried for a long, long time over it. Then had put it away, saved it in her closet.

It was pure luck it hadn't burned. Luck that Nick could find it, when most of the town had burned down in the fire months ago. Luck that Nick had found it, and luck that it was wrapped up in a tight place, saved in their dresser, waiting for Christmas day.

A day where she would have Gus, and her friends, her *family* now, shrug off the burden of what they were doing and just enjoy each other for a moment. Relax in the early morning feel of hot chocolate and opening presents, of laughing and sausage rolls, of a toy train circling around a Christmas tree, of a few hours of being away from it all. Relax in that safe, secure way that Christmas had, as everyone sat next to each other, with wrapping paper all over the place, some music playing in the background, and a big, brightly colored tree.

Now, though, Christmas seemed so far away. Even if it was right around the corner, even if it was a week away. Jen had pinned too much hope on the gift, on that card, had pinned too much of herself on that day. It was beginning to feel like, if that moment couldn't fix her, couldn't help her let go of her fears, then they would keep driving her, taking her to an ugly place where she questioned everything she did and everything she didn't do. Where she would race between all the people who needed her for the fear they might be gone soon. Where she would do a million things she wouldn't worry about normally because she feared she might die.

She had been dead once. If she died again, would it be even possible for Gus to save her, twice? She had the same questions the others did. Only, she had had her one strike. Could Gus save her again?

Her hands clenched, even tighter. Her nails pressed into her palms.

She was broken. And she didn't know how to put the pieces of herself back together. She didn't know how to stop worrying now. She didn't know how to be the Jen she was before. The strong Jen. The person who took care of everything. The person who was there for Gus when he needed it. The foundation he could stand on.

Once Jen had been stronger. She had been the one who had told Gus he needed to go on, no matter what happened. She had realized that death was a possibility for any of them.

Before she had died, before Azazel had killed her, she had tried to get Gus to see that he couldn't always be there for his friends. That he would have to count on them to come through for him. That —no matter what he did—some of them might die. Could die.

Gus had fought her. But she had made him promise. *You have to be the person who stays strong, if any of us die. Any of us. Even me.*

Not you, he had said back in that garage, and the look on his face had torn deeply inside Jen. Not a serious face, but a stone-like face. Unreadable, except Jen could feel it, close to cracking. He always carried so much. Too much.

Just promise me… Your word, Gus.

Fine, he had said, and Jen relaxed a bit. Once Gus gave his word on something, it was good. Forever. *You have it.*

And she had gone and gotten herself killed.

Her hand went to her chest. To where the bullet Azazel had fired and entered. There was no scar there, nothing to remind her, nothing but the memory of the bullet passing through skin, slicing through muscle, shattering bone, and tunneling through her heart.

There was a soft memory of her dying. Something in a soft white light. A gathering of her ghost into warm arms. Gus's arms. And a fading away, she had thought at the time, into death.

It had been the key. Gus had found a way to keep her spirit alive. And he had come after her. Had even brought her back from death.

Most people might have been happy with that.

And Jen was, but now she felt nagged by something. She had lost something when she had died. Before, she had felt, well, if not invincible, *strong*. She had been young and full of power, and even as she had asked Gus for his word, she hadn't quite understood what that really meant.

You can't ask someone for something you're unwilling to give yourself.

What might happen if Jen died again? Or what if she lived, but Sarah was killed? Nick? Or, heaven help her, Gus himself?

Would Jen keep going? Could she? Was she strong enough?

Jen didn't know.

And she hated that.

It wasn't a fair feeling. Jen knew that. It wasn't fair to ask Gus to go on, if Jen couldn't face those same fears.

She had been, once.

Then she had died.

And now she was living the aftermath. Trying to figure it out. Trying to be strong in a place she had never been weak.

Was that fair? Was there such a thing as fair?

Jen didn't know. All she had was the memory of his face, the stone-like face almost breaking in the garage. Many faces afterwards, the faces she had seen as a ghost, the darkness Gus had carried. The sadness. The despair.

She understood it. All the times she had floated above him, as a spirit. The times he had seen, and the times he hadn't. The two unable to hold on to one another, and both carrying the fear that they never would again...

And here he was again. Out in the graveyard with Zoe. She could feel Gus, battered by the spirits he fought. The fear and the sickness he felt, living their memories. She could feel all that through his bond as Jen sat alone on the couch, her hands balled up tight. Wondering if she could go on without him. If she was strong enough to lose him. To lose any of them.

Tears leaked down her face.

Wondering how she could help.

Wondering if she *could* help.

It was a fear she couldn't fix. It was something she didn't quite understand in herself. It was a knowledge, a truth that she knew once and couldn't grasp again. Not when the truth was about *her*.

Could she still be the same Jen if she lost her sister? Or Johnny, Nick?

Gus himself?

Once, she would have said yes.

A sudden sharp pain erupted from the bond. It stabbed at her. Gus, scared. A fear, something deep and wild. A rage, as he fought for his survival.

She had felt the like from him, from the bond, during these fights. It brought her own fears to her, and those fears bouncing back and forth along the bond could quickly escalate into something uncontrollable.

So Jen had kept that knowledge—that she could feel him live these memories, live these evil spirits—from Gus. As much as she could hide it from him with their bond. In some ways, Jen felt it was a test. Could she be strong enough? Would she?

The pain doubled. She folded over herself, sobbing into her lap. Pulling herself into a fetal position. Pushing comfort and a sense of *being there* back along the bond. Something she wasn't sure Gus could feel in the state he was in.

It was what she could do.

Then it was over. She could feel Gus putting himself together. His first thoughts, of her. The words *I'm okay* came over the bond, over and over.

Was he? The question escaped her. *You sure?*

Jen felt his chuckle. It felt short. Harsh. Grim. *Sure enough.*

She could feel him behind the words. Trying to put himself back together. His heart raced, he was panting, and still worried about something. A lost ghost? A vanished spirit?

Jen had made him do this. Not the knives, but had made him go with Zoe to figure that part out. The evil spirits. She had made him go and perhaps shouldn't have.

Gus...

She could feel him pause, in all his pain and fear. There was a moment where she could feel him focus on her through the bond. It felt like... like he was swinging a telescope towards her.

Safety radiated to her. He was okay, and trying to convince Jen. *Really. I'm good. We're good.*

A pause.

We're coming back now.

She took a deep breath and let it out. It shuddered in her chest, and felt like something escaped with it. Jen took a slow moment and uncurled herself. Sat back straight on the hard couch pillows. Stared out the window. Thought about sitting on a warm couch by a stubborn kid with a happy *just-for-her* smile. About the large flakes of snow outside back in that moment in time, about a warm fire in the fireplace, the crackling of the logs, the sound of a scratchy Frank Sinatra from an old record. The brightly colored blinking Christmas tree, a warm mug of hot chocolate in her hands, with big, melted marshmallows on top, and the childlike wonder of Gus in his first real Christmas.

Okay, she said, back along the bond. Wondering if she would ever have the strength she had once had. If she would ever have his strength. If she could be the part of them she had always been, for him. *Okay*.

And, *hurry back*.

CHAPTER TWENTY-FIVE

The storm broke out on our way back. Fitful bursts of rain blasted the windshield. As happy as I was to have some rain, some damp coolness, now might have been the worst time for it. Instead of being refreshing, it felt like the final exhale of the graveyard behind us. A final blow from the mad spirit there.

The drops of rain against the windshield like a splash of a promise, a hint of a final meet. I turned the wipers on high, letting them rub that promise away. The rain fell, the rubbing of the wipers on the glass repeated, leaving little streaks of wetness unbroken behind each long travel of the rubber arms.

I focused on driving. The safe house wasn't far. Thirty minutes or so. A little longer in the night, in this storm, with the yellow headlamps barely lighting the road ahead.

Even if the storm hadn't hit, I wasn't going to hammer down on the gas anyway. The sedan didn't really respond to the need for speed. This was a slow and steady kind of car. The kind that would get you there, in time.

For a while it was just the hum of the engine, the occasional pelting of the rain on the windshield, the rubbing of the wiper. With the windows closed, the cabin of the car seemed to echo the sounds louder inside, so the crunching of the tires on the dirt became the snapping of bones, the occasional squeal of a bouncy suspension became the angry cry of hungry rats, eating parts of me in Hector's coffin.

This one, like the others, was going to stick with me a while.

The storm quickly drizzled out. The headlights pointed out the road, weakly. The night rolled on underneath us. The stars remained high in the sky, the tiny pinpricks unmoving, for all the motion underneath them. For a while we followed Ursa Major, and occasionally I caught sight of the moon in the rearview, a few clouds masking its face.

I was exhausted. Zoe was too. After the rain stopped we cracked the windows, getting a little cool breeze to keep us awake. Well, relatively cool for this December. It was still hot, still that unusual heat in late fall in Mexico, but the movement of air felt cool on my skin, and for now that was what counted.

It wasn't quite midnight, yet. Zoe didn't say much. Anything, really. She sat there staring straight ahead, her orb tucked safely back into her purse. She didn't look afraid, or angry, she just looked like she was processing. I thought that was the word.

Hell, I would need to process this, too. Jen would help with that, some. A hot shower, too. But maybe, mostly, a drink.

Yeah, I could use a drink.

I felt the keydrop on my chest. Asked the question. It was late in the night, but I recalled the bar next to the safe house stayed open most of the time. Jen answered with a *meet you there.*

Then it was the final bits of the drive. All the time me wondering about Hector. The ghost had been on the edge of banishment, his tap gone, all but gone, and then Zoe had stopped everything.

Well, that wasn't fair. Hector had been at his end, but maybe me too. I had been attacked by spirits in a way that had never happened before, in a way that had me fighting for my survival in a way that had never happened before, either. And it hadn't been just Hector, but all the ghosts around him. Some of those had been his victims, and in a normal world, they should have been helping me.

You would think.

These hadn't. They had boxed me in. Fought me, if not as hard as Hector, but in larger amounts, like a mob. I had pulled and pulled from them all, and they had piled on, higher and higher, pushing me back down into Hector's memories.

Behavior I hadn't seen in ghosts.

Worse had been the whistle. The hellish cry of an unseen train. A train thundering down upon spirits, spirits who seemed lost, who seemed to flee.

All but one, at least. Hector. Dragging me down into his memories. Over and over. Not letting me go. Dunking my head, over and over into his well of madness, each time holding my head down until I sputtered under his dark madness, drowning in his brutal, twisted essence. Until I could no longer take it, until I fled from his memory, finding the ghosts back around me, penning me in, holding me until Hector could grab me again...

Until there was just him and me.

Me pulling all the energy from him.

Hector drowning me, again. In the foulness of his life. In his murderous rage and mad lust.

My groin stirred a bit in the car.

My stomach turned.

And the car lurched again. A large lurch, the sedan twisting to the right. We had drifted off the shoulder a bit, and I wrestled the wheel to get the car back on the road. Zoe looked over, briefly. Her hand on the handle of the door, holding it tightly. Her eyes a little closed, almost as if she was squinting, thinking.

Me too. Only I needed to make sure I could think and drive.

Apparently some people couldn't.

I shook myself. Not literally, but figuratively. Grabbed the wheel in both hands. We had gotten onto a real road, well as real a road as there could be in the middle of Mexico. It was tarred and flat and didn't have too many potholes. I placed the sedan in the center of its lane and drove.

The sedan weakly followed.

I missed my Camaro. Leaving it had been necessary at the time. Azazel knew it was mine, knew what I drove, and now that we were wanted, every police department knew it too. It had taken a minor miracle to get out of the country, as it was.

Still, some things you always missed. Even if you understood why they were gone. Sometimes, you had to make do with what you had. The hand you were dealt. And not the spirit or the power you wanted, but the ghost that was there.

These things searched me out. The ghosts like Hector, and Jo, the warrior. They blazed with power, but as I neared them I also felt them wanting me. Wanting to... attack me was the wrong word. They wanted to pull me under. Drag me down with them. They wanted to swallow me in all their darkness.

But a part of me searched for them, too. I realized that now. I wasn't one to back down from a fight, but some little part inside me wanted to face that darkness. Wanted to fight it and remove it from the world. As much as I felt like it stained me, as much as I felt like these—evil, for lack of a better term—spirits wore me down, I also was still fighting the biggest fight I could find.

Something I had done even as a kid. Standing up to the bully, like Raphael. That had led to me as an adult. Standing up to Azazel. To Dominic, Victor. Standing up to ghosts like Jo, the Aztec, Hector.

I had never seen one reform their tap. I looked back to the moment. Hector, seeing the ethereal energy. His eyes widening at the realization. Then he had cupped his hands and taken a large drink.

His tap had reformed. More malevolent, whipping underneath him. He had laughed and looked at me and grinned and then—

Disappeared.

I had checked the radar after that. The ethereal radar. And while it had been more empty than when Zoe and I had arrived, and although a few spirits remained, none of them were Hector.

And I checked the radar now. Like I had a dozen times, leaving the graveyard. There was still no sign of Hector. Not back at the graveyard. Not anywhere around the sedan. Not in the small town ahead, our town with the safe house, whose lights I saw glowing over the horizon.

I had never seen a tap reform itself. In the beginning, years ago, when I realized I could use the ethereal energy through the spirit, I had always left enough for the spirit. I had only used what I needed to survive. Whether that was because I feared where they went, if I used them up, or if it had been that I didn't want to live their memories, whatever the reason, I had left them.

But I realized what I was doing, then. Maybe what angels should have been doing in my place. Michael himself was supposed to transport the souls of the dead to Heaven. I guessed those that deserved it. Maybe other angels, angels that were no longer around, maybe their jobs were supposed to perform the judgement, send the souls left in limbo, those on the ethereal plane, to heaven or hell.

Maybe that job shouldn't be for me. I was mostly human. Only partly angel. Maybe something in my DNA had screwed all this up, where I lived the memories of the ghosts, angels could just view them.

I wanted to push those questions aside, but I would need to ask them. Need to ask Michael if I saw him again. As much as I wanted to push aside what that meant, in the larger scope of things.

Like I had said, seeing was believing. And I had seen more of the one side than the other. It had led me to not be a great believer in heaven. Or what heaven meant. Not for myself.

I could admit that I believed in it for others. Or that I wanted to believe. I had seen Jen, her spirit back in Red Rock, climbing up the stairs, white stairs leading up into clouds.

If anyone deserved heaven…

But not for me. Not for a stained soul like myself. I might descend from angels, but I also was what I was. A fighter. A warrior. Someone who took vengeance on those that oppressed. Someone who had to learn to live with the pieces of Jo, the pieces of the Aztec, the pieces of the grandma, and even the mad pieces of Hector, took all those pieces staining my insides and learned to live with them.

Those pieces would be there. I couldn't forget them. They piled up, piled together, and washed across me each time I picked that fight. And though each of the pieces might be small, over time, collectively, they grew larger with each spirit I fought. They grew larger, and heavier, and seemed to weigh me down. Seemed to drag me under. The evil was like the ocean, like the tide rushing against the shore, swelling larger and larger with the moon overhead. Washing me away.

Hector's memories were just the latest piece. Another life from another evil spirit I had lived and kept something of, after the spirit was gone.

Although Hector hadn't left.

He had remained. I kept hearing his mad laugh in the back of my mind.

I felt like he was going to be a problem.

But I had picked him. I had started that fight. And I wasn't one to back down once it started. Even if it bothered me that this fight felt different from the others.

CHAPTER TWENTY-SIX

We entered the town from the northeast. Along the large road that ran through it on its way to Mexico City. Like any town, we passed a few smaller buildings first, little shops, small homes, a long brown building with its windows all boarded up. A gas station, a large blue and red and white sign brightly lit above the alphabet sign showing the current price of gas. A large number, but then, it was all in pesos, so I had no idea what it really was.

The main road seemed a little slick in places, a little darker in spots, the headlights picking up tatters of puddles here and there, as if the storm had hit here too, briefly, and dispersed. Like the storm had come up against the heat of the Dead Zone, given one big puff, and blown itself out.

Most of the rain had already evaporated, leaving darker, shinier patches of tar scattered along the road. At first the spots had been large, the tires whushing through them, but they shrank quickly. By the time we got to the town only little stains of puddles were left, as the rain was sucked back up into the unusual heat of Mexico's December night.

I turned us into the side street that led to our safe house. The car turned off quietly after I parked, with barely a shudder, not like the Camaro at all, and I pulled the emergency brake up. It ratcheted loudly, violently, echoing in the cabin.

Zoe hadn't said a word the whole time. Maybe she could use the same thing I could use.

I unbuckled my seat belt with a snick. "You drink?"

In our planning sessions, I had never seen her with a Medallia, the local beer, her or her mother. It hadn't occurred to me they might not. Part of me grinned a bit inside at the image of a librarian in a library, shushing people while knocking back a six-pack.

Sometimes my brain takes a left when it should take a right.

"What?" Zoe asked, blinking.

"You drink?" I mimicked the motion with my hand.

There was a pause. Her seatbelt snicked open. "I don't not drink."

"Then let's go." The tiny sedan rocked as we got out, giving the slightest, ever-so-small squeal of the suspension that had me shudder. It would take a bit before I stopped associating that sound with rats. I reached into the backseat and grabbed both of the Five-Fold blades, sticking them together down the back of my pants, feeling the hard steel press against my back.

I shook my hand. The hilts had thrummed a bit in my hand and left a little echo in my palm. My nerves tingled with it. Like holding a drill, a power saw, or a jackhammer too long. Even now, the blades felt *funny* against the back of my shirt and the cheek of my ass.

Zoe let me drag her around the building. Down the blocks of main street a bit. The night was still warm, but cooler than when we had first headed to the graveyard. I was still sweaty, and my shirt was still stained with my bile, but I had been in worse bars with worse stains.

We walked past the older buildings. Doors and windows shuttered, covered with boards in some places, but broken into in most. Just a few stores open. A mom-and-pop place, down the street, a little grocery store where we bought what food we could. Not far from it was a Mexican version of a dollar store, with cheap things to buy, touristy things, T-shirts, and other items like knives and plates and cups, water pistols, squeaky dog toys. A nail salon, not far from those stores, still had its lights on.

Those that remained here, like back in Grafton, seemed to have no place to go. A lot of older people, grandmothers and grandfathers, though a few younger kids remained. Teenagers, unsupervised, would randomly appear throughout our time here.

One day I had seen four of them, two boys and two girls, go screaming down the street in a cherry-red Mustang, its top down. Something blaring across the radio, a thumping beat. The group had been laughing and holding bottles in their hand, shouting in Spanish, one of the girls leaning over the side of the car and waving at me as the car roared by. The engine had revved and rumbled in the distance, long after they had passed.

The world changed, but teenagers kind of stayed the same. It seemed. Those I saw, at least. An occasional kid, a few women and men, gray-haired and stooped as they walked, that seemed to be it. Most of the townspeople had left. Or—thinking about La Familia Diablo—some of the people may have been taken, just to be given later. Like livestock.

I guessed, for those who remained, there was a reason the bar was still open in town.

The neon sign flickered ahead. Red and yellow letters, El Muerde Amargo, the big M in Muerde the brightest yellow light, the big A flickering a dark red. It was a small place, but the sign was always on, the lights were always on, the A was always flickering, and the door was always open.

We walked in. Inside was just as hot and humid as outside, though there was a little air movement in the place, a breeze caught my face, and cigarette smoke drifted lazily around the ceiling, spun around by a lazy, loping fan up there.

A small chain from the fan waved back and forth, *tinking* against the bottom part of the fan. It was the only sound in the room, otherwise it was quiet. No music played from an older juke-box, off to the side of the door.

A long bar sat along the wall to the left of us, stools in front, an easy thing to walk up to and order a drink. Plenty of bottles lay on a shelf behind it, all kinds of tequilas, the bottles ranging from a smooth glass to all kinds of multi-colored skeleton shapes. One bottle was a big yellow skull, a cork right on the forehead. The skull was grinning.

A guy stood behind the bar. The same guy I had seen wave to Nick the other day. I thought he was in the same flowered shirt, but who was I to knock another guy about wearing the same shirt a few days in the row, especially with what I was currently walking around in? And he seemed happy enough, waving us in with the same gap-tooth grin I had seen before.

Round tables scattered the floor. Five or six of them, black wooden things with square-back chairs around each. The one closest to us had a game of dominoes laid out on it, the blocks facing up, the pips of numbers, sixes and twos, the fives and fours, the spinner, a pair of ones, all staring blankly up at the ceiling.

Jen sat at a table in the corner. Not drinking anything. She smiled when we walked in, the smile had me give her one in return, and Hector's memories retreated a bit further back in my mind.

She had a few cold beers on the table. I didn't think just beers would do. I waved at the bartender as I headed Jen's way, motioning the drinking motion all people do when they want shots.

The same motion I had with Zoe, cupping my fingers slightly and tilting my hand towards my mouth a couple of times.

The bartender grinned and nodded. I held up three fingers. He nodded again and winked. Then turned to search his stack of bottles.

Zoe had gotten ahead of me, taking the seat to the right of Jen. The two of them had their backs to the wall, so that they faced the bar and the door. She remained quiet, though she was in the middle of grabbing one of the bottles off the table. I pulled the chair out on the other side, sliding it closer to her before sitting.

Jen took one look at my shirt, shook her head, just a little. "Gus..." Her voice was a little exasperated, but I knew she was teasing me. I did seem to go through a lot of shirts.

I grinned, falling into the best part of us. The comforting match of being with someone who understood who you were, and who you weren't. Jen was a safe harbor, no matter what the storm.

I was what I was, a fighter, a warrior, a guy who would still stand up for those he wanted to protect. I was also an angel, whether I wanted to think about it or not. I might get angry sometimes, sullen others, but a part of me was also the same kid I had been as a child. Who got excited when it rained, and played army with Nick and Danny in the mud. Running around in the rain with stick guns shouting *pow-pow-pow*.

I had always found a way to slide into third. Or get covered in muck. Or turned up at Jen's house, covered in muck and leaves and brambles, after playing kick the can.

I grinned and waggled my eyebrows like Johnny did. Jen was worried, we both were worried, and I knew she didn't like what had happened in the graveyard any more than I had.

This was us, helping each other after that storm.

I laid the knives on the table. The hilts still thrummed a bit in my hand, though a bit less now. Like they were settling down. Still,

202 • CHRIS J CRANFORD

I rubbed my wrist briefly. There was a memory after holding them, like an electric shock, that my nerves seemed to remember.

The Five-Fold Symbols still glistened on each. Like the metal of the etched symbol, the circles, was wet. Occasionally I thought I saw a slight bluish-white light trace around the curves, into the petals of the flowers and back around again.

Jen's hand reached out and grabbed mine. Hard. So hard it surprised me. Her eyes glistening. "It worked?"

I nodded. Grabbed a beer. It went down cold and fast, and tasted malty and bitter, with a strong, dark coffee flavor. Not Medallia, but a label I couldn't read.

"Was it bad?"

She already knew, but was asking. Sharing these things helped, sharing them *aloud* helped, as much as I wanted to internalize it and go on. I was one of those people that would power through, and one of the older arguments between us, well, one of the older *debates*, was about me allowing my friends to take more of the burden. To allow Jen to shoulder more of my load.

Sharing is caring, after all.

And I was trying her way. Sometimes I needed prodding. It wasn't easy, saying these things out loud. Describing what I had done, as Hector. What his ghost had put me through was still a bit raw, but I could talk about it. I *would* talk about it.

Haltingly at first. Knocking back more beer. As I talked about the experience, the memories seemed to recede; at first just a little, than a little bit more with every sentence. I could push them back, further and further, deeper into that place in my mind where I hid all the others, the grandmas with the gingersnaps, the murdering Aztecs, the raping Jo's of the world.

Jen listened, quietly. Zoe was quiet as well, though she gave a nod here and there. As if confirming something she had seen. Or watched. Or heard.

There was a small interruption when the bartender brought our shots. Three little glasses, the glass not quite clear, I thought because they were old enough to have picked up some color in their age. Amber liquid rested in them, something swirling a little in the middle, like it was cloudy. I looked back to see the big yellow skull bottle uncorked on the bar. An empty shot glass next to it.

Well, it was a shot. I tossed back mine.

It wasn't cloudy, but smoky.

It wasn't tequila, not the regular kind, but Mezcal.

I coughed right after knocking it back. The taste was smoky, thickly hinted with ash in the agave, and if it wasn't horrible, it was shockingly ashy enough to make my face do something weird.

The bartender grinned, like he was sharing the world's best secret with me.

I coughed more. Tried to grin back. I'm sure it all looked just like the bartender wanted.

The taste of the Mezcal matched the smell in the air. Cigarette smoke, sharp in my throat. I tried chasing the shot with a beer, but even the beer now tasted like ash.

I wondered where all the smoke came from, with us being the only people in the bar. It seemed a force all on its own, remaining from the thousands of people who had smoked here over the years, forcing its way into every skull-shaped bottle in the bar, every bottle of beer, so that alcohol no longer existed in its own form, and everything was Mezcal.

Zoe, surprisingly, tossed back hers. Jen, after a pause, followed. Both of them grimaced a bit too. Jen managed not to cough, but Zoe covered her mouth with her hand and—I thought—looked much like I must have.

The bartender grinned even wider, the gap in his front teeth large. It was an odd look, because his nose had been broken many times, so the gap in his teeth didn't line up with the bridge. "Good, sì?"

I didn't know how to respond, so I nodded.

"Three more?"

More shots wouldn't be a bad thing, but I stopped him with my hand on his arm.

"Sì, señor," he said. "Three more."

I shook my head. "Not Mezcal. Añejo?"

He didn't try to hide his disappointment. "Sì."

I let him go. Tried to swallow more beer, still grimacing. The smoky aftertaste was strong in this one.

Then I finished the story, ending with all the spirits piled around. Hector, pulling me back in, over and over. Talking about Zoe, where everything had *stopped*, and what I had seen her do.

The bartender came back with more shots, and brought a metal bucket with six beers in it. The bucket was full of ice, and the beers dripped in condensation. The bucket thumped on the table, but each placement of a shot glass was accompanied by its own slight, fragile tap against the wood.

I checked. No smoky swirl in these. The bartender waited a moment and then seemed to realize we weren't going to immediately toss these shots back.

I guess I couldn't blame him. We might have been the only people here today. Maybe this week. But I couldn't blame us either. The next shots might be more of the sipping kind. "Sir."

His gap-tooth grin came back. The bridge of his nose oddly off the center of his mouth. "Renaldo, señor."

"Grimm." I answered. Giving a good look at the man. He looked twice as old as me, but still young. Mid to late forties, with the weathered dark skin of someone who had spent their whole life in Mexico. Face wrinkled more than it should be, with thick crow's feet around each eye. "Most of the town is gone, Renaldo. Why stay?"

He stood there a moment before motioning to the drinks. The beers and the shots. It was a wave and a shrugging motion, at the same time, though his voice remained cheerful enough. "Where would I go, señor? What would I do? Who would be here for those that want the drinks?"

All valid questions, I guess. But his answer reminded me a lot of Miss Tammie, back in Grafton. She had stayed because she had nowhere else to go, because she had felt like she hadn't had many other options, but mostly for those that needed her.

For feeding those who remained. She had been a mother of sorts to me as a kid, and her voice still shook slightly inside of me; words from one of the last things she would ever say to me, talking about *the children*, and asking who would take care of them.

I pushed a dark feeling down. It fought me some, so I worked it down with a large swallow of beer. And then another.

Renaldo sensed the turn in mood, though it didn't seem to affect his smile, and went back to his bar. I fiddled more with my beer and finished it, picked a new one out of the bucket, ice shifting and sliding as I pulled the bottle out, the glass chilled and damp.

Zoe kept sipping her bottle, but it looked like she was catching up. Jen still held her original beer, just holding it, not really drinking. Her eyes had a great depth to them. I could see all the worry and concern in them after I finished my story. Telling them about Hector's spirit at the end, and what he had done.

"I had wondered, I guess," Zoe said. She waved her bottle at Jen. "When she talked about what you do, I always wondered where you found these ghosts. The really bad ones. Why they were where you found them.

"For me, I can't see them," her eyes shot to mine. "Not normally. The spirits are voices to me, whispers, answers, replies.

Sometimes I can see faded outlines, little white trails, like the barest white silhouette against a field of black. Not a silhouette, not really, but a tracing of the silhouette, like someone had traced the outside of a shadowed body with a white pen."

Maybe her seeing them had something to do with what I did. Zoe normally couldn't see the ghosts she spoke with, but she had tonight. And when she had, it was kind of how I saw them, in my ethereal vision. With Zoe though, she had seen them without the ethereal energy, without that bluish glow, just their outlines, in white wispy trails.

Zoe pulled a long drink of her beer, her swallow hard. "This time, I saw it all. I saw Hector there, I saw you get pulled into him, and I saw the struggle. Your struggle. I saw what he did. I saw you fighting him. I saw, at times, him looking at you while you fought him, and that spirit was laughing at you. Laughing and pulling you down. Laughing and raping that girl. Laughing and killing and holding you down in all of it…"

She finished her beer. Grabbed another and popped the top off on the edge of the table with the flat of her hand, taking another big sip of it, even as the beer foamed out the top.

Way to go, librarian.

"You might have saved me," I admitted, not looking at Jen. I had been at the bottom of a well of hundreds of ghosts, and it had been hard to get out of Hector's memories. Too hard. I had drained all of the ghosts, well most of them, their taps had been empty, they all were on their way below, but… "It was a struggle."

Zoe's eyes went between me and Jen. Her voice grew intense as she spoke. "It was evil. That's the only way I can describe it. I've seen good and bad, talking to spirits. But this wasn't bad, it wasn't small, it was dominating, it was *malignant*. I could see that ghost, and I saw pieces of him drift off and attach themselves to you as you fought, like pieces of a spiderweb. Those pieces would float away and stick to you. Not just threads from Hector, but threads from all the spirits, thousands of pieces of web flew from them, they tangled around you, stuck to you, and there those threads seemed to melt, blurring out the white outline that I knew was you."

Her voice shook at the end. I thought she had taken back as much as I had from my experience with Hector. She had lived his memories, in her way, same as I had in mine.

Well, that was telling me what I knew, I guessed. I got the feeling that both Jen and Zoe felt bad for what they had put me through, but I had been doing this long before they had asked me. And I would keep doing it. I would just have to find a way to keep doing it and keep pushing the memories back.

Those that stared into the abyss, and all that. I knew the abyss stared back. That contest had been going on between me and it a long, long time.

So that's what I said. Or words to that effect.

Jen smiled a little, an inward smile, as if she knew what I was trying to do. Well, she knew me. Still, she took one of the shots and knocked it back. Wiping her mouth on the back of her arm.

Then her hand found mine. Gripped it tightly. A white-knuckled kind of grip.

I wondered what she had felt along the bond, back when I was living Hector's memories. Was it just what I felt? Or had she lived on the edge of those memories, herself?

"So," I said, looking at Zoe. Remembering what had happened at the end. "What was the stop about?"

Zoe's eyes glistened a bit. "There was a point where you were more dark than light. I could see your shape, falling and getting up, over and over. Hector's spirit, it had gotten, well, lighter isn't the right word, but more faded. I couldn't tell who was winning, if winning is the right word.

"But I saw all the spirits pressed around, and there were more of them now, it seemed, and all their threads seemed to be holding you down. Blurring you, more and more."

She shrugged. "So I stopped them. I used the orb and stopped them."

I *had* gotten the feeling that I had been inside the orb. It had felt that way, with the tolling of her command, the world, just me, and all the ghosts piled around me. With Hector at the bottom of the well. The place had felt small and contained, like it was just us and swirling grays and misty whites. And Zoe, walking amongst us.

"It's something I've learned to do," she said. "When I talk to a particularly strong spirit. But..." Her head shook, little slow motions, left and right, left and right. "Never like this."

"They talked to you," I said. "I saw them."

Her head tilted. She went to say something and stopped.

"I couldn't hear them," I said. "Not most of them. But I heard Hector, he shouted something in Spanish. I couldn't make it out."

Zoe looked sad. Her words were quiet. "Bienvenido a mi mundo."

Jen's eyes narrowed. "Welcome to my world?"

She had always been the better one in class.

Zoe nodded. "Other spirits there said something similar. The ones that would talk. It was like a chant."

Jen's hand tightened on mine. By others, Zoe meant the bad ones.

"It felt weird to me, talking to them," she said. "You ever walk by a bad neighborhood and feel like you should be anywhere but there, in that place?"

I nodded. I had been by those plenty, especially when Azazel had been dogging my heels. In those types of places, actually, more often than not. When you're on the run, those were the spots where it was easier to hide.

"It felt like I should be somewhere else. That if they could, they would drag me down with them," Zoe said. "I think that's the thing. That's what they want. Just like bad neighborhoods. They don't want to get better themselves; they don't want to clean up, or paint their homes, or get a job. They are ridden with envy, soaked in jealousy, bathed in evil, and instead of trying to redeem themselves they make themselves better by dragging you down to their world."

I tested the words out. "Bienvenido a mi mundo."

"Just so," Zoe said. "To me, they're the type of people that the better you try to make yourself, your life, the more they want to drag you down into theirs. The brighter you get, the more they want to stain you. They want to bring you down to their level. They want you to be as evil as they are."

She spat. "It's an excuse. It's like saying what chance could they have, if someone like you can't make it? It gives them an excuse. And evil feeds off these excuses. Evil hates the hard work it takes to be good, to be forgiven. They want you to live in their world because it's easier for them, showing that you can be corrupted, rather than undertake the work required to become good themselves."

Her face twisted a little, angry. Or upset. It felt like this was a topic Zoe had fought before, with other spirits. She took another drink. "And there's more. Something worse, I think."

Jen and I exchanged a glance. That didn't sound great, if that was the good news. "What could be worse?"

If Zoe's first words had been quiet, these were a whisper. "Recompensa del rey del inframundo."

I looked over at Jen. "Reward of the king of the underworld," she translated, looking worried.

"It's what I thought they said," Zoe said. "The worst of the evil spirits. One of the my things they said: reward of the king, judgement of the king, bounty of the king... maybe devil judge. It was hard to distinguish. The spirits were saying it together, talking over each other, like a crowd does. But I got the idea that someone had put a bounty on you. Or a contract."

"A contract?" The only contract I had signed had been with Belial. Who would take one out on me?

"Like a hit," Zoe said. "The ghost that takes you down, that spirit will be elevated when they go below. Put above other spirits."

She shrugged. "I don't know what it means, but a lot of them were excited about it. Not just the bad ones, but even the other, smaller spirits. The ones just standing around, not doing anything."

It wouldn't make sense for them to put a hit on me. I thought of Belial. Would she go behind my back and put one on me? Would Lucifer? I didn't think so, but what did I know about hell or those that ran it? One of the other demons from the Dead Zones seemed more likely, but who in hell would work with them? Who else was king of the underworld?

I kept thinking about it, and it kept not making sense. Neither did what Zoe had just said. All the ghosts I had seen in the graveyard had been fighting me. "What did you mean by the ones standing around?"

"I think those are the ones you talk about, the normal ghosts you say you see on your radar," she said. "Those. And I could sense even more, hidden spirits, neither good nor evil." Zoe looked down, like she was searching the underworld, trying to find them. Her gaze seemed a little lost. "Those hidden spirits, there are so many. It was unbelievable to me that so many could exist and me not see them. So many that... *waver* in my senses, for lack of a better word."

More things that didn't make sense. How could there be such a crowd of spirits around and not be on my radar? How could I not see them, and tap them? "Are you sure? Is this something you know, or something you just think you felt?"

"I'm just telling you what I sensed," Zoe said, frustrated. As if she knew how it sounded. "There's more there than we know.

There's something hidden, something swimming in the currents. Like a hidden world, a world of spirits, and I could feel this swell of excitement in all of them as Hector fought you, the sheer amount of that excitement, it almost overwhelmed me."

Great. Something else for me to worry about. It was bad enough what I had to live, pulling ethereal energy from ghosts. Living their lives. Now I had to find out there were more of them, hidden from me, spirits somehow wavering, but also cheering on my possible demise.

Spirits cheering. Spirits wandering, lost. Ghosts pulling me down with them. A bounty. And the long, mournful cry of a lost train. I shivered and found myself looking down, like Zoe.

Why now? What had happened?

"This all began back in Lewiston," Jen said. Knowing my thoughts.

It had. I had lived bad memories before. But I had lived them, and banished them. Well, I didn't know I was banishing them below at the time, but that's what I had done.

Jo had been the first ghost to *see* me. To fight me. To drag me to his side of the world.

What had happened before then?

Not much, in Lewiston.

But a lot, in Grafton.

I had finally figured out who I was. What I had been born as. Who I should be. And although I had problems accepting the fact that I had some angel in me, and I wasn't at all sure there was a place where good spirits like Danny could go, I had since that moment tried to be a little better. Just in case.

I had grown in power. But I also had gotten better, as a person. And like Zoe had said, these were the type of evil people who, once they saw something bright and shiny and good, wanted to tear it down and stain it with their evil. Color it with their sin. Drag you down to where they lived, and never let you go.

Tearing things down was always easier than building yourself up.

Jen knew my thoughts. They weren't hard to follow. "More knowledge is better than less."

She wanted answers, that was why she had put Zoe up to this, but we had more questions than ever now. I was no closer to understanding the evil ghosts like Hector, like Jo, like the Aztec warrior, than I had ever been. And now, now there was even more.

I shook my head. "It hasn't gotten easier."

There was a little moment, there, where we all looked at each other. Zoe's eyes looked more glassy behind her glasses, and she was playing with the label on her beer. Jen's smile looked a little wistful. It was more somber than any face I had seen her put on, lately. Jen tipped back her beer and finished it quickly, in a few hard gulps. Set it down on the table with a light thunk. "Nope, it has not."

Well, dammit. I had hoped she would have responded with something a little more... positive. More Jen. Not this Jen, the one who had argued with Gertrude.

We're not getting anything free...

The three of us sat in silence a bit longer. Finishing what was on the table. Bitter beer and the sweeter agave, the ashy taste of the Mezcal a memory. All of us lost in our own thoughts. Zoe finally got the label off her beer bottle, leaning more forward over the table, her shoulders slumped, eyes more and more glassy. Occasionally Jen reached over, her fingers twisting quickly through mine, touching my hand, her hand patting my leg.

Reassuring me, I hoped. Because if she was reassuring herself, Jen was more worried than she let on. It was very un-Jen-like.

In the end, I had to put it all away. I had a job to do—we had a job to do—and this was just another thing in the way of that job. So I pushed it all down to the place inside me, likely a locker right next to the one holding all the ghostly memories of Hector and Jo and the warrior. It didn't really matter, I didn't think, who promised the reward. Who had put the hit out. It didn't matter these dark spirits were hunting me because of that. All that mattered was I knew about it, and knowing about it allowed me to fight it.

What doesn't kill me makes me stronger.

Not a particularly happy thought. But one accompanied by a memory of my mother. The same one I had thought about, leaving Michael.

The image of her scar, the thin white line circling her neck, the one that had been so bad her powers couldn't heal it completely. The memory of all the smaller scars, the white lines crisscrossing her skin. And with those scars, some words she had spoken to me once. Maybe not advice at the time, from mother to son, but advice I had taken, nevertheless.

You find a small part of yourself… you tuck it away, and hope that part is stronger than the evil.

Jen had always been that part for me. And she was stronger than anything. The bedrock of my foundation. But now she had me worried. And so, for the first time I could remember, I was *hoping* more about her, than really *knowing*.

More knowledge was better than less, I guessed.

It was time I found out more there, too.

I looked out the front door. A light mist covered the street, a fog of humidity, what was left of the brief rain. As hot as it was here, I knew the mist would dissipate before morning. The rest of the night was black, dark, and it was more time to go to sleep and recover than dig into things a little deeper.

But other words of my mother came by, unbidden. The world was never fair. It was never even. It was never balanced between good and evil. There was no guarantee we would win, there was only stroke and counterstroke, and the winning side would likely be the last ones standing.

I was a fighter. It was what I did. I took a deep breath, felt my chest expand with it, the blood stir through my body, my heart get ready to race, as if I was looking ahead at Sabnock and the Dead Zone and our plan, and this minor complication to it.

Instead, I'd be talking with Jen.

I needed her to be there. I needed her to be my bedrock. So we would need to have the talk we hadn't had yet.

Jen caught an echo of my feelings, and the bond must have had her puzzled. She looked over, her head tilted a bit as if she could figure it out. I was surprised to see her eyes shimmer, too, as if she was on the verge of crying, and I realized all her touching me hadn't been Jen trying to comfort *me*.

I grabbed her hand then, in both of mine, and squeezed it hard.

It was her and me. Forever. And we'd figure it out, together.

We had what we had.

CHAPTER TWENTY-SEVEN

W e hadn't drank a lot.
I swear.

Well, maybe we had more than usual. Renaldo had come back a time or two, with another bucket of beers, and then another round of ashless shots. I had gotten some pesos from the bartender and wandered over to the jukebox, punching in a few random numbers. I couldn't read Spanish. Well, not much of it. The music that came out was random, sometimes a pop song, sometimes mariachi, sometimes the slow playing of a Spanish guitar.

I thought I recognized one of the last ones. It sounded like Stairway to Heaven, just done with a Spanish guitar. There was plucking the strings to the same chords, and a thumping as someone beat on the body of the guitar. The beat picked up and got faster, and faster, and all of a sudden the plucking of the strings became the fast-picking playing of a master guitarist. I liked it. I tried to find it again with no luck, and I couldn't describe the song well enough to Renaldo for him to find it, so as soon as I heard the song, it was gone.

We *drank* more than usual. Much more. For much longer. The very edge of the eastern horizon was lightly tinged with the morning sun, a thin, bare line of yellow, when we left the bar.

So, we stumbled more back to the safe house, than walked. Well, I walked. Jen walked, holding the Five-Fold blades. The two of us were a little slow, a little more precise with our steps. Zoe was the stumbler. I ended up mostly carrying her, one arm around her shoulders, and actually fully carrying her up the stairs to her and her mother's apartment on the second floor.

Tabitha hadn't been pleased, opening the door.

Mothers, right?

Jen and I gave a brief apology. I only mentioned the graveyard had been worse than what we had thought and that Zoe had been a part of it. Tabitha grunted and said something under her breath that sounded much like the word *children*, and took Zoe into the room.

Jen and I headed back to our place. Jen made me shower. I put up no protest there. The clothes I had on went right into the trash. She joined me, briefly, to clean up, and there was a moment where there was the two of us, holding each other tightly, warm water cascading over the both of us, as our arms refused to let go.

I could have sworn there was more than water running down her cheeks. Though I didn't point it out, because she could have said the same to me. So we hid our words and let the shower run.

We got ready for bed. Sure, it was early. And the windows in the bedroom faced the east, and the apartment was brighter than it needed to be. I pulled the curtains shut, reducing the light in the bedroom from a *time-to-wake* kind of light to more of a warm, *sleep-in-if-you-need-to* kind of glow.

And we lay there. Both of us on our backs. Our heads on slightly lumpy pillows. My arm around Jen's shoulders, underneath her and her pillow. Her head, as usual, lying against the side of my chest. I could feel her breasts press against me, with each deep inhale. Feel her breath, warm, stirring the hair on my chest with each exhale.

A slight thumping came from overhead. Someone walking, a little heavy. We were directly underneath the planning room. A few thumps as they walked to where I thought the kitchen was, a pause as maybe the refrigerator was opened and closed, and a few more thumps as they walked over to where the couch should be. Jen's arm snuck across me, lying across my belly, her hand picking at the sheet in little, random motions.

And, I thought, I had put it off long enough.

"Hey."

I felt her smile on my chest, the press of her lips against my skin, more than saw it.

"Hey."

Then a long wait, a wait that swelled with what was not being said.

"Tell me what's up, Jen."

A longer wait. A rise and fall of her chest against my side, inhales and exhales and stirrings of hair. Then a warm wetness spread along my chest, directly under her cheek.

And her voice. Cracking. "I can't."

I was surprised. Enough to pause longer than I should have. We told each other everything. We always had. I thought we always would. "You can't?"

The cracking in her voice became a sob. Her hand grabbed the sheet in a big ball, in frustration, her knuckles white. "Gus, I don't *know.*"

"Hey," I said. It was a good word with us, and I used it now. Pulling her more into me, harder. Holding her in a big hug, my voice soft. "Hey, hey hey…"

Jen was frustrated, and worried, not worried but full of fear, scared at something she could not see or feel or identify, and that made it worse, for her.

Her worry magnified along our bond, swelled between us. It was a thing that made me scared, it was so large. The anxious wave swelled between us, and I tried to hide my side. The fear I felt, but it was impossible this close, with the bond. Maybe it would have been impossible anyway. The wave rose and rose, Jen's sobbing grew with it, rode that wave, until the crest broke, and her sobbing broke with it.

"Gus, I don't know what's wrong with me." Her fingers squeezed the life from the sheet, her voice sharp with tension, so sharp it cracked, and another sob broke out. "I don't know, I don't know, I can't figure it out and *I don't know*."

The last came with a slap of her hand on the bed. Hard enough that her arm caught my belly, right in that tender spot where all the air sits, and I gave a slight *oof*.

The sound made her look at me.

In my defense I was trying to catch my breath. But still look serious and comforting, the kind of look all the heroes of all the stories gave in these moments. The kind of look that said *don't worry, I'm here, and I'll take care of it*.

Which was hard, you know, being out of breath and all.

I'm sure my face looked a little, well, it had to have looked silly. Because Jen went from crying to laughing, a hard belly-like laugh, and pressed her face against my chest. The switch was instantaneous and caught me by surprise. The warm wetness against my chest grew, but they were happy tears now. Jen kept laughing and laughing, and her laugh had me laugh, you know, when I was finally able to breathe, and then it was the both of us laughing for a good, long while.

After a bit, the two of us settled into smaller laughs. Quieter things. Giggling occasionally. Well, she giggled. I chuckled. But it went on like that until Jen relaxed, lying over me, calm. Occasionally sniffing a bit, little tiny inhales, and her hand came up to wipe her face, her nose.

"I'm a big baby," she finally said.

Which had me chuckle a little more, but only briefly. Only until Jen looked at me.

"Babe," I said, smiling at the word. "You are the least amount of baby of anyone I know."

She sniffed again. Her voice a little thick. "I don't feel that way."

"I know you don't now," I said. "But it's what I'm here for. To remind you how strong you are. How strong you've been. What you mean to me, what you have always *meant* to me."

She was quiet then. It had me realize she was waiting for more. More of the same words I had just spoken. Which, to be honest, I had never been good at. And it needed to be something I got better at. There was a reason Nick kept prodding me about a Christmas gift, and I was a little ashamed I hadn't seen Jen like this before now. Seen that she might need me.

Her next words were small. Tiny. "I know what I mean to you," she said. "You came after me."

She was talking about after she had died. But that had been an easy decision. The easiest I had ever made. When someone like Jen dies, you move heaven and Earth to get her back. There simply had never been another choice to make.

"I will always come after you," I said, kissing the top of her head, feeling the soft strands of her hair on my lips. "Always."

I felt her breathe against me. A shuddering breath. And while I would always come after her, those words wouldn't make her feel strong. They wouldn't make her feel safe. They wouldn't help her in this fight, when there was so much going on in our lives that even Jen felt overwhelmed.

She had died not too long ago. It was hard to remember now,

because it was something I didn't want to remember. But she had been a ghost. She had hung on, barely, inside a stone prison, using her ethereal energy up as a spirit to keep me alive.

She had come back the same person, but also different. A little harder. I had been surprised when she had brought up the plan. I thought she would want Azazel dead. But she didn't just want him dead, she wanted to take everything from the demon, first.

She had never been soft. But this was a much harder Jen. And being hard came with a price. A brittleness. A place inside you that could break, when you least expected it to.

Jen had always been the person to take care of the group. The person we all gravitated towards, to feel comfort. Safe.

Me especially.

I could see a little of her fear. Sarah seemed sad a lot of the time, and was spending that time with Jen. I knew some of it was because of Sarah's power, it had grown into something deadly and uncontrollable, and it had changed something in her sister, just like Jen had changed. Something that had Sarah finger the locket on her chest, more and more.

Johnny and Gabrielle also had to weigh on Jen. They were back and forth. They fought a lot, in private, and made up. We all knew the reason, but none of us could *make* Johnny drink blood. To be honest, I wasn't sure we should. But, if we didn't, he would eventually die.

I was sure Jen felt responsible for that. If she hadn't died, none of us would have been headed to Colorado. To the Conclave there.

Gertrude's doubt, on top of that. Her fear. The Dead Zone, Sabnock. The sheer outweighing of numbers, us versus them. Jen's fear that I could be caught inside, where Sabnock could easily kill me. Sarah's likely fear about Nick, for the same reason.

It was anything and everything, all at once. I had seen this some in soldiers after a particularly intense fight. They had been fine, deadly killers, during any battle, had stormed through doors and killed and watched their brothers die, and had come out fine. Most of those soldiers had gone right back in, death all around them, over and over.

Then, a minute later, a day, sometimes weeks, even years, it would all hit them.

All at once.

"I remember your smile when you first came to class," I said. And I felt, more than saw, her frown. Trying to understand where I was going. "The first day we met, it was the first time I saw you, and at the time, I couldn't say anything. Something had come over me, something big, and I couldn't figure it out. All I could do was stare at you."

Jen sniffed. But I felt a tiny smile. "I remember."

"Remember what you told me then?"

"Yes." Mopey.

"You told me I ought to try smiling more." I smiled, too, at the memory of us as kids. Her first words to me, said laughingly, teasingly. *You ought to smile more. It might make your face look better...*

I almost laughed, but held it in. "I figured it out later. Much later. The feeling. The world had changed for me the moment I met you. I was too young to know it then, to understand it, but I remembered that moment, always, I thought about it, always, and when it finally hit me, I completely understood the feeling. The day I met you, my world changed."

"For the better?"

"Always," I said. "Always. I couldn't be the person I am now without you. I couldn't be the person I want to be, if you weren't here."

I wanted that to be true for her, as well. I knew she felt the same, but maybe her death had clouded those feelings for her. Introduced some doubt. Not in her, and not in us, but in her ability to always *be there*.

That should have been my job. Helping her to feel that way. I had been busy, with this whole nullifying the Dead Zone thing, but I realized I needed to be better, be there more, for Jen. At least, for right now.

"Remember back with Kimaris," I said, and I felt, more than saw, her frown. "It was you and me against his whole army. All his demon-clones. We were fighting them, and you had that lightning shield going, throwing bolts everywhere, and there was this moment where Kimaris and I were fighting, and I threw him, and at the same time you threw a bolt of lightning where he landed, and I just thought—"

"What a badass woman I'm with?"

I laughed. "Yeah," I said. "But right then, in the middle of the fight, I had this thought about how we completed each other. About how perfect we were together. Here we are, the two of us in the middle of a fight for our lives, one we had to win to save your sister, and we're still *together*. Like in a dance, where we know each other's move, long before the beat."

"You don't dance," she said. A small protest.

"Babe, we've been dancing since we met. That song has gone on for us, forever. Wherever either of us were. There were times I knew, *I knew*, I could look up at the night and know you were doing the same, whether it was in Grafton, or me in New York, or me overseas. Even in New Orleans, saving your sister. Anywhere, any *when*, I could almost always know what you were thinking."

It was even that way in New Orleans, with our backs against the tomb, getting ready to face Azazel and Buné. We had both sat there, shoulder to shoulder, ready to go out, guns blazing. Knowing what each of us thought, knowing what each of us were capable of, and complementing each other to the end.

I squeezed her a bit. The next words were hard for me to say, as well. "It was even that way after New Orleans. When you weren't there, not physically. We could feel each other in the bond, and when I needed you, no matter what was happening with you, no matter that you were a ghost, that you had your own fight in the key, you were there for me.

"When I had fallen in Red Rock, when I couldn't move, you kept fighting. When the geas had me completely in control, you picked up the fight. When all of us were moments from death, you were ready to give everything you are. Until you were ready to—"

I left those words unsaid. The ghostly water tower in the clouds, that moment was still raw.

"You know how strong you are." I paused. "So whatever this is, whatever is bothering you, whatever you can't figure out, well, we'll weather that storm. We'll handle it. That's what we do. We'll weather the storm, figure it out, and come back stronger."

She waited a bit. Her breath evened out a little. Her voice less pained, more like she had been as a little girl. Soft. Questioning. "How can we figure it out, if I don't know what it is?"

"We just will," I said. "It's what we've done, so far."

And it was. It was what worked for us. Not the plans, not even the fights, but the getting back up. The *continuing*, when things were at their darkest. Picking ourselves back up and marching right back into the fire.

"Part of me thinks of that, Gus," she said. "Thinks of that water tower, the dream of you and me, and the stairs going up into the clouds, that place, and watching you jump off the tower, jump towards those stairs…"

Another breath. "I wonder if I'll have to be that strong, if something happens to you."

I hadn't considered that strength. I had just known it was necessary. She had deserved it, more than anyone I had ever met. The world had changed the day I met her, and together, we would continue to change it. For the better.

"Oh, you'll have to be stronger," I said, chuckling a bit, but making my tone mock-serious. "I mean, I had it easy."

Her head shifted, I felt her looking up at me. I met her eyes, and knew mine had a bit of a gleam in them. A little, devilish, if you'll forgive the term.

"After all, you'll have to save me from *down there*." I whispered the last words, still mockingly serious, using the forefinger of my free hand to point downward, over and over. I even waggled my eyebrows a bit, in time with each point of the finger, for the effect.

It took her a moment, but her laughing got me laughing again. It lasted a little while, again, and lightened something heavy in the room we hadn't known was there. Then the laughing became chuckling, or even giggling, though I would never admit it.

And the giggling got to kissing, and the kissing got to, well, it got to other things.

CHAPTER TWENTY-EIGHT

W e got up later than we should have.

There was no real set time for the planning session, but most of the time it happened in the middle of the afternoon. If there was big news, like the other day, then earlier. But for the most part we all worked the night shift. We slept as much as we could during the day. We all had gotten used to it.

I got up, working myself out of the soft mattress, and moved the curtain a bit, peering outside. The bright glow of morning sunlight had been replaced by the shadowy dim light of late afternoon. I groaned, stretched, and felt something pop along my spine. Then a few more smaller pops.

"You're too young for all that cracking," Jen murmured, from under the blankets.

I grinned. Sometimes, rarely, Jen would get up first. For the most part she liked to sleep in. And then, if a certain ritual wasn't performed, she would be grumpy.

I slid into a pair of jeans, then went into the kitchen to start the coffee. I grabbed the bag of beans and poured some into the grinder and hit start, smelling the rich expresso scent of them as the grinder worked, as the burrs dug into each bean and released all the caffeine and unlocked all the flavor.

Or, that was what I imagined happened. Coffee beans were their own kind of magic.

I hit brew, and the scent of coffee came another way, hot, rich, and bitter. The steam carried it further through the apartment, from the kitchen through the open door of the bedroom, and, hopefully, under a certain blanket to a certain someone.

The Five-Fold knives lay on the kitchen counter, still in their sheaths, just the hilts and the Five-Fold Symbol showing on each. The blades were crossed a bit and looked as normal as blades could be, though the circles of the symbols still looked shiny and wet.

I tried looking at them in my ethereal vision and had to blink it off quickly. Both of the blades radiated like small suns. Small, blue-white suns.

Wow. I wasn't exactly sure what I had done, but it was something. I thought I had built weapons, but at the least I had made ethereal batteries. Blades I could bring into the Dead Zone and pull energy from. Blades my friends could bring into the Dead Zone and maybe stabbity-stab a demon with.

They would need testing. It would be easy to see if I could pull energy from one inside the zone. The stabbing-a-demon, though, that would need a little more care in the planning.

And heaven forbid I lose a blade. I did not want to have to make more. Not with a wanted poster of my grinning face spread all through the spirit world.

I dug through the cupboard, finding a box of Mexican cereal, something called Mini Cinnamon Churros, little tiny circles of oat covered in cinnamon and sugar. Everything a body needed. And plenty it didn't.

Breakfast of champions.

I poured some into a bowl. Followed it up with some milk. Crunched my way through them as the coffee brewed. The cinnamon had just the right amount of sugar in it. The taste reminded me of being a kid, at Parker's. Sometime breakfast there had been a piece of toast with butter and a sprinkle of cinnamon and sugar on top.

I thought of the old man who had run the halfway house Nick, Danny, and I had grown up in. He was dead now, a gruesome death that I always pushed away. The two of us had always been at odds, and I felt bad that he couldn't see me as I was now. He had thought me a coward, and he had died before I had taken the next step. I was much farther along my path than I had been back in Grafton.

The last time I had seen him, he had been angry because I had run. Because I had kept running for a decade. He thought he had raised a fighter.

Not the best thoughts to have, eating cereal. But that's where the taste of something takes you, sometimes. Old memories and thoughts, things long gone, surfacing at the bite of a pancake in the morning, slathered in maple syrup. The taste of a hot cocoa on a winter night. A spoonful of cereal, in midafternoon in Mexico.

The coffee finished. I poured some heavy cream into a tall cup, sprinkled some nutmeg in it, along with a pinch of sugar, and heated it for a few seconds in the microwave. Then I beat the mixture with a tiny whisk, working it until I saw the smallest bit of foam. As ghetto a latte as there ever was.

Still, it would fulfill the requirement. Hopefully. I delivered it to a pair of hands reaching out from beneath the blanket and a grumpy thanks. Then I grabbed a shirt and put it on, noticing as I did, the drawer of T-shirts was growing low.

Back to the kitchen. There I poured my own coffee, black; though I had gotten the taste of better lattes and liked them, I didn't put that much work into my own cup. Maybe I needed to find one of those super automatic machines that made your coffee in that fancy way the baristas in the shops did.

There was a knock on the door. Light. I opened it and—not surprisingly—found Sarah. She smiled, though her smile was always a little sad, and her eyes carried more of the sadness than the grin.

I motioned her in. "Coffee?"

She shrugged. I got her a cup anyway. Did the same thing with hers that I did with Jen's. Which had her smile a little wider.

"Grumpster still sleeping?"

I shook my head, a smile on my lips. Then looked up at the ceiling with one eyebrow arched. Trying to listen. If there was any movement in the bedroom, it was slow and steady, and I may or may not have heard it. I rolled my eyes a bit, having a little fun. "I think so." A pause as I thought I heard something, and a frown. "Or not. Maybe?"

My voice trailed off as I genuinely wondered. Which brought a laugh from Sarah. Which was good. We all needed more of that.

"Is she okay?" Sarah looked worried. But she looked that way a lot. Maybe I was reading into her expression too much.

"Yeah," I said, wanting to keep what happened between Jen and I, between Jen and I. If she was the rock for everyone, I would be the rock for her. A very silent, quiet rock. "Yeah."

Sarah drank her coffee in little sips. I finished my cereal, the sweet cinnamon a nice complement to the bitter blackness on my cup. The bits and pieces of churros still crunchy in the milk. It was quiet in the kitchen, except for that.

Crunch, crunch, crunch.

Stilllll crunchy.

"How are things with you?" I asked. The question felt silly, with us all together, and with us taking on Sabnock. Plus, Sarah was like a sister, yet I was getting to know her again, after being away for so long from Grafton.

But I wanted to follow through on the promise I had made to myself this morning. Of trying to help Jen. Of sharing some of her burden. Of trying to help Jen be more Jen.

Sarah tilted her head a bit, left and right. Then shrugged.

I wasn't good at this, but I tried something else anyway.

"How about with Nick?"

She blushed then, and that was funny to see. Sarah had been like a younger sister when I had left. I had come back to a woman who was the plaything, putting it kindly, to Raphael and his vampires. I was a little surprised, and a little happy, to see her embarrassed.

"Nick and Sarah, sitting in a tree…"

"Stop," Sarah said, laughing openly now.

I did. Quickly. The word reminded me of last night, and I couldn't help but feel a cold chill descend over me. A remembered fear, and anger, at Hector's memories. His ghost. Who could be anywhere now.

Sarah saw the change and frowned.

That quickly, both of us went back to our usual places. Grim and Sad.

Dammit.

"Something last night," I tried to explain. "Zoe and I, with the ghosts."

"Oh," Sarah said. "Is that why you guys were at the bar?"

I wondered how she knew.

"Maybe," I said. "It's fine, though. It's fine." I hated that we had lost that bit of happiness we had just had. I wanted to recapture the moment of a moment ago. The laughing for the sake of laughing. But time is like that; what passes you by, you can enjoy it, but it always passes. It never stays.

Sarah seemed to understand that as well. That things never

returned to how they had been, that change was inevitable, and sometimes for the better, but also for the worse. The better was always fleeting, while the worse always seemed to wait there, looming underneath us, poised to pounce whenever the bottom fell out.

Like me, Sarah just moved forward. Dealing with it as she went. Taking the good while she could, but ready for the bad.

I had learned her power, what she had grown up with, was much like the powers of the Sirens of ancient Greece. She could call people, promise things, control them, with a light touch. Often, she hadn't even needed a touch, her voice, a song, a humming thought, could influence a person enough to have them act on her wish.

But Raphael and Azazel had bastardized that when they had created the drug that would control vampires back in Grafton. The rites they had put Sarah through, the magic and demonic powers and the drugs, had turned her into something else. Had changed her, irrevocably.

They had made a monster. Her powers now exploded wildly out of control, and they were almost impossible for her to control. The draining of a will could quickly turn into the draining of a life. I had seen what was left, after that had happened. Sarah had turned from a Siren into a Medusa, where the barest gaze, the tiniest flickering touch, left someone a statue. Motionless. Dead.

The worst example had been at Red Rock. Although it might have been necessary at the time. There were hundreds, if not thousands, of vampires there at the Conclave. Sarah had been a dark cloud of *something*, tentacles swarming, flicking out, licking vampires and thralls alike, killing all. Killing anything that neared her. Leaving no one behind.

I couldn't pretend to understand how that kind of power could affect someone. Not just that kind of power, but not being able to control it. To have the power of death, barely leashed, barely able to control, that could kill everything and everyone around you. Maybe even those you loved.

How much control did Sarah have? I hadn't asked. Maybe there was a reason she was always sad. I hadn't asked about that, either. It was something I had put aside for later, in my mind. Something for Jen to take care of, or Nick. Not because I was that type of person, but because there had been so much going on that I just couldn't do it all.

Maybe what Jen had been feeling lately.

I finished the bowl of cereal churros, not really tasting it anymore, and quickly washed it in the sink. Sarah watched me, quiet, sipping her coffee, her face back to its mask of sad eyes and tiny smile. She looked at the knives on the table, off to the side, and then back to me, her face a question.

"I'm hoping they're weapons," I said. Toweling the bowel dry, putting it back in the cupboard. I had come a long way from the guy who just threw his empty energy drink cans into the back of his car.

"Knives *are* weapons," Sarah said.

"True enough," I said, grinning. "But these, I'm hoping these work inside the Dead Zone. That they might help us kill a demon."

Sarah cocked her head, reached out and touched one lightly, as if afraid the knife much bite her. Then she put her hand on the hilt, frowning a bit.

"They feel… heavy. Or maybe full is the word."

I was hoping they were full. Full of ethereal energy. Like a battery, supercharged.

"I've been thinking," Sarah said.

"That I make the world's greatest latte?"

Sarah snorted. "No. About the Dead Zone. The Dead Zones."

She had always been quiet in the sessions. Timid. Playing her guitar softly. Being around Nick, just to be around him, I thought. "Let's hear it."

"It's like hell on Earth, right," she said. "Your powers don't work there. Jen's, neither. But Nick's does. Gabrielle, too."

Left unsaid were Tabitha and Zoe and Gertrude. None of them had made it into the Dead Zone yet. And Johnny, because, well, he was being Johnny.

"You think it's because some people's powers are good?" Sarah asked. "And some people's are bad?"

I paused. I hadn't really thought of it that way. I could see where Sarah was going. That because her power, and Nick's, worked in the Dead Zone, that the two of them might be evil.

Jen's powers didn't work in the Dead Zone. We both knew that. I remembered her lightning shield, the shield of bolts that circled around her, fading right before Azazel had shot her in New Orleans.

The Dead Zone seemed to have its own rules. I wasn't sure Azazel would build something so limiting. Though I could understand a piece of hell not letting an angel have power, much as I assumed, if heaven did exist, that demons would have no power there.

But Nick's power did work. Sarah's, and vampires too. Was it because their powers were evil in nature? Or more demonic? I didn't know.

I did know that Nick had felt that way once. He had told me, outside of a barn, in the middle of nowhere, that he had searched forever, read the Bible, talked to Father Benjamin, looked at everything, everywhere, because he felt like what he did was evil.

Nick had come to the realization it wasn't the power, though, it was what you did with it.

"I don't know," I said to Sarah, finally. "I mean, look at what I do. What I have to do in order to do it. I wouldn't necessarily say it's good." All the horrible memories I had to live, the murderers, rapists, and thieves. It would be easy for a person to fall victim to living those lives.

To becoming the evil they lived in order to access power. I hadn't though, and maybe that was a point of pride. Or stubbornness. "I think, in the end, it's always what you choose to do with the power you have. Whatever it is. I think that choice matters more, in the end, to make you who you are than whatever you were born. Whatever power you have."

The words of my mother, as always. *You find a little part of yourself, and you tuck it away, where nothing can get to it...*

Sarah needed to find her something. She looked thoughtful. Maybe she had heard variations of the same thing from Nick.

"I used to sing," she said, wistfully. "I could bring people together with my songs. Make them sad. Make them happy..." Sarah shrugged. "Now all I bring is death. All I do is take from people, until they die. And I don't know if I can stop it. I don't know where these powers will end if I really let go."

She sighed. Fingers of one hand playing with the locket around her neck. "Will it take me, too, in the end?"

I didn't know how to answer that. Not really. Even if the two of us had something in common. Our powers left us feeling like monsters. I could understand her fear, her worry, about losing control to the taint of something that may never leave you, if you succumbed to it. Not to the evil, but to the *power* of what you could do.

And I understood the helplessness of it. The swelling evil, the shadow inside that just wanted you to slip one time, so it could take over. That kind of feeling only grew each time you used your power. Each time you used it *more*.

I opened my mouth to tell Sarah that. At the same time the bedroom door opened, Jen peeking out. She held her cup of coffee in one hand so that it hid her face. She saw Sarah, and I saw the edges of a smile. "Be right out."

The door snicked shut again.

Sarah looked at me, looked up at the ceiling, much like I had a minute ago. Maybe, just maybe, rolling her eyes. Slightly.

I laughed. And, for good or bad, the previous moment between us passed. The one where I wanted to share that I might understand a little how Sarah felt.

And, like all moments, it was impossible to recapture.

CHAPTER TWENTY-NINE

The planning session room was a little less lively today than the day before. The room faced east, it was right above our apartment, and the late afternoon sun left the room in a somber light, the deepening shadow of the oncoming evening. If light, or the lack of it, the *darkening* of it, could cast a pall, then this light did. Over everyone there.

It was certainly quiet. Nick was stretched back along the couch, his eyes partly closed. He looked tired but nodded as the three of us came in. His feet were on the coffee table, his phone next to them. Johnny and Gabrielle were there, too, by the island. Johnny with a beer in his hand, and Gabrielle standing close to him, as if by being close, she could keep him.

Alejandro too, with his second-in-command, Millie. The small vampire with the scar along her face, the girl who never looked happy. Tabitha and Zoe, in the same place on the couch as the day before. Zoe looked like she could use more sleep as well, with her eyes looking a little pinched, but she gave me a tiny wave of her hand, something that said, *what a night, right?* Tabitha still didn't look happy, and Gertrude stood behind them both.

What an army, right?

I had the Five-Fold knives in my hand, thinking for a brief moment, here I was, here we were, about to take on a demon in the middle of a city of millions, millions of people, millions of creatures, or some combination of both. A demon in the center of his power, on his own turf, with who knows what kind of armaments, weapons, armies.

And we had us, and now, two knives.

I laughed a bit, inside.

We had what we had.

I took the end of the couch opposite Nick. Arched my eyebrows at him. Put the knives on the table next to his phone.

He frowned, pulling his feet from the table. Leaning forward. "What are those?"

"I'm hoping the key to the fight," I said.

"They look funny," Johnny said. His voice a little thick. It made me wonder how much he had drunk today. "Shimmery."

I was a little surprised he could see that, but Johnny had mentioned that he caught glimpses of spirits and other ethereal traces, the things I could see in my ethereal vision. He seemed to have picked that up after we had healed him back at the airport, in Denver.

Another change in one of us, another moment where my mother would have said our side was growing stronger, becoming *more*, though honestly I couldn't tell you what had happened. Johnny was dying, Gabrielle bit him, and I had tried to heal him in the same way I tried to heal myself. All done in a rush.

Johnny lifted a shoulder and dropped it. His glance was a little blurry, like he was still sleepy. At least I hoped it was sleep. He and Nick and Gabrielle had been out late last night.

"The knives are full of ethereal energy," I explained. "We went out last night and made them. I'm hoping they work in the Dead Zone, and if they do—"

Nick was suddenly alert. "I'll have a weapon that could kill Sabnock."

I nodded. Though I wanted this to be the last resort. I didn't want Nick to go in solo and try to kill Sabnock with a blade that may or may not be able to do it.

At the very least, though, this Five-Fold blade should help nullify the Dead Zone. It wasn't like there was a switch to flip. The center of the pentagram, the center of the power, would need to be broken in some way. Cut. And this knife would do that better than any other.

He picked up one of the blades. Pulled it quickly from the sheath, the entire foot of it, and whistled, low. Did the thing with knives people did in the movies, feeling the edge, testing the blade's balance. He flipped it around his wrist in a couple of circles, the metal of the blade flashing a bit under the light, the slight shimmering of the Five-Fold Symbols leaving a little afterimage in the air, before sliding the knife back into the sheathe.

"I get both?"

I smiled, shaking my head. Nick would want both. He was a dark fucker. And I meant that in the best possible way. "One's for me."

I was hoping to use the blade too, but in a different way. I wanted to use it to draw power from. I was hoping to use my powers in the Dead Zone by draining what I could from the knife. Kind of like a battery of ethereal energy that I could bring with me into the zone.

I thought it could work.

And I thought that would make all our jobs easier.

Because the Dead Zone would be a much easier nut to crack, if Sabnock was dead.

I had never been comfortable with sending Nick in to kill a demon I felt responsible for. If the blade worked like I thought it would, if I could use the ethereal energy in it to fuel my powers inside the Dead Zone, then we could get back to Plan A.

Nick understood that, and maybe even accepted it, lifting one eyebrow, briefly.

For now though, we were going to stick with the original plan. Bringing in a convoy from Cuernavaca. Attacking the Dead Zone from that direction. Hopefully pulling Sabnock's attention that way.

Sneaking in Nick. Cutting the power to the Dead Zone. Then killing the demon.

Nick pushed the phone across the table. "Took pictures last night."

I grabbed the phone and opened up the photos, taking a look. Jen leaned over my shoulder, looking with me as I swiped from one picture to the next.

The first one was of the stadium. Oddly, whether it was the angle of the photo or just the phone's camera, the stadium looked much smaller than I would have thought. Especially for something that once had held over a hundred thousand people. To me, it looked more like a parking garage than a stadium.

It was an oval structure. Flat, angled concrete arms circled the outside, each bone-like arm reaching up from the ground, stretching all the way up and over the top of the stadium, the ends of the bony arms looking much like crenellations might look on a castle wall.

Actually, the whole thing looked much like a crown, such as a king might wear. Each of the arms just lay vertically on the crown, ringing the crown like a crown of thorns.

Not a crown of thorns. Not even a kingly crown.

It was a crown of bones.

I shivered and swiped to the next picture.

A dark gray sign over the front of the stadium read Estadio Azteca in big white letters. Flat planes of glass over the doors. Cables stretched from the top points of each bone-like arm, circling the crown.

Swipe.

New construction. Mounds of dirt to the side of the stadium. An earth mover there, a super-sized dump truck, big enough it made the stadium look small. Smaller figures, people, workers, in the middle of whatever they were doing. Some by the mounds of dirt. Some walking in and out of the stadium. Some of those looked to be workers, some looked to be armored, like knights of old, taller figures with what looked like helmets and shields and chest plates, greaves.

The armor appeared old. It might not even be armor. The knights looked like large creatures, with flat-sided arms and chests and bodies. Like they had been chiseled from dark, sickly green rock. Like golems.

That was the word that came to mind. Their bodies weren't shiny, or silver, like a knight. They *were* armored, just not in metal, but maybe stone. The creatures were tall. And thick. Like granite. Covered, or colored, in the same gangrene I had seen covering the tops of the taller buildings in Mexico City. Their stone-like bodies lined with streaks of rusty red.

Weird.

Swipe.

Lines of people around the back of the stadium. Thousands of them. Funneled as if they were going to the game. Standing among them, taller than the people by a head or two, were those knights. As if keeping order among those in line. As if they were taking tickets. I wondered if Sabnock was selling seats to the upcoming demon versus Grimm match.

Swipe.

More workers on top of the stadium. This picture caught something sparking there, as if someone was welding. Some of the girders seemed to be getting attached to the top of the crown, long pieces of iron lay in the air between each bony arm, as if the workers were building the crown higher.

Flat sheets of metal were being lifted up to the new girders, were being welded in place between each. The sheets were angled down, as if looking on the head wearing the crown. I thought I caught a reflection of what might be inside, on the field. At least one of the metal sheets was polished enough to catch some kind of bright glare there.

Hmmmm.

Swipe.

More pictures of the stadium, from different angles. Mostly the same. At least, not different enough to matter. Lots of eighteen-wheelers. Lots of vehicles. Lots of figures. More sheets of metal, some being lowered inside the stadium, as if they might be building a cage to hold something in. More earth movers. More welding.

Swipe.

Pause.

Sabnock himself. The picture was too far away to really see great detail, but there was no mistaking the demon that Nick had described. Tall, far taller than humans. Dark, in all the lights surrounding the stadium, like polished ebony. There were a couple of pictures, and one of them caught the pauldron-like shoulder covering Nick had described. The golden lion's head, resting above the demon's arm.

I could see no expression there on the lion's face. Or the demon's. The pictures were at the largest zoom the camera could manage, with everything slightly pixelated. So it could have been the picture when I thought the lion was looking directly into the camera. It was still hard to hold back a shiver.

I couldn't make heads or tails of what was going on. The welding. The lines of people, the knights. People being funneled to the stadium. But the sight of the Sabnock locked this in for me. My heart started its usual racing, getting ready for a fight. The sight of the demon made all of it, whatever it was, more real.

"Notice anything?" Nick asked.

Obviously, he had seen something I had missed. I went through the pictures again, faster this time. Pausing at a few. The first picture, of the front of the stadium, one of the knights or golems off to the side. The next focused on one of the bone-like arms circling the crown. The best one of Sabnock, I looked at again for a long while. That picture of someone welding at the top, the sheets of metal circling the crown, as if Sabnock was keeping something in. The huge crowd, as if going to a game.

Jen gave a *hmph*. I felt the same. I shook my head.

"Think about it," Nick said. "We see a lot of trucks going in. A lot of the eighteen-wheelers."

I didn't see what he was talking about. The pictures showed the trucks. All the steel girders piled up around the stadium. The tools needed to build whatever they were building. Some of that, maybe most of that, would have to get brought in. I pulled up a picture showing the pile of girders off to the side, the pallets of metal sheets, and showed that to Nick.

He shook his head.

"All that's already there," he said. "So what are they bringing in *now*?"

I froze. That was a good question. The trucks came in nightly. A lot of trucks came in nightly. Lines and lines of them.

But the trucks also left nightly.

We had assumed—I had assumed—all the trucks were bringing

in supplies, tools, and metals to a demon that was an architect. Sabnock had designed Pandemonium, a palace in hell. It wasn't much of a stretch to believe the same demon would be forting up, building his own personal kingdom here in Mexico.

Had we gotten it wrong? From the start?

What if Sabnock wasn't building? What if he wasn't *only* building? Was he taking things out with the trucks instead? Shipping something out?

If so, what?

"He's not just an architect," Johnny said. "He outfits armies. Arms them. Armors them."

The knights.

I cursed myself. The Dead Zones wouldn't have been the end game for Azazel. He would have had plans for after. The demons wouldn't just want kingdoms of their own to rule. They would want to do more.

And Mexico City had millions of people. Mexico the country had millions more. All of the demons had Dead Zones around places in the world with large populations. Places with histories of large populations.

But we had found the surrounding towns, the cities, were mostly empty.

We had assumed those people had fled. And those that hadn't fled, possibly captured by Sabnock to offer as food to clans like La Familia Diablo. And those people that hadn't fled or been captured, maybe they had flocked to the Dead Zone instead.

I had seen that in New Orleans. There was good and evil in the world. We had seen some people trying to leave the Dead Zone. But just as people would want to leave, there would be those that wanted power. Wanted what the demons could offer. And they would flock to the Dead Zones.

I hadn't given the massive emptiness we found here in Mexico enough thought. The dead towns, the empty cities. What if Sabnock was building something, building someones, some-*creatures*, and shipping those out to the other Dead Zones? What if he was taking one of the largest centers of population in the world and building an army from them?

What if our initial assumption was wrong? And the trucks coming in were actually taking people out, taking armies out, instead of bringing supplies in?

Did we need to know more? Would it matter what the demon was doing as long as we killed Sabnock? I didn't know.

I looked up from the phone. I'm sure my face looked frustrated, because I felt like I should have seen it earlier. I mean, it wasn't like Mexico City didn't already have its own construction tools, metals, girders, all of that. They wouldn't have needed to bring all that in.

What was Sabnock building?

"I know," Nick said. "I'm going to try to find out more tonight."

In the end, I had to hope it didn't matter. Did I care what the trucks were carrying? We were going to kill the demon anyway. What would his plans matter if he was six feet under the ground? Or wherever it was that demons were buried. "If you can do it safely."

That earned me a Nick look.

"What about the stadium?" Jen asked. The lines of people up there. "Did you see inside?"

He shook his head. "It's going to be a problem. There are too many people. And the stadium lights, they're pretty bright." He winced. "Even at night, I'm going to have to be careful."

The stadium had to be the center of the Dead Zone. And to find the construction there... Sabnock. The weird nights, the lines of people. There was a puzzle there, and likely the key to the puzzle itself, both the question and the answer in the same place.

If Sabnock was making an army, why the stadium? Just because it had the capacity to hold a lot of people? Or something more?

244 · CHRIS J CRANFORD

"There's something he needs there," Jen said.

"Yeah," I said. "But what does he need it for?"

The stadium had to be the place of power, where we could nullify the zone. The location fit. The power in the center of the stadium. The concentrated place of the pentagram, the center of the center of the center, all focused on one spot.

Those same things were of use to Sabnock. We just didn't know why. Or really, what.

"We need more information," I said, looking to Nick.

He lifted his shoulder in a little shrug. *No big thing.* "I can go back in tonight and find out."

The talk in the room died off a bit after that. There wasn't much more we could do until that. Nick was the critical part of the plan. He needed to nullify the Dead Zone, get into the stadium and somehow release the power that was binding the Dead Zone to the Earth.

Then, and only then, could I kill Sabnock.

The rest of the plan was just show. The Mad Max convoy, rolling in from the south. Lots of show, lots of whistles. A *look at me* distraction, so that Nick could get in, make it to the center of the stadium, and cut the power to the Dead Zone.

A lot rested on Nick. Even our recon, tonight. Nick getting inside, past all the creatures, into the stadium and taking a peek. Just to see if there was something *to* nullify.

The stadium's picture came back to mind. The Crown of Bones. Large, imposing, white arms cradling the stadium, bone-like arms circling the rim of the crown. Concrete arms stretching into the air.

That would be a lot for one person to do. Our plan, such as it was, depended a lot on Nick. But we didn't have a lot of extra people standing around. We would all be busy, over the next few days.

CHAPTER THIRTY

We waited until evening to make the recon run. We took the Camaro, Nick and I. Both of us took our Five-Fold blades. A little surprisingly, Jen and Sarah decided to join us. Like it was a night out for the four of us.

The girls took the backseat. Jen reached forward, patting my shoulder, smiling at me through the rearview. I took a big breath of it, always a little stunned at how that smile could make me feel.

Nick slid into the passenger seat. The windows were down, and he held his arm out of it, elbow on the door, tapping the roof of the Camaro with his hand a couple of times. Like he was testing it. Then he looked at me, not quite rolling his eyes, but not quite not rolling them, either.

"You always find one," he said. "You know Mustangs are better."

"Better?"

"In every way. Better power. Faster. Smoother looking. More iconic." His grin took me in. "It's the ponies, man. Even the rumble sounds better."

Well, Nick was the mechanic. And I couldn't argue the sound thing. There was something different about the exhaust from a Mustang, but if a car was made specifically to have that rumble, then that wasn't a car I wanted to drive. I wanted a car designed to be a car and not just the rumble.

Though I did like both, in my '68.

So I not quite rolled my eyes back at Nick. And patted the steering wheel of this Camaro. It wasn't my old one, but it would do. We all liked what we liked.

I mean, it fired up nice. The car shook a bit under the power of the engine. Even if, being a newer model, the shaking was a little smoother. A little less loppy than my old Camaro, a little less like the roar of a lion. A little more purring, like a puma.

It all had me laughing. I held the brake down and goosed the gas pedal a few times, looking at Nick. Raising my eyebrows. Pushed down hard on the gas one time, all of us feeling the car tilt a little in anticipation.

He laughed.

We took off. Headed back to our spot. The night was quiet above us, stars poked out in their spots, though it was muggy enough that a few clouds lay low over the earth, and where the clouds were, the stars weren't. A bunch lay behind us in the east, hiding the moon as well. A bright white shine radiated out from the dark bank in the rearview.

It felt almost like we were going on a picnic. Just two guys and their girls, heading out to spend an idyllic day under some trees somewhere. Likely next to a bubbling brook.

Well, not a day, so not a picnic. It was night, so maybe a drive-in movie. With popcorn and cold pink lemonade in a big cup with two straws, the screen large in front of your car and flickering with images, the radio tuned to the movie, and your girl curled up next to you in the seat...

You know the feeling.

We headed west along the paved road, the only car on the highway. The wind was brisk, and we rolled the windows up. Nick fiddled with the radio for a bit until he found nothing. He kept pushing the media button until the compact disc fired up with a spin, and all of a sudden, reggaeton filled the cabin. The words were in Spanish, but it sounded like the guy was rapping, and there were all kinds of cymbals and a synthesizer and one of those steel drums they beat in the Caribbean. I heard words like *al garete* and *broki*, and once or twice I heard *jah*, whatever that meant.

The song ended, and the next one fired up with the banging of a steel drum. Crashing of cymbals. And a synthesized scream that didn't quite seem to end.

I pushed the mute button on the steering wheel.

There were some things about the newer cars that, even if I didn't quite like them, I still found convenient.

"Brother," Nick said, grinning. "Navigator picks the music."

"I'd let him, if he were navigating." I pointed forward. "We're almost there."

We were. I turned off the paved road, onto the little dirt trail that led up to the hill we had watched Mexico City from earlier. The Camaro handled it a little rough. I went slow, the car bouncing a bit here and there. I had us go as far as we could, then shut the car off, setting the emergency brake.

We all got out. Jen naturally sliding next to me. Nick with one arm around Sarah, the other holding his blade. The four of us headed to the top of the hill. Looking out over the muted, sporadic lights of Mexico City, still some distance to the southwest.

Below us, the Dead Zone began. A few hundred feet from the bottom of the hill. I imagined how large this zone must be, how much power must have gone into its creation. Larger than Texas, was my guess.

Nick said something to Sarah. She hugged him. They kissed, quickly. I made fun of the kiss, and Jen bumped my hip with hers. But laughed as she did it.

I could feel Jen trying to be more happy than she was. To try to find her old self. There was a shell there, something surrounding a part of her she couldn't understand, something that she was worried about still, but hadn't been able to tell me. Because she didn't know what it was herself.

We all told Nick to be careful. He tried to not roll his eyes. He was antsy to go, to get the deed done, but I pulled him aside.

"Just recon," I said.

Nick looked surprised. Like he hadn't been planning on anything else.

"I'm serious," I said. "No trying to kill Sabnock with the blade. No trying to cut the power to the Dead Zone. Not with the rest of us just sitting here."

"Sure," he finally said. His response hesitant.

"None of us are ready to back you up," I said. "Let's do it once. And do it right."

He nodded, a little less reluctant this time.

And then he was gone.

Kind of a cool power. I blinked on my ethereal sight, trying to catch a glimpse of Nick as he walked the shadows. I knew he could go anywhere he could see, or anywhere he had been, where a shadow still lay.

I thought I saw him once. At the farthest edge of my vision. A tiny shimmering of white, and then he was gone.

If that had been Nick at all.

I blinked back. Sarah looked a little worried, and a lot sad, and Jen was already in the middle of pulling her back to the car. The two sisters spoke in low voices, the fun of the car, the feeling of the trip, all gone now.

I pulled out my binoculars and looked at the city. Found the tall towers of the high-rises far in the distance. Far in my ethereal sight. The glimmering darkish green shine at the tops of the buildings, as if rot was eating each one from the top down.

So tough to see. I sat there like I had many nights in the past, looking at things I couldn't see. Even with my sight. Even with the highest power of binoculars we could find.

Not a lot of detail. Not enough detail at all. To really see these things, I needed to go in like Nick.

Where my powers wouldn't work.

A little more time passed. An idea occurred to me. I looked at the edge of the Dead Zone. Right there at the bottom of the hill. I had left my Five-Fold blade in the Camaro.

Nothing like a little testing while we waited.

I headed back to the Camaro. Jen and Sarah lay back there, both on the hood, their backs on the windshield. Talking in low voices and looking up at the night.

"Nick back?" Sarah asked.

I shook my head, opened up the driver's door. Grabbed the blade I had left there, in that space between the door and the seat. "Going to test the blade."

Jen cocked an eyebrow. "Didn't you tell Nick not to?"

"I told him not to kill Sabnock," I said. "Or try to cut power to the stadium all by himself."

I waggled the blade in its sheath. "This is a little bit different."

"Nick'd say different," Jen said.

"Sure he would," I said. "But he's not here. And we're waiting, and we might as well kill two birds with one stone."

Jen wasn't wrong. There was always the chance that summoning the sword might ping Sabnock's radar and pull his attention this way. Something I had worked hard to avoid this past week.

Still, I was just going to summon it. Briefly. And then let it go. If it was anything, it would be a momentary blip on the demon's screen, there and gone before it could really register.

Jen sighed. Pulled herself off the front of the car. She was going with me. And where Jen went, Sarah was going too.

I was going to have company while I tested. Which made it more important to be quick. Not just to make sure Nick didn't come back while I was testing and point out that I was doing something along the lines of what I had asked him not to do, but also just to keep us all safe.

We picked our way down the hill. Right to where I knew the line rested. The line that no one else could see, just me. The cool night air surrounding us would be hazed in red, with one more step. The rusty tinge colored everything, the ground, the grass, even the gangrene goo far in the distance, miles away.

"Hey there," Jen said, next to me. She knew where I was standing, and why, and what I was looking at, and wondering. "Testing anytime soon? Like tonight?"

I looked at her. She arched an eyebrow and took one large step. Into the Dead Zone.

I took a step to follow.

And slammed into a wall. I wasn't expecting it and dropped the knife. My face collided with the outer bubble of the Dead Zone, where it hadn't before. Hadn't ever before. I had taken a step and slammed my nose into something that shouldn't be there.

"Gus?" I heard Jen say.

My eyes watered. I pressed my palms to them, pressed my little fingers hard against my nose, waiting for the smarting to pass. I shook my head a bit and wiped my eyes.

Jen stood there in front of me. Just a foot into the Dead Zone. Not far at all. She had reached down and grabbed the Five-Fold blade and was holding it in front of her. As if handing it to me to grab.

I reached for it.

My hand hit the wall of the Dead Zone again.

I swore and shook it. "What the hell?"

Jen stepped towards me, saying my name again. Worried and waving her hand in front of my face. To her, I must have been a sight. I must have immediately flipped the crazy switch. It might have been like watching someone in the distance walk into a spider-web, seeing that person throw their arms wildly in the air. They are just trying to get the web off, but that person in the distance observing them would be saying to themselves, *stay away from that guy.*

She held the knife out, the blade in its sheath piercing the line of the Dead Zone. I pulled it back out, her hands came with it and found mine. Each of her hands outside on my arms.

Her eyes were worried. And puzzled. I took a step forward, one large step, to right beside Jen.

My foot kicked the wall. The knife flew backwards. I fell back-wards, pulling Jen with me before letting her go and falling flat on my ass. I swore, but Jen was laughing, and Sarah too.

Everyone loves an audience.

At least the two of them helped me up. I dusted myself off. Tried to take one more step into the Dead Zone.

And went right in.

So smoothly I stopped. Surprised. Jen stood next to Sarah, both of them standing fully out of the Dead Zone. Jen had just picked up the Five-Fold blade. Again.

Her head was cocked, still looking at me with a curious expression.

Then she took a step towards me.

And I got to see what I had looked like, when I hit the wall of the Dead Zone and fell backwards on my ass.

Needless to say, I laughed. I might not have wanted to, but I did.

Jen looked a little piqued, getting up. But she was smarter than me on the second try. She held her hand out until she found the outer edge of the Dead Zone. The edge of the bubble. And then she smoothed her hand around it. As if trying to find a way in.

Her eyes were intense. Worried. A bit of fear in the irises. More worry than I thought she should have been.

"Gus?" she said. Or asked.

It was then that I saw her keydrop. It had fallen out of her T-shirt. It glowed a bit on her chest.

I pulled mine out. It was glowing the same amount. Which was to say, barely. A shimmering of ethereal blue over the polished rock.

Jen held hers in her hand. She looked worried. She looked like she had back in the hallway, puzzled. Worried. Concerned.

"What the hell is happening to us, Gus?"

This. Feeling Jen in the bedroom, her feeling me feel her, and her feeling me. Really feeling. The communication between us with the key, some residual thing between Jen and I had grown in power, became larger in scope and feel. We felt more with each other. A piece of me was always in Jen, and a piece of her was always in me. Like our hearts were pieces of each other.

The bond between Jen and I had existed long before the key. Though she had been in the stone a while. Maybe that had left a residue, of sorts, between us. It was hard to know. It was hard to tell.

We both were one of a kind.

That thought rang around in my skull. It meant something. I wasn't sure what.

"Gus," Jen's voice was still worried, and she handed the Five-Fold blade to Sarah. "Come out."

I shook my head. Stepped out. Jen held me in place with one hand and then placed a leg back into the Dead Zone. It went in fine, so she pulled it back out. Like she was doing the hokey pokey.

Since that was the case, she placed her foot back in. Next, she grabbed my hand with hers and tried to move it back into the Dead Zone. My hand stopped. Jen's didn't. It felt a little funny, like Jen's fingers were trying to pull mine through a brick wall.

Then it felt less funny, and more *pinchy*. Her fingers had twisted mine into a bind in the wall. I yanked my hand out. Shaking it.

"It seems like only one of us can buy a ticket to the show," I said. Whoever went into the Dead Zone first, either Jen or myself, the second person wasn't going to be allowed to follow. Which didn't really change our plans at all. I was going in to kill Sabnock, after all.

Jen's concerned face didn't change. She pulled her keydrop out, holding the rope that held the key in two fingers, so that the stone lay in the air between us. The key no longer glowed now.

She did the hokey pokey again. The stone blinked on and off.

Huh.

"At least we know if one of us is in, right?" I said, trying a grin. Trying a joke. "No sneaking off for this guy."

Jen just grunted. She was thinking. I was too.

The key had changed. From being a prison for demons, to holding the ghost of Jen. We had formed a bond during her captivity. Something that existed even when she came back.

And from there, after Red Rock, the key had changed further. Jen had been dead. Well, as close to dead as you can get. I had carried her in the key, we had created the bond through it, she had even helped me in my fight back at Red Rock. She had manipulated ethereal energy I had pulled, and helped me fight the geas. We had fought as one. Became one.

Maybe the key hadn't changed so much as we had. Maybe our

bond wasn't morphing so much as testing our limits. There were rules and powers in play. Maybe when I thought the key was changing, that our bond was changing, it was really Jen and I breaking free of a constraint we hadn't realized was there.

Either way, it didn't change the concern. Jen worried about what was happening with us. I wasn't worried, per se, but I guess you could say I was highly interested in the possible outcome. I had gone a long way to get Jen.

I wasn't going to let anything happen to her now.

To us, now.

So I was going to file this away as another variable in the equation that was us, an equation where the answer was unknown, like one of those whiteboards professors had with x's and y's and algebraic constants scattered across it.

I knew Jen. I knew me. I knew us. That was what I would go with. For now.

"Hey," a voice shouted. The three of us glanced up at the top of the hill, surprised.

Nick was back, waving his arm. "There a reason you guys are down there?"

We went to see what he had found out.

CHAPTER THIRTY-ONE

Nick waited by the Camaro. His ass against the front fender. Holding his phone in one hand. Looking bored.

"I couldn't get everything," he said, handing the phone over. "There are too many people. Too many of those golem creatures, the knights. And Sabnock, always around."

He had the pictures up. I started to swipe through them. These were different from the photos he had taken before. Each photo had part of a blocky shadow along the side, as if Nick took the photo hiding behind a wall. A door. Or... a shadow.

Some of those were blurry. Others weren't entirely clear. Most had that shadowed line taking at least a third of the shot up. Those were the worst, as if the shadows had thrown off the phone's focus.

I looked at Nick.

"Best I could do," he said. "I was on the move."

It was like Nick had flicked into a place, took a quick shot, and flicked back out. Walking shadows non-stop. Moving from place to place and grabbing what photos he could.

"I'm pretty sure they didn't see me."

Some of the photos were too busy to make out. But, swiping through, there seemed to be an order to them. As if Nick had started in one place and made his way around. The first dozen or so were of humans, everywhere. Crowds of them. Lines of them. In some places their faces looked worried. Others, tired. A few, expectant.

Humans threaded through the gates. Packed in a certain order, standing in single file lines, one line stacked to the next. As if they were going to a game. The game of the century. Of the centuries.

Grimm versus Sabnock. A battle to the death. Like in the coliseums of old.

Maybe the demon wanted a crowd.

None of the lines bulged here and there, though, like some of the times I had gone to a game. There were no groups of friends, all standing together. Not one person looked like they were jumping or cutting the line. Not one family of people stood huddled together, organizing who was sitting where. Everyone stood in a precise order.

Sabnock must have been hell on anyone stepping out of line.

The photos went on. The lines of people were funneled into the stadium, and the hallways circling the field were the same. People standing in line. People, not going to the bathroom. People, not getting a beer or hot dog at a concession stand, of which all were closed.

Just the lines of people. Waiting. Expectant. Tired.

The shots grew blurry. I swiped past a few, stopped at a photo looking down at the field from above. Like it had been taken from one of the tops of the concrete arms, right back from the circle on the top of the roof of the stadium. I imagined there being a shadow there, between the arm and the girders being mounted to the arms and the plates being welded to those girders, and Nick had found that shadow, laying down to see over the edge of the roof's rim, in a quick moment.

"I had a window," he said.

So we got a picture of inside the stadium. From the very top. The long square field in the shot, way down below. The field was small in the camera's focus. Tiny.

On one side of the field were large containers, like the kind eighteen-wheelers would carry. The containers were stacked up, one after another, in the end zone beside the field's entrance ramp. It looked like they were being pulled in and out along that ramp. The doors on the containers closest to the ramp were closed.

The rest of the field was full of lines. Not lines like on a soccer pitch. Not the talcum powder lines of a baseball diamond, or a football field. The lines of people from outside the stadium. Even more concentrated on the field below. More packed.

There were so many figures below. The containers, some open, some closed. The lines of the people, almost swirling into the center of the stadium. The center of the field. The center of where we believed the pentagram was. To the very center of the power of the Dead Zone.

Which seemed... smudged.

I wiped the face of the phone. The smudge remained, as if someone had smeared the very center of the phone with an ink-stained thumb. I peered at it closer. Was it a stain? A smudge? Or was there just so much activity there in the center the phone couldn't capture it all?

"I can't figure it out either," Nick said.

Jen was quiet, looking at the photo over my shoulder. Sarah hummed something, something brief and short, from my right.

Jen was doing the same, over my shoulder. Sarah on my left.

I swiped a few photos forward, there were no more shots of the field. The rest looked to be from the other side of the stadium. As if Nick had taken all the photos in one run, from one side of the stadium to the other, with a brief one-pic stop at the top.

The final pictures were of less-crowded hallways. At least, there were none of the lines of people from the other side. There were more workers running around, construction hats on, some of them wearing safety harnesses for getting into the bucket trucks.

It had me wondering, briefly, about how a person could work for a demon, in a top-side version of hell on Earth, and still be worried about hitting their head on a girder, or falling off a ladder. I mean, where did they think they were going to go if they died on the job? Some kind of OSHA version of heaven?

I had worked construction jobs. Some of the rules there had seemed zealous, at best. Checklists for everything. Proximity switches on gates, gates that never lined up, gates that vibrated with the operation of the machine, so that the switch would always shake out of place and stop the machine.

One place I had been, they had wanted safety switches lined up to let them know when other safety switches were tripped. It made it so that a person had to work out a jigsaw puzzle to stop a machine. Usually solving that puzzle took so long the machine broke. People I had worked with would get around that by reaching in while the machine was running, trying to yank out whatever it was the machine was caught on. Trying to keep whatever drum spinning, whatever arm carrying whatever load to wherever it was trying to go. Trying to keep the machine running, because more product meant more sales, and a higher paycheck.

My eyes narrowed a bit. Maybe the Occupational Safety and Health Administration had a little more devil in them than I had thought.

I moved on. These last sets of photos, on the other side of the hallway, were more empty. Fewer people. No lines. Workers, and the occasional knight. The ones I saw were in the distance, as if Nick hadn't dared get too close. Even if the light seemed dim around the knights. None of the photos captured their faces. Everything about the knights seemed dark, from their shadowed helms, their armor, their skin. A dark, rusty, gangrene type of color.

I reached the last of the photos. These final shots looked much like Nick's first trip. Pictures of the construction outside the stadium. A picture of a crane, its large boom swung out overtop the stadium, its cables holding a large, polished steel plate in midair. More of the plates being mounted on the top of the stadium, around the hole in the roof. Making the crown taller.

There was a knight standing guard, the construction workers climbing around the stadium, the tall piles of girders and pallets of steel plates in front. The picture of the side of the stadium, much like the first shot I had seen of it. The crown of bones shot.

I didn't like that name. But it had stuck. The stadium did look like a crown. Placed on the very large earth. Especially with the bone-white concrete pillars reaching up around the stadium. Hundreds of pillars, hundreds of concrete bones, circling it. The very tops of each pillar curved in, reached in over the roof of the stadium, like bony fingers.

I swiped back to the photo from the top of the stadium. The one looking down on the field. The one with the smudge in the center.

Trying something, I flicked on my ethereal sight.

And immediately slapped my hand over my eyes. Instinctively. Like I had been blinded.

And I had. The smudge in the photo was a ball of ethereal energy. It had burned like the hottest sun in my sight. Burned so brightly in the center of the stadium it left an afterimage of bluish-white in my sight.

I tried to blink the afterimage away. The ball still burned brightly in the back of my eyelids, a bright ball with a tiny black center. I waved my hand until someone took the phone. I kept blinking and wiping my eyes with the palms of both hands.

"Gus?" Jen asked.

I blinked some more. Trying to get the bright blue ball in the back of my eyelids to go away. The ball softened, dimmed, and as it did I noticed little afterimages swirling around the ball. Like thousands of motes of light being flushed into the center of the stadium.

I closed my eyes and focused on those motes. The little afterimages on the back of my eyelids. The tiniest images swirling around. I pressed my hands tightly over my eyes, so that no other light interrupted my focus.

They weren't little afterimages.

Those motes were spirits. Little spirits, circling the center of the stadium like it was the eye of a tornado. The spirits whirled around as if seeking the power inside. As if drawn to it, like insects to a light.

Ghosts.

Thousands, I thought.

Maybe hundreds of thousands.

Flying in a circle around the center of the Dead Zone. So much ethereal energy concentrated there, the brilliance of it had almost blinded me. From a photo.

Were they being called? Or created?

I could think of reasons for both. Ethereal energy called. It bound spirits. It was in the tap of every ghost I had found. The plane that bound them, the tap accessed infinite energy. Ghosts seemed to use that energy to remain in this world, to remain in limbo, and the center of a Dead Zone held a lot of that energy.

Or were the ghosts being created there? I had seen the dot in the afterimage of blazing blue. A dot of power, hidden behind all that ethereal energy. The power of the Dead Zone itself, in the very center of the pentagon.

The power Sabnock likely used. There were thousands of people in those lines. Tens of thousands. All of them looked as if they were being forced in. Resigned. One after another, being marched to the center of the field, where...

What?

I had no idea.

But I was worried. Whatever we wanted to do in the center of the Dead Zone, however we thought we could nullify it, Sabnock already had plans for it. Was actively using the power there. For an unknown reason.

Time, all of a sudden, felt shorter than it needed to be.

CHAPTER THIRTY-TWO

We raced back into the Camaro. I explained what I had seen in the top photo.

None of them liked it any more than I had.

And no one had a good explanation.

So I was taking the side of—if I couldn't explain it—it was likely bad.

We got to the safe house. Gertrude was up in the planning room, sitting on the couch by herself and looking out the large windows, at the clouds to the east, the moon, now above the clouds. There was some music playing from the radio, something poppy with a beat and someone singing in Spanish. Oddly enough, Millie was there, too.

Most everyone else was sleeping. I wanted to get them all up. It was Jen that stopped me. "You won't have time," she said, looking at the window outside. At the moon.

It was close to midnight. It would take longer to drive to Cuernavaca. Especially if we skirted the Dead Zone like we always had. We would have to drive through the sunrise to get there.

"We'll be fine," Millie said. For once looking not-quite-so murdery. The vampire was actually being helpful, as if she wanted to get back. "Our trucks are made to handle the sunrise. Our gear, too."

I looked at Jen.

She smiled in understanding, even if something behind the smile felt a little worried. "You feel something, don't you?"

I did. Something in that photo had resonated with something inside me. I wasn't sure if it was the angel-side, or something in my history that warned me. I didn't think it mattered.

"Whatever Sabnock's doing," I said, "it's more than building his kingdom here on Earth."

We had seen two Dead Zones. The one in New Orleans, and the one here. Both had been short on people, although I had met people trying to leave New Orleans, who may or may not have made it.

But New Orleans had felt different. The United States Army had tried to go. The Navy had surrounded it. There had been fighting, for weeks.

Some of the same things had been reported overseas. The Dead Zone around Rome. The one in Paris. Walls being constructed. Monsters fighting back.

Here, in Mexico City, there was nothing. No government left. No armies trying to fight their way inside. No monsters fighting back. Just an empty city, an empty country, with something unknown at the center.

That something was getting shipped out. To the other Dead Zones, maybe. I talked to Gertrude and Millie. And retold the story as we woke everyone else up.

Tabitha and Zoe came first. Millie found Alejandro. It took us a bit to get Johnny and Gabrielle, at least, until we found Johnny. Gabrielle was in their apartment. Johnny had been next door in the bar. Renaldo asked me if I wanted more of the Mezcal, and laughingly grinned after I shook my head.

With everyone back in the room, I showed the picture again. Described what I had seen. A few of the group nodded, as if they could understand. Johnny. Jen. Zoe. Others took what I said on faith.

We went back to our plan. The one we had formed earlier in the day. Now with a little more urgency. At least, from me.

There were two major parts. I would go to Cuernavaca. We would hit Mexico City from the south with a large convoy and draw Sabnock's attention. While we did, Nick would sneak in from the north and nullify the Dead Zone.

Simple is as simple does.

People offered suggestions, having some time to think about it. They tweaked parts of it. In the end, it wasn't fancy, which I preferred. It was flexible, and I liked adjusting on the fly.

General Patton might have laughed at it. General Custer might have applauded. I understood each and at the same time worried about both. It wasn't much of a plan, but there was very little that I could screw up about each, so I felt like it had a chance to work.

Though calling it a plan was possibly mocking military commanders through the history of the world.

It was what we had.

Alejandro and Millie would go with me. We would start organizing the convoy. Alejandro would get more of his people to drive the trucks in. Millie was unhappy with that part, but the vampire just shrugged.

"We don't have a lot of real fighters left," he explained. As if that explained Millie. The tactical team he had brought had been what was left of their best. What they were using now was what was left of their clan. Vampires, but also those humans that made the clan their family.

I understood. Millie probably didn't like being a pawn in the larger game. After all, there was a good chance a lot of the convoy might not come back. She knew, we all knew, that the convoy would take the most casualties.

But we had what we had. I was going to be there. We would see what we could do in order to protect those coming with the convoy. Part of that was going to be me, drawing as much attention as I could. I could be a big nuisance. I had to hope that would be enough to get most of those that came in with me, out.

"You've seen the stadium," Gertrude said, pointing out the obvious. "Do you think we can draw all of them away?"

There were thousands of people there. Maybe more. I thought it would depend on how close the convoy could get. The more things we could blow up along the way. The closer we got, the more Sabnock would be forced to respond.

Of course, the closer we got, the harder it would be to get out.

We would have to work on that part of the plan a bit more.

Alejandro mentioned an armory down in Cuernavaca. The police had established a base there, placed to fight local drug lords, and the vampires had hopes we could find serious weaponry down there. Not just assault rifles, but hopefully more.

That was one of the flexible parts of the plan.

Tabitha would come too. She would use her Earth magic to strengthen the vehicles. Make each car a tank. Each truck a massively armored beast. The larger the vehicle the more damage it could withstand. Something about what she did hardened the steel, caused it almost to be self-healing.

I had seen her work. My old Camaro looked as new as the day it had come off the assembly line, and I was slightly easier on cars than I was on T-shirts. Accidental scratches in the paint disappeared moments after they happened. Someone had dented my door with theirs in a parking lot somewhere, and later that day the dent was just gone.

So Tabitha would do that, just on a larger scale.

There was a little discussion in figuring out if her Earth magic would hold, if the vehicles would last once they crossed into the Dead Zone, but much like the Five-Fold blades, I was hoping that anything created outside Mexico City would retain its energy as it crossed over.

Nick's trip inside the zone had proved it to me. His blade looked fine after he had come back. The energy there still potently bright in the center of the Five-Fold blade.

I thought the blades, the cars with Tabitha's Earth magic, they all would function like batteries. Like that battery powering the hazard lights of that car I had seen by the wall of cars north of Cuernavaca.

They would be magical batteries. Holding supernatural powers. Powers we couldn't call, once we crossed the Dead Zone line, but powers I hoped we could access, once in.

It was a crazy shot in the dark, but I had tried worse with less. If we could make a vehicle, or a blade, and if we could store supernatural powers in them, like a battery, and they retained that power once we crossed the zone's barrier...

Well then, we'd have a chance.

It was a lot of *ifs*.

I was on the right track with the Five-Fold blades. I could feel it. Power could exist in the Dead Zone, because various powers *did*, and it wasn't the power itself but the actual calling of the power was what was preventing my sword from appearing. After all, my powers worked before and after leaving the Dead Zone. They just didn't work inside. Was that because the powers disappeared, or just because the Dead Zone was preventing me from accessing it? I thought the latter, that the Dead Zone was a "no angels allowed" type of place.

I hadn't been able to test that theory last night. The thing between Jen and I had interrupted that. Another thing we needed to figure out. But at least I would find out about the sword. I would test that theory as soon as I got down to Cuernavaca.

I had hope.

Gertrude was coming with Tabitha. She said that with an eye towards me. I nodded in return. A promise was a promise.

Jen and Sarah were staying here, with Johnny and Nick. Zoe was going to stay here too. There seemed to be an argument there of sorts, between Tabitha and Zoe, that was carried out in mostly looks and facial expressions, and ended with Zoe saying she was staying.

Gabrielle, maybe surprisingly, maybe not, was coming with me. Johnny didn't look up as she volunteered. She thought she could best help Alejandro with the clan by representing the Dumonts. That name could pull in more help.

I wasn't going to turn down another fighter.

We needed as many as we could get. The convoy had to be big. We would take in what we had, but right now, what we had likely wouldn't be enough.

Nick would be doing Nick things. Scoping out the best way in. A path to walk as close to the center of the stadium as he could.

Sarah was staying with him. Johnny as well. It made sense, Johnny could go into the Dead Zone, and while he couldn't travel like Nick, he thought he could put together an operating base inside the zone, somewhere safe that Nick could shadow walk from. Watch his back.

Jen, with a look at me and a look at Sarah, was staying.

I understood. Sarah needed her. And Jen needed to be needed, or rather, there was something inside her she needed to work on.

Something she couldn't figure out inside herself. Which I under-stood as well.

I wanted to be there for her. I wanted her to be able to tell me. But I also understood some things took time. Some things you didn't know until they hit you in the face. And until that moment, all you could do was worry about what you weren't understanding. Weren't seeing.

It wasn't easy to leave her like that. To leave us like that. Espe-cially after the Dead Zone thing. But I had to be in Cuernavaca. I was the largest part of that plan. Nick had to be here. He *was* the plan. And Sarah was staying with Nick. And Sarah needed some-one, while he was in the zone. So I understood Jen needing to stay, though my hands might have tightened into brief fists, thinking about her being apart, when she seemed to need something. Need me.

"We starting now?" Johnny asked. As if he had missed the urgency.

"As soon as we're done here."

"Okay," he said. Not looking up so much as sipping his bottle of beer.

So that was the plan. We all started heading out. It was late enough we'd have to stop for sunrise. Or have Gabrielle ride in the vampire truck. Other than being close to midnight, it was as good a time to begin as any other.

We packed. I would go to Cuernavaca and get everything started. Test out the Five-Fold blade. Put together the attack force. Then, we'd do the Mad Max thing. Only we would be heading the convoy in for battle, into a city full of crazy demons, and not fleeing from them.

Things blurred together. The packing. The little conversations among the packing. Did you remember this? Do you need that? A moment where I looked at Jen and she looked at me and we both knew that we needed to talk, but also understanding that talk could come later.

I was rushing and I knew it, but that picture had me worried. We weren't ready, and I knew we weren't ready, but that much ethereal energy in one place couldn't be good. It could only be bad.

And, if I was being honest, there was no way to really be ready. We had a decent plan. We'd give it a shot.

The whirlwind stopped. I found myself leaning back against the trunk of the blue Camaro, the car running, a soft rumble of the vehicle running through me. Jen was next to me, leaning into me a bit, her head tucked on my shoulder. The night was dark around us, bringing a quiet of shadows, the muffled silence of the horizon closing in around us, through which we heard tiny bits of goodbyes and the low rumbling of the car.

"I'm a little nervous," I said.

Jen smiled, a playful thing. "Really? You?"

"Eh," I said. "Yeah."

Maybe it was just nerves. The pictures I had seen of Sabnock. The photo of the stadium. The feeling of being monitored from the Dead Zone when I was in Cuernavaca.

Maybe it was just the upcoming battle. The one I would lead into the Dead Zone. My body could have been looking at that and starting its usual ramp up. Anticipating the fight. Worrying about who might get hurt, who might not make it back.

"Stay safe," she said. Giving me a quick kiss.

"Yes ma'am."

She punched me. Just a little thing. "I'm serious."

"Me too," I said. I was worried, like she was. The bond was changing us. Or maybe we had been changing it. In how we communicated, in how we felt each other, not just with our emotions, but really feel, like in bed, like when I had come back from Cuernavaca.

And now this, the Dead Zone thing. The hokey pokey thing. One Jen in, one Grimm out.

Things were changing, and we lacked the time to really understand it.

I could only hope that lack of time wouldn't come back to bite us.

I knew Jen felt the same way as I did. We both could feel each other, emotions and thoughts, backgrounds of thoughts, that running stream of consciousness we all have in our minds, both Jen and I could sense those currents in each other. We could feel those thoughts form, this close together.

So we both were worried. We both knew we both were worried. And we both could almost laugh as we tracked that in each other. The concern, the frantic thoughts, running subsurface in us both.

And I was used to leaning on Jen. She was my foundation. Her being worried, it was like having a favorite chair with a leg about to break. You could sit on it, and feel the leg underneath, giving way.

I brushed that thought away. Knowing Jen could sense it. Knowing if I gave her time, she would really sense why, and I did not want her to have that from me. I wanted to be her rock if I could. The subsurface worry running under us both was enough to keep Big Pharm in business, all on our own.

She was mostly herself, but I could feel something missing. The same something she knew was missing, but also at the same time not knowing what the missing thing was. Concern lay waiting in the back of her eyes, always there, and out a little more now with us saying goodbye.

There was a lack of confidence in her, the knowledge of Jen knowing she was Jen. I tried on a comforting smile. "You going to be okay?"

The concern disappeared from her eyes, mostly. They became

glittering remnants of old Jen, twin twinkles of mischief. "You think we can't survive a couple of days without you?"

My grin widened. "Well, now that you mention it…"

That earned me a harder punch. And a deeper kiss. It was worth it.

We held each other for a bit, leaning against the back of the Camaro. Feeling the car shake a bit underneath us. Nick came by, wished me luck. Funny to me, but Nick had become a rock. The guy who took care of things. A guy who was always just there. Backing me up. Some of the worry I had was about him going in alone, and what might happen if things went south. It would just be Nick in the Dead Zone, alone, facing the demon and his entire army.

Nick didn't smile a lot. Sometimes he grinned. Here, a corner of his lips curled up, just a bit. "I know what you're doing."

"Yeah?" Sometimes I didn't. But we both knew what Nick was talking about.

He shrugged. "It'll be interesting to see which of us gets him."

And that was that. I had been worried that Nick would feel like I didn't trust him, that I didn't think he could complete the task. Kill Sabnock. Apparently, that was only a worry I carried. Nick was going to be there. Joke about it a bit. Make it a competition of sorts.

"You get a gift yet?"

Out of the sides of my eyes I caught Jen looking at me. Watching carefully. "We aren't getting each other anything."

His smile spread a little. I didn't miss his glance over to Jen. Her now slightly wider eyes. Her heart beating just a little faster through the bond.

Nick's head cocked a little. His smile was something like one I would use. The grin of a man who knew something others might not. "You sure?"

It was funny, me not wanting to break a tradition. Even if Jen had gotten me something. For me our Christmas was enough. Or had been. Snow outside, and a fire inside. Christmas music and mugs of hot chocolate. A colored, blinking tree with a slanted star on top. The two of us, with her family. Later on, Nick, and then Danny.

I laughed, which surprised them both. "Of anything at all? Hell, no. I'm just taking this one crazy demon at a time." The two of us bumped fists. "Hold the fort down, brother."

He winked.

I wished everyone could feel like Nick. Have his confidence. He walked over to Sarah, who stood apart from the group, arms wrapped around her shoulders, as if the night was cold. Even though, like all the nights here, it was too warm for the night, too hot for December.

Johnny was separate from us, too. Maybe in ways more than the physical. Gabrielle stood in front of him. They were talking, well, she was talking, in tiny, muted tones. Jen and I both watched, my arms around her back, her still leaning into me, so we both watched Johnny let Gabrielle's hand go, maybe a little more easily than he should.

The vampire stopped, her fingertips on edges of his, and Johnny looked aside, looked past Gabrielle, not really looking back at her. His face was blank. Cold.

Gabrielle let Johnny go and left. Walked past me and Jen, around to the other side of the Camaro and got into the passenger seat. Slamming the door.

I gave Jen a last, quick kiss, a press of my lips on her forehead. Then walked over to Johnny. His eyes narrowed a bit as I walked up.

"You know," I said. "I told you once to stop being an ass."

That had been back in Denver. Right after we had brought him back to life, and he had discovered Gabrielle had turned him.

Johnny had been angry and furious, instead of thankful he was alive.

His eyes remained narrowed. He took a long moment to answer, and when he did, his voice was dark and thick, dark with emotion, thick with alcohol. "You know, I remember something happening to you once. Something you couldn't handle. I remember you running away, running for ten years."

Johnny didn't just sound dark, darker than anything I had ever heard from the guy who was the comedian in our group, but he also sounded frustrated, as if a hunger gnawed at him, a hunger he couldn't fill. Each word was a bite of all of that. "So maybe give me more than a month."

He was talking about Danny. And even now, after the past few months and what we had done for each other, those words hurt. I *had* run away, after finding out I could see ghosts. After Raphael had found out he could control me with the geas. After he had tried to control me, and had killed Danny, doing so.

That had been the beginning of all of this. It had taken years for me to come to terms with it. And, honestly, I never would have been able to, had I not come back to my friends. Had they not been there for me. I had only gotten to where I was today, the person I was today, because of my friends.

But in some ways, I still struggled with it. With Danny's death. With me running. But the struggle now was in finding a way to get better. To be a better person. To be there when my friends needed me.

A worry spread through me, an unrecognized fear. Had I been too focused on Sabnock and the Dead Zone? Ending the demons? Because my friends were suffering. Johnny. Sarah. And Jen. All of them were struggling with their own worries, trying to overcome them on their own.

And losing.

Johnny's gaze softened a bit. "Sorry man, it's just..." He shrugged, not able to explain it, the frustration tearing up his eyes.

I put my hand on his shoulder. It felt thin. "I wouldn't follow my example in anything," I said. "Ten years was ten too many."

His eyes shimmered wetly. The whites of them were streaked with red lines. He was drunk. I had seen the signs, and I had ignored them. I could use everything I was doing as an excuse, and that's exactly what it would be. Shame washed over me, hot. My skin flushed with it.

"You ever see a vampire that was really thirsty?" he asked. "Really hungry?"

I nodded. I had. I had seen feral vampires munching on dead bodies, sucking what fluids they could from them. Anything for them would be food. I had seen vampires, in the middle of a fight, with limbs torn from them, trying to bite a human to try to heal themselves. No matter the wound.

In those times, vampires lost all sense of themselves. Or what had made them. They might no longer remember they were human. There was only the hunger.

"I don't want to end up like that," he said. Forming each word slow. "What if that happens to me. What if that happens, and only Nick is around? Or Sarah. Or Jen."

They weren't questions to him. But statements. It had already happened in his mind. He had already drained us all of our blood to keep himself going. He had drank and drank to keep the hunger from swallowing him whole.

He was fighting that image. As much as he had ever fought anything. And that fight was killing him. And killing Gabrielle.

The Camaro's horn blared. One long blare. Even though the car faced away from us. I saw Gabrielle in the passenger seat, not looking back at us.

We *were* burning nightlight. It was a long drive. We needed to make sure we got to Cuernavaca before sunrise.

I squeezed Johnny's shoulder. Carefully. "Man, we'll figure it out."

His eyes watered more. A tear broke loose, and Johnny wiped it away with the back of his hand. The same hand that held a half-empty beer. His voice, a whisper, still broke. "How, Grimm? How?"

"Hey." I shook his shoulder. Carefully. It did feel thin. I wonder when the last time was that he ate something, and got real nourishment from that food.

I focused on his face, his eyes. "We will. We've done it before. Grafton. New Orleans. Denver. Each time, we've figured it out. There's something that will fix this."

He nodded. But stood there, still a little lost. Eyes empty.

Broken.

Not believing.

But staying as long as he could. Hanging on as long as he could. For his friends.

I slammed the Camaro's door myself, getting in. Pulled the car out faster than I should. Gabrielle didn't look at me. I didn't look at her.

My friends hung in the rearview mirror. Jen and Nick and Sarah and Johnny. They stood loosely together, Jen giving a little wave. Nick standing solid. Sarah's arm around Nick. Johnny, standing where I had left him, not even looking our way.

It was a hell of a group. The best of friends. And maybe a group that was falling apart. Sarah's worry that her power was evil. Her lack of control. Her fear of what she may let loose. And that she may be evil because of it, and because of her past and her power now, that she might not be worthy of Nick.

Nick wanted his shot, he wanted to help our group of friends, and he would do what he could. Maybe he would do too much, wanting to be there for us. He had complete trust in me, confidence in himself, and wasn't worried about things like staying alive. He would go in, guns blazing, counting on himself to come back out.

Johnny, still standing there. As if lost. I couldn't tell if he was watching the Camaro drive away or staring at some unknown future. One in which he had become what he feared. One in which he was draining his friends of their blood, sucking blood from any human he found, like we had both seen in the club back in Grafton, because he had given into a hunger he couldn't control.

And Jen. Struggling with her own issue. Something she couldn't identify, something missing that used to be a part of her, but now that something missing was chained around her leg. It was dragging her down into the depths of her own despair, because she didn't know what that missing something was. All she could do was fight that feeling with every fiber of her being, but even fighting it, she thought she was losing.

You could only swing blindly for so long.

My mother had told me that we all were becoming more. That the good side was growing, swelling, into a tidal wave that would rise up against the evils that had taken over this world. What she hadn't said was that there would be growing pains, and that the pains might be too much to bear.

I balled my fist. Hit the steering wheel. Not hard, but not soft. I wondered if I was doing the right thing. If we were doing the right thing. If I had killed Azazel right after Red Rock, if we had gone to Charleston and killed him in that coffee shop, would we all be like this now? Or would we have found the time to help one another, to heal our wounds?

The thing about wounds, though, is that they do heal. Sometimes it takes longer, but a lot of the times the healing also makes us stronger. Makes us more.

I had to hope this was the case here. Because I felt like we were in it now. If we weren't fully committed to this, we were close. No one was backing down. We all kept staring into the abyss, no matter the wounds we carried. No matter the fear that held us, hovering over the edge.

And if those wounds killed us? Changed us? Instead of making us more, made us somehow less?

Well then, killing Sabnock, nullifying the Dead Zone, hunting down all of the other demons and killing Azazel? None of that would really have been worth it.

Evil would already have won. The abyss would have gazed back.

CHAPTER THIRTY-THREE

The drive started out quiet. I was working through my thoughts, and Gabrielle through hers. The Camaro rolled along, the engine at a constant thrum, the tires rolling perfectly along the highway, the headlights catching the painted lines of the highway. The cabin silent, no music playing, not that I had ever looked to see if a station existed. I took a breath, with the windows up I caught a whiff of the new car scent, the smell that somehow people had packaged into little scent jars and sprays, keeping a car smelling new long after it had been sold.

Though this car was new. I was nearing ten thousand miles. Whoever had left it in the street hadn't wanted to stay around. I wondered for the thousandth time why they hadn't taken the car when they had fled.

So it was that way for a bit. The headlights picking out the dark road, rolling out of the darker night. The stars hanging in the night-time sky. The moon, not hiding behind the clouds tonight, to the east. The headlights of Tabitha's sedan behind us, and Alejandro's car behind her, as well as his team. The quiet of the cabin, the thrumming of the engine, the occasional whipping of the wind against the front windshield, big bursts of air that beat against us.

"I was not supposed to be like this," Gabrielle said.

I glanced over. She was looking straight ahead. Her face pale, a scattering of freckles on her skin. One hand pressed against the door, right underneath the window, as if holding her there.

She wanted me to ask, though I knew part of the story. Johnny had told me, back in Grafton. "Like this?"

She smiled; it was a nasty thing. Acknowledging the obvious. And she explained anyway. "The way the clans work, the larger ones, they have bloodlines. Human bloodlines, families that live alongside their vampire brothers and sisters. So that the Dumonts are a real bloodline, they go back thousands of years. Mother births daughter. Father sires son."

"Johnny told me something about that," I said. Gabrielle was supposed to be one of the daughters, raised to be human. She had older brothers, the eldest of which, when he got to a certain age, would have succeeded Victor Dumont as the head of the clan.

Then her brothers had been killed. All of them. I had found out later that had been my mother, doing the bidding of Dominic Antonado. A war had begun between the Dumonts and the Antonados, after the Dumonts had exiled Dominic to the Americas, hundreds of years ago.

"I knew about the clan," Gabrielle said. "I was taught. Instructed. But I had many brothers. And, although I knew, I also understood I would never be called to the clan. I would never be raised. I would be what you call a thrall," her mouth twisted on the word, "and serve my family that way.

"I would be assigned a husband. I was young. I still dreamed of love. I had hope. My dreams as a little girl, had been to be in love.

Have a family. Have children, and provide that service to the family. It was my *path*."

Her voice hardened. "I never wanted to be a vampire."

I don't know if I was surprised or not. Watching the movies, reading the books, there was an attractiveness to it. After all, it was power. Power and immortality. Those things called to some.

Her voice, as hard as it was, broke. "All I wanted was a child."

I knew she had one. That she had been forced to conceive before being turned. Because she was the last of the Dumonts, the last of the progeny of the original Dumont, after all her brothers were killed.

Gabrielle had been raised to continue the bloodline of the Dumonts. She was part of the family, a direct descendant of the first Dumont. She was going to be part of the family that kept the Dumont bloodline going.

Her brothers had been killed. All of them. So the girl that wanted a family became a young woman force to have a child. Her family had taken the babe from her and hidden the child instead. Victor Dumont had. Keeping his bloodline safe, and alive.

Then they had turned her.

I glanced over again. Then I focused on the road. I didn't know vampires could cry.

I wondered about that little girl who had dreamed of love, a family, children. Wondered about who had forced themselves on her, so that she could conceive. I was betting love didn't have any part of it.

Her voice shook. Sobbed. Her sentence tough to come out. "For a hundred years, I served. I grew. I became what my father wanted. And—finally—in Grafton, I found something. Something I had dreamed about as a kid. I found *him*, and now he, now he, he—"

She couldn't get the words out. Just shook, silently, in the seat next to me. Her hand still pressed against the door. Her other hand in her lap. Gabrielle didn't wrap herself up, didn't hold herself in. She sat there, looking straight ahead, arms held still, as if she didn't know how to cry.

It went on like that for a while. I didn't know what to say. I didn't know what to do. I wasn't really good at the comforting thing. After a while, as the thrumming of the engine went on, her sobs lessened. Became sniffs. And occasional wipe of the nose.

Until Gabrielle was herself again. Still looking straight ahead. As if, by looking ahead, she would not think of what she had left behind.

I had to say something. So I said what everyone might say. The words that you try to say just to say them, that don't really mean anything. "He'll come around."

Her snort told me what she thought about that.

"He loved that part of me," she said. "Before. He loved providing for me."

I wondered if that was their word. I had never heard it before. By providing, I knew she didn't mean money. Or a place to stay.

"He loved that part of us." Another sniff. "And now, he can't stand it. Can't stand me."

It wasn't that black and white. Johnny had gotten a little past that, from what he had told me. I hoped it meant that he had accepted that he had been bitten, that he might have no choice but to become a vampire, but that he was afraid of what that might mean.

Not that black and white. More of a swirl of grays.

"I don't think that's it."

"What else could it be?"

"Have you," I tried to find the word, "has he *provided* for you since?"

She shook her head. "He's in the middle of the turn."

"But he's still human, right?" I said. At least, that's what the books said. Until the human took their first bite of a person, the first suckle of human blood—I almost shivered thinking those words—the person who was bit remained human.

Her mouth frowned. She looked as if I had just said something wrong. I realized I might have. She believed humans and vampires could coexist. She was living proof they could, and that vampires weren't the bloodsuckers the stories made them out to be.

I shrugged. I didn't mean the word like it had come out. But I couldn't take it back.

Her frown became something more thoughtful. "You are right."

So he was still human. He hadn't turned. And Johnny didn't want to turn because in his mind, he could become something that might turn on his friends in a moment of weakness. Maybe, also, a part of him had never wanted to turn, because that part of his relationship with Gabrielle would be over.

He had never wanted to be a vampire, but he had loved being a thrall to Gabrielle. I know that wasn't the word they used, but I thought there might still be hope Johnny could still be the same thing he had been with Gabrielle before. The provider. At least, it sounded like it was possible. If he could find a way to not turn.

Johnny drinking. Johnny forcing food down. Johnny, bottle in his hand, leaning back against the wall of the planning room, eyes looking out the windows, staring at everything and nothing at all.

He feared what he might become. He feared what he might do if he turned. Who he might do it to. And maybe, he feared most of all that he would lose that part of him that he enjoyed giving to Gabrielle.

He had been violently introduced into a world Gabrielle had been raised among. Before he was ready. Before he had the same understanding Gabrielle had, the same... maybe a better word was control. The belief that whoever you were, even a vampire, you could be good in this world. Do good.

It was an understanding I had only recently come to myself. Before Gabrielle, I had killed any vampire I had met. It wasn't something I set out to do, but the ones I met, well, it was a them-or-me situation. So I could understand Johnny, standing on the edge of that realization, not wanting to take the next step. Not knowing if he could have that control, not knowing if he could continue to do good.

"He wastes away."

"I know," I said. The only thing I could say is what I believed. And I realized I really did believe it. Each of us in our group had our struggles, but each of us were also becoming more. "We'll figure it out."

Her head turned then, and she looked at me. Face pale in the dark of the car, the wetness on her cheeks reflecting the little light coming from the Camaro's console, the whites and blues and reds of the head unit, the ventilation controls.

There was a way through this. I had to believe it. Believe that all of this should mean something. We had been through too much, for too long, from a little town like Grafton to taking on a demon in Mexico City. We couldn't fall apart now. There would be a way.

If not, I would make one. Gabrielle was one of us. Johnny too. Wolverines.

I tried to smile. Or at least grin. "I told him the same thing."

Something in my expression must have registered with her because Gabrielle nodded, as if to herself. Facing front again. Composed, in her normal way. As if none of our conversation had happened.

The drive continued in much the same way as it started. Quiet in the cabin. The Camaro rolling along the road. The thrum of the engine. The headlights picking out things far ahead in the night.

The silence seemed more comfortable now. At least, less pained. The moon seemed brighter, off to my right. Larger, in the night. We would have to find a place to stop soon, just for sunrise, but otherwise we were making good time. The wind no longer beat against the windshield but flowed around us, and for a while the ride was smooth enough I could believe we were flying.

CHAPTER THIRTY-FOUR

Alejandro's place was a minor fortress, and it sat right in the center of Cuernavaca. A tall complex, more than an apartment building, less than a rich condo. The building was a big U-shape, with the front doors in the center, six stories high. A brick wall surrounded the land around it, red brick, freshly built, separating the complex from the buildings around it. An evenly paved road took us in a semi-circle to the front door. I imagined, back in the day, before the Dead Zone, there would likely be a concierge there, offering to get your bags, activities for the day, what time dinner would be.

Nice.

I let Gabrielle out at the front. The moon had made its journey west, the night sky lay quiet above, though the horizon to the east had already lightened, a burning sliver of orange pushing away the somber black. Sunrise would be soon; I was a little tired, and still a little hungover from the night before, but I wanted to test the Five-Fold blade out as soon as I could.

They were a large part of the plan.

Gabrielle headed up the steps. We hadn't really talked much after what we had talked about. There had been the drive, the town of the ambush, a quick stop at a gas station where we checked on Tabitha and Gertrude, Alejandro and Millie, and their team.

Speaking of, the rest of them got out. All heading to the building. Gertrude came over to the driver's side of the Camaro. I pushed the button and let the window wind its way down. I told her my plan at her question.

"Need company? Or backup?"

I told her I had it. I was going to test the blade out and see if I could access my powers there. I'd be right back.

Gertrude shrugged and followed Tabitha up into the complex.

So I drove back around the semi-circle. Gave a quick wave to Alejandro. Headed back out and north along the streets, The blocks of the city rose around me. Empty. Windows gazing back like empty eyes. It was weird. Occasionally I saw people, and I wasn't sure if it was so quiet because it was early in the morning, or if it was so quiet because everyone was gone.

The city felt like people had left in a hurry. Sometimes I had to slow down and pick my way along the street. Avoiding all the dead cars and trucks parked along the road, some still stopped at stop-lights or stop signs. A large package truck, brown, was parked in mid-turn. All of the vehicles abandoned, left like the Camaro, some with their doors open, some, I was sure, with their gas tanks dry, having idled their way to empty.

I wondered, if people were here, why all the cars were still parked that way. Could it be that the city was really empty? Or only that there weren't enough people left to move the cars, to straighten out the mess left by a population that had fled? And had they fled because of La Familia Diablo, Sabnock, or had it been something else entirely?

A question for Alejandro, certainly.

Anyway, north. Picking my way along. The Camaro responded quicker than my older one; a slight press on the gas pedal sometimes had me shoot forward. I didn't like it. Liked the feel of power I felt in the pedal of my older car. But that was newer technology for you, fuel injection instead of carburetors, something like that. Quicker responses. Maybe even more power. But harder to control. Harder to feel.

I touched the key. Tried to feel Jen. Send her something, the *I'm okay* signal. I thought I felt an answer, but it was faint, and if it was an answer I couldn't tell what it might be.

I wasn't happy with how I had left my friends. It seemed like the closer we got to our goal here, to nullifying the Dead Zone and killing Sabnock, the worse off we got. As if everything in the world fought us.

There was a saying. Most people said it in jest. Whatever doesn't kill you makes you stronger. I felt like what was happening was that, but I was worried that some of us would get stronger, and some of us, well...

I didn't want that to happen. But I didn't know how to stop it. I didn't know how to help Johnny. I could think that what Sarah and I were going through was the same, but when she let go, let her power really go, she was draining people of their lives. And Jen, how could I help her, when she didn't really know what it was that was bothering her?

The sliver of orange on the horizon became an orb. The sky lightened from the black of night to the early gray-blue of dawn. Here and there was a cloud, solitary puffs in the sky, so far away from each other that I wondered if they were searching for each other.

Soon I was back at the street I had been when I had met Michael. The archangel. I paused and looked at the patio. It wasn't as white. The coffee shop looked closed. I could see the expresso machine through the window, but no one inside. The white dogwood was empty, no longer white, the green bushes along the wall a dry brown, and no flowers bloomed anywhere. No smell of poppies or poinsettias, no fresh bitter scent of expresso.

I wasn't surprised.

I turned off the Camaro. It shut down like it was designed to, no extra lops of the engine, no sputtering. Then I got out, grabbing the Five-Fold blade from behind my seat.

Ahead of me, a mile away, was that wall of cars. The wall of destroyed vehicles, stacked three or four high. The wall broken almost in half with the eighteen-wheeler jackknifed through the center. The cab of the truck facing Cuernavaca, as if someone had been driving out of the Dead Zone.

I thought about what Nick and Johnny had said, and wondered if Sabnock was bringing something out of the Dead Zone. And if someone, long ago, maybe when the Dead Zone had first come around, had been trying to stop those trucks.

The car with the blinking hazard lights was still there. Closer up I thought it was a Tesla. One of those electronic vehicles. All battery and no sound. No engine. Maybe the battery had finally kicked the can, and the car was drained. At least, the lights no longer blinked. The on and off had become just off. No deep current warning from the buoy. No lighthouse, warning sailors of a shoal ahead.

I searched for it, but couldn't find the feeling. The one where I thought someone had been watching me. I relaxed a bit, thinking I had made it up. That it had just been nerves.

The conversation in the planning session yesterday had me thinking differently about the wall of vehicles and the eighteen-wheeler. Maybe the truck hadn't been fleeing. Maybe someone here had seen what was happening, with the knights, the army Sabnock was creating, and the wall of cars had been their way of stopping it.

I didn't think I could know, now.

But I was here, so might as well check. I was a little curious. Nothing ever bad happened from that, right? And we were looking for what those trucks were carrying. I thought it would be nice to kill two birds with one stone.

I took my first step into the Dead Zone. The feel and smell of hot coals with gingersnaps came again, like before. There might have been a slight tingling through my body, over my skin. There certainly were a few goosebumps on my arms. Those might be the only signs I would get that here, my powers were lost to me.

I tried summoning my sword.

Nothing.

I looked over my ethereal radar.

Blank.

I blinked, pulling up my ethereal vision. Still walking down the road. Heading deeper into the Dead Zone.

The entire landscape around me looked tinged with red. Like a bad filter on a photo. Everything took on that dusky feel. Little dust trails swirled in the wind, crimson motes circling in the breeze. Blue cars became purple, white trucks became pinkish red, green became an ugly brown. The brown dirt darkened into something mottled, ugly, as if the skin of the Earth was cancerous.

I tested the blade with a little pull. Ethereal energy swelled into me from the blade, much like it did when I pulled from a ghost. This felt cleaner though. There was no living of memories, just a faint murmuring of them in the background. Like a muttering of angry voices, far, far, away.

Maybe it felt cleaner because I had already lived the memories, in creating the blade. Or maybe because there was no spirit in the symbol for me to live. Just energy held there in the blade.

I liked it. And well, I had paid for it. I had lived the lives of spirits to power this. It was nice, almost a relief, to be able to access my power without having to go through some of the memories I had, as I had in the past. I hadn't known what this could feel like, and now that I had it, I didn't want to access my power any other way.

Faint footsteps lay scattered in front of me, tiny prints left, echoes of ethereal energy from humans. At least, likely human. They were faint enough that I thought they had been left for at least a week, maybe more. Shimmering outlines of shoes and boots. Enough prints for a few people, a tiny crowd, facing the opposite way.

Leaving. Or running.

I kept walking. I felt a buzzing on my chest. The keydrop. It hummed, and I almost felt like Jen was telling me something. Her voice stronger. Maybe she was responding to me reaching out earlier. I thought I was closer, being a bit further north, but was still surprised I could feel anything from the bond. It could be another benefit of the Five-Fold blade, and the ethereal energy stored there.

I got to the wall of cars. The crushed cars, three or four high. The cab of the tractor trailer had pushed through the middle a little before the truck had jackknifed, so the wall swelled out towards me, leaving a broken and flattened car staircase. Of sorts.

I picked my way over it, looking for bodies in any of the vehicles and finding none. I did recognize the spiderwebbing of cracks in the windows, the dents and punched finger-like holes that indicated gunfire in the side panels of the cars. Closer up I saw the same along the side of the truck, bullet holes scattered all the way down the side, dozens of dark empty holes glimmering a purple-crimson, tiny hints of what the container might once have held.

The silver side of the eighteen-wheeler, the long run of the container, reflected a shimmering angry orb, a purplish-red sky, as I walked along it. I wanted to blink my ethereal vision off, not seeing anything recent, and if I was being honest, the overload of the crimson filter on my sight was just too much. But I kept my sight up, tapping the side of the trailer with the hilt of the knife as I walked along, hearing an empty *thunk-thunk* echo from inside.

This all spoke of something long past.

Still, I got to the back of the jackknifed rig. The end of it stood alone, pointed out to the side of the road, both doors wide open. I stood there, holding the Five-Fold blade in my hand, not ready to look inside, so staring north instead. Towards Mexico City. The road ran north, empty, the tiny buildings in the distance swelling in the distance, growing larger the closer to the city the road got.

A pair of doors sat at the rear of the truck, both open. Thick plastic curtains hung behind them, yellowed with age. I parted them to take a peek inside the container. It was one of those refrigerated trucks. With a big unit up in the front of the container, hanging from the top. Had all the trucks we'd seen been refrigerated, all the trailers heading in and out? I hadn't paid enough attention, but I thought the answer was yes.

There was a little light. Shots of light came in from the bullet holes in the sides of the container. Beams crisscrossing the shadows, but the sunlight wasn't strong enough to break through the darkness of the container. Shots of light in a world of black.

Whatever lay inside was hidden from the sun. Mired in blackness. There was a musty scent in the air, musty and sick, like you might take a breath of near a crypt. I didn't like it; I flicked on my ethereal sight, and when I did crimson flared up through the unit. Lines of it, twisting in my sight, thick and dark and mired in the darkness, the crimson trails darkening until each line became a hard purple.

The lines in the air were like the swirls you see in cartoons, the swirls people drew to represent a hard-blowing wind, except that these lines were real in the air. They hung through the container. Each line held power, almost vibrated with it, as if someone had captured a photo of a windy day. As if each gust held a malevolent power and was ready to blow.

All the gusts needed was someone to give the word.

The crimson-purple lines thickened up at the front of the container where something dark lay, hidden in shadows of black, covered by the darkness and the lines like a large blanket. The shadows swelling with a certain shape, the shape of someone sleeping, the crimson-purple lines swirling over it.

It was a body.

I didn't want to, all the movies I had ever watched told me not to, but I climbed in. The Five-Fold knife tight in my hand. Tapped into the blade and ready to access its power. Curiosity had me tight in its grasp. I worked my way down the container, towards the front. My feet stirred up little dark flakes of whatever had been in here before, my shoes kicked aside thin shadowy casings, flimsy black hulls. The things crunched as I walked through them, whatever they had been a part of.

I got to the front. The body was large. Larger than human. Big. Bigger than any human I had seen. This was like a professional wrestler's body. Big and tall and thick, laying there. Inert.

And covered in scales.

It was a kind of golem. One of the knights. From the photos. I had thought the armor looked odd, funny; rock tinged in a green ichor. Instead, the knights were covered in thick plates of scales. Shaped like armor like knights might wear thousands of years ago.

The granite-like scales covered the body's chest and back, like armor. Thick over the arms and legs and chest. The only thing I had seen in the photos that wasn't grown was the helmet on the creature. The helmet was compact, almost square, and pressed down hard over the skull, as if it was meant to never come off. It actually looked like metal. Maybe iron. It wasn't shiny, but a darker metal. Not aged, or rusty, but splotchy with that gangrene color.

I grinned. There was a plume of something poking up from the back of the helmet, like the feathers of knights of old. It wasn't a feather, though, it was fuzzy and seemed... decorative. Which didn't fit the creature, or anything else I saw.

The crimson and purple lines ran thick over the body. But inside the body's center was the ethereal blue-white light I recognized from ghosts. The light there was blue and white, carrying a thick center of red. Not red like the crimson lines around me, but more of a stoplight red. The kind of red that warned me away from the very bad spirits on my ethereal radar.

Back in Grafton I had run into wights. Bodies from the grave, human bodies, with animal spirits trapped inside, animating them. Creatures with large hungers, massive strength, and not a lot of control.

This seemed similar, but different. Almost opposite. Some kind of ancient creature, ancient human creature, but with a human spirit trapped inside. Like a rock someone had stuffed a ghost into.

The face itself looked human. Or some kind of weird human-lizard mix. Dark skin, like an alligator's, knobbed in places. But all the right features. A chin, lips. A nose. And eyes, closed eyes, under a thick ridge that looked like a long eyebrow.

The eyes opened. Eyes I recognized. Unfortunately.

I knew this ghost.

Shit.

The body grabbed me before I could swing the blade. The massive hands crunching into each of my arms, right at the tops, the fingers painfully digging into my flesh like ten individual vices. Crushing the bones.

I bit back a scream. Focused on the blade. Pulled ethereal energy and strengthened my bones, my muscles, my skin. Old hat now, something I did almost from memory. Just from the blade instead of a ghost.

We stayed locked there for a moment. The body holding me above it. A silent war of wills. Hector's eyes lit into mine. The mad eyes of a man who, all his life, wanted power over others. Wanted to exert his power over others. Wanted dominion over all for the sheer pleasure of inflicting pain.

He laughed. It wasn't the high-pitched laugh I remembered from his memories. It was a thick laugh of a monster's voice, a cavernous chuckle.

I wriggled in his grip, hanging in the air. Kicking. My feet connected with his legs. It was like kicking concrete.

The body sat up. Straight from the waist. Like someone sitting up from a coffin. I shifted in the air with the motion, my legs still flailing. I thought I might have connected with something between his legs, and I couldn't tell you what that might be, only that Hector gave a grunt and swung me to the side. More of a toss than a swing, actually, like he was throwing something aside.

Only I went much farther. And faster. I burst through the container and tumbled over the wall of cars. More glass broke, more metal crunched, sharp jagged edges of broken cars tore along my clothes and skin as I rolled along the broken vehicles. I held onto the Five-Fold blade like it was a lifeline, healing each tear as metal ripped down my skin, healing bones that broke as I bounced off of cars, pulling and healing and rolling, pulling and healing and rolling.

A final roll. A final bounce. I slid off the last car, over the edge of a silver hatchback with a rugby sticker that said I should Give Blood and Play Rugby.

I gave a snort, slapped the sticker with one hand. Then plopped to the ground.

At the feet of someone else. Something else.

Demon-else.

When it rains it pours.

I was covered in some kind of black shells. Dead husks of insects. Whatever had been in the container with Hector. I tried to brush them off and groaned. Feeling every bruise as if I had been hit with a car.

I pulled from the Five-Fold blade as fast as I could. Healing as fast as I could. I thought I would need it.

Sabnock stood above me. Tall, like his knights, taller even, with plates of gold over his skin. Dark ebony skin. A long face, with almond-shaped eyes. Covered in armor, real armor, the lion's face a massive work of metal over his shoulder.

The long face looked down. His lips curled in a grin. Dark lips on a dark face.

"Well, Fergus Grimm," the voice said. It was everything a demon's voice should be. Rumbling with power. Deep. Sonorous. With an echo, as if Sabnock spoke with more than one voice. "We finally meet."

CHAPTER THIRTY-FIVE

I t was a quick thought, but with the lion pauldron-thing, the tall dark skin, the golden armor, Sabnock reminded me of Anubis. The Egyptian god of death. Or the guardian of the underworld, the protector of the gateway to the dead, the gatherer of souls.

Something struck me. Rattled around my brain, and though it seemed important, in the present moment I wasn't going to focus on whatever it was calling for my attention. Maybe there was an Aztec deity that looked the same, triggering something in the back of my mind, some pictures of the god I had seen somewhere. I certainly recognized the link to Anubis, but Sabnock's armor was in a style I hadn't seen before: pieces of gold linked around his midsection by golden chains, part of that plate covering his dark-skinned chest on the same side as his lion. More gold, a necklace, or collar, holding two metal orbs, twin golden eyes below his throat.

Anubis—or some other god of death, some guardian of gateways, or taker of souls—the association was closer than I wanted it to be. Especially with the dry heat of the Dead Zone, with the mottled, cancerous dirt around the two of us, and an empty blue sky above, bereft of but a few clouds, the scene felt like out of a movie, like *Death on the Nile*.

All I needed was a few pyramids in the background and a few jackals, a tall golden staff with some kind of gold medal on the top of it, and Sabnock would look exactly like the pictures of the hiero-glyphs I'd seen. Especially with his long face. Cheekbones sharply protruding, almost skull-like, it looked like the face of a jackal.

Not that I'd say that aloud, right now.

I mean, even I have some sense, sometimes.

Sabnock stood there. Massive. Smiling. Blocking out some of the sun. I pushed myself away, scrambling back, until my back hit the wall of cars.

They… were just a few feet away.

Not a lot of room to go. But I had a trump card. I swapped the Five-Fold blade to my other hand and went to summon the sword in my usual one. With a bit of luck, I could send Sabnock back to his own personal valley of the dead. Or associated Aztec mythological realm.

My hand remained empty.

So I summoned the sword. Again. Pulling energy from the Five-Fold blade. Feeling the usual rush of power, of energy, the beating heart and the quickening along my nerves. Feeling the ethereal energy work in its usual way.

And yet, the sword didn't appear.

That wasn't great. A bit of fear rolled up my spine, though I tried to not let it show on my face. I mean, I had fought Azazel for a decade without a demon-killing sword.

Still, I was pretty sure my face paled a bit. Although Sabnock didn't seem to see it. Or notice. He remained where he had been, where I had landed after Hector's toss.

"I wanted to see you for myself," the demon said. His large, elongated head tilted to the side. Man it was long. He had taken a step closer, keeping an intimate distance between us. "There have been few humans that can kill one of us."

He seemed to talk slow, although he was so big, maybe it took some time for his mouth to form the words. There was definitely an echo in his voice, as if a hundred other speakers spoke the same words as Sabnock, in the same deep voice. "And you have killed two."

I swallowed. Put on a show. It was my fallback option, something I had honed over the years, running from Azazel. There was nothing like a good bluff. "Why don't we make it three?"

The snort was less human, more like something that came from a horse. Hot breath, something wet spat over me. I wiped my face with the sleeve of my shirt. It came away a little sticky. I kept wiping until I could open my eyes.

Other than the snort, the face so far above me hadn't moved. The demon hadn't moved. His eyes, almost white, with the tiniest center of black, bore down on me. Cataloging me, filing me away like materials for one of his buildings.

Sabnock held one hand up, extending only his index finger.

"Kimaris was always a fool," he said. "A born fighter, though, so we can say you were lucky with him. I would bet that he overestimated himself. He likely had you surrounded, with his *klons,* and thought he could take you out man to man."

Had Sabnock said clones? I thought he had. The word sounded similar, but also different. As if it had been another language. The demon smiled. The voice, if it could be, was deeper. The rumble greater. As if he was musing aloud. "Or man to demon."

Then a second finger came up. "Buné was never a fighter. And he was always a means to an end. An end he was unaware of, perhaps, but an end nonetheless. Whether it was by you or someone else Azazel manipulated, he had always been marked for death. For a sacrifice."

There was no need for Sabnock to say it. We both knew what he meant. *The* sacrifice. The one that had allowed Azazel to create the Dead Zones.

The lips spread wider over the demon's teeth. He was dark all over, even his lips were black, and that darkness made his teeth stand out starkly white in his face. Sabnock was smiling, but it was a mocking smile. "As you can see, by where you stand, that worked to plan."

"I get it," I said. Pulling myself up to stand. I came up to the demon's chest. Still, a bluff was a bluff. I dusted myself off. "You demons formed your Dead Zones. You have your little kingdoms here on Earth, for each of you to rule. Your plan worked."

The head tilt became more pronounced. As if I had said something incorrect. Sabnock's smile grew wider. His voice carrying a hint of incredulousness. "Humans. Always thinking they know everything."

The words carried a mocking hint of laughter. I thought about what I had said. Felt like I had it right. "Demons, always thinking they have the right of things."

The giant head shook. The smile hung between his skull-like cheekbones. "Human, I am a *builder*. I built Xertezie, Cthulaton, Pandemonium. Places you have never seen, wonders you will never lay your eyes on. What could you possibly have done to compare to that?"

His arm swung out, as if encompassing the entire Dead Zone. "Does this look like a finished product? Do you think I undertake something *small* here?"

I didn't see anything but a dead land. Brown grass. Hard earth. Empty buildings.

Yet the rumble of Sabnock's voice promised something *more*. "This is but the first block."

The first block of what? Had the Dead Zones not been Azazel's end goal, but the beginning of something else?

If that was the case, what was Sabnock doing here?

What were the other demons doing? What were the Dead Zones for?

I guessed all questions that could wait. Sabnock was laughing quietly, as if to himself. I didn't think he was going to explain what he had said. And, even a larger worry, I needed to figure out how to survive to puzzle it out.

There was a large squeal of metal on metal behind me, down the line of cars. Tiny pops of breaking glass. Hector, I thought, getting out of the trailer and working his way down the vehicles. Probably flattening each car more, as big as he was.

I could definitely outrun *that*, or him, whatever the knight thing was. There was a chance Sabnock wasn't a long-distance runner either. So, all I had to do was get to the edge of the Dead Zone, maybe a mile away. There, the sword *would* appear.

There I could pretend I was safe.

I went back to the bluff. Pretending I had a pocket pair of aces. Maybe I could get Sabnock to back away a few steps. He was tall enough one or two backsteps would do. Then I could start running. "You going to sit there mocking me, Chuckles, or am I going three for three in demon killing? I don't have all day."

The quiet laughter slowed. Stopped. The demon's voice rumbled in its echoey way, proclaimed to us tiny humans—by tiny humans, I meant me—standing below.

"You are impertinent, human," he said.

"I get that a lot," I said. "You going to tell me why you're here?"

If it was only to kill me, he'd have done that before I had known I was there. Sabnock had something more to tell me. That was the builder in him; he wanted an audience. Someone to appreciate his design coming to fruition.

Just like Azazel.

Demons. No matter who they are, they feel the same. Having lived thousands of years, and they couldn't appreciate things for themselves. They always wanted someone to bask in the glory of what they created.

Sabnock's smile got larger until all I saw was brilliant white teeth underneath black lips. He spoke. Words I hadn't expected. Words that drummed through me in his deep voice with the echoing voices underneath it. Words that carried a malevolence which beat into me.

"Human, you threatened us. You came to us and promised to destroy us all. To take us, one at a time. To take away each of our kingdoms, our lives." Sabnock's eyes bored through me, twin pits of malicious malice and glee. "There can't be even a small piece of you that believes you can speak so to us and walk away unscathed."

The demon was talking about my threat to Azazel. To kill each of his friends before I killed him. To not only kill them, but to send the Dead Zones back as well. To make it all go away, everything Azazel had worked for, before coming for Azazel himself.

I wanted to run, flee, get away.

Even if Sabnock would strike me down from behind.

The demon saw the fear. Understood where it came from. "You dare to threaten us. I will instruct you on what the term really means. I come to you now, *human*, to let you know I will take everything from *you*. I come to let you know that I will personally kill each of your friends, every one of your Wolverines, before coming back to you and finishing you off."

A real fear sprung up from my belly. A cold fear that gave me the shakes. My heart had been thumping before, now it was hammering. Now I couldn't seem to get enough of the warm air of December in Mexico into my lungs. Every breath felt thin.

I forced a smile to my lips. Put on my best Grimm. "A bit unoriginal, Sabby. Taking my plan and turning it around on me? I thought you could do better."

"Plan?" The demon snorted. It sounded like a horse. "You have no plan. You look and you flounder. You poke and you guess. You change your thoughts on a whim."

His white irises, glimmering with dark intent, focused on me. The demon's gaze almost physically bore down on me now. He stood taller over me, the armor glistening, seeming to swell even larger, one hand cupping his chin. "I am an architect. I build things to last, and my plan is already in motion. Already in place, from the first of your shadow walker's pictures. The axe has already begun to fall."

The fingers stroked his chin, as if the demon was thinking. He gave me his challenge. "You want to kill me, human? You want to take what I built from me? Perhaps, *perhaps*, save your friends?" The hand dropped from his face to hang next to him. The other hand clenched itself into a fist, with a glimmering of red around it. One leg slid a little behind the other.

"I await."

The rumble finished, like the final reverberation of the last barrage of cannon-fire, slowly dying off as the words traveled further and further away.

I didn't have a chance to run. I wouldn't have a chance to run. I felt like my pocket aces were more like an off suited two and a seven. Nothing like calling a man's bluff on his first all-in.

I had nothing. And my hand was getting worse. The crunching and squealing behind me only kept getting louder. Hector's new body must weigh a ton. It was slow, but making its way.

Hell, if I was Sabnock I'd be confident too. The demon was in his place of power. He himself was huge, and I was sure the glowy-red fist wasn't there for looks. To top it all off, he had a hell of a monstrous creature—both in size and in deed—for backup.

There was nothing like backup to build confidence.

I was beginning to regret not bringing any myself.

"I thought so," the demon said. "I still wonder what your thought was. Coming this way." His eyes stayed locked onto me, his rumbling voice echoed around me, his eyes stayed locked onto me, as if he was ready to fight, yet the architect part of him still wanted to understand every brick in my plan. "Did you plan to sneak in? Perhaps get to the center of the *Zatar*? Disable it?"

The musing continued. "Or, kill me?"

I didn't want to tell him I was checking things out. That there had been no plan today, that I was trying to figure out if the Five-Fold blade worked. It would only confirm what the demon had just said about me not having a plan. About me doing things on a whim. Sure, the testing and poking got the better of me, curiosity had tempted me to look inside the eighteen-wheeler. Sure, Sabnock had hit the mark.

No need to let the demon know. And the squealing in the back-ground told me Hector was getting closer. It wouldn't be long before I would have to fight Sabnock and Hector. In Hector's new-and-improved form.

"Ushabti are slow," Sabnock said. "But powerful."

I didn't like the name. I also didn't like the odds now that the golem, the knight, the Ushabti, whatever Hector was got here. Hell, I didn't like any of my odds, against Sabnock or Hector, but I'd rather take them on one at a time. I could get a lucky strike in and start running for the edge of the zone before Hector arrived.

It was now or never. I pulled everything I could from the blade. My heart raced. My nerves sped up. Muscles grew stronger. Skin and bones harder.

The world around me slowed as I got faster. Faster than a bullet. My arm, my body, a smear in anyone's sight. Moving too fast to be seen. Swinging the blade for all I was worth at Sabnock's chest.

I didn't catch him by surprise. He had waited, watching. Matching me in speed.

Pulling back from my swing as if we both were in the same dance. The same slow step of time. The same speed.

The next second later a staff appeared in his hands, a real staff, something tall with a gold point at the top of it, a sharp gold point with a burst of rays underneath the head of the staff, like a sun.

Anubis. Even as scared as I was, I couldn't stop the grin. Nailed it.

Then I didn't have time to think. Both of us were as fast as the other, but the staff was almost faster, a blur in the air. For a few seconds it was the two of us, both smears in the air, moving so fast we would be just two smudges, two indistinct clouds, whirlwinds of motion around each other.

The staff was harder to dodge than my blade. Pure physics. It was thin and long and moved lightning quick. My knife was short; I needed to get inside the staff, inside Sabnock's reach just to get close enough to the demon to strike. All he had to do was keep me away with a ten-foot pole.

Plus, the pointed end of his staff was the dangerous side. The blade was sharp and long and glistened in the sunlight. It was everything I could do to make sure it didn't spear me, and once or twice it did slice along my shirt. One time drawing a thin line of blood over my stomach.

I could barely threaten Sabnock with the Five-Fold blade. Not him, but his arms. Each time he swung, I aimed for the center of the staff, where his hands rested, both of them glowing now, but the demon was always too quick, twirling the staff back in the next attack.

So there we were, in the whirlwind of a stalemate. For a heart-beat of a few seconds. Two smudges in the air, a blur of a human and a bigger blur of a demon, his hands leaving little red streaks behind them in the air, both of us striking out at each other and avoiding the other's strike.

I ducked the tall swing of his blade. Made a slight misstep. A small slip of my foot over the hard, dead ground. And I found the bottom of the staff sweeping around and connecting with my side.

After which I found myself in the air, again.

This time I lost my grip on the Five-Fold blade. I watched tumble away in the air. Both of us hit the ground, me bouncing off the wall of cars and landing a few feet away with a giant *whuufff*.

The blade stuck point first in the ground, a dozen feet away, the hilt of the knife pointing a little drunkenly, a little slantedly, into the air.

I immediately felt the loss of energy. Felt slower. Pain radiated from my side, hot.

I didn't have time for that. I couldn't have time for that if I wanted to live.

Sabnock pounced on me. That was the word that came to mind, if something that large could pounce. His body leapt in the air, the staff overhead, swinging down at me with a mighty two-handed chop. Like he was about to split a piece of wood with an axe.

I used the dwindling ethereal energy in me. Rolled as fast as I could. Barely got out of the way in time. The staff connected with the earth behind me. There was a splitting sound, a *whomp*, and the ground burst open there.

Rocks and dirt erupted into the air, landing around both of us. Pebbles struck me as I rolled. A cloud of dust washed over me, but I kept rolling and reached out by memory, grabbing the Five-Fold blade as I passed before jumping in the air. Out of the cloud of dust. Onto Sabnock's back.

Back in the game.

I swung down, but the demon twisted. The blade ended up connecting with his staff, right over his heart. I was assuming he had a heart. The blade hit the staff, a clinging sound rung the air, and Sabnock lunged and threw me over his front.

My hand reaching out to grab anything. My elbow ended up catching his staff, me hanging from it. The demon shook me, like a dog shook something it had its mouth around, and all I could do was hold on for dear life and swipe blindly at Sabnock's arm with the Five-Fold blade.

I felt the knife connect.

There was a burst of blue-white light. A flare of crimson. And a scream.

It was loud. Ear-splitting. Like the air-horn of a train. There was a tiny boom, and we both were tossed away. The staff one way. Me another, thankfully holding on tight to the knife. Sabnock, falling back, one giant demon hand pressed against his forearm.

The scream ended. Though the air still vibrated with its memory. The sound had been concussive, and I staggered up, trying to find my balance. My sight seemed a little blurry. Maybe it was the scream, maybe I had been hit one too many times, but there were multiple Sabnocks in front of me.

I pulled from the blade as fast as I could. The two or three Sabnocks became one or two. Then just one, kneeling on the ground. And even kneeling, still as tall as me.

The demon looked furious. It was an ugly anger. Liquid ran down his forearm and spilled onto the earth, burning the ground. Little puffs of super-heated earth rose up from each drop. The brown grass sparked at the touch of it, little flares of quick greenish flames that burned out quickly and left something gangrenous behind.

Well, well, well, I thought. I had pocket aces after all. I held the knife in front of me, like I was in a martial arts movie, my legs spread a little a part, for balance, my free hand right behind the hand holding the blade.

I grinned my most Grimmish grin. "Like I said, three for three."

The demon snarled. Bloody drops continued to flare up as they struck the ground underneath his arm. He looked angry. Then, oddly enough, an extremely happy expression appeared on his face.

He grinned back. A very Grimm-like grin. Completely copying me.

Two very large, very scaled arms encircled me in a bear hug. The arms collapsed over me and pinned my arms to their sides. The arms pulled me back into Hector's chest, and it was like being encased in concrete.

Concrete trying to pop you.

I swung my head back, trying to connect the back of my head with his face, but I clipped the ghost's chin, and it was like someone sledgehammered my brain. My head rang, Hector's arms tightened, and I couldn't find the energy to even thrash. I wanted to throw up as his arms squeezed me.

It was everything I could do to hold on to the knife. The two of us stood there, well he stood there, at the edge of the wall of cars, compressing everything I had inside me. All I could do was pull energy, strengthen my bones and muscles and skin and try to keep my insides, well, inside. I looked down and saw his feet, large and thick and stone-like, blending into the sand. I couldn't tell where the sand started and where the big feet began, and I wondered when my last breath of oxygen was.

Hector stopped, though, at a certain point. The point where I was almost blacking out. Where tiny flashing dots circled in front of my eyes. I shook my head again, trying to see Sabnock.

The demon was standing now. The blood poured down his arm. The cut seemed to be closing. I thought traces of blue-white light trickled along the edges of the wound. Maybe slowing the healing process. Or maybe just wishful thinking.

"It will be nice to get rid of you," Sabnock said. "Maybe you have the right of it, and plans should be something that should change, upon a whim."

I would have replied, but air was in short supply.

The demon found his staff. Picked it up. The trail of blood drops burning up the earth slowed. Each drop became a single, green-flamed puff against the grass. I pulled and fought and struggled, but barely moved.

The key warmed on my chest. I could almost feel Jen reaching out. Knowing something was wrong. I pulled energy from the knife and tried to push it into the key. Wanting to let her know I had made a mistake. That I loved her. That she loved a dummy back who had gotten himself killed because he had been curious.

Dammit.

Something slammed into Hector. From behind us. One moment the knight was there, holding me, and I was reaching out to Jen in the key. A moment later, he was a few dozen feet away. Rolling on the ground. Like a car had hit him.

I had fallen to my feet. Well, my knees. Trying to gasp air back into my lungs.

Sabnock had paused. His eyes widened, but they weren't looking at me. They were looking behind me. His voice shocked and thrilled and very, very angry. Furious. "You."

I glanced back. The white Tesla was behind me. Running, but quiet in the way electric cars were. It had a very large dent along its front. And the driver's window down.

Michael was behind the wheel.

"Get in," the archangel shouted. Looking past me, at Sabnock. "Quickly."

I was still trying to get air inside me. But I could breathe later. I found myself sliding across the dented front of the Tesla. Getting into the passenger side. The archangel had the car moving before I had shut the door. The vehicle moved violently, lurching to one side as if the alignment was out.

Hitting concrete will do that to a car.

I got my lungs working. Michael fought the wheel. Pushed the pedal down. The center console, the big thing in the middle of the dash that looked like a small television, had a map on its screen. Showing the road between Mexico City and Cuernavaca.

We headed south. Bouncing over the hard ground. The front left side of the car whined like something was locked up there, maybe a tire, but it still drove.

In a minute, hopefully more or less, the Tesla might cross the Dead Zone barrier with me and Michael. I turned and looked back. Hector was picking himself up and heading this way. But Sabnock stopped him.

The builder demon just stood there, staff propped against the ground. Golden blade pointed at the sky. Watching us with what I would bet was an angry, thoughtful expression. Behind him, behind both of them, I thought I saw a dark cloud low on the horizon. A thin black line to the north. But I couldn't be sure the way the car was bouncing.

Either way, they faded into the distance. Quickly. The tall demon the last thing to disappear from sight. Sabnock stood there with a hand to his chin. Like he had found a problem in his blueprint. Like something hadn't measured quite right.

A fly in the works was a saying that came to mind. It made me frown. But also smile. I had almost died; if it hadn't been for Michael I would have died, but I had accomplished what I wanted to do here. And I had pulled Sabnock's attention this way. Looking out his front door, so Nick could sneak in through the back window.

The demon knew about Nick. He said he knew about the rest of us. But the best part of my plan was the fact that it wasn't a real plan. Sabnock wasn't wrong, it had been built on a whim. It had changed already; it would likely change again.

Fly like a butterfly, sting like a bee. Sabnock might think he had planned for us, and that worried me. I had no idea what the demon could bring to bear. The one comfort I had was that the demon thought he had made plans for us, and every demon and monster that had that same thought in the past had found out they had underestimated the Wolverines.

Still, seeing Sabnock's face. The focused concentration of the large demon throughout the fight. The utter confidence he had in his plan, standing in front of me. The furious anger at the fly in the works as I had jumped into the Tesla.

All of it had me worried. Especially the part where Sabnock had said things were in motion. What things? And where were they moving? What trap had just been sprung?

The demon didn't appear to like any changes to his blueprint. I could only hope that whatever Sabnock was planning, I remained front and center in his sights. That I had convinced him I was the problem he needed to solve.

CHAPTER THIRTY-SIX

The Tesla bounced its way south. Somehow I buckled my seatbelt, but honestly it was everything I could do to stay in the seat, even after I got it on. It felt like we were off-roading, and we were *on* the road. Teslas were built to be maintenance-free, but something in the front left suspension was going to need a lot of work.

We just needed to go a mile, though. Then the car could have all the maintenance it wanted. So we kept bouncing down the road, Michael's hands tight on the steering wheel, me with one hand on my seatbelt, the other holding the Five-Fold blade so that it didn't accidentally stab someone in one of the larger jerks of the car. The sheath was somewhere back by the tractor trailer. I had definitely lost that.

A Christmas tree, hanging from the rearview mirror, jumped around. It was a green-colored thing hanging right above the large console on the front dash, one of those air fresheners shaped like a pine tree, yet for some reason carried the smell of marshmallows.

Which seemed odd, but what did I know? I guess Christmas and toasted marshmallows kind of went together.

Other than the whine coming from the front left wheel, the car was oddly quiet. Michael kept wrestling the wheel. Grunting occasionally. His face was still the serious angel face from when I had first met him, back on the patio, but it also had a slight grin. Like he was excited to be back in the fight.

"Better late than never?" I asked.

His grin grew wider. Not a real smile, but something that spoke of acceptance. "More like, if not now, when?"

Whatever got him here, I couldn't have asked for better timing. It literally had been a life-and-death moment. "It's appreciated."

Another wrench of the wheel. The angel's hands slipped, and the Tesla took a quick dive off the road before Michael got us back on the blacktop. His glance at me looked… Angry. Surprised. Frustrated. All three. "I can't believe you went in."

"Went in?" I looked back, towards the wall of cars. "There?"

"Sabnock has been waiting," Michael said. "He loves setting a trap. He's been monitoring you since you started showing up around here."

That was something new about the demon. It made sense. Traps involved plans, plans are something you build. Building is something an architect loves. And I hated to hear that Sabnock loved them since it was a skill I hadn't really developed.

Though at least I knew my plan was working, if Sabnock was looking for me here. Still, Michael had said he had cautioned me against it. I didn't remember that from our conversation. "You said you warned me?"

"I left you a sign." Michael was having a hard time keeping us on the road. Maybe angels didn't get to be student drivers. After a particularly good bounce, he patted the steering wheel. "The hazard lights."

It clicked. The Tesla sitting off to the side. The lights flicking on and off. I had even thought of it a beacon, though I hadn't really dove deeper into that idea at the time. To me, it had been a random thought.

And then I had met Michael. Right after seeing the car. There had been the whole patio scene with the angel.

"You could have just told me," I said.

"I could have. That was the plan," Michael said. "But meeting you brought up some painful... memories. And the conversation went elsewhere."

And, a moment later. "I have gotten too used to leaving signs. Our side is not usually direct, you know."

Well, he wasn't wrong there. His side certainly couldn't be accused of that. At the very least, they were the great hemmer-and-hawwers of the past few millennia.

Still, Michael had talked to me. The least he could have done was share a little warning. Even just give me the double-time-it signal. A little fist raised above the head. That would have been sign enough.

Or so I thought. I hadn't been happy leaving that meeting. Maybe, like me, he had left angry.

His voice still sounded that way. Angry, but a focused anger. Something that had developed an edge over a long period of time. "I have not seen Sabnock, the others, for thousands of years."

By the others, he must have been talking about the demons trapped in the key. Because Azazel had been around. I'm sure he had a history with all of them, he was the leader of Heaven's armies, but Sabnock seemed to get a particular rise out of the angel. Michael had known enough to want to warn me.

The angel nodded when asked. "Those trapped by Solomon, they were some of the worst. The unhappy. The malcontents."

"Unhappy with what?"

Michael's eyebrow raised. "The natural order."

Well, that explained it. The natural order of heaven and hell? Of angels and demons and Earth? Of peanut butter cups being the one seed of candy bars?

Hemming-and-hawwing had been too kind. I hoped he'd explain it better when we weren't running for our lives in a three-wheeled Tesla.

In front of us, the outer edge of the Dead Zone neared. Blinking, I could see the red tinge that marked the barrier, the crimson bubble, get closer and closer. I recognized the place I had entered the zone from. The road passing the patio, with the blue Camaro waiting.

All of it bouncing in my sight. The whine of the Tesla grew sharper. A higher pitch. I started to smell something burning, the acrid thick smell of melting rubber. Smoke flooded out of the front of the car, from the left front tire well. Black smoke.

I looked back. The wall of cars was smaller. I did not see Sabnock or Hector, though I wondered if they were still watching.

The Tesla passed through the edge of the zone. Bounced out into the regular world. I felt it, more than saw it, with the tiniest of shivers along my skin. The smallest of goosebumps.

Michael pulled the car over. Flexed his hands like they still vibrated. I understood, because my whole body felt the same way.

Something popped from the front left of the car, with us sitting there. There a burst of black smog, and tiny trails of gray drifted up, thinning out in the air. Like the vehicle had finally given up. The Tesla sat at a decided angle, pitched forward and a little to the left.

My hand was still tight on the Five-Fold blade.

Michael's eyes had found it.

"I see you've found a way to fight them."

I had. But not in the way I wanted. I couldn't summon the sword. But the Five-Fold blade had done real damage. It had worked. And—I hoped—it would kill Sabnock. Or at least, I thought it could kill the demon, and if not kill, hurt him enough for us to nullify the Dead Zone. Whether it was me or Nick wielding the blade.

"Does this mean you're in?" I asked.

The smile came back. The self-deprecating unhappy grin of amusement. "If not now, when."

A repeat of what he had said a minute ago, but his words weren't a question.

Michael got out and walked to the front of the car. I followed the angel, unclicking the seatbelt and pulling myself up and out of my side. The Tesla definitely had a slight lean to the driver's side.

The front left of the car didn't look any better than it had a few minutes ago. The huge dent was still there, folding the front of the bumper inward, inverting a bit of the wheel well and the hood. The smoke still drifted from the tire there. Tiny trails of gray wafting upward. The thick smell of burned rubber was strong; the tire looked mostly shredded where it wasn't melted.

Michael popped the hood. It took a moment. The hood seemed stuck with the dent, and the angel finally reached down to yank the hood up with a plasticky pop. I was surprised, there wasn't an engine there underneath. The front of Teslas apparently was a trunk, instead. The engine was in the back, like the old Volkswagen Beetles.

Under the hood lay Michael's sword and shield. I got the feeling they hadn't been there long. A minute or two since crossing the border. His sword with the gold cross in its hilt still in its sheath. His shield still a brilliant white.

"Do you summon those?" I asked. And at his questioning look. "Do you call your sword to you…" I waved my hands, trying to explain how I called my sword to appear, and not really finding the words. "Do you make it appear and disappear?"

His eyebrow arched. He held the sword in front of me by its sheath. A moment later the sword disappeared in a fancy burst of white motes. Not bright white light, but something more subtle, as if the blade had instantly become millions of brilliant white dots, each slowly fading away in the air.

A moment later, the sword was there again. In its sheath. Gold cross facing me. The hint of fiery red playing across the metal.

The motion, like the sword, was very showy. But also very apparent. There was no doubt who Michael was. If the two of us were angels, we must have been distant cousins. Very distant.

His sword looked much like a real sword would. It was a shiny silver, or even a white gold. That would fit a real angel. My blade was almost transparent, the outline of it colored in the blue-white ethereal energy I pulled from the plane so that the edge looked like it trickled with a lightning-like pulse.

Michael held the sword like it had real weight. It was long, and looked heavy. Like there was a heft to it. His forearm flexed a bit, holding it up in the air.

My blade had always felt different. There was more of an imaginary weight to it. It balanced in my hand. There was some weight I felt when I swung; I could feel it in my wrist. When I really swung the sword, it felt like I was swinging a crowbar. Yet at the same time, it felt light as a feather. That was the best I could explain it.

His shield looked real, too. Like it had come right from a blacksmith's forge. I wonder if he had armor, too. Like King Arthur, or Lancelot.

I looked at the Tesla's hood. I meant trunk. Whatever you wanted to call the place the engine should be in a regular car. "So why not just call them when you need them?"

Michael thought about it a moment. He seemed to find the question interesting. "I find it better, to go through the motions."

And at my questioning look, he mimicked popping the Tesla's

hood. He pulled the sword a bit from its sheath. The metal caught the light, and I couldn't say why, I wasn't someone who worked in metals, but the feeling of white gold came over me again. Then he sheathed it again. "The motions. It helps me to remember who I am. What I am not."

That didn't really explain it to me.

The angel put a shoulder through the strap holding his sheath. Slung the blade around his back. The shield next, over his back and sword.

The two of us were of a similar build and size, although he felt taller. More commanding. A guess a few thousand years leading Heaven's armies gave you that kind of gravitas.

That patio was nearby. The old man and woman weren't there. The dogwood's blossoms were like I had seen them before, when I had passed by earlier. Wilted and—for the most part—missing. The bushes brown. The poinsettias gone.

But two cups of coffee rested on the table. I could smell the espresso from here. I could almost taste the first sip.

If this was going through the motions, I could grow to like this guy.

Michael headed that way. Grabbed the cup he had held a few days ago at the same place on the table, taking a large sip. His eyes looking past me, towards the Dead Zone.

I echoed his motion. The latte was much like it had been before. The perfect blend of bitterness and cream. I savored it, and while savoring it, let the adrenaline rush out of me. Feeling the shakes and the cold, thrilling sensation that came with them, the thing that said *you almost bit it that time, Grimm.*

I had almost bit it. No matter how many times you hear the words *curiosity killed the cat*, you never think they apply to you. You always take that one extra step, wanting to see. Wanting to find out.

Just a little idle curiosity, a little wanting to know, and that had been enough to get me almost killed.

Still, I had made it. And not only made it, but found another ally. Someone in charge of an army. At the time when we needed one more than ever.

Maybe it was the coffee. The caffeine in the beans. Maybe it was the pure excitement at being alive. I knew my voice sounded more animated than usual. "Where are the rest of your troops?"

With the commander of Heaven's armies leading them into the Dead Zone, we could have a real chance of pulling off the whole shebang. Nullifying the pentagram. Killing the demon. Taking one ally away from Azazel, yanking one pillar out from the demon.

And going after the next one.

Michael took another sip of his coffee. His eyes shifted. Glancing at me, then back to the Dead Zone. Measuring the threat. Staying aware.

"Grimm," he finally said. "This is it."

CHAPTER THIRTY-SEVEN

Like our meeting before, the latte had gotten too bitter, too fast. The cream was lost in it. Nothing but a sharp black sourness.

At first, I was confused. There was a host up there. A large army of angels and whatever else came with them. I was looking at their commander. "All the stories say—" I started.

Michael was already stopping me with a slight wave of his hand. Shaking his head. Taking another drink of his own coffee. Finishing it with a slight grimace. "I know what they say."

He wanted to say something else. We both paused. His mouth started to open, closed again. Then repeated, as if Michael was rephrasing what he wanted to say, or didn't know how to start.

Finally, he exhaled. "I think your misunderstanding is, three thousand years ago, when Solomon bound up the demons in his keys, I think you think my side was *winning*."

I hadn't known what he was going to say.

It took a moment for his meaning to sift in.

His words hit me like a brick.

Michael had said it. He was it. He was his side.

We had all been taught that forces usually have an equal and opposite force. It's a basic concept. Push something, and that something resists your push. I mean, if moving things were easy, we wouldn't have to buy pizza and beer for friends to help us after buying a new place.

And I spent my lifetime denying it, but if hell exists, there needed to be a heaven. Equal but opposite, right? Demons meant there were angels. Lucifer meant there should be a God, no matter how much I've fought that thought, with what had happened to people like Danny, Miss Tammie, Parker...

I put that thought away again. It wouldn't help me now. It never had, thinking those people might be alive, that if someone, or *something*, had only cared enough to stop them. That we lived in kind of a fucked-up world if those kinds of people could be beaten with a bat. Burned alive. Executed.

Putting that thought away was tough. I had to fight it. Because I was what I was, now. Angel or part angel. I had grown to accept my responsibility with my friends, but I didn't want to think that they might grow. That I might have to become *more*.

Dammit. Fuck you, I thought.

I was angry. Angry might have been an understatement. Michael was it, the only reinforcements we would get. After everything I had been through. Everything my friends had been through. Everything my parents had been through, and their parents. Danny and Miss Tammie and Parker and Father Benjamin and ...

Recruitment numbers were low, Greg had said. Talking about the Templars. Then he had died.

It wasn't *fair*. They had demons and Dead Zones and vampire-demons coming back to life. They had humans and vampires and other creatures flocking to the Dead Zones to grab a part of their power. They had giant crabs, some kind of monstrous creature in

Lake Pontchartrain, lizard knights with ghosts like Hector in them, and even a dragon.

Our side should have something too.

Our side shouldn't just be us.

The war hadn't even started with us. With me. I had been pulled into it, much like my mother and father had before me. *We* had been pulled into it, the Wolverines, with Raphael and Azazel back in Grafton. Our group, Jen, Nick and Sarah, Johnny and... Gabrielle, we were just a small group of friends. Trying to do the right thing.

My mother had told me that evil had been winning a while. But that it was time for good to rise again. That there was a pendulum; it had swung as far as it could toward evil, and was beginning to swing back our way. I had the feeling, back when she talked about it, that the good side was like a wave, slowly gathering strength, getting taller and thicker out there in the ocean, a towering tidal force of good, waiting to crash over the vast shore of evil.

But if Michael was it. If he was all our side had to offer us, for help... how long had our side been losing? Since even before the geas? How long before? Since the Flood? Since Sodom? Since the time a serpent found its way into a garden?

The angel watched me work through it all. His coffee forgotten, just like mine. I had no idea if I had stood there for a minute or an hour.

"Think about what happened with the cross," he said, softly. "The crucifixion. Is that something you do if you're winning the game? Or is it more of a Hail Mary kind of thing?"

Oh.

I let out a big breath. Something I hadn't known I was holding. I had thought this had begun with the geas, the whole good and evil thing. With my mother telling me about it, fighting the call of the geas inside her.

I had thought this had been all about me. Maybe it was ego. Or arrogance. But a part of me still couldn't believe what I was hearing. The geas had colored most of my life. My parents' lives. Their parents. It had been such a part of my world for so long that I couldn't believe it wasn't the beginning of all of this. Of Azazel, his demon friends, and their plan.

Their plan that wasn't the end. But was only the beginning. Sabnock had hinted at that very thing.

The beginning of one thing was the end of another. In this case, the Dead Zones marked something that had just now begun. But what had ended?

One long battle? Between good and evil? And if the good side had already been losing since before the geas, since thousands of years before that moment that had meant so much to my life, what had happened over all those years? How many losses had our side taken? How many angels did Michael have left to command?

This is it.

Michael was it.

That was his army.

I guessed there was a reason he had stayed out of things. I felt a little bad about accusing him earlier. But only a little. Because whatever his losses, however his side had fought, it still led to the here and now. Not just Azazel and his Dead Zones, not just Raphael and his plans, not just Lucifer and Belial and whatever they wanted, but to everything me and my friends currently faced.

And that plate was full.

All of these thoughts were like bombshells. One explosive realization after another. Followed by the largest of all. If Michael was here helping me, because *if not now, when*, and if he was it—the only angel left to help us—that meant me and my friends *were* the good side.

All of it.

Which meant I was leading the charge.

Against an array of evil that had beaten everything in its path. Had wiped Michael and his host from the face of the Earth. Had been growing since, hell, I don't know how long, and been winning larger stakes the longer the game had been played. That could add the Dead Zones, Azazel, *and* his demon friends to their list of triumphs.

My eyes must have opened with the enormity of it all. I realized at some point I had set the coffee back down on its little plate. I couldn't tell you when that had happened.

Michael's grin was a little cynical. Or maybe it was self-flagellating. If that was the way to say what I was thinking. As if he knew who was to blame for this. For everything.

"I see you understand." Those were his only words.

I did. I understood it all. And yet, at the same time, the idea was too enormous for my brain to hold it all. A few months ago, I was running from Azazel. Trying to help Sarah. Finding a way to save Jen.

And now this. The end of the world.

What I was fighting had grown exponentially, so fast I couldn't keep up.

From the look of it, the angel felt the same way. His face, I was sure, looked much like mine. He may be thinking along the same lines, but in reverse. He had led a host of angels. He had watched that host get winnowed away with attrition, through his war with demons. And, at the end, Azazel had trapped his remaining brothers and sisters in the geas.

"You know what they call me?" Michael asked, looking past me. His voice near a whisper. "The one who escaped."

The whole idea was too enormous. Before, we were killing demons and attacking the Dead Zones because we wanted to take everything away from Azazel, before killing him. We were doing it because Jen thought it best, and because I thought I owed her that, for what the demon had done to her.

Now the whole thing had much higher stakes. Stakes Sabnock had mentioned. Stakes the demons of the key were playing for.

"You know what they're planning," I said. "Azazel and the others."

He nodded. "I do."

"It's not about building kingdoms for themselves on Earth," I said. "It's not about a place they can have that's neither in heaven or hell."

He nodded again. "It isn't."

To me, there was only one thing it could be. With the world the way it was. And the good side as weak as it had ever been. "It's a full rebellion. Against all sides. If these are the malcontents, the worst of the worst, then all they could want..."

Maybe it was the enormity of it all that kept me from grasping it. I couldn't see it. I just knew it was bad.

"Is the total annihilation of it all," Michael said. "You. Me. Humans. Angels. Even heaven and hell. They want to wipe it all out."

The thought of it froze me. It was beyond anything I could think of. Why would they want that, unless it was to build something of their own? "To start over?"

"Maybe. Maybe not. Azazel has never been easy to read." The angel shrugged. "But at that point, will it matter to us?"

CHAPTER THIRTY-EIGHT

M *ore.*
We could be more.

That word, every time I thought about it, brought my mother back to mind.

She had told me that she thought it was time for our side to win again. That we would grow stronger, that even as the pendulum completed its swing for evil, our side was building its response. That even as we suffered, we were growing stronger, ready for our time, ready for the weight to return to our side. She had said that, seen it in me.

Believed it enough to die for it.

There was no way she could have seen this, though. Dead Zones across the Earth. Demons running rampant, creating new monsters, bringing old monsters from the history of the world. There was no way, when she had said I could be more, we could be more, me and my friends, there was no way she could have seen *this*.

Versus us.

The Wolverines. Five kids from a small town. One vampire. *Us.* Plus some friends, some witches. Some allies, in the vampires of Cuernavaca. And Michael, the only angel left. Against...

I looked at the Dead Zone. The narrow line of darkness swelled a bit more over the northern horizon. Like a thin black cloud, gathering. Maybe some rain, finally, although I had never seen it rain in a zone.

Sabnock was building something. Something with his fellow demons. I didn't know what it was, but there was a dark plan underneath all the smaller plans. Something Azazel had designed long ago, perhaps even before his fall. Something to wipe us out. Humans. Angels. Demons, at least those still serving Lucifer.

Something to destroy it all. Everything.

How the hell could we do this? Defeat a plan that evil? Something that large?

It was too big to think of. It was so large, all I could do was stare north at the swelling storm. It was so large I was unaware of time passing while I did.

At least, until the keydrop hummed a bit. A tiny vibration, as if Jen was trying to reach me. Which reminded me of my last attempt to reach her.

Guiltily. She might be in a panic. I needed to make a call.

"Be right back."

I walked over to the Camaro and pulled my cell phone from where it had been sitting between the seats, attached to the charging cable. I stood by the driver's door, hand on the Camaro, and dialed Jen. For a wonder, the lines seemed to be working. She answered on the first ring. Her voice a little worried.

"Gus?"

"Here," I said. "Though I almost bought it."

"You're safe now?"

I looked around. Michael still stood on the patio, staring north like I had been doing. The sword and shield on his back. Otherwise, it was the two of us. The street was empty. And the upcoming storm.

"Safe enough," I said.

"Good," she said, and the word held more relief than I would have thought. It was almost shaky with it. I wondered how much of what I had sent had reached her, how much of me almost dying had gotten to her. Jen had been dealing with her own thing, and that had me worried, and now she had me almost dying on top of that.

"I could tell you went in," Jen said. "The key glowed. Faint. It woke me up."

"Look, I–"

"Gus," she said, her voice still shaky, but also carrying a smile. "I've gotten used to the whole you almost dying thing. It happens more than it should. But you reaching out that way, and me not being able to feel you that far away, to know…"

She was talking about the slam of emotions I had hit the bond with, when I thought Sabnock and Hector were about to kill me. The apology for dying. For being stupid. A little fear and a lot of guilt ran through me. I had reached out, trying to let her know that I was about to be killed, pushing that rush of emotion through the bond. And had left it there. Had left her not really knowing. She had seen the bond wink on, felt the rush of emotion from me, and then the wink off.

Jen tried a lighter tone. "Just let me know a bit faster next time, you know, if you survive."

I closed my eyes, and it was like she was there, right next to me. It made me feel good, the teasing, the laughter. *Us.* I wanted her there, right next to me, right now. The feeling overwhelmed me enough that I put a hand on the roof of the Camaro, feeling the coldness of the metal.

How had I ever been away from her for ten years? When just this short time away had me missing her this much?

"Deal," I said. Opening my eyes. Trying to smile, even though I wanted her there. "But you said it, it's part of the deal. You can only hold me to it if I survive."

She laughed, even if it was a little strained. I grinned in much the same way. And we both missed each other.

I told her what happened. I could have sugar-coated the news; she would have known. And she would have called me out on it. We could always tell if the other was trying to hide something. Well, if I was being honest, Jen could always tell if I was trying to hide something. I had no idea if I had that same superpower.

I didn't give her all the details. About Sabnock wanting to kill all my friends before coming after me. About my threat to Azazel. But I gave her the rest. Telling her mostly everything. The knights. Hector. Sabnock and his trap. Michael saving me. Sabnock and his plan, a plan the demons were just beginning. A plan Michael had expounded upon.

Finishing with that little thing, the annihilation of everything and everyone. All of us.

There was a pause when I finished. Both of us had gotten serious, and her voice sounded small. It carried a little uncertainty, regret, some mixture of the two. Small. "Maybe we should have just killed him."

I was confused. "Who? Sabnock?" We *were* trying to kill him.

"No," she said. "Azazel. Back in Charleston. You know I talked you out of it. All this is because of me. Because of what I wanted."

Oh. I suddenly was glad I hadn't told her what Sabnock had said. And I had that happiness, although maybe Jen felt *something* from me in our bond.

I mean, words were just words, right? A promise was something else. I had learned a short time ago that the word was the deed. But when people are just speaking... anyone can say anything, any demon can say anything. The trap is in believing what they say. The way to not fall into that trap is to believe in the thing you were doing, more than the fear of what those words might mean.

I had learned that from Jen.

I ached for her. Small wasn't the word to describe how she felt. Not sad, either. Sadness described the feeling better. Sad implied something temporary. Sadness carried a weight with it, a persistence. Sadness bore you down; it was the heaviest of anchors, dragging you down into a world you could never, ever leave.

All of that echoed over the phone, and at the same time, the slightest bit of it crossed over our bond. I could feel it from both places. An echoing of sadness and uncertainty. Jen thought killing Azazel might have stopped this, the demon's plan of wiping the Earth of all of us. She thought she had been selfish, back then. And now she thought that particular piece of selfishness was endangering all of us.

It wasn't.

She wasn't.

I mean, I was worried. But I was worried about how we could win. How our side could come through in the fight. I struggled with the very idea of it. With what the demons were planning, and how we could possibly beat something like that. I had no idea, it was too large in scope, and we were too few.

And I also knew that we would try. It was in us. It was how we were made. It was who we were. To get back up and keep fighting. To take the loss and put ourselves back together. Stronger. Better. *More*.

It didn't matter if there was one angel coming to help, or a thousand. The realization was strong; it never mattered. No matter how big the evil grew. It didn't matter what the evil thought, or told me.

It would never matter. The whole world could be taken over by

330 · CHRIS J CRANFORD

demons and Dead Zones. The whole world could be destroyed, and if there was one part of it left, one tiny parcel of land anywhere, that's where you would find us. The Wolverines. That's where you would find me and Jen, Nick and Sarah, Johnny and Gabrielle. We all would be there. Getting ourselves back up. Continuing the fight.

It was who we were. We would gamble everything on us. We were always going to try. Win or lose, those dice were going to get thrown.

And Jen knew that. But something she carried had her doubt it. Doubt herself?

I went back to our thing. The word that said it all between us. The one that made me think of us two as kids, the nighttime sky, me staring out my window at the stars, her staring out of hers. Both of us knowing, feeling, each of us one with the other, even back then. Even before the bond.

"Hey."

She heard it. The word resonated between us. And she even knew what I was doing, trying to give her something to stand on. And even her knowing all that didn't stop it from working. While I still heard that sadness in her voice, there was a little smile as well. Growing. "Hey."

Silence on the line, after that. Silence from the key, with the distance between us. And then a breath from Jen, something deep and long, almost sensual. Like she was taking everything in and then letting it all out in a shuddering exhale.

"You done with blaming yourself over there?"

If I could hear something like rolling of the eyes, I'm sure I would have. Her voice was thick, though, like she was crying. Or about to cry. "Yeah. For now."

"Good," I said. "I got enough of that over here with the angel."

Boy, I wasn't too great at this. The comforting thing. I was trying. However small a role she thought she played, Jen blamed herself for what was going on.

Michael carried a lot of guilt. I could see it in his eyes. I had seen it when he first told me I was late to his party. If the angel had once led a great host, and if he was all that was left, then all he could carry was blame. For thousands of years.

A lot of weight to carry, and it would only grow as he hid from the world.

I understood the feelings coming from both of them. The weight of blame. The depth of despair.

I had felt much the same about Danny. I had hidden from the world, from my world, from Jen, for ten years. I knew what blaming yourself could do.

Blame was evil in its purest form, and even though I knew that I still had to watch for it. Even now, Jen would point it out to me because things like blame snuck up on you. It was a feeling that started small, taking little bites here and there. It would slowly take larger bites, and it would grow, and take even larger bites, and swell, until all that was left was the blame.

And nothing left of you.

There was no way I was going to let that happen to Jen.

"You had every right to want to take everything from Azazel," I said. "Maybe now you think it was too much. Maybe you think it was selfish. Whatever the reason, your instincts were right."

She should see it. She was always the smart one, and she could always see it in me. It was harder, though, looking at yourself.

"Killing Azazel would have felt good. Hell, it would have felt great. I would have loved it," I said. "But it wouldn't have fixed *this*. It wouldn't have stopped what's going on here or in any of the other Dead Zones."

There was a pause. A little sniff. Her voice still thick. "Go on."

"What if I had killed Azazel?" I asked. "Where would we be

now? Would we be here? Would we even be trying to nullify all the zones?"

It might have been easy for me to see. Jen might even see it, but there's a difference between seeing and knowing. Between the idea and the understanding. I had fought it before. "It was your idea to nullify them. It was your idea to take them all out. All the demons. It was your idea to get friends to help us, and find allies."

Her voice still carried doubt. "Gus, we would have done that anyway."

"Would we?" I asked. "Maybe. Maybe not. Maybe differently. Maybe we would have tried another Dead Zone. Maybe we would've went to Europe. And then, whatever chain of events followed, maybe we don't learn about the plan to destroy everything. Maybe Michael doesn't show up. Maybe I don't see a way to create the Five-Fold blades. Maybe Sabnock and I don't get to chat."

A long pause, this time.

"All that's pretty thin, Gus," she finally said. "It's a lot of maybes."

A laugh escaped me, something real that I couldn't stop, at the memory of telling her a little of the same thing, not so long a time past, and yet at the same time ages ago. "Hell, I live with thin. I thrive on maybes. Thin, seat-of-the-pants stuff is what I *do*. You point the same things out to me all the time. You just think it's different because it's you looking in the mirror now."

"Gus." Jen sounded… irritated.

I was definitely not great at this.

Actually, I might have been really bad.

But I kept trying. It's another thing I did. Kept swinging.

"How many times have you pointed out the same thing to my thick head?"

A heavy exhale through her nose. A moment of thought. I could feel her coming to a realization, the way a stubborn mule gives in and finally follows the tug of his rope. "Yeah, but that's you." She sounded a little less mad. Maybe. "You take a lot of work."

I grinned at the sound of the old Jen, working her way back. I *did* take a lot of work. Between us, I was definitely the stubborn mule. "All I'm saying is that you can't go back and blame yourself for that decision. That decision led to here. We've found out the demons have a plan to kill us all. And we've found a way to kill Sabnock. We have a chance to nullify the Dead Zone. And we have more allies, more friends, and a way to put a kink in their works."

I could hear her eyebrow raise. Not really. But the tone brought that image of her. "Kink in their works?"

The phrase didn't quite fit the occasion, but the words were out. I couldn't take them back. So I did like anyone would do and doubled down.

"Kink in their works," I repeated. "All I'm saying is that somewhere inside of you, you knew the right thing to do. *You* put us on this path. And here we are, with a chance. All we're ever going to get is a chance. And we've got one, now. So let's not waste time thinking about what we might have done, or might not have done. Let's just take it."

There was a moment, and I let her work through it. I was working through the same process myself. I had looked too far ahead, and the task had gotten too big. For a moment, that mountain had been too tall, too heavy.

Though to be fair, the annihilation of all the Earth, of heaven and hell, that was a pretty big thing. Almost too big to even comprehend. How the hell could I possibly deal with something like that?

Well, it was easy. Take the smaller task. Accomplish that. Move on to the next small task. Climb the mountain one step at a time.

Anything else would overwhelm us.

"You know, for a guy who takes a lot of work," Jen said.

"You're pretty bright sometimes." A long pause, her voice losing a little bit of recrimination, and gaining a little more of her humor. Of her inner Jen. Of the person who waited ten years for me to come to my senses. "Occasionally. Once in a long, long while."

I let out a breath. Away from the phone. All the worry I had been holding about Jen left with the exhale. Well, most of it.

"It's why you love me," I said.

And paused. The Dead Zone in my view, looking normal, yet not. That thin black line of clouds to the north. Something flitted around the back of my brain right then, but I couldn't catch it. Something I knew I needed. Maybe that we needed.

Jen interrupted the thought. "If we're being honest, I only love you because you bring me coffee in the morning."

The thought escaped me. And I wasn't sure it mattered. Jen seemed to be Jen again. As much as she could be. As much as I could tell, this far away.

Motion caught the corner of my eye. I looked over and saw Michael, waving. Pointing at the Dead Zone. That I was already looking at.

Was it a storm? After so long being hot and dry, had a real storm decided to hydrate the lands again? Wash us all clean? I didn't think so, coming out of the Dead Zone.

I narrowed my eyes. Flicked on the ethereal sight, trying to see further. It felt like the thin black line was getting thicker. Much, much thicker. It was really hard to see anything, it was so far away.

"Good?" I asked. Not wanting to rush Jen. Whatever was happening, it could wait.

"Yeah," she said. "I feel foolish."

That hit on the other something I had been feeling from her. The hidden something she wasn't ready to share. The problem she couldn't find a way to deal with. I could feel that coming from her, the self-recrimination about Azazel, and that other feeling, all washed together. From the phone, and a little from the key.

"Good," I said again, although this time I wasn't asking it. "Because I'm usually on the other side of these conversations. This side feels weird."

She laughed, a real Jen laugh. It felt good to me. She had always been the person to hold me up. To make me believe I was better than I was. I needed that. I would always need that.

Michael waved harder.

Back to work.

"The angel needs me," I said.

"Something happening?"

"Maybe." I looked at the thin black line. It was definitely growing larger. If Sabnock wasn't going to chase us from the Dead Zone, where the fight would be more even, if he wasn't happy about us getting out, well, apparently the demon had another plan in mind.

"Gus."

Well, I had said she could always tell if I was sugar-coating something.

"Something's happening," I said. "Not sure what, but I'll be fine."

"Sure," her voice was teasing again. It felt better, normal, us.

"Is it storming up there?"

A moment, and the ringing swish of a sound of curtains getting pulled along a curtain rod. "No rain," she said. Corrected herself. "Maybe some clouds. In the west."

"Same thing here," I said. "Coming from the Dead Zone."

"That doesn't sound good."

"When does it ever?" I said. "Stay inside today, if you guys will. Just to be safe."

"Really?" Jen said, poking fun at me. "*You* telling others to be safe?"

"I'm evolving," I said, smiling. "Tell Nick the blades work. They may not kill Sabnock, but they hurt him." I was sure I had seen a trickle of ethereal energy along the edge of the wound I had given Sabnock. "But stay away from where he cuts. The blood burns."

"Burns?"

It was the only way to describe it. The blood had puffed up in fiery green blooms, with every drop striking the ground. That couldn't be good for skin. Or humans.

I wasn't sure if the blades could kill him. But they could hurt demons in the Dead Zone. Badly. I was sure part of the anger I had seen in Sabnock's face had been surprise. And if we couldn't kill him, I thought we could still hurt him badly enough to get to the center of the Dead Zone, the part Sabnock had called the Zatar, and nullify it.

You know, if Hector and the demon's army of weird ass knights would let us.

"Burns," I said. "Tell him to be careful."

Knowing Nick, he may or may not be. He was taking chances, going as far into the Dead Zone as he was. But he was also more cautious than me. At least, I was pretty sure he was. Especially with recent evidence.

"Will do," she said. "Be safe."

"Always," I said. "You know me."

She laughed again. "I do. It's why I keep saying it."

I didn't want to, and she didn't want to, but we ended the connection after that weird pause where neither party wanted to hang up. That moment seemed like forever, then it was over, and I had to be content with the smallest feel of Jen in the key. I took a breath and walked over to the patio. Michael stood there, before the table, looking north. I could feel the urgency in his voice.

"What's up?"

"Locusts," he said. As if the word explained everything.

I looked at the thin black line, swelling just a bit larger. And a bit more larger. Even as I watched. Could it be that many insects? A swarm of them? Millions?

It was… as biblical a thing as I could think of.

"Really?"

The angel nodded. "I recognize the signs."

The black line, swelling. Locusts, harbingers of disease and pestilence. I imagined how many insects would have to be a part of that. Surely more than millions. Trillions. Infina-billions.

Sure, I made that number up. Because I couldn't simply imagine a number large enough. I wasn't sure anyone could.

"Aren't locusts a 'your side' thing?"

His reply was simple. I was beginning to think that was the angel's fallback. "What do you call a swarm of locusts?"

I hadn't been the best at English. Or math, or any of the subjects back in school. But, for some reason, the answer popped into my head. I had a big ah-ha moment. Dammit. "A plague."

Sabnock was a demon of pestilence. And nothing brings pestilence like a plague. I had the answer, as far as what trap had been sprung, and what trap-springer it was headed to. "What do we do?"

His eyebrows rose. "We find a place to hide, and wait it out."

I kind of had hoped for more. Something angel-like. "Is that all?"

Michael looked like he was remembering something unpleasant. "Once you've seen a body peeled by locusts, getting eaten in tiny bites, tiny shreds, you don't want to find yourself in the open."

Grasshoppers had never looked evil to me. Not for that image. "They eat people?"

He nodded. "These do."

Well, that meant we needed to get back to Alejandro's place. We needed to warn them. And we all needed to hide. With doors and windows shuttered. I thought they'd have a good place. Vampires normally did.

"You got a problem with vampires?" I asked.

The angel's eyes never left the cloud of insects, growing larger by the moment. "What you are isn't always who you are."

Funny that had come up a few times with him. I didn't know if it was answer enough, but I guessed it would have to be.

CHAPTER THIRTY-NINE

We raced back in the new Camaro. I didn't worry so much this time that it wasn't like my old '68 Camaro. I was just happy it was fast. I didn't slow down much along the streets, like I had coming north. The stoplights and corners where cars were still parked, doors open in the middle of the intersections, I blew through those. Swapping paint on occasion in a squeal of brakes and the crunching sound of metal hitting metal.

Michael remained quiet the whole time. No backseat driving. Which had me worried even more about the plague.

Both of us looked back in different moments. After a while I stopped turning my head. The plague could be seen easy enough in the rearview. Swelling bigger and bigger, like some evil tidal wave of insects that was going to crash down on all of Cuernavaca.

I feathered the brakes, sliding into a turn. Hammered down on the gas to pull out of it. Bounced a bit as the rear fender of the Camaro smacked a tiny Toyota truck.

Then we were off again. The car surged forward, if not with the meaty rumble of my other Camaro, something that felt very much like a roar. It seemed the car also could feel the need for speed.

Soon enough we came up on the block holding Alejandro's home. The tall U-shaped fortress-like condominium of vampires. The gate in the brick wall was open, and I swung the car into the curved road, heading to the center of the U of the building, breaking in a long squeal.

There were already a few large trucks in the semi-circle in front of the building. Duallys. A few welding machines. Plates of metal. Gertrude stood by a truck with a torch in her hand, blue flame spurting out at the tip. She had a welding mask on, flipped up, and was looking at me curiously.

It looked like they were starting. Tabitha leaned against one of the trucks with a fire extinguisher nearby. She had the same expression as Gertrude, her brows furrowed over her glasses.

I switched the Camaro off and jumped out. My foot tangled on the side plate of the car and I almost fell. I narrowly avoided stabbing myself with the Five-Fold blade. Michael got out of his side no less quickly, but a lot more elegantly.

"Run," I shouted. Still trying to catch my balance, but also looking back at the cloud. It hung over the northern edge of the city, and grew. A low sound, like the screeching of a train whistle, hung at the very bottom of my hearing. The chirping of an infina-trillion locusts.

I stumbled, thinking of the train I had heard recently. The ghostly train in Hector's spirit world, the lonely, mournful cry of a hellish machine, the mechanical rumble like the stampede of a thousand bulls. Could these locusts be that sound?

I kept stumbling, it seemed to be hard for me to run and think, but got to the trucks.

"What's going on?" Tabitha asked, her face worried, but no part of her was running.

"RUN!" I screamed, grabbing her and pulling her with me.

Although having more to do with her, Gertrude was faster. The Valkyrie was out of the welding outfit, the welder off, and right next to us, running up the walk to the front door. Michael right behind us.

A vampire was at the door. Covered in a dark tactical suit, goggles and all. The sun itself wouldn't kill them, but it could be painful. Especially to the newer ones. I didn't recognize him, and wasn't sure if he knew me, but I blew past him, pulling Tabitha with me. Gertrude followed. And Michael.

I slammed shut the door. It was a fancy glass thing, tinted heavily against the sun. I didn't think it would hold against locusts. Which was a funny thought to have. Still, I looked a question at Michael.

The angel shook his head.

"Who is he?" Gertrude asked.

"A friend," I said.

"But who?"

"We can do all the specifics later," I said. "I'll make all the introductions. Right now, we need to find a place to hide."

The vampire in the tactical suit was getting up from where I had knocked him down. He took off his tactical mask. Actually, she took off her tactical mask. Millie. All suited up, she looked more like a boy than a girl.

Her face was angry. Furious. I had the feeling she didn't like me, but that, too, could wait until later. "How many people you have here?"

"People?"

"Vampires. Humans," I explained. Trying not to use the word thralls. "Whatever you want to call them."

"Not many," she said. "Some are out looking for a large truck."

Fear ran through me. Was Gabrielle one of those? Alejandro? How many people, how many allies would we lose today?

"However many," I said. "Get us to a basement. Whoever is here, get them down there. Now."

They would have a place for all of them. The whole clan. A place like in the movies, where coffins lay scattered for the vampires to sleep. A crypt, a place deep in the earth, hidden from the sun and safe.

It wasn't something vampires had to have. Or at least, most of them. Most of them would sleep in beds, in homes, in condos. But it was a place they needed. A safe place, from sunlight. A place they could hide and feel protected.

Her jaw set. The scar flashed on her face. "It's not a place we allow strangers."

"You will today," I said, staring at her. Knowing I was giving her my Grimm face. The one ready for a fight.

Still, it took Millie a second. She nodded, once. Motioned to an elevator a little down the hallway from where we stood.

"Stairs?" I asked.

Millie shook her head. "One way in. One way out."

That was exactly what we needed.

I pushed Tabitha towards Gertrude. "Get everyone down below. Make sure nothing can get in." I looked at Michael. "You too."

The angel just raised an eyebrow.

"Explain it to them," I told him.

"Where are you going?" Gertrude asked.

The screech of the train grew louder. I thought we had fifteen minutes or so. Jen was right. This did seem to happen a lot.

Boy was she going to be mad if I got eaten by locusts.

"To get who I can," I said. Shaking my own head. And running back out the door.

The screeching kept growing louder.

CHAPTER FORTY

I paused, looking back north. The black cloud covered half the sky. This close, it was less of a cloud, more of a billion black dots, darkest in the center, but black specks circled the edges, trailed down to the ground. Like little particles of darkness reaching down below.

The screeching was everywhere. It pounded in my head. And it didn't let me hear the little ticks and pops I might normally hear, as locusts begun to plop on the street around me.

I didn't have a moment to waste. I couldn't even search for a ghost on the radar. Every second counted. At least, that's what I told myself, holding onto the Five-Fold blade and pulling from it.

A part of me wondered, briefly, if I was scared of tapping another ghost. The blade was easier. Cleaner. Less of a struggle.

But that was all the thought I gave it. Like I said, time was a'wasting.

The energy poured through me. Clean. Pure. Powerful. I leapt into the air and flew. Ethereal wings spread out behind me, trailing sparks of blue and white.

The blade was strong. The symbol seemed to have endless energy. I was a fan.

I started out circling the block. Then the blocks around this block. It wasn't long before I saw a group of people near what looked to be a rail yard. At least, there was a platform, with a lot of cars lined up there, but no engine. Which seemed odd.

There was a large parking lot to the side. Acres of pavement, holding all kinds of big vans. The ones you see delivering packages. In the corner of the lot were a couple of big rigs, and a couple of the sport utility trucks I associated with Alejandro's people. The black Escalades with the tinted windows. All of them, the two eighteen-wheelers, the trucks, the vampires, were in the far corner of the parking lot. Mostly looking north.

Some of those people were dressed like Millie. In the full tactical kit that covered every bit of skin. Some of those people weren't, and I was guessing those were human.

I had found them.

Something hit my face with a pop. Then another. I spat out pieces of locust, sharp little bits of legs, ignoring the globby wormy mess that had broke open on my upper lip, thinking in a crazy way that I needed a windshield while I was flying up here.

Angel problems, right?

Anyway, I landed. Fast and hard. The ground thumped around me, hard enough that some of the humans fell, and a few vampires pulled out guns as they turned.

Alejandro was one. The vampire looked concerned, his brow furrowed, one hand on his gun. He gave a little shake of his head and put the gun away.

"That you?" he said, loudly, motioning north. The screeching had begun to pulse in a weird rhythm, like the locusts were calling. Hunting. Loud and soft, loud and soft, as they got closer and closer.

"Yeah," I said. Though the locusts weren't me, but it was definitely about me. "Well, yes and no."

His grin said it all. Like I felt. Though the vampire still looked confused.

"You guys got to get back," I said. "To your crypt."

His frown remained.

"The place under your building," I explained. The crypt. "The one the elevator goes to."

"Ah," he said. As if understanding, and not understanding. "The vault."

"Just trust me," I said. Almost shouting to be heard above the screeching. "We're all going to want to be there. Or we're all going to get eaten."

The locusts had covered three-fourths of the sky now. They began to block out the sun. A shadow crept over us. The city darkened, like a huge storm was passing over it.

The pulsing grew louder. It felt like a large bass speaker at a concert. There was the screeching, and the underlying rhythm, a subsonic type of feeling. Insects began to drop to the ground around us, drop like rain, they looked like black crickets, thick, each as large as my finger.

Alejandro gave a quick whistle and a circle of his fist above his head. Pulling his hand down sharply. A part of my brain wanted to record it and show it to Michael, the next time he wanted to tell me to run away from something.

Everyone there understood and jumped to it. Vampires and humans ran to a couple of sport utility vehicles nearby. Big trucks with shaded windows. Ran for all they were worth.

Alejandro paused. "Miss Dumont." And pointed south. Towards the building. "She's looking for keys."

"Go," I said. Pushing the vampire toward his vehicles, and ran for the train center. Pulling more energy from the blade and running faster, fast enough that the locusts felt like bullets as they hit me. It was like running through a thick storm of hail, just hail that popped their guts out when they struck.

I kept running. A blur through the air. I must have looked like the Flash. Though he wasn't covered in a bunch of twitching black legs and snot-like goo, just a red jumpsuit. I had built up enough speed I had a hard time stopping at the door. So I broke through it.

The door twisted off its hinges and danced through the inside of the center before falling to the floor. The center seemed smaller on the inside, with a tall ceiling but a compact center room. There was the door on the ground, benches lined up in a row for people to sit, and a long counter to one side where I assumed people bought tickets. Or all the delivery drivers, to pick up their routes. I wasn't sure if this was a passenger train line or some kind of freight line.

A huge clock was on a far wall, the second hand ticking around in a long arc. I couldn't hear the clock over the screeching, but I could feel each tick of every second. Locusts fluttered into the building after me, dropping to the benches and the floor here and there, single insects, exploring. Looking. Searching.

I could see and feel those things, but I could not see Gabrielle.

I rushed over to the counter, then behind it. There were two doors there, each on the left and right of the wall. Like people would come out one door, walk down the counter, and back into the other door in one large circle.

Each of the doors led to the same place, a large room with a lot of shelves and even more boxes on the shelves. I was thinking more freight train center now, or some kind of package delivery service. A cargo depot. The shelves were tall and dusty, and the room carried the musty smell all rooms holding a lot of cardboard did.

No one moved. There wasn't any sound, except for the muffled screeching from outside, getting louder and louder. And the bass-like pulsing. I yelled out for Gabrielle, but I didn't think there was any way she could hear me over the locusts now. Not even here.

I ran back to the middle room. The one with a clock. The exploring locusts had become groups of insects, searching and seeking. Hopping over the benches, fluttering through the air. I ran past them. There was a large set of double doors on the far side, and I flew toward those. Not literally, but running as fast as I could, feeling the screeching, the pulsing in my blood.

I was scared. And angry that I was scared. The pulsing reminded me too much of the geas. The heartbeat rhythm that had demanded I do whatever it was Raphael and his father had wanted. Although it wasn't controlling me, the sound pulled at me in a way that made me both wary and furious.

I broke through the double doors. It was a large bay, like a maintenance area, with house-sized roll-up doors on either side. Like garage doors, on a much larger scale.

Train tracks led inside from underneath each door. A train engine sat on the tracks facing one set of roll-up doors. A large engine, white and streaked horizontally with red lines. A few flat cars strung out behind the engine, still attached to the locomotive. Like someone had driven the train in to be worked on.

I wondered, briefly, what its whistle might sound like.

Gabrielle was standing by that engine. Looking at it. One hand on her chin. Like she was lost in thought. Like the other vampires, she was in full tactical, her hair tucked into a beret-type hat.

I shouted at her. Twice. She turned and looked, a puzzled expression on her face that quickly turned to alarm when she recognized me.

I got closer. The screeching was so loud now that I had to yell, but what was more alarming were the hard thunks that were hitting the top of the maintenance bay. Like hail, striking the roof. Hail that could eat you.

"Gabrielle! Let's go!"

I'll say this. Gabrielle asked no questions. She saw my face, and at the same time, the screeching must have registered, because she took off running.

We both took off running. Next to one of the roll-up doors was a thick emergency door, the ones that say emergency exit only. I kind of felt like this situation applied. The door held a tiny square window at head level, and that window had black things fluttering around it. Like the locusts were trying to break in.

We burst out that door into a hail of locusts. They bounced off both of us. Gabrielle let out a shocked yell of surprise, or pain. The insects popped over everyone, and where they didn't pop they clung to our clothes, our hair, and even in that moment I could feel tiny painful bites on my skin.

Gabrielle's eyes were wide in fear, or wonder, or puzzlement. I got it. I was having trouble with the idea too. But there wasn't much time, and we needed to get to the vault. I pulled energy from the blade, grabbed Gabrielle, who was light, even for as tiny as the vampire was, and flew.

The vampire let out a second yell and bit back on it as we took off through the cloud of insects.

Locusts burst around us. I flew through the cloud almost blind. It was that many. That dark. I flew up and in what I felt like was the right direction, and as I did tiny claws and wings beat at my face. Tiny exoskeletons broke and cracked over my head, always popping with a burst of goo, so much I kept wiping my eyes with the back of my hand. Next time a swarm of locusts headed my way, I needed to grab a motorcycle helmet.

It was all I could do to keep us in the right direction. Flying as fast as the swarm would let me. Pulling ethereal energy and hardening my eyes and skin. After a bit, I found myself holding the Five-Fold blade right on my forehead, trying to give my face more protection. There was a glow around the hilt of the blade, something I thought I could see only because it was so dark, a blue-white glow radiating from the Five-Fold symbol.

I held Gabrielle in the other hand, my arm around her waist. She had balled up, her arms over her head. Locusts hit us both. They tore through my clothes, her tactical suit, shredding parts of my shirt, my jeans. Blood began to run freely down her back, and though the vampire jerked as though she bit back screams, she didn't yell out loud.

I flew faster. I was healing each open wound as soon as the locust tore along my arms and legs. I was using ethereal energy to harden my skin, over and over, with each collision of every insect. With every painful tear down my side.

Gabrielle had none of that.

I kept pumping ethereal energy into my skin. Holding Gabrielle close. I finally twisted in the air, placing my back first, flying so that the locusts hit more of me than her. Trying to force my way through them, like a bowling ball going a hundred miles an hour down a lane holding nothing but insect-like pins.

It just got worse. The insect pins numbered more and more, hundreds at first, thousands a moment later, and then millions. I could feel myself slow in the air. No matter how much energy I pulled from the blade, it just wasn't enough to push me through the thickening swamp of locusts.

The weight of the insects grew heavier and heavier. The screeching louder and louder. The pulsing rhythm pushed at me, a dull bass-like undertone to everything. A sharp pain broke over my arm, the back of my hand, and then a monstrous one bit into my hip. I looked down, watching half my jeans just get ripped away, lost in the storm.

The locusts pounded the back of my head. They *rat-tat-tatted* my skull like bullets. Bullets that burst open as they hit me. The ones that survived, for the briefest of moments, survived only to tear at me.

The vampire let out a scream of pain, or maybe she had been screaming, and it had been muffled by her arms. She kept her face hidden, but even balled up, even hidden as much as I could hide her with my own body, locusts were striking her. The tactical suit on her back was nothing but tattered remnants of black nylon, leaving her back open and exposed and thick with trails of blood. Her beret was gone, and her hair was crawling with the insects, the locusts clinging to the dark strands.

I glanced in front of us, turning my head, feeling the bullets of locusts work their way across my face. The building appeared and disappeared in front of me. Hidden by the thick darkness of the plague of locusts. I was aiming for the front door, but it seemed so far away. I didn't think we'd make it.

Well, I might. If I kept pulling ethereal energy. Gabrielle wouldn't.

The air beat at me. The pulsing beat at me. The locusts striking my head beat at me. Everything beat and wore me down, as much as I pulled energy from the Five-Fold blade. Repairing my wounds. Hardening my skin. Trying to make myself a human tank, shielding Gabrielle from the storm.

The last of my shirt ripped away.

There was a moment of me looking at it, a brief flash of whiteness lost in a storm of black. Another T-shirt lost, this one torn from me. Gone. A silly thing, but also the final straw.

All there was left was anger. Anger at losing. Anger at the locusts bursting over my skin. My one-legged jeans. The insects eating Gabrielle alive with every bite.

I kept pushing. It was all I could do. Flying blind, steering towards the front of the building, backwards through the air. An ever-slowing flight. Towards a destination I might reach, but my passenger wouldn't.

The locusts burst all over my back, the goo washing away in the sea of air and other insects bursting in the same place. I gathered Gabrielle like a child in my lap. Encircled her with my arms, the ethereal glow of the Five-Fold blade lighting a small nimbus around us. All I could do was this, protect the vampire as much as I could, and even so, watching all the blood run down the ragged remains of her suit.

With no outlet, nothing but an infinite amount of insects to punish, my anger just grew. This was a lousy way to die. Not me, or likely not me, but her. Gabrielle would die a very painful, very messy death. Likely was already dying, her muffled screams trailed off, she no longer jerked at a particular large bite.

My anger found somewhere to go. Something burst from my back. At first I thought it was a larger locust. Maybe they made them car-sized now. It felt like something slammed into my back, or out of my back, either way the reverberation of the collision certainly felt like a car had hit me head on.

But it wasn't a car-sized locust. Electricity burst out of me, too, sparks shooting outward, briefly, blue-white trails like small fireworks. Fireworks with forks of lightning.

Whatever it was, or whatever it had been, flapped over my head, like a hood, but higher. Taller. Fluttering a bit in the air above me.

I almost stopped flying. I almost dropped Gabrielle in surprise. Shock.

They were wings.

Real wings.

Real, like a real angel. Not the ethereal ones. Real wings had burst from my back. Feeling them slice through the air, funnel the currents of wind around us, like the wings of a Boeing 747.

I brought Gabrielle in closer. Huddled around her. Feeling, as I did so, things slide out of my arms. My legs. My chest and back. Everywhere around me, and all at once.

It was so dark now it was hard to see, and the things were black. A bluish black. Like a shiny metal. Or hard, polished leather.

Armor.

Like back in Grafton.

The armor plated me. Or I became plated with it. It was thick and big and made me half-again as tall. Half-again as wide.

A moment before I was a slowing down, a human weighed down with the thickest of the plague of locusts around him. Drowning in a sea of insects that tore through both me and my passenger.

Now I was a plow. A thickly armored vehicle hurtling through the air. My wings spread in a way that they funneled through the locusts, diverting them to either side of us. Like an arrow splitting the air.

Just a well-armored arrow. An arrow trailing spits and sparks of blue and white. The few insects that made it past us splatted harmlessly on the armor plate. I never felt a thing. I was hoping Gabrielle didn't, either.

There was a moment of silence. Like everything was quiet inside the pocket of air around us. Well, relative silence, in the middle of all the screeching. Gabrielle's head lolled back from her arms, her eyes were slits, and they seemed to widen a moment before rolling up into the top of her head.

Then we crashed through the vampire's building. The front of it, luckily. Right by the door. My aiming was mostly true. I slammed up against the wall of the hallway, going halfway through it before stopping in an immediate and painful stop. Gabrielle flying out of my hands and rolling down the hall.

I blinked. Took a deep breath. I had made an angel-sized door in the wall, right next to the front door of Alejandro's building. Like one of the old Road Runner cartoons. And, for the moment, locusts weren't swirling right in after me. They were bouncing around the edges of the hole. Trickling in. As if wondering where we had gone.

I shrugged myself out of the hole with a groan. My armor began to slip back under my skin. An uncomfortable feeling. Not tingly, but that type of sensation. Like the type of feeling you get watching something you can't turn away from, like a television show on pimple popping, or a doctor making that first long incision across the belly in a surgery. A feeling I couldn't turn away from because I wasn't watching it. The feeling was all around and *in* me.

It felt like forever, but in a moment, the armor was all gone. The wings, gone. Back to wherever it went inside me.

I shivered.

The trickling locusts all paused. At the same moment. Almost like someone was directing them. The closest ones in the hallway found me, and then all of them, each of the creatures faced me at exactly the same time.

I turned down the hall, pulling Gabrielle with me as fast as I could. Slapped the elevator button. Screamed as the doors opened, too slowly, far too slowly, the doors dawdling in their speed. Revealing the elegant cab inside like they were unveiling a secret.

I couldn't wait. As soon as the doors had parted enough, I pushed Gabrielle in. Stepping over her and tugging her body to the corner of the cab. She wasn't moving much. My hands slipped on her arms, covered in blood. Mostly, I thought, hers.

Her body fell back against the corner, limp. She let out a soft moan. I pounded the door close button, once, twice, a hundred times. Locusts followed us in, and I slapped the ones I could out of the air, feeling them burst on my palm.

Slowly, in their dawdling manner, the doors shut. The screeching lessened as they did, muffled by the thick elevator walls. A trickle of insects continued to slip through the narrowing crack. I kept up my game of locust-pong, hitting the ones that flew in with my open hand. Smacking them into the walls of the cab. Hearing them *snick-snack* against the metal like a ping-pong ball.

The doors finally shut.

There was a dinging sound. Announcing we were moving. The same dinging sound every elevator had all across the world.

We descended. At a pretty good pace. I could feel the floor dropping in the pit of my stomach. It went on for a while.

I crushed a final locust under my foot.

Gabrielle's eyes were closed. Her face, even unconscious, scrunched up in pain. There were hundreds, if not thousands, of cuts over her skin. Dark liquid ran from all of them.

It was then that the adrenaline fell out of me. One moment I had energy; I was standing and slapping locusts and screaming. The next I found myself on the floor of the cab. I worked myself up next to Gabrielle. Since I was there, I checked to make sure she was still breathing.

She was. It was a wonder. Her tactical suit was in shreds. Locusts, mostly dead locusts, still lay tangled in her hair. Some of the insects I thought stirred, but I lacked the energy to pluck them out.

I wondered how I looked. Missing a leg of my jeans. T-shirt gone. Covered not in blood, well, not mostly my blood, but a mix of mine and Gabrielle's and the green goo of a million exploded locusts.

I was sure I wasn't a pretty sight. But at least I was a live one. And Gabrielle too, for the moment.

I thought, maybe, we had made it.

CHAPTER FORTY-ONE

The falling pit sensation of the elevator ended with the ringing of a bell. The same one that elevators around the door used, a tiny ding announcing our arrival. I opened my eyes, not realizing I had closed them.

I was tired. Exhausted. Beat.

The doors slid open.

Millie stood there. Alejandro. Gertrude and Michael.

Their eyes opened wide at seeing us.

I must have missed a locust. Or one had hidden from me. Locust-pong was a violent game. The locust fluttered out. It looked a little lost, a little drunk, and kept hitting the wall opposite the elevator with a little *ticking* sound. A sound that ended when Michael smacked it with the flat of his hand.

Locust-pong was also not a spectator sport. The thought had me chuckle. Or at least try. My throat was dry.

None of them looked surprised to see the insect. Or the crushed ones in the car. Or the condition of me and Gabrielle.

"Help her," I croaked.

I felt the vampire still breathing, slightly. She had leaned closer to me, and one of my arms lay around her back. I was exhausted. More than exhausted, used up. Spent. I couldn't get up, couldn't move my legs, hell I had to let Alejandro move my arm as he and Millie worked Gabrielle up.

She groaned a bit at that.

I hoped that was a good sign.

They took her away, gently and carefully.

Gertrude and Michael got me up in much the same way, helping me out of the elevator. Once they did, once blood started moving in my arms and legs, I found I could help. At least take a small step or two, here and there. Move my legs in a weak approximation of walking so that they weren't dragged.

The two of them pulled me out of the elevator, down a short cubby area, and into a large room. Kind of like the area they have at the top of nice apartment complexes. The areas that tenants can reserve for a large party, with doors leading to balconies and the elevator cubby in the middle of one wall.

It was a tall area, the ceiling fifteen or twenty feet above us. Tiny, elegant chandeliers ran along the ceiling, golden things with tiny globes of light dangling from them. A large bar ran along one side, a wall-sized television mounted on the wall above the bar. The bar held sinks and refrigerators, bottles of wine on racks inside them.

Couches and seats were everywhere. Most of them filled. Vampires I had seen in the tactical gear, but also vampires in normal clothes. Humans, too. A fair mix of all. Fifty of them, or a hundred. The place felt packed, like a refugee camp.

And still, it was a large area. Alejandro and Millie were carrying Gabrielle to one of the doors in a far corner. The door was open. A few of the humans and vampires helped them, one holding the door. Others looking questioningly at me.

I couldn't blame them; I knew I looked a sight.

Gertrude and Michael brought me over to the bar. I was able to stand there, leaning with my lower back holding most of my weight against the bar. Gertrude pulled a bottle of water out of the fridge and gave it to me, something tall and long. I held it, unopened, and waited.

"We have to tell you something," Gertrude said.

Michael's eyebrows raised, as if he was asking, *now?*

I wasn't sure what it was, but it wasn't going to be good.

I nodded.

"You have your phone on you?"

I didn't. I had left it in the car. I shook my head.

"Jen tried to call us," Gertrude began.

The words hit me so hard I almost didn't hear the rest. They hit me with the realization that something was wrong. Something I hadn't counted on.

I almost didn't hear the rest.

"We were in the elevator," the Valkyrie explained. "So we're not sure if that's why the signal cut out. But she was calling and shouting about something. I heard yelling in the background. Maybe explosions."

Those were brutal words, bringing a more brutal realization.

The cloud had been out there too.

I had asked Jen about it. Warned her to stay indoors for a bit. I went lost in that thought, wondering if she had taken me seriously. Would I have, if the shoe was on the other foot?

Explosions. Shouting. Where had Jen been? Had Sarah been close by? Nick and Johnny? Had Jen had to run out and find them? Had she been out in the open when the locusts hit? Had all my friends?

Had the explosions been the last gasp of my four best friends?

Thought after thought poured out. None of them good. But they kept pouring.

I stood there for I don't know how long.

Something slapped my face.

Gertrude.

I wasn't holding the bottle of water anymore. It had fallen to the ground. Empty and crinkled, the way the plastic bottles are when someone crushes them in their fist.

My hand was wet.

"Grimm," the Valkyrie said. "It doesn't have to be bad."

It didn't, but I knew better. I had lived this before.

"They can take care of themselves," she said.

I knew she was worried about Zoe, but the Valkyrie looked like she knew the deal. Her words were the words people gave to those who had survived a real battle. A war. Something like, hey, we know a lot of people died, but hey, you're alive, and we won.

But we hadn't won.

And I should have known. I had enough of the bad feelings to know. Something monitoring me from Mexico City when I had first looked at the Dead Zone from Cuernavaca. Nick's pictures, the wondering thought of the lion's head of Sabnock looking right at the camera. Feelings of something being off. Making me uneasy.

Michael had said Sabnock loved a trap.

Sabnock had even told me the trap had been sprung. I had convinced myself I was the center of the demon's attention, but I hadn't really listened to him. I hadn't paid close enough attention.

The trap hadn't been just for me.

It had been for us all.

I hadn't fooled the demon at all, with my flying around the southern edge of the Dead Zone. With appearing here and there and killing creatures where I found them. With my showy flying around the southern edge of the zone, like a fighter jet on patrol. I hadn't fooled him, and I hadn't pulled his attention to me and me alone. Hadn't been close.

Sabnock had known, had laid the trap, and had waited for the perfect moment to strike. He had waited until I was separated from my friends. Until I was too far away to help them at all. Until all I could do was hide, and wonder.

I closed my eyes. Trying to feel Jen in the key, and not feeling anything. Not this far away from her, not this deep underground.

I hadn't felt anything from her along the bond, but would I have, flying through the plague of locusts? While trying to keep Gabrielle safe? With a million insects tearing at us? While becoming some kind of armored angel?

There had been too much going on.

I pushed Gertrude's arms away. Staggered through the large room in a direction I knew, without knowing how, was northeast. I walked like a drunk man, passing by vampire and human, not seeing either, until I pressed against the wall there.

It was cold. Flat. Unresponsive.

Much like the key.

I stayed like that for a long time, with my forehead lying against the wall. My arms above me, my palms pressed flat, too. Taking large, empty breaths.

Reaching out from the keydrop. Pushing what I could along it. Trying to feel Jen along our bond, stretching from here to there. From Cuernavaca to that small town, north-northeast of us. Wondering if that same storm of locusts, that same plague, had struck my friends there and wiped them out. Having that image, the one I had just barely survived, go through my head over and over, with my friends at the middle of the plague of locusts, and not me.

A hand placed itself on my shoulder.

Michael.

He handed me that same bottle of water.

But remained quiet.

I thought about everything a long time. As I did, I became aware of how thirsty I was. It burned inside me. Finally, I opened the bottle. The plastic top broke from the plastic ring holding it in place with a little snick. I took a sip. It was a little cool, not quite warm, and I took another. Then another. Until it was finished.

Michael had another.

I took it too. Did the same there. As I drank, a little feeling came back into me. Maybe the blood in me started moving again, now that I was giving it liquid. My arms and legs and back hurt, like they had been beaten with baseball bats. I was sore, everywhere.

At some point I turned around. Leaned my back against the wall. Drank more. Slowly slid down the wall, my back sticking occasionally to the paint, leaving a locust-goo streak as I slid, until I was seated on the floor.

I needed a shower.

And a new T-shirt.

My eyes shimmered with water. Thoughts of Jen and T-shirts and breakfast in our apartment. Showers. The bacon fight. Bringing her coffee. Laughter. Us holding each other in the bed. Her feeling like a big baby. Me telling her it was all okay.

Blame washed over me. I recognized it, hell I knew all about that emotion, and knew it wouldn't matter. That was what was insidious about blame. About doubt and despair. They could twist you up even when the feeling was wrong. But when they were right, well, the twisting only got worse. Like the sharpest knife digging right under your ribcage.

I thought I was passing out. At the same time, I knew I was trying to stand. But my body wasn't moving. Wasn't doing either.

I could make it to our little hideout. All I needed was the Five-Fold blade. All I needed was a little ethereal energy, and I'd take it from it or all the ghosts everywhere around. I could move, as long as I could keep tapping into ghosts.

"You will not make it." The angel had read my thoughts.

I still tried to move. I think my leg twitched. My arm, the one holding the bottle of water, let the bottle go.

"The plague will pass. Then we will go."

Still, I looked around for the blade. The fingers of my open hand opened and closed, as if they were holding it. But the blade wasn't there. I couldn't find it.

My hand found its way to the floor. I tried to lever myself up.

Michael's palm on my chest stopped me. Held me in place. Lightly.

"Stop," his voice said. Soft. Comforting. But commanding.

I looked at him. His eyes shimmered, too. "Rest, brother. Rest. Then we will go."

My throat still felt hoarse. Torn. The voice, broken. "It'll be too late."

His hand stayed on my chest. Palm flat. Fingers splayed. Warm.

"It is too late already," he said. "What has happened, has happened."

"We can't save them," I said.

"No," he said. "We can't. Not now. Not anymore."

His voice still soft, and I wondered about what had happened to him, so long ago, to cause him to hide for two thousand years. "It is now you have to trust them. You have to believe in them. You should know, I know you know, we cannot be everywhere. Not all the time."

My eyes crunched up. Tears ran from them. Warm trails sliding down my cheeks. My shout, broken and hoarse, erupted throughout the room. "What good can we do, then?"

And even that little bit of energy failed me. My hand collapsed, limp. My legs lay there like a corpse. It hurt to breathe, to pull in air and let it back out. It all seemed like a chore.

Some of the vampires around us had jumped. A few of them, vampire and human, stepped back. With little worried glances at each other.

"Fergus Grimm," Michael said, then stopped. His hand flexed against my chest, as if an anger had briefly ridden through him. As if his fingers would have spasmed into a fist, had he not held them back.

He pulled his hand away. Michael's voice, next, no longer soft. It carried a surprising amount of iron in it. Hot iron. "We will do what we can. What we should."

His eyes no longer shimmered with water. His irises were black in their intensity. They burned with anger. In that moment, they felt as black as my soul.

"After all," he said. "I am the angel of death."

CHAPTER FORTY-TWO

Jen hung up with Gus. As always, feeling the connection of the phone end with a muted click. Missing him already.

The bond was still there, weak with the distance. It had pulsed so hard earlier, Jen had felt sorrow and love and guilt, all mixed together, those emotions had washed strongly over her from the bond, from Gus... her heart still beat hard with the memory of it. With the fear that he had died.

Then the bond had gone quiet. Jen had gotten used to always feeling him there. The maleness of him. Stubborn. Hard-headed. Worried. He was a contradiction of strength and weakness, of fight and self-doubt, and had been since the day she had met him.

If you smile it might make your face look better...

Jen smiled.

She glanced out the window, looking southwest. There were clouds there, massing above Mexico City. Thick clouds, and they felt wrong. That and Gus's warning was enough for her to start gathering people together.

Better safe than sorry.

Jen had found Sarah in the planning session. Zoe, resting in her apartment, the one she shared with Gertrude and her mother. The two of them went back to the top of the safe house. They crawled up the ladder and stood on the roof, facing the clouds.

They had gotten bigger. The clouds didn't look like real clouds, they were almost pixelated, as if they were made of millions and millions of black dots. Jen might have been imagining it, but she thought she heard a whistling in the distance.

Sarah called Nick. Her sister's eyes were worried. Jen tried Johnny's cell and got a busy signal. They all went back to the planning room, and Nick had appeared shortly, with a few bags of groceries and a questioning look. The cloud was larger, they could see the edges of it in the large windows of the planning room, and the whistling had become a low-lying keening, something Jen felt almost in the air.

Still no Johnny. And he wasn't answering his phone. Jen had watched Gabrielle and Johnny when they separated, and the look on the vampire's face reminded her of how she had looked one morning, when she had woken up and found Gus gone, and Danny dead.

Johnny's face had looked darker. More withdrawn. As if he was pushing deep down anything he was feeling. Pushing it down and replacing it with alcohol.

Jen had been leaning against Gus. Enjoying her moment of togetherness, of feeling Gus's strength on the outside, and doubts on the inside. She loved that he was complicated, and that he was good, and that he was hers.

So it had been hard watching Gabrielle and Johnny. Not every relationship worked, Jen knew that, but there was a part of her that wanted her friends to have what she had. She wanted Sarah and Nick and Johnny and Gabrielle to have what she had with Gus.

Someone who would come for them, even after death. Who would come no matter what.

A tough ask, but it was what she wanted.

She had leaned there, against Gus, watching the two of them. Johnny and Gabrielle. Feeling Gus through the bond, the worry he was trying to hide from her, about her, and wondering if he could feel her hiding her worry from him.

Round and round.

Gus smiled at me. He didn't smile often, he grinned in a way that men did, thinking it made them look tough, but his smiles did make his face look better.

"You going to be okay?" he asked, keeping his voice light.

Jen raised her eyebrows. "You think we can't survive a couple of days without you?"

His smile turned into his Gus grin. "Well, now that you mention it…"

She punched him. Hard. And pressed up tight against Gus and kissed him for all she was worth. For all the moments they had been together. And all the moments in the future. He had wrapped his arms around her, and Jen had taken a big breath of him, smelling the sandalwood scent he thought was piney, but wore for her.

Then he let her go. The warmth of him leaving quickly, being replaced by the coolness of the night air. His eyes firmed up, as if Gus had seen something, and he walked over to say something to Johnny.

Something beat against the windows. Thrummed, like a light rain. The sound brought Jen back to the now, to standing in the planning session room.

Something black and small bounced off the plate-glass windows there. Little objects, maybe the size of her fingers.

"Are those… cockroaches?" Sarah asked. Both her sister and Nick had come up to stand next to Jen, and they both watched the rain of insects start dribbling down from the skies. Just a few smacked against the window, others fell down to the street below, too small to really make out.

One of the black things caught on the bottom lip of the window. Paused there a second. Black-winged, black-legged, long carapace, with tiny mandibles.

"Grasshopper," Nick said, bending down to really peer at it. Placing his face right on the glass.

The creature reared up a moment, facing the window, and started bobbing up and down. She could almost hear the thing scream an alert. Like the insect was shouting *Found Them, Found Them, Found Them...*

Then a burst of wind took the thing from the window.

"Not a grasshopper," Jen said. Her voice flat. "Locusts."

"Locusts?" Nick turned, and his eyes widened at the realization. "Shit."

"What does that mean?" Zoe asked from the kitchen. Her hand on the fridge door.

Jen walked away from the window. "We need to find Johnny." She tried his phone again, and it rang and rang until voice mail picked up: *You've reached Johnny. Speak up, drink up, or hang up...*

Jen swore. The group ran down to his apartment, the place he shared with Gabrielle. It was littered with empty bottles, and a half-eaten enchilada on a plate on the kitchen counter, but there was no Johnny passed out in the bed. No Johnny taking a long, hungover shower.

Their apartment faced the west, away from sunrise, so it was easy to see the cloud from Mexico City through the windows there. The ever-swelling cloud with its ever-increasing whistling sounding through the air. A whistling, a keening. Screeching.

The light hail-tapping sound of insects against the glass of the window became a heavy thrumming of a hard rain. The black things began to pop against the glass windows. Literally popped, the creature leaving a green goo behind.

"What the fuck?" Nick asked, standing in the kitchen, watching the locusts beat against the glass until—one by one—they exploded.

Jen went right to the window. Trying to see through the hail of locusts thrumming against the glass. Trying to peer through the stains of green goo sliding down the window. Trying to see behind and through all that, looking at the storm of insects flooding main street, as if a tidal wave of locusts smashed over the town.

"You have got to be kidding me," she said. Softly. The locusts blew by as if heavy gusts of wind carried them, one black tidal wave after the next. Like the air was an ocean, the winds a heavy current, and the insects carried over the town in great washes of waves. Waves brought by an ocean of storms.

"Bar." Nick's voice abruptly broke through Jen's thoughts. She looked over at him with a raised eyebrow. Still watching, out of the corner of her eyes, the black waves of insects crash over the town.

He held an empty beer bottle in his hand. Motioned to the rest of the empties. "Bar. That's where he is."

Johnny.

None of them spoke. They all turned and ran. Their feet thudding down the hall, down the stairs. The thrumming of hail became the breaking of glass. Windows broke behind them, above them, the glass popped and tinkled from the apartments they ran past.

The four of them got to the entrance at the bottom of the stairs. The thick door there, always locked behind with bar across it. The walls of the apartment complex were sturdy, and so was the door, but even still the keening of the insects broke through, muffled only slightly by the brick and the wood. And behind the keening were little popping sounds, as if the insects were dive-bombing the ground, cracking their carapaces on the sidewalk. It sounded like hail.

Sarah grabbed Jen's hand; the sisters exchanged glances, a million things passing between them. Worry. Knowledge. Fear. It felt like death was knocking at the door. Death was outside, waiting for them all.

Her heart thudded in her chest. Jen had already died once. She wasn't about to do it again. There was the briefest thought of staying inside, of hiding in the building, just flicker through her mind that went away just as quickly as glass tinkled above them, broken windows from the apartments upstairs.

The whistling, screeching, keening of the locusts swelled inside the building.

As if that was the cue, Nick worked the bar off the door, swinging it open. The whistling became a high-pitched screaming, a screeching. Black dots zipped through the air, sounding, feeling almost like bullets to Jen.

Like the bullet that had killed her.

For a moment she couldn't move. Couldn't breathe. *There was the shot, the final shot, the zipping sound of the bullet through the air, and then pain, pain in her chest...*

Then her sister pulled her out. Nick was there in the street, dancing, swatting insects as they hit him. Making his way down the alley. Sarah tugged Jen along, and Jen followed, a little numb. Still thinking of the bullet. Of the black gun that had fired it. And that whistling, zipping sound that had signaled the end of her life.

Jen's skin stung in places. Her neck. Her arms. She couldn't shake her fear. Couldn't shake the sound. And couldn't shake the feeling that, like the gun firing the bullet that had killed her, something else was behind it all.

Nick stumbled through the alley. He was at the corner there, at where the alley met main street, pressing himself against the little stucco wall there as if it would protect him. Zoe ran by, yelling, her hands over her face. They weren't far behind either of them, Jen and her sister; Sarah kept tugging her along, constantly looking back at Jen. Worried.

There was something out there.

The feeling shook Jen. Got her moving. The black waves of the insects washed down the street in front of them all, hiding everything in darkness, but even so Jen thought she saw a form hiding there. Something tall. Someone dark but also glinty. As if sunlight caught something there, whatever rays could break through the dark cloud of insects.

There was something out there. The dark and glinty something, or someone. Someone who might be pulling the trigger right now.

And somehow, Jen's fear turned into anger. Into fury. It got her moving, got her running. Now Jen was pulling Sarah along, screaming for them all to get into the bar.

The screeching sound was so loud, she didn't know if anyone heard her. But they all knew where they were going. She ran with her sister, hand in hand, Zoe and Nick in front of them. All of them now swatting as sharp mandibles, mandibles too big for the insects, took tiny chunks from their skin.

The locust waves crashed over them. Chittering and screeching and biting and zipping. The whistling hissing sound of a thousand bullets passing overhead. Jen and her friends slowing down, more and more, as they spent their time trying to get the insects off of them. They clung to their thin shirts, their jeans, their hair. They hung from their mandibles, dangling from skin. Drops of blood came as Jen swatted them away.

The bar wasn't far away, but they weren't going to make it. Not with the locusts surrounding them. Not with that thing hiding behind them.

Jen's fury swelled, became something larger. Greater. Something that burned inside her, burned with a fiery anger that she could not control. Something that wanted to burn away the locusts, burn away the thing hiding behind them, burn it all away—

She stopped, tugging her hand from Sarah's. Then she raised both arms in the air, screaming defiance. Raised her face to the sky and ignored the bullet-like sounds of locusts buzzing by, the bites of the insects, the burns from all the tiny scratches and tears in her skin.

If the locusts, if that glinting thing hiding out there wanted a storm, she could bring one.

She would *be* the storm.

The waves of insects slowed over the street, as if they were moving in slow motion. A gust of wind blew over them all, not the waving gusts of the locusts, but a gust that brought the awareness of a coming storm. The burning bites faded as the refreshing coolness of a coming rain washed over Jen and her friends. Not a real rain, just the feeling and scent of the drops in the air, the lightest haze in the air, a cool wetness. A feeling of a chill, as if the rain was coming from clouds miles above the stratosphere, as if a storm was coming from the glacial voids of space.

The coolness brought a boom of thunder.

Nick turned to look at Jen. His eyes open. His face with an understanding grin. His hand smacking a locust hanging from his chin.

The refreshing coolness burst over them as a second boom rumbled through the air. A rumbling felt underneath the screaming of the locusts. The boom was followed by an ear-splitting crack, a sound that snapped through the screeching of locusts around them.

A bolt of power struck nearby. Not something that could be seen clearly through the cloud of insects. But something that could be felt.

The power surge through Jen. The *electricity* of it. The tingling ran over her skin, through her bones, her muscles, from the top of her head to the tips of her toes. Like always, it thrilled her. It powered her. It rose her from being just Jen, to being the storm.

A second bolt snapped to the ground. Closer to the group. Locusts burst and scattered under the strike. The wave of them broke. Ozone wafted, thick in the air.

Then a third bolt.

Then a rain of them. A barrage. Bolts struck everywhere along the street. All around the group. Jen directed each bolt, calling it down from up high in the atmosphere, pulling the lightning down to strike around them all. Strike down the street. Poke and prod at the waves of insects hiding the glinty man.

Each strike blazed briefly in a snap of electric blue. The street flashed with it as Jen brought the storm over them all. The locusts no longer dive-bombed the street, sounding like hail. They no longer zipped by like a bullet.

They fled. In a quick moment, in the strikes of lightning around them, they had turned from a coordinated mass of attackers into fleeing individual insects. Flopping and twitching as the lightning struck all around them. Floating in circles, dizzy from the flashing bright blue light.

And then rain burst down. A chilly, soaking rain. It came down like a thick curtain, sweeping over the group and cleansing them, briefly, from locusts and bites.

Nick was the first person to break from the shock of it all. He grabbed Sarah in one hand, Zoe in the other, and was dashing down the street. Towards the bar. El Muerde Amargo. The yellow letters a dull glow in the blackness of the locust cloud, the neon sign still flickering its big letter A in glaring red.

Jen took a few steps and stopped. Took a look around. The sense of that glinty person was still out there, strong. Hidden from her lightning.

Then she ran too. Her feet stomping on the shells of locusts.

372 • CHRIS J CRANFORD

Crushing them underfoot, feeling them pop under the soles of her shoes. Feeling the electricity of the storm run along her skin.

They all got to the bar. Nick burst through the door first, pulling Sarah and Zoe behind him. Jen followed them up, Nick slamming the door shut behind her.

The jukebox was still playing inside. Something with a marimba. It was small and hard to hear after the booming thunder outside.

The two of them looked through the dirty glass of the door. The locusts swirled lazily outside, gathering themselves together in little flocks, the flocks becoming swirls, the swirls becoming thick black tendrils of insects, circling around the bar.

"What're we looking at?" Nick asked.

"Something's out there," Jen said.

"Something?"

Jen's eyes traced the circling tendrils of locusts. "Someone."

Nick's following grunt was, well, Nick.

Jen balled her fist, feeling the spark of the storm inside her hand, the call of electric power. The storm raged overhead, raged up in the exosphere, and Jen pulled some lightning down. Tiny, thin bolts that stabbed up and down the street. Probing for the glinty man.

She thought she heard a laugh. A deep voice, a rough one, a voice that sounded like a hundred voices. Jen thought it might have been in her head, but then Nick glanced at her, his eyebrow raised.

"Damn," Jen said.

She turned around, looking around the bar. She had been there just a few days ago with Gus and Zoe. So it was easy to gather it all back in, see the bartender—Renaldo—standing by the large window by the front of the bar, a stained rag in the older man's hand, his mouth open, his eyes looking through the glass to the street outside.

The insects there moved across the glass, crawling, glistening with water.

And there was Johnny, sitting at a table by himself, a bunch of empties on the table in front of him. Empty bottles sitting around a game of dominoes he had been playing. His eyes stared at the group, blurry.

"Guys," he said. His words making the *S* sound more of a *Ssshhh*. "I'm seeing the damndest thing."

More insects followed Jen in. Zoe shut the door. Jen faced the street, feeling the bolts come down through the air, directing them in front of the bar. There was a *snap-snap-snap*, a rattling long *cracking* sound, like the splitting of a forest of giant trees, and a row of lightning bolts rattled the street. Leaving blue zigzags as an after-image in her eyes.

The bartender said something low. In Spanish. One of his hands made the sign of the cross in front of him.

"We need to find a place to hide," Jen said aloud. She could only call lightning down so long. Well, she would call it as long as she could, but it would be a battle between her and the cloud of locusts. And that cloud had seemed large. Larger than Mexico City. Larger than Mexico. Jen had no illusions that she could keep her storm around long enough to protect them all from a sea of *that*.

The song ended. The marimba died out. Then a flare came from the bond. Something sharp and pained and full of wonder. The surprise and pain of it caused Jen to stumble to a knee.

Gus, Jen wondered, a hand going to the bond. *Gus, are you okay?*

That moment was all the locusts needed.

They redoubled their fury. Their attack. The big window by the front door burst open, and a flood of insects streamed in. Their buzzing angry. Their screeching large cries for blood.

Jen pulled lightning down on top of them all. The bolts stitched the area around the bar. They struck the roof. They struck the windows. They struck the waves of insects trying to fly in. Ozone flooded her nose; it became all Jen could smell.

The bartender stepped back. Looked at the group with his badly broken nose. Something in the man's brain clicked. "Freezer," he shouted. His accent making the word come out fast.

Nick got it first. He pulled Johnny out of his chair and ran to the back of the bar. There was a door there, and he got Johnny through it. Sarah and Zoe, and the bartender behind him. Jen behind them all, walking slower, calling lightning over them all.

The insects redoubled, tripled their fury. It was as if the locusts could feel the group slipping away. Jen made it to the door, now calling lightning from her hand. Shooting it behind her through the bar. Watching the bolts zigzag through the air, instantly super-heating the insects, bursting the locusts in midair.

Past the door was a kitchen. It held ovens, fryers, a standing fridge. Pots and pans hung from hooks over a center island, a long steel table. The walls were metal too, not quite shiny, but a dull metal, and past the kitchen were a couple of doors. One looked to be an exit door to the back of the building. The other door was a thick piece of stainless steel, like it opened to a walk-in freezer.

Nick already had that door open. Sarah and Zoe and Johnny were already through it. He was helping Renaldo in. The bartender kept looking back at the kitchen. At the bar. At Jen and the locusts streaming in past her. At the locusts streaming in from *above* her.

Was there a hole in the roof?

The glinty man struck then.

The power went out. The kitchen fell into an instant blackness. Jen couldn't see a foot in front of her. Much less the door.

"Storm Witch!" the voice she had heard earlier, the rough, deep laughing voice of a thousand voices, called.

It sounded right behind her.

She spun. Called the lightning shield around her just as something struck her. It felt like a pole. There was a zipping whip-like sound, and all of a sudden, she was tumbling over the ground. The lightning shield blazed a brilliant blue. It popped and sizzled and burned part of the metal of the table. It fried insects trying to bite her.

She hit the ground on her back. A bolt of lightning flew from her hand, suddenly, without a target. Like her hand had spasmed under a bite and thrown the bolt accidentally, electricity zapped along the stainless-steel table and exploded against the far wall.

Her shield, that bolt, illuminated the kitchen in flashes. She saw Nick, briefly, shutting the freezer door. His eyes connected with hers, and she saw fear there, fear of something, but also anger. His eyes—behind wire-rim glasses—full of determination. His lips twisted in an angry snarl.

Then Jen understood the fear. The flashing blue of her shield had also shown her what had struck her. *Who* had struck her. It lit up in front of her, the demon. Sabnock. A tall, dark man with a black staff in one hand, and that gold lion thing on his shoulder.

Smiling.

She tried to back up until her back hit the wall. The fear overwhelmed her. The demon was her. With Jen. Coming after her and her friends while Gus was far away. While Gus wasn't there.

The demon was here. He was here to kill her, to kill her friends. He was here with the bullet-like locusts swirling in the clouds around her. He was here, the shadow behind it all, the shadow with a weapon, a weapon aimed at Jen and about to fire.

She screamed. Called bolts of lightning down between her and the demon. Watched one burn along the table, dance until it struck him. Then another bolt, a direct hit. And then a third pounded the demon, driving Sabnock to one knee.

A glow of red appeared in his hand, the hand not holding a staff, and the demon struck back. Red blasts of force came from his fist, at first bouncing off her shield, and then sticking to the lightning circling her for a moment. The red *attaching* itself to the blue until deep swirling purple tendrils spat and hissed.

And then disappeared.

Her shield was getting eaten. Was evaporating. She called more lightning, but could also feel the exhaustion setting in. The storm, so much storm, so much *power*, being called so quickly.

Fear came back then. Fear of death. Of her friends, just a few feet away. Of Jen dying and leaving them all at the mercy of Sabnock. Of her lying there, looking up at her death, just like she had watched the bullet from Azazel crash into her chest.

She found a way to turn the fear into fury. Found a way to dig a little deeper. To call one more bolt, a large thing, the size of a car, and pull it down from space to drive into the demon like a thousand-pound hammer driving a spike into the earth.

The demon screamed. The scream became a roar of pain, of a hundred, thousand voices screaming in agony.

And then the lightning bolt was gone. Jen's lightning shield was gone. There was nothing left but the blackness of the kitchen. The chittering of the locusts. A small pause, as if the insects realized they were no longer being burned.

Only seconds had passed in the fight between her and Sabnock. Brief, fleeting moments. And now Jen was exhausted, and the insects were back and biting her.

They were everywhere, suddenly and thickly. Jen couldn't see anything in front of her. She tried crawling through the darkness, and her head bumped painfully against the center island. She knew the door to the freezer was somewhere in the room, but she had no real idea where.

All she could hear was the screeching. It was loud and everywhere. A pulsing could be underneath the sound, something rhythmic. The pulsing, like the beating of her heart, slowly slowing down. Jen tried to huddle into herself, rolled underneath what she felt was the table, whatever it was she had cracked her head on. It was too dark, she couldn't see, didn't know where the door was.

There was nothing but the locusts. Nothing but the bites. Nothing but darkness, a darkness growing darker, her heart loudly pounding in her chest. Jen didn't want to die. But she also didn't want to be scared anymore of death. It made no sense to her, the fear —

Arms huddled around her, quickly. Lean arms. Nick.

He pulled her face hard into his chest. As if he had just appeared from the shadows above her. Walking the short distance from the freezer to her.

Jen could smell Nick, something woody but also floral. Citrus.

Fahrenheit, she had time to think.

"Hold on," he told her. "I've never done this before."

Then there was a blink. If Jen could actually feel something like a blink. Then another. She felt tugged to a certain direction. Towards the freezer, if she had to guess. Her whole body shifted with the motion. Then there was a snapping feel.

And then nothing but the chilling cold of the inside of the freezer. The metal floor icy against Jen's skin. The bites of locusts instantly ceased. She could feel the insects stumble off of her as if shocked by the change in temperature.

Jen lay there on the floor, exhausted. The fear still there, shaking in her hands, her arms, her legs. The trembling of her chest as she drew in a deep, tremulous breath.

"Did you get her?" Jen heard Sarah ask from somewhere in the depths of the small room.

"I think so," Nick's voice came. His arms released Jen, and the warmth of his body pulled away from her. Leaving the chill air of the freezer. "I got you, right?"

"Yeah," Jen said. And laughed. A shaky laugh. She was alive. They were alive. For the moment.

The screeching of the locusts grew louder, even if their cries were muted by the thick walls of the freezer. The hail-tapping sound of the insects, like back at the windows, started again. This time lighter, but Jen could still hear it. Right at the front of the freezer door.

She shivered. The temperature inside was cold. Too cold. With the power out it would warm up, but other than that, the group would have to huddle and wait. Her powers could do a lot, but lightning bolts weren't the greatest source of warmth. They were more of a brutal, destructive heat. Flashing in power. Less of a campfire.

The group huddled together and waited. Sarah hugged her sister. Every now and then one of them found one of the locusts that had made their way in with them. Those insects moved slowly. Wandering around like they were lost.

They couldn't see them, none of them could. They could only hear the hands of one of them slapping something on the chilly metal floor.

And like that, they waited.

Jen didn't know for what. Or for how long. All they could do, though, was wait. Her hand felt the key on her chest, and she held the stone tightly in her palm, feeling it against her skin. She tried pushing herself along the bond, reaching out to Gus, letting him know that they were okay, for now. That they might need help.

If he was okay.

There had been the flash of pain. Of surprise. Of wonder and... fear?

He had to be okay.

Jen held onto that thought. Held onto the stone. Pushed her thoughts along the bond. Felt a tiredness creep over her, and fought that too.

CHAPTER FORTY-THREE

S omehow I slept. It wasn't restful. I had a dream, one I had before, one I had many times, though not recently.

I was in a dark cloud, a faceless fog. A black soup. Almost swimming in it. A light appeared, like those lights do, dim, and from far away. Not lighting anything around me, but farther away. Making the surrounding blackness more black, because in the distance there was light. As if I was standing in a tunnel, a dark mist swirling around me, my feet spread over the tracks of a train.

I had had this dream before.

A horn blew. Muted in the distance. Muted under the thundering of metal beating the tracks. Millions of ghosts hid from me. Other faces swirled around me and past me. Countless faces. Faces of the dead.

My Ranger unit. Master Sargent Bradley, eyes opened for the last time, not seeing. His body flat, trapped under a boulder the size of a Buick. The sergeant's ghost, the last words he had heard the man say. *Help me understand, Grimm.*

Shit. If I could.

The blackness swirled. The horn sounded, closer. The light, stronger. The thundering, louder.

There were the others from my unit. Gorilla, stubble on his face, cradling his MK in one hand. Suzy Q, the first ghost he had ever remembered living, flew by. Patty Ice, with his Benelli. The one I still had in the back of my Camaro.

And Lilly. Flower Power. Her head crushed by a rock.

Even in the dream, a man can throw up.

The dark mist swirled. More faces blew by. Miss Tammie, skin peeling from the flames that had consumed her. Parker, body covered in the same flames, a hole in the center of his forehead. Parents of my childhood, as much as I had ever had them.

Mrs. Cooper. Jen's mom. Making us pancakes. Her eyes wild and crazy with a thirst for blood. The back of her head missing.

The chugging of something heavy coming this way. The tracks under my feet rumbled. Then a fast face. Blowing quickly past me. Father Benjamin, lips moving as if he still whispered for me to *see*.

Followed by Danny. Not the kid I remembered, and not the ghost at the end. Not the happy boy singing *Take Me Back to the Ball Game*. Tossing a baseball up and down in the air. And not his spirit I had seen at the end, a happy, blazing ethereal blue ghost, but what came at me was the image of the moment of his death. His head split open by the swing of a bat, his jaw hanging oddly out of his mouth as if he was trying to smile.

His face grew larger, flew over me, flew *through* me, and then zoomed past.

Gone.

Rumbling of the tracks.

Swirling of the mist.

The train horn long and low and vibrating the air around me. A deep screeching, a screaming whistle from a thundering machine. A metallic stampede.

The engine was closer. Rushing to meet me. Rushing with all the faces. My mother. My father. Blood staining their teeth. Their faces. My father, telling me not to be a pussy, over and over. My mother's eyes sad and knowing.

And then the worst ones. I turned to avoid them. Found I couldn't. My feet were stuck, stuck like concrete on the train tracks. The ground vibrated with a deep, dark, rumble. The light from the distance was closer, but no more bright. Just larger, smeared, as if the lamp of the train fought the blackness of the tunnel.

The sound of the horn pierced the air. A hot breath washed over me, bringing Johnny. Johnny, thin and cavernous. Eating himself from the inside.

Nick next. Glasses open. Eyes open, as if in shock. As if he hadn't seen what had killed him. As if something had struck him from the shadows.

Sarah, her face sad like my mother. Face dark with veins of blackness. Worms, black worms, wriggling under her skin.

She screamed as she went by.

The smear of the headlamp of the train swelled. Grew larger. My vision blurred; the smear became a nimbus of light. Above the smear was blonde hair, like a halo.

I did not want to see this face.

I could not turn away.

Hair, floating above the nimbus. The tiniest scent of honey-suckle. A tiny laugh, something just between us, floated by in the blackness so quick I almost missed it.

I did not want to see this face.

I knew this dream.

I knew it for what it was, but I also knew life for what it was. It was never fair. Never safe, no matter what I did or could do or had done.

I closed my eyes. It didn't matter. The light of the train burned them open again. The train neared; the tunnel felt like it was collapsing around me.

The shimmering light. Blue eyes in the smeared glow of the nimbus. Blue eyes, the blue of the deepest ocean. Not smiling at me, but weeping. The smear resolved, the nimbus cleared, and *I DID NOT WANT TO SEE THIS FACE.*

I yanked. Turned. Screamed.

SCREAMED.

The face came closer. The tracks jerked underneath me. Her eyes wept from a face torn to shreds by a million locusts, blood streaming from thousands of little smiles. Her mouth opened, wider and wider, a shriek came, the shriek loud and blasting my eyes.

Everything happened in the moment. The shriek, the train's horn. The rumbling of an avalanche loose in the tunnel.

The tracks bounced underneath me. I screamed and yanked and pulled, and then the plow hit me. The first sharp strike, the very tip of thousands of tons of rumbling metal.

The cowcatcher bored into me, the splitting pain of the thick angled metal striking me right in the center of the chest. That moment held, everything paused, all the faces and the darkness swimming around me and the smear of light. Then the plow burst through me, blasted over me, the sharp point somehow hot in the center of my chest like something burned there, like something bored into me, drilling a fiery message to the very fiber of my being...

CHAPTER FORTY-FOUR

I woke with a start. Jerking myself off the wall. Trying to take a deep breath, trying to recover from a gasp that came from holding my breath for far too long.

I had slept for far too long.

My chest was covered in spittle. Cold spit. My heart beat erratically; spasming in my chest. A lopsided rhythm that had me breathing in the same way. Trying to catch a breath. Trying to slow the beat of my heart.

I rolled to the side, and realized something else.

The bond beat at me. Urgently. Weakly.

No words I could feel. No signal I could identify. Nothing but a slight warmth on the center of my chest, right above my heart. Nothing but the knowledge that Jen was there.

Out there. Somewhere.

Alive.

God, I did not want to have that dream again.

I softly cupped the key in my hand. Held it, feeling warmth radiate from it, in the tiniest, weakest of pulses. Reveling in the knowledge she was alive. Trying to push the same warmth back into our bond. Letting her know the same.

And then the key went quiet. Flickered out, like a candle spent.

It took a bit, but I let it go.

And let out a deep breath. The deepest of breaths. I didn't know what kind of shape my friends were in. But at least I knew they were alive. At least, I hoped. I knew Jen was alive, and she wouldn't be, if any of our friends weren't. She would have done everything she could to keep them alive.

What kind of shape they were in, I'd have to find out.

But I would start with alive. And go from there.

I turned back. My back ached from sleeping in a sitting position. My body still ached from the battering of locusts it had taken. A groan might have escaped me.

Michael was sitting there, cross-legged. A towel in his lap. His clothes more white under the dim light of the vault. I had remembered the area brighter. He was alone, though the chairs and couches around were empty, as if the vampires and humans there had found other places to be.

He had a few bottles of water next to him. The same ones with the blue drops on the bottles. He handed me one.

"We didn't know whether to wake you," he said.

I nodded. Took the water he handed me. It was cool, cold really, and delicious. I swallowed a couple gulps down. My voice was ragged and rough, even with the water. "They're alive."

The angel nodded. His eyes flicked to the side, and I followed the motion. Tabitha was sleeping on a chair.

"All of them?"

I wasn't sure. But I thought so. Because my friends would have done everything they could.

"I think so."

Another nod. Michael grabbed the towel and wiped my chest.

CROWN OF BONES • 385

The spit there was cold and sticky, and the angel made a butchering of the job, but the towel came away more dirty than clean. The experience felt oddly maternal.

He looked at the towel, made a funny face. Part puzzlement. Part curiosity. Part disgust. I *was* covered in dried goo, snotty goo, and flakes of shells. None of it came off easy.

"How did you survive?"

I blinked. Michael's question didn't make sense. Did he not know? "I summoned the armor."

"Armor?"

"Armor," I confirmed. Like I was part of some angel club. "The plates that slide out of you."

It took a moment for Michael to answer. The towel dangled from his hand, forgotten. "Plates that slide out of you?"

It sounded like the both of us were confused. Didn't he have the same thing? He had summoned his sword, like I had summoned mine, and even if the two blades looked different, I thought they would cut the same.

Like the blades would be the armor. Michael certainly wouldn't spend an hour putting on a full suit of armor before rolling into battle, even if he did carry around his shield. It made a kind of sense.

"Plates of armor," I explained, making my hand flat. Running it along my arm, as if showing Michael how the armor slid out of my skin. My throat was dry, and my voice sounded like I had smoked a million cigarettes. "They appeared out of me, everywhere. Overlapped my body. Thick enough that they took most of the blows."

A change came over the angel. His face looked almost shocked, and a few words escaped him in a whisper. I barely caught them, and didn't think I could have heard them right.

Armor of faith?

I snorted. I was anything but a believer. I believed in myself, but honestly, that was all Jen. She had gotten me there. Anything else was a stretch, in my world. I believed I had some angelic powers. But that was it. I wasn't what they call, all in, on the faith thing. Which is what I told the angel.

"You humans are funny," he said. "You think belief has to be like a switch. It is either on or off. It is there, or isn't. You must have it, or you must not."

"Yeah," I said. "That sums it up." People seemed that way to me. There were believers, and there were non-believers. There were people who went to church just to go, and there were those, like me, who wondered where, in a world of evil, good actually existed.

"I have watched you all for thousands of years and still can't understand you," Michael said. "How can something like truth, righteousness, salvation, how can those concepts be either on or off?"

"People believe, or people don't," I said. "Pretty simple."

That was belief to me. Simple. People either believed in something, or, not seeing evidence of the thing, didn't.

"Faith is like a boat," Michael explained. "A boat in an infinite ocean, sailing under foreign stars. You set course on a *feeling*, a part of you that says this is just. This is right. This is the direction I head. No matter the winds that fight you. The currents that rob you of any headway. You head out, you sometimes find others searching for the same thing, in the same waters. Always sailing to a horizon you may not find, but you *know* must be there."

I wondered what Father Benjamin would say about that. He believed. He had believed strongly enough to use his belief as a power. It had seemed like an on-and-off thing with the priest, at least. I had never not known him not to believe.

And he had died, despite it. Horribly. The fate of a lot of people I had known. Miss Tammie. Parker. *Danny*.

"So, faith is like sailing a boat across an infinite ocean. To a place I may or not make." I shrugged. "Sounds about right."

"On and off," Michael said, his nose twisting, as if he had caught a bad odor. "It is not good enough for you to have this armor when your friends needed it most. You must know why you don't always have it. Why you didn't have the armor, your sword, from the very beginning."

He leaned closer. "The best answer I can give you is, time."

Our eyes locked. I knew mine were angry. His were, too, but anger of a different sort. The anger maybe of a parent, trying to keep their children safe. Like a father, telling a child not to climb a tree so high, even as the kid reached for the next branch.

"The ocean is large because you all need *time*," Michael said. "You have to be *forged*. The knowledge doesn't come easy. A child must touch a burner to discover how hot it is. How hot they are *told* it is. And then, sometimes, they have to touch it again. *Why?*"

He let out a large breath, as if this had been a puzzle he had worked his life on. Thousands of years of it. "The best answer is time. You need time to experience life. Everything it has to offer. To see all the evil people can hold, and, finally, to know that there can be just as much good in it."

"If there's so much evil in the world," I said, thinking I had him. There were literal zones of hell on Earth. People had died, likely by the millions. Demons roamed the Earth. Anger did color my voice, and, rough as it was, my words came out almost guttural. "Where is this good? Who's pulling people out of this fucking ocean? Who's saving them and sailing to that fucking unknown horizon?"

The angel's smile became real. "Grimm," he said. "Why do you think I am *here*? Helping *you*?"

Well.

Well, well.

Like on the patio, he still had the turnabout thing down.

If not now, when?

Those words took on a much darker overtone. More grim. I could see myself color the thoughts, much in the manner Michael had said. I could see myself look high in the air and scream out why me? Why them? Why Danny and Miss Tammie and Parker and Lilly and all the others, the friends and people I had tried to protect over the years? Friends, family, people I had known? Hell, people the angel had known, like my father? My mother?

The thick line crossing her neck. The scar that had never healed. The one I would never know about. Never understand where she had gotten it from. Or how she had lived.

The angel had said the answer was time. I didn't know that I had enough. He had said the horizon was there, but I knew I would never see it. The ocean was too big. Too large. The winds, the currents, all against me. All too strong.

Still, I fought the thought. Resisted it. Pushed it away. I wasn't righteous. I didn't have something like faith. I wasn't even particularly good; at least, I had done questionable things. If not evil. And likely would do them again.

Michael saw all of that play over my face.

"When you first saw me," he said. "What did you do?"

I had pulled out my sword. And tested him with it. I had made sure he wasn't a demon.

"Do you know what your blade is called?"

I shook my head.

"The sword of spirit," he said. "It is the Word of God." A moment, while he let that sink in, before asking, "Can you guess why?"

The sword was fairly new to me, to my life. I had run from Azazel for a long time, and if I had it then, maybe the demon would be gone. Maybe none of this would be happening.

But what if the sword wasn't about killing demons. What if it wasn't about being there because evil was around. What if it had been waiting for a time when I was ready for it?

A feeling like vertigo came over me. I shook my head. The perspective was too different. It was like walking the stairs in one of those M. C. Escher drawings. The one with the stairs leading everywhere, on the floor and the ceiling, right side up and upside down, leading every which way.

However I tried to walk it, I got lost.

I thought I had been doing good things at the time, running from the demon, keeping the key from him. I thought I was protecting the world. Keeping the most people safe that I could.

But I had found out differently. I had found out, while thinking I was saving the world, all the people I knew and loved had suffered. I had come back to Grafton and seen all that there. People who had been hurt because I had thought I was doing something larger. People who had been killed because I had taken my eye away from them, and instead looked to protect the world.

That thought, those thoughts, were part of this different perspective. But the view had shifted too much. Like looking out the windshield of your car, seeing the road lead far ahead, before another car crashes into you, violently shifting your world.

It was too fast a shift for me, too violent a collision, for me to grab the thoughts racing through me. All I really knew was that I had made a promise. And I had kept it. That promise, keeping those I loved safe, *trying* to keep them safe, seemed to allow me to call the sword. That promise, along with others. Those words that meant, even with their loss, even if they died, I would continue to stand and fight against evil.

Had the sword not come as a weapon for me to kill demons? To help me defeat the evil in the world, the evil that had since grown to towering heights? With demons and Dead Zones scattered over the Earth?

Had the sword actually only come because something had changed in *me*?

Michael summoned his sword, holding it right in front of me, the blade blocking his face. The blade of white gold, the golden cross on the hilt, the hint of flames licking the sharp edges. "I was born on the horizon I speak of. This sword was *given* to me. It has always existed, in my hands. It is, like you think, on and off. For me."

Michael said for him, but I thought he meant for angels.

His sword disappeared. The blade subsumed itself in a glow of golden sparks. Sparks that hid his face, sparks that drifted lazily around us, floating in the air as if from a campfire.

His words came to me, through them. "You weren't born on that same horizon. In that same world. With that knowledge. You have to make your way to it. The Word of God is an active thing. It lives and grows. You must sharpen it. You stroke whetstone over steel, over and over, until the word knows the division of the soul, of your spirit; until it discerns the thoughts and intentions of your heart."

The intentions of the heart.

The word is the deed.

The last showy mote drifted past Michael. Its spark was lazy, zigging and zagging in an unseen current of air. "None of that comes easy for you humans. None of that just appears; none of it is on and off. It must be forged. The right fire has to be found. A heavy anvil must be paired with the hardest hammer. It must be molded in the hardest of lives, quenched in the deepest of doubts, polished with heartrending pain."

His hand had remained out, and that last spark lit onto the back of it, winking out. His face appeared as if the angel was looking back in time. At a memory. "None of that happens without time. It all needs time. The life. The pain. The forging. It is easier, perhaps, to be on and off. To say you believe."

His final words, simple. Somber. "Much harder to carry the faith."

I wrestled with the concept. The change in view. But the collision had been too large. My car still tumbled across the road, the windshield shattered, the road I had been driving on wrenched away from sight.

Michael watched me. And could see the moment I gave up on it.

"Rest," he said, simply. "The ocean is large."

I still struggled. My mind still tried to gather it all in. I ran staircase after staircase, looking up at the floor. Down at the ceiling.

The ocean was large. Too large. This armor of faith. The sword of spirit. Why they appeared didn't matter so much to me as that they did. They were tools I could use. Tools to save those I could. To protect those I loved. That was large enough an ocean for me.

I was a fighter. I would fight. It was something I was good at. It was something I could do.

Those were the thoughts I wrestled with. That wrestled me. Collisions of perspectives. Upside-down stairs leading to the place I started from.

My eyes opened wide, briefly, then closed again. The lids tight. My mind raced; I fought all the thoughts. Everything that came at me: my friends trapped somewhere, out in the world among insects that ate anything and everything, anyone and everyone. Locusts above us, throwing their bodies against the vault. Hector, smiling from his new body, his grip crushing my chest. And Sabnock, building an army, working his plan to destroy my world, to take the lives of my friends, to do to us what we had threatened to do to them.

A storm of locusts raged above us. There were ships and oceans and horizons to cross. There were towering waves surrounding me, waves of the unknown. Waves of uncertainty. And waves of chitinous creatures battering Mexico.

392 • CHRIS J CRANFORD

And in the center of everything, the stadium, the Crown of Bones. There was our answer. There was *one* answer. Our place to end one part of the demon's plans. Where the Ushabti seemed to be made, the golem-knights. Where the Dead Zone could be nullified, the Zatar broken. Where, if anything at all went well, we could do all of the above and still kill Sabnock.

Those were my thoughts, as I huddled back to sleep. As the storm of Sabnock's making assailed all of Mexico. As everyone, as *everything*, above was eaten by the plague of locusts. A sea of mandibles that could chew through skin, bone, and stone alike.

A ship and an infinite ocean and an unreachable horizon, locusts and demons and ghosts circling the waters around me. I would have to become more to survive it all. My friends would have to become more, for us to swim out of that ocean, to find our horizon, to have a *chance* at victory. Not just here in Mexico, but victory for the world.

After a time, there came a final close of the eyes, as I finally fell into a fitful sleep.

Enjoy *Crown of Bones*, and maybe looking for the sequel?

Great news—*Storm of Souls* is ready for you right now.

I'm a little biased, but I kind of love this story. I was excited when I finished writing it, and can't wait for you to read it.

Feel free to take moment and visit chrisjcranford.com. Be a part of the Grimm Universe. Discover all the other worlds I'm building.

Or just reach out and say hello.

ABOUT THE AUTHOR

When Chris isn't trying to figure out how to write a bio, he spends time contemplating the fate of the universe. Probably while walking into a door jamb. He's accepted that the two go hand-in-hand.

He currently resides in Florida, though he has some Magellan in him, and loves to wander.

It is his dream to write stories that – through their telling – influence others to live a little better. Stand a little taller. Smile a little wider. Hold someone a little longer. Fiction should be the dream real life aspires to be.

Dogs are his buddies. Football is his hobby. Books are his passion.

Find out more about Chris here:

www.chrisjcranford.com

 facebook.com/chrisjcranford

X x.com/chrisjcranford

 instagram.com/chrisjcranford

www.ingramcontent.com/pod-product-compliance
Lightning Source LLC
Chambersburg PA
CBHW060220030726
47499CB00004B/1126